D1010598

A Private Sorcery

A Private Sorcery

A NOVEL BY Lisa Gornick

Algonquin Books of Chapel Hill 2002

Published by
Algonquin Books of Chapel Hill
Post Office Box 2225
Chapel Hill, North Carolina 27515-2225

a division of
Workman Publishing
708 Broadway
New York, New York 10003

Printed in the United States of America.
Published simultaneously in Canada by Thomas Allen & Son Limited.
Design by Anne Winslow.

This is a work of fiction. While, as in all fiction, the literary perceptions and insights are based on experience, all names, characters, places, and incidents are either products of the author's imagination or are used fictitiously. No reference to any real person is intended or should be inferred.

Library of Congress Cataloging-in-Publication Data
Gornick, Lisa, 1956–
A private sorcery : a novel / by Lisa Gornick.— 1st ed.
p. cm.
ISBN 1-56512-341-7
1. Psychiatrists—Fiction. 2. Psychotherapist and patient—Fiction. 3. Fathers and sons—Fiction. 4. Married people—Fiction. 5. Drug abuse—Fiction. 6. Prisoners—Fiction. I. Title.
PS3607.0598 P7 2002
813'.6—dc21 2002033249

10 9 8 7 6 5 4 3 2 1
First Edition

For
Ken, Zack and Damon

As for the symptoms, they are a private sorcery.
They transform one thing into another.

A Private Sorcery

Prologue

They come in the middle of the night. There's a ruckus on the stairs, then the bell ringing. Once, twice, quickly three more times. Saul, naked, sits up in the bed as Rena, lost in his pajamas, moves forward. She clutches the neck above the buttons, swipes the tangle from her eyes. Through the peephole, she sees men's faces: a pale, a dark. Behind them, more.

Chain in place, she opens the door a crack. The pale one, brillo hair, a faded strawberry mark on his cheek, stuffs a paper through the space. "Warrant. For Dr. Saul Dubinsky."

"My robe." She turns. There's a rush in her chest. From the rear, she hears the grates to the fire escape opening. A bullhorn blasts. A voice, loud, staccato: "At the window. He's at the window."

Trash cans clatter. "Don't move, Dubinsky. Stay where you are."

From the front: "Open the door. *Now,* missy."

She swings around. Above the chain, the snout of a gun. The old guns explode inside her. The pistol Nick waved while her mother scrambled to gather her panties from the parking lot. The one Sammy kept loaded under the bed. Joe's rifle mounted in the room where she slept.

"I said *now.*"

She unlatches the chain. Men run past her toward the bedroom. The doughy rookie grabs her around the waist, an arm yanked sharply behind her, the other caught at the wrist.

"Let go of me." Her voice—a trickle of sound.

He tightens his grip. His boot touches her bare foot. "Don't struggle, ma'am. It'll only make it worse."

The reverb from the bullhorn surrounds them. "Dubinsky, we're counting to ten. You better be off that fire escape by then."

The rookie's heartbeat is on her back. He's scared, too.

"I'd recommend you get your naked butt inside."

The grates bang closed.

"Okay, Doc. We're going to take this a step at a time."

A few seconds later, Saul is pushed into the living room ringed by three of the men, his long neck spindly among their thick ones, his dark hair frizzed like a clown's. She can see the hollow where his breastbone is concave, just large enough for two robin's eggs, she'd once told him, her finger tracing the spot. His hands are cuffed behind him.

"Oh my God."

"It's okay," the rookie whispers. He pulls her closer as though she's his date, the two of them swaying together, and then she remembers that today is her birthday.

Saul's eyes are circles of panic.

Rena looks at the one with the brillo hair. "You can let him put some pants on, at least."

Her left eyelid is twitching, the pajama top twisted under her arms. She can see Brillo taking her in—calculating something.

"Bring her in to get Doc here some clothes."

In the bedroom, she opens Saul's dresser drawers: the mismatched balls of socks, the T-shirts and jeans thrown willy-nilly. She searches for underwear without holes. From Saul's closet, she takes khaki pants, a button-down shirt, a tweed jacket worn at the elbows.

They undo the cuffs. Saul moves slowly, his fine fingers fumbling with the buttons. Brillo takes out a handkerchief and blows his nose. "All right, Pretty Boy. You'll get the fashion award down at MCC."

The rookie takes the rear. At the door, he turns and tips his cap.

"Night, ma'am. Lock up tight."

Part One

BURNING CHILD

1 Leonard

A regimented man, I rise as always at five, lowering my big white feet onto the cold wood floor. I am thinking of you, Saul, my second-born son. You would laugh to hear me call you my second-born. *So biblical,* you would say. *Begat, begat, begat.* Your mother—a flowered bonnet over her beauty parlor hair, her chin slack, the inhaled *clu-hah* with the slight gasp in the middle, the exhale through the Grecian nose that turned somewhere in the past thirty-seven years from regal to beak—still has a morning's sleep before her and then her daily litany: not a wink all night, such a torture to lie there just watching the clock.

Downstairs, I make coffee and struggle to peel an orange. I toy with the night's dream fragment, partly a compulsion like a dog worrying a bone, partly an exercise from my old psychiatry days when residents still spent six months studying Chapter Seven of *The Interpretation of Dreams*. So different from your training three decades later when, you bitterly complained, no one read books, reading relegated to four-page articles in the green journal, terse pieces correlating drug dosages and symptom checklists. In the dream fragment, I'm with my sisters: Rose, Eunice and Lillian. We're in a room with pocket doors and a clawfoot dining table, so it must be when the six of us lived in the back of my Aunt Mindyl and Uncle Jack's apartment—the dining room, the maid's room and the miniature maid's bath our delegated quarters. Then the scene changes and Carmelita Erendira Gomez, the subject of the accursed biography I've been trying to write these past twelve years, is sitting with my sisters, showing them something I either can't see or can't now recall.

I eat standing at the kitchen sink. It's a habit your mother has always hated. "Only laborers eat on their feet," she would hiss in the years when I still existed enough in her consciousness to merit criticism, willfully dumb to the knowledge that my father had spent twenty-nine of his forty-two years breaking his back, the last six leaning over a pressing machine in my Uncle Jack's factory—the job, a gift in Depression years, bestowed only after my father had promised not to utter on the premises so much as a word of what Jack had called *your Commie union filth*.

I stare out the window, trying to lift the thick cheesy covering from my mind. A soapy light washes across the lawns, filtering through the two Japanese maples and the Canadian spruce we planted thirty-two years ago when the development was still new. I think, as I have every morning since, about how dissatisfied I feel with the view before me: the colors, muted and tasteful as befit a neighborhood where property values have consistently risen and the homes have gracefully aged, the uniformity of the colonials and ranches and split-levels hidden behind varying additions. How every person needs to live in a place imbued with substance, with personal meaning, how these surrounds have for me never ceased feeling weak, dilute, perfectly pleasant, with nothing discordant to the eye, but with nothing, either, upon which the eye would linger.

At six, I enter my study. Unable to face a blank page or yesterday's scrawl, I take out the red leather album where I keep the Mexican newspaper clippings about Carmelita. They're in chronological order, the first from a local paper when Carmelita started having visions, the last from a Oaxacan paper after her death in prison. I am midway through the album, feeling as always daunted about how to convey the many ways the events surrounding Carmelita were experienced—her family and the village priest saw her as a virgin saint with the baby miraculously conceived, the local police pointed to vindictive villagers jealous that her father had prospered in the new copper mine, the doctors suggested command hallucinations that had driven her to drown her own child—when the phone rings.

I pick up immediately.

"Leonard."

Hearing your wife's soft, chilly voice at this hour, my stomach clutches. Rena is not the sort of daughter-in-law who calls simply to see how we are doing, perhaps because any call would involve listening to your mother's catalog of symptoms, each preceded by the phrase *I'm doing better, better than last week,* a reminder to callers that they'd failed her when she was really down.

"Leonard," she repeats. I am envisioning the bluish skin under her gold-flecked eyes, so large they bulge slightly and make one wonder about thyroid levels, her willowy form, the almost-perfect posture broken every now and then by a slight slouch, pentimento, I've always imagined, of some earlier, awkward self.

"Are you sitting down? You should sit down."

"I'm sitting."

She sucks in air. "Saul's been arrested. Last night, in the middle of the night."

"What?" I stammer, not because I haven't heard but rather because I can't connect this to anything I know about you: your blue lips at the neighborhood pool, your wobbly ankles and eyeglasses the butt of so many pranks.

Saul's been arrested. The words sit outside my mind like three steamer trunks that cannot fit into an already packed car.

"Why?" I whisper. I hold the receiver in my hand, paralyzed, staring at the Japanese maples, their limbs knotted with baby buds.

"Something to do with drugs, a burglary of the pharmacy at his hospital. He tried to escape through the back window, but they had police in the garden."

I'm gripping the phone, having the oddest sensation, as if I can't quite make out what is being said. This uncomfortable thought I've had on occasion about your wife returns: that there'd been some other life before she came east, before you met her, things you hinted at when you married three years ago, black holes between the few facts you told us—that she'd grown up over an Italian restaurant in San Francisco where her mother was a waitress, was helped to go to Yale by a community organizer who'd then died of breast cancer, had her half brother living with her for several years.

Did she say drugs?

"I need a lawyer. I thought maybe Marc would know someone. I . . ." For the first time, her voice falters, a tiny fissure between the words. "I don't have his number."

A surge of protectiveness wells up in me. It's a relief to feel something recognizable, to discern the outlines of something to grasp onto. "Wait," I say. "I'll take the next train."

I SHOWER QUICKLY. In reaction to your mother's hypochondriasis, I have refused to purchase the blood pressure cuffs so many men my age keep in their bathroom cabinets but find myself now anxiously worrying about my diastolic reading. I soap my flabby chest, forcing myself to concentrate on the circles of suds I make over the gray hairs, duck under a showerhead not installed for men my height, remembering the years of taking you and Marc into the shower with me, when you were little little, still in diapers, being sure to clean all the creases, the indent where we once had tails.

My hands shake as I write a note to your mother: "Gone to the city to use the library. I'll call later to let you know when I'll be home." I prop it next to the coffeemaker and lock the kitchen door behind me.

It takes twenty minutes to walk to the train station, the streets empty this early on a Sunday morning. I ride on the platform between the cars, staring out at the cruddy landscape grown around the tracks—the junked cars, the aluminum-sided houses with their clotheslines and swing sets, at one spot something that looks like a dead dog. I'm feeling sorry for myself, that I can't tell your mother what with her hysterical response to everything: the fainting or feigning of fainting, the need to call Dr. Stone for tranquilizers, the way anyone else's problems are immediately co-opted as her property, her tragedy. Guilty because I'm saved from another morning facing a blank page, as though Rena's call announced a snow day. We're in the tunnel coming into New York before I can focus on you and then I feel so awful, so sick in my soul, the air acrid with fumes, I have to move inside and take a seat.

Of course, I'd sensed you were having trouble this past year; for the first time, we'd hardly seen you. But I'd assumed it had to do with your job, with what had happened to that boy in the subway. I count back the weeks to mid-December, when you asked to borrow my credit card. You said you wanted to buy holiday presents for Rena, didn't want her to see the bill. I didn't question you, didn't let myself entertain any concerns about why you'd been so insistent, taking the train out to New Jersey on a Tuesday evening to get the card. Even your mother was suspicious. "Maybe he's having an affair," she said smugly, unable to disguise the touch of glee the idea gave her, revenge on Rena for not having provided any family of note for a *Times* wedding announcement, for keeping a distance from the dear-dear cluckers who listen to her complaints.

Your mother's bemusement disappeared when the bill (the only thing about the household to which she still attends being bills and bank statements) arrived and there were twenty-six hundred dollars of charges: a gold chain, a man's leather coat, a television set. "You call him, Leonard," she commanded. "Right this minute." When I'd not reached you, your brother, usually dutiful but brief in his phone calls with your mother, was, for once, happy to be her sounding board. He threw out his own theory, *gambling, does he go to Atlantic City, you know what a gullible person he is,* but it was easy to brush this aside as his old antagonism to you, the usurper whom he'd pronounced on your arrival home from the hospital to be an icky-wicky, his opinion of you having gone only downhill from there when he'd felt burdened with the job of protecting you from the very neighborhood bullies whose friendships he sought.

At Penn Station, I buy a bag of bagels and a tub of cream cheese, and then feel idiotic for having done so, for having blindly followed my mother's rule never to arrive at anyone's door empty-handed. I consider handing the bag to one of the homeless women splayed near the Eighth Avenue exit but, superstitiously, I clutch it to me.

Outside, it's cold and drizzling. The rain hits the bald spot on the top of my head. I hail a cab. Coptic crosses jangle against the rearview mirror and I recognize the radio station as the listener-funded one you support, the shows put together with Scotch tape and chewing gum, the topic today the environmental racism behind a Harlem incinerator. It's a little after nine when I climb the brownstone steps and ring your bell.

She's wearing what must be your pajamas. Her tawny hair is wild and uncombed, and my first thought is how alike the two of you look: two long-limbed ectomorphs, she the pale-complected reflection of your darker hues. A thread of blood has formed in a crack in her lower lip. I resist drawing her toward me. I know that she could not stand it.

I follow her to your galley kitchen, a chopped-off corner of what had once been the parlor of an elegant house. She puts the bagels on a platter, turns on the kettle. "Tea or coffee?" she asks.

"Whatever you're having."

She scoops green leaves into two mesh balls. Although her white couch and sleigh bed replaced your ratty corduroy couch and mattress on the floor when she'd moved in with you, it still feels like your apartment: the brick-and-board shelves overflowing with books and old records, the crates of unfiled papers, your cheaply framed political prints. Rather than overhauling the place, she has, it seems, carved out areas as her domain—your previously swampy bathroom now meticulously clean with sea-green hand towels and a glass shelf holding an aloe plant, the blue mugs into which she now pours hot water having ousted your drug company and radio station handouts.

She carries the mugs of tea. I follow her into the living room with the platter of bagels. She sits with her legs folded under her on the couch, cradling her cup, and I take the chair across. She rubs her shoulder as she talks. It takes quite a while for me to piece together even the most basic things. I can't tell if the ellipses are because she is editing what she knows or because she, too, is bewildered, but I find myself thinking the way I did when patients would tell me their stories and I learned to let the first version have some breathing room before pushing at the contradictions, before insisting on details.

IT STARTED, SHE TELLS ME, when that boy jumped in front of the train. She calls him Mitch as though he is a frequent subject of discussion between the two of you, this boy dumped on your caseload New Year's Day, over a year ago, when the clinic's other psychiatrist quit and suddenly you were responsible for twice as many patients. From the perfunctory note left about him, you had no clue that he was rapidly decompensating and should not be grouped among the less urgent cases to be seen the following week. No one blamed you. The head of the service said it was fully his responsibility for giving you an unmanageable task. The lawyers skipped right over you to the doctor who'd left the inadequate sign-off note. You'd never even met the boy until his first night in intensive care, by then a double amputee.

"Saul couldn't sleep. His eyes wouldn't even shut. He'd pace in the hallway. I was the one who suggested he take a sleeping pill." She tells me this with the steadiness of someone confessing. I refrain from reassuring her that it was an innocent thing to do, remembering all too well how the reassurances I tried to give you those first weeks after Mitch's jump made you feel worse, lonelier, as if you were the only one who could see your failure—how the nurses' reassurances on the ward that my patient Maria's actions were independent of me (when I knew they were entirely about me) left me unable to work as a psychiatrist anymore.

Every night, she tells me, you took your Nembutals: first one, then two, then four. Convinced that you could not sleep without them, you would wake groggy and then panic that the grogginess would cause another mistake. She doesn't know when you began prescribing for yourself, maybe March, maybe April, only that she discovered it Memorial Day weekend when the two of you went to visit your old supervisor, Sylvia Jacobs, at her house in Montauk.

"Yes, I know her," I say.

Rena looks at me with confusion.

"She was chief resident when I was an intern. Twenty-six with orthopedic shoes. We used to joke that she'd make the *Guinness Book of World Records* for being the youngest little old lady in the Bronx."

Your wife does not smile. She continues: You were napping on the beach. She'd gone into your camera bag because the sky had filled with flocks of gulls and she'd been overtaken with the desire to photograph Sylvia's wonderful house, set itself like a bird alit on the cliff, with the gulls overhead. She unzipped the inner pocket to get the lens cloth and found instead a candy store of pills: the Dexedrine, Methedrine and Ritalin bottles with her name on them; the phenobarbital, Tuinals and Dalmane with Santiago Domengo's name; the Valium and Librium with yours.

"When I saw those vials, the reality of what had been going on hit me. All those messages from his job on our machine. The nurses calling to say they needed certain orders written. His boss, Dr. Fishkin, asking if Dr. Dubinsky would grace them today with his presence."

Rena removes the mesh ball from her mug. I copy her. "The real clue, I don't know how I hadn't seen it, was Santiago—his message that he hoped Saul and family were not ill. You know Saul never missed his Tuesday nights reading to Santiago. When we got back to the city, I went to stay with Ruth and Maggie. Maggie found a doctor who specializes in treating addicted medical professionals. After I was gone for six nights, Saul agreed to go."

She stands, opens the window a crack. She stretches in front of the window, fingertips reaching toward the ceiling, and for a moment I remember Maria standing in my office before a barred window, stretching her arms up to the green ceiling, the fan whirring above, her thick black braid touching her round plump bottom, and I am disgusted to feel heat in my groin as I recall her bottom and the way her braid swung back and forth like a horse's tail.

"This doctor, Arlen, seemed to help for a while. He detoxed Saul from the sleeping pills. By the end of June, Saul was sleeping without anything. He took up jogging—Arlen recommended it to reduce stress—and started listening at night to these relaxation tapes. Then, in August, I had to go out to Colorado for three weeks to work on the Braner campaign. I think that's when he started up again."

She sits, hugging her knees, seemingly going over in her mind the events of last summer. It occurs to me that she probably has no idea how much I know about her work, how it was partly our discussion of the anonymous op-ed piece she'd written about the way people vote for their childhood images of the *übermutter* or *überfater,* the quality of the candidate as irrelevant as the nutritional value of a potato chip, that had initially prompted you to write her care of the *Times*. A second-year psychiatry resident, still enamored of the critical theorists introduced to you by Santiago Domengo, disappointed by the anti-intellectual atmosphere of your residency, you'd neither known nor cared if you were contacting a man or a woman.

I'd seen you, I recall now, last August while Rena was in Colorado. Of course, there'd been other times when I'd sensed lagoons of privacy, things you'd rather not discuss, but for the first time between us it had felt like an ocean. When I asked how you were doing, you said fine, better, you were jogging every day. You said nothing about Mitch and I didn't want to press you. Instead, you talked about Rena and how upset she was by the merger of Muskowitz & Kerrigan—the originally Democratic but, you told me, increasingly centrist political consulting firm where she'd risen from assistant pollster to something called physical presentation director—with Cassen & Silvano, a firm with long ties to the Republican party. Cassen, you said, had a thing for Rena, got a perverse kick out of forcing her to work with the candidates she found most repugnant. She was sickened, you told me, at having to work with Braner, a gubernatorial candidate propped up by gun lobbyists and antiabortion activists—repulsed at having to touch Braner's hands as she coached him to present himself as closer to what they called the man in the streets rather than the son of the real estate developer that he was.

"By the end of my first week in Denver," she continues, "I knew Saul had slipped. I could just sense it. He adamantly denied it. I was imagining things. I was ruining our marriage by acting like his social worker. Yes, he was having more trouble sleeping, but no, he wasn't going back to the pills. We'd see each other in ten days when he'd come out for a long weekend. Then he canceled the trip. He told me the other staff psychiatrist had a death in the family and he had to cover the unit. I was sure he was lying. I called Arlen, who lectured me about letting go."

I take my first sip of the tea, lukewarm and bitter. September, October, November, December, January, February. Six months between then and now.

"I knew Saul was lying, but I let myself be lulled by Arlen into backing off. All fall I backed off. At work, they were running me ragged, sending me out to Colorado eight times, insisting that I accompany Braner on his town meeting tour."

She stops as though afraid of sounding like she's defending herself.

"The way we worked it, Saul paid the major bills—the rent, Con Ed, the phone—and I bought the food and what we needed for the apartment. I guess he must have kept up since nothing's been turned off."

It occurs to me that you must have been determined to pay those bills.

"I didn't call Arlen again until Christmas eve, when I came home to find this ominous-looking guy sitting on our steps, threatening that if the doctor didn't pay up there was going to be trouble." She shudders. "Saul brushed the whole thing off. He said it was a psychotic patient he'd treated in the clinic. It was the holidays. I let myself buy it."

Her hands move up her face, pushing the hair off her forehead. Without the fringe of hair, she looks young, like a girl emerging sleek-headed from a lake. She stands. Her shoulders sag. She must have been up all night. "I need to take a shower. Help yourself to more tea, whatever."

IT TAKES ME a moment to realize that this is all she is going to tell me. I wait until I hear the water running before getting the phone. I dial your brother's number.

Susan answers in her chronically chipper voice. After three miscarriages, the last occurring in the fifth month, she had her tubes tied, unable to bear seeing the sonograms, the little hands floating on the screen, but never having the baby. Since then, they've devoted themselves to what they refer to as their *lifestyle,* moving last year to a Spanish-style house on a golf course outside Atlanta, going every January to their time-share in Hawaii, hiking in the summers in one of the western state parks—a doggedly serious pursuit of pleasure.

"Good timing. Marc just came in from his morning run. It's glorious here today, in the sixties already. Sweetheart," she calls out, "it's your father."

"Hi," Marc says. "What a day! A nine-holer at least."

As always, I am taken aback that an offspring of mine could sound so much like a talk-show host, everything he says the buttery small talk that greases impersonal interactions, people you find yourself standing with in an elevator, the spouses of colleagues, talk whose purpose is not to communicate anything in particular but rather to signal that we're on the same side. But with Marc and the other partners in his law firm and the members of his country club, the backslapping and exchange of clichés go on and on. It took me a while to connect the depressed feeling I have after visiting him with the hostility that underlies all this forced pleasantness of speech and environment, its purpose being to shut out people who look or smell different. It took me even longer to see that I am, in fact, one of the people being shut out, that I carry the scent of the shtetl my mother left, of the poverty my father struggled against, and that although Marc and Susan belong to the conservative synagogue of Atlanta and, had there been children, would have had them bas mitzvahed or bar mitzvahed, the Jews they associate with have sanitized themselves of not only the Old World but also the landing spots—the Lower East Side and Brooklyn and Newark, with their pushcarts and tenements and rallies and the suspect ideas that constituted my father's politics and now both your work and mine.

I deliver it straight. "Saul's been arrested."

Marc exhales loudly. "What the fuck . . ."

I imagine the dark circle of perspiration in the middle of his University of Pennsylvania T-shirt, his bulging legs, the muscles still engorged from his run, his thick neck, the black hair trellised from belly button to collarbone.

"Hold on." I hear water running, gulping sounds as he drinks. The glass bangs on the table. "What happened?"

"It's not clear. Rena says he'd been using drugs, prescription drugs he began taking after that boy lost his legs. He'd started seeing someone for help, but I guess it didn't stick."

"Yeah, but why was he arrested?"

"A burglary of the pharmacy at the hospital where he works. It sounds like he's being linked with that."

"Great. Breaking and entering. Conspiracy to distribute controlled substances. Revocation of his license."

"He needs a lawyer. A criminal lawyer, obviously. Do you know anyone here in New York?"

In the background, I can hear Susan's little screeches. "Look, I have to talk to Susan. I'll call you back. Where are you?"

"With Rena. At their apartment."

"Give me the number."

Your brother doesn't know your phone number—a place you've lived for eight years.

I carry the mugs and platter into the kitchen, scattering dank tea leaves over the counter as I try to empty the mesh balls. I turn on the kettle, stand at the living room window waiting for the water to boil. The block association has put metal cages up around the trees. Bags of garbage lean against the sides.

Two women in ski jackets climb the steps and the doorbell rings. The shower is still running in the back. I go to the intercom and ask who's there.

"Ruth, Maggie. Rena and Saul's friends."

I buzz them in. You introduced me to them shortly after you and Rena started living together: Ruth, who you said had been a classmate of Rena's at Yale and then later told me only became her friend after they'd bumped into one another in Riverside Park; Maggie, whom you called Ruth's lover.

I open the door and Ruth gives me a peck on the cheek. She's wearing a wool cap that makes her face look small and cramped, and she stomps her work boots on the mat before coming in. Maggie towers a good half-foot over Ruth. She pats my arm and runs her fingers through her cropped blond hair. She unwraps a scarf from her neck and untangles her dangling earrings. Although they're both in jeans and turtlenecks, on Ruth the effect is of a squat woman who has opted out whereas on Maggie the clothes suggest an urban chic.

"How are you holding up?" Ruth asks.

"Rena called us at eight," Maggie says. "We wanted to give you some time alone with her before coming over."

The phone rings and Rena picks up on the extension in back. Maggie heads into the kitchen as the kettle starts to whistle. Ruth plops onto the couch.

"Thanks for the letter," I say. "It was very thought-provoking. I should have written you then to say so."

I think back to when I last saw Ruth. July. At your birthday party. Piecing things together with what Rena has told me, this must have been after you'd gone to see that doctor, during the interlude when you were doing okay. You donned a chef's apron and positioned yourself in the garden next to the charcoal grill Rena had bought you for your birthday, flipping chicken pieces and these marinated slices of something Maggie, who'd made them, told me was ground soy. Although I'd known Ruth was a historian, we'd never discussed our work at any length. I'd felt too insecure about my historical skills, afraid that my first two books would strike her as amateurish, riding on an unused medical degree, my methods slipshod.

Perhaps I was buoyed by your looking better, perhaps it was just the desperation I've felt this past year about the Carmelita project, but that night I threw caution to the wind. I settled into the folding chair next to Ruth, probed her about her work on nineteenth-century women living outside of marriage, the choices she'd made in focusing on the history of three prototypical women, her narrative strategies. Then, for the first time, I tried to explain what I've been struggling with in the Carmelita story, the multiple frames through which I've been examining Carmelita's life.

A week later, Ruth's letter arrived—two single-spaced pages of additional thoughts she'd had about my project. She knew, she wrote, that I was interested in comparing the religious, psychiatric and economic interpretations of the Carmelita story, but had I considered the sexual politics of the situation? Assuming that Carmelita's pregnancy resulted from intercourse, what were the conditions of this copulation? Was it rape or passionate mutual consent? Perhaps it was a monetary transaction. A paragraph followed on how she'd learned about the centrality of understanding the sex industry in the lives of disenfranchised women from her research on Lydia Johnston, a Presbyterian minister's daughter who until the age of thirty-three had been her widowed father's housekeeper only to find herself destitute on his death, after which she'd become a prostitute and alcoholic around the shipyards of Richmond. Reading her letter, my head spun. I felt keenly aware of how unaccustomed I was to this level of intellectual vigor.

Ruth waves a hand as though to brush away my pesky apology. She reaches for the plate of quartered muffins Maggie has set on the coffee table. Rena comes in from the back. Her hair is wet, combed off her face, and she's wearing a loose white shirt that makes her appear even more pale and sylphish. She squints, steadies herself on the doorjamb.

Maggie moves toward Rena. Rena leans into her. Ruth opens out her arms to Rena, who sinks into the sofa beside her, head touching raised knees. She's still barefoot. Awkwardly, I watch as Ruth massages Rena's shoulder blades.

After a minute, Rena sits up. "That was Marc." Beneath the even words, I can hear the disdain, faint like the whispering of children who've been bid good night. "He discussed it with Susan, and they've agreed that it would be colluding with Saul to help find him an attorney. Marc said that Susan pointed out what a codependent family we are and how this would be a continuation of that."

Ruth snorts. "Can you believe the bullshit level of discourse?"

Maggie glares at Ruth as if to remind her that you don't comment on other people's relations.

I feel mortified, oddly more mortified by your brother's behavior than by yours. It's so mean-spirited, and Ruth's comment has highlighted for me what I can only call the deep insult for Marc to use this commercial pop-psychological analysis given that he knows how seriously we've both struggled with understanding human behavior. I remember our debate years ago, back when you were in college, about the ethics of hostility: Is hostility unconsciously expressed better or worse than hostility consciously expressed? (You were insistent that we include *expressed,* not wanting to imply that it is the hostility itself that is ethically negative. "That would make us Catholics," you said, "where thought and deed are judged as one.") I took the position that hostility unconsciously expressed is less evil because the perpetrator is himself innocent of the act—suggesting that he, too, finds the act abhorrent. You took the position that hostility unconsciously expressed is, in fact, worse since the perpetrator is guilty both of the aggressive act and of not taking responsibility for what he has done. I was so proud of you, barely twenty, of the elegance of your argument, and for a moment I indulge in the reminiscence—until the image of fingers curled around iron bars presses against my escape.

Ruth stands. It's nearly eleven, still dim inside, the scant light blocked by the brownstones across the street. "I'm calling Ann."

Maggie shoots Ruth a quizzical look. "This is kind of far afield for Ann, isn't it?" She turns to me to explain. "Ruth's sister does—what the hell is it she does?"

"Corporate litigation. But she'll know someone. Their clients, those Fortune 500 VPs, have kids who get in hot water and need bailing out."

2 Rena

Rena and Leonard take the subway to meet Michael Morton. Rena doesn't know or care what he owes Ruth's sister, only that he's agreed to meet them even though it's a Sunday. They get off at Chambers Street and walk east into a biting wind. She bows her head, cutting the wind with her forehead, relieved that the effort excuses her silence. City Hall looms like a gigantic wedding cake set down on a construction site. They pick their way over ramps and head north through Foley Square, Rena navigating the way she's always done with Saul, whom, absorbed in the pursuit of some line of thought, she's often thought she could lead right off the edge of a bluff.

Everything is closed, the row of kiosks that during the week sell hot dogs and souvlaki and falafel covered with rolled tin fronts. She reads the signs: Criminal Courts, Municipal Building, U.S. Courthouse, New York County Courthouse, Family Court, Customs Courthouse. Her hair blows up from her neck. She quickens her pace, too numb and cold to slow down when Leonard falls a step or two behind. They turn left on Worth Street and look for the number Morton gave her. It's a twenties office building with bubble-letter graffiti sprayed on the red brick: FUCK YOU JUAN. She tries the door but it's locked.

"He said he'd be here by one-fifteen." She looks at her watch, not yet one, takes shelter in the doorway. Saul, naked and handcuffed, sticks stubbornly in her mind.

Leonard marches in place. Across the street, there's a typewriter repair store and a sign, STENOGRAPHERS-CLERKS-TYPISTS: HOUR, DAY, WEEK. The setting, a stark contrast from the mahogany-and-marble offices of her clients, is making her nervous; it seems more like the location for a pawnshop, somewhere she and her mother might have gone, than a lawyer's office.

"A lawyer's lawyer," Ruth's sister had said about Morton. "A former U.S. assistant attorney, street-smart and sharp as a tack. Don't be put off by the shabby office, that's just part of his demeanor—doing what's practical, which for him is to be close to the courts. The courthouse locals call him Monk, for monkey, because he has this big forehead and long, thick arms. They tell this story about when he first came to the U.S. attorney's office and how he was riding the B train late one night and some guy approached him from the rear with a knife, to mug him, and how he spun around and slammed the guy into the platform. The detectives like to tell it that the mugger was left brain-dead, but what happened was a broken pelvic bone. The Monk is also a kind of joke because all he does is work and spend Saturdays going up to Yonkers to see his kid and pine over his ex-wife, who left him because all he did was work."

At one-twenty, a man rounds the corner. He's not wearing an overcoat and he's running, his arms swinging loosely and the sides of his sport coat blown back so he looks half airborne. Reaching them, he dances around like a child who needs to pee. "Goddamn freezing," he says, the comment addressed more to the street than to them. He extends a hand to Rena. "Mrs. Dubinsky?"

"Rena Peretti. This is Saul's father, Leonard Dubinsky."

Morton fumbles in his pockets for keys. They follow him through a tiled lobby to the freight elevator on the right. He blows on his hands and wiggles his fingers. On the fifth floor, he leads them down a dim corridor. He unlocks a door, flips a light switch, then turns toward them, offering a hand first to Rena and then to Leonard as if the greeting downstairs had not occurred.

"Sorry I'm late. I wanted to see the client, and there were some things that had to be taken care of."

It's the first time he's looked straight at her and she's startled by his eyes: a brilliant pale blue that unnerves her, suggesting, it seems, either utter sincerity or madness. They pass through a waiting area with a secretary's cubicle and then into his office. She'd expected a room with dirty windows and overflowing trash cans, but it's clean and orderly with large windows facing east. The Brooklyn Bridge looms so close and clear, it appears unreal. The opposite wall is covered with photographs: Morton with judges, Morton with a group of men in baseball uniforms, Morton with the Pope. On top of the desk, there's a picture of a little boy, three or four, grinning beside a fishing pole with a silver bucket by his feet.

Morton sits behind the desk and they sit in two chairs across from him. He takes a legal pad from a bottom drawer, pushes back his chair and swings his feet up onto the desk. "Okay, you tell me first what you know. Then I'll tell you what I learned today and we'll talk about where to go from here."

It takes Rena about ten minutes to tell Morton basically the same story she told Leonard. Morton takes copious notes, interjecting with questions of the *when precisely was that* and *how do you spell that* variety. When she gets to the arrest, he asks a lot of questions about what the police did and where they looked.

"Anything else? Anything at all?"

She catches Morton's glance at Leonard, and it occurs to her that he's thinking maybe she doesn't want to talk in front of Saul's father, an idea that hadn't crossed her mind before but is, she realizes now, partly the case.

"There's something I thought of on the subway here." She pauses, reluctant to open this door. "There's someone I know, Reed—actually, he's a lawyer, too—from a long time ago. We were roommates in San Francisco. He used to have a drug problem, before I met him, when he was a kid, really. Marijuana, LSD, psilocybin mushrooms, that sort of hippie experimental stuff. We lost touch for quite a while. Then Saul and I bumped into him. We were at the Whitney Museum and we ran into him in the stairwell. We went for lunch, the three of us, got together a couple more times after that. Saul and Reed started doing things, just the two of them, and I remember feeling pleased because there aren't too many people Saul finds as interesting as a book."

Hearing herself, she feels embarrassed—the excess words, the apologetic tone that Saul, master of nuance, had taught her to notice in herself.

"What would they do?"

"Basketball games, mostly. Reed would get box seats at the Garden through clients and he'd take Saul."

Leonard looks at her, confused, she imagines, to hear about Saul, who's always viewed his arms and legs as little more than vehicles to transport his mind, attending basketball games.

"It didn't last long. By the end of the year, Reed started flaking out. Once, we invited him for dinner and he showed up two hours late with some story about the subway. Another time, he and Saul were out somewhere and Reed went to the men's room and never came back. Saul said Reed was edgy, like he was jumping out of his skin. It seemed clear to me he was using something."

Rena can feel Leonard staring at her, and she doesn't know if it's because he's stunned that she'd introduced someone like Reed to Saul or because her face betrays how upset, in fact, she'd been to realize that Reed was using drugs again—Reed, who'd taught Gene, her half-brother, how to throw a football, been her only friend when she'd first moved east.

"I left a half-dozen messages on his home machine. Finally I called him at work, only to discover that he'd either been fired or quit. I guess it's possible that Saul was in touch with him without my knowing it. I don't know, it was just a thought I had."

Morton keeps his poker face, but it dawns on Rena from the way he doesn't ask her for Reed's last name that Saul has already told him about Reed, and then she wonders if Morton's not asking is purposeful, that he can't tell them what Saul has told him so he's leaving them this clue.

"Anybody else he'd see regularly?"

"How about Santiago?" Leonard says. "Didn't he read to him every week?"

"Who's that?"

"He was a professor of Saul's at Swarthmore," Leonard says. "A political scientist from Cuba. He came here in the fifties to take a position at Temple University, then lost his visa during the McCarthy era and had to leave to teach in Mexico. When he came back, he and his wife settled here in New York and he did some visiting teaching jobs. He was in his seventies by then, but still a marvelous teacher."

Morton glances at Rena, checking her reaction.

"Santiago had a big influence on Saul," Leonard continues. "He introduced him to Marxist theory, really made it come alive for him. Then, the year after Saul met him, Santiago's son disappeared in Guatemala. It was clearly a kidnapping, but unclear who had done it. Saul was convinced it was a paramilitary police faction and that the CIA had been involved. He organized a committee to help raise money for Santiago and his wife to carry on their search."

"Did they find him?"

"No. Not even a trace. Then Santiago went blind. He was too old and dispirited to learn braille. When Saul came to New York for medical school, he became one of Santiago's readers."

"How often would he see him?"

"Every Tuesday," Rena says. "Though this past year, I think it was pretty irregular."

"What's your take on him?" Morton asks Rena.

"I never met him. He and Saul had their routine, and . . ." She stops, reluctant to admit that she'd never wanted to meet Santiago, not because he didn't sound interesting—she'd enjoyed hearing Saul's stories about him—but rather because of a wariness about getting drawn into his life, into someone else's grief.

To Rena's relief, Morton abruptly shifts gears, turning his inquiry to Leonard's demographics: age, address, occupation, legal history. At occupation, he raises an eyebrow. "Two shrinks?"

"Well, not really. I haven't seen patients since 1955. I taught the history of psychiatry to medical students and residents. I retired two years ago."

"So let's hear your two cents on what might have happened here."

Leonard adds very little to what Rena has already said: he knew Saul had been having a hard time since the boy who threw himself in front of the train, they'd been less in touch this past year, he guesses he'd placed too much stock in the good cheer Saul had shown at his birthday party.

Listening to Leonard, Rena's fatigue surfaces—a dry burning around her eyes, her thoughts slow and muffled as though they've traveled down a long corridor to reach her mind. A sharp tone in Leonard's voice jolts her back to alertness.

"I'd been hoping this would be a two-way exchange, that you'd tell us how Saul is, what's going to happen next, what we can do."

Morton lowers his feet. He folds his hands and leans forward, a sequence so often repeated, she can see, it's no longer deliberate. "Look, this is a complicated thing and I'm going to talk to you two straight because you're both educated people, not like some of the know-nothings I see in this office. The law says that what the client tells me belongs to the client and I can't reveal that to anyone, not even our creator above. But you know and I know that that's not how the clock ticks and I wouldn't be able to get anything done for my clients if I couldn't share any information with relevant parties like you folks. I'm going to tell you some of what Saul told me this morning, but it has to be with the understanding that, as far as you're concerned, information has flowed in only one direction—from you to me. Whatever you know about Saul, you figured out yourselves. Agreed?"

Rena nods.

"Agreed," Leonard says.

"Okay. First of all, he's strung out. Barbiturates and cocaine. He says he's physically dependent on the barbiturates and if he doesn't get some into his system by tomorrow, he could have a seizure."

Rena's cheeks burn—not so much surprise at Morton's confirmation that Saul has been using again as humiliated anger that Saul had again hidden it from her. A hundred lies. Twice as many times she'd let herself be fooled.

"He's right," Leonard says. "Absolutely. Neuronal firing is slowed by barbiturates, and too rapid a withdrawal can lead to too rapid firing and a seizure."

"I've already called Medical. They'll be on top of it because they're all scared shitless about malpractice suits. So don't sweat over that. Detox is their bread-and-butter. That's the easy part."

"Where is he exactly?" Leonard asks.

"He's in a cell with three other guys at the MCC. It's a federal holding facility. It ain't the Plaza, but it's not as bad as what you see on TV. He's lucky this is a federal offense, because otherwise he'd be at Rikers and that can be ugly. Right now, though, the accommodations are irrelevant to him. His mind is on those pills."

Morton rotates a pencil between his fingers. "The biggest problem is his mea culpa syndrome. I've seen it before, especially with the white-collars. They just keep repeating, I deserve whatever I get. You're the shrink," he says, looking at Leonard. "You explain it to me. They want to plead guilty to everything. I had to struggle with Saul about entering an NG, a not-guilty plea. If I'd arrived fifteen minutes later, he would have already given them a signed confession. We don't want that. We've got to start with an NG. Otherwise we've got nowhere to go."

Leonard closes his eyes, all of this, she realizes, even more of a shock to him than to her.

"Can we see him?" she asks.

"That's the other thing. He doesn't want to see anyone. It's common, and in my experience you're better off, for now, staying away. They get into these tearful reconciliations with the family and they lose their focus for the arraignment. The most important thing these next twenty-four hours is keeping him focused for that arraignment. We pass that hurdle and we could have him out on bail by tomorrow night."

"Tomorrow night?" Leonard repeats.

"Unless there's some bullshit I don't know about, this should be a light lift. First offense. An accused with strong contacts in the community. Perfect bail-release candidate. So what you folks need to do is get yourselves organized to post bail. I'm guessing a hundred K, which means you need to put up ten. Is that going to be a problem?"

"I can handle it," Leonard says. "How about the arraignment? Can we come to that?"

Morton drops the pencil. He turns his hands palms up like a judge's balance. "I can't tell you not to come, it's open to the public. But the fewer distractions, the better, and you're going to be a big distraction. We're on the nine o'clock docket with Dunney, who's a pretty straight shooter. She goes fast. Still, there will probably be eight, nine other cases up, it being a Monday morning. So let's say two. I'll meet you here then."

RENA AND LEONARD walk back together to the subway. She hugs her arms, unable to stay warm. She's thinking about her discomfort with Leonard's offer to pay the bail, about her account balances.

"The bail," she says. "I should be able to come up with most of it."

"Don't worry about it. It's just an escrow, to guarantee court appearance."

Leonard buries his face in his collar, not wanting, she thinks, for her to see the doubt etched in his brow. A year ago, anyone who knew Saul would have said he was incapable of deception. As a child, he'd told her, his mother had to teach him not to volunteer his misdemeanors. His first-grade teacher would come back after stepping out into the hall and she'd say, who was talking, I could hear talking, and Saul would raise his hand. But now, Rena thinks, in his condition, does anything still apply?

She imagines Saul's retort, soft-spoken, but quick and deft as his grandfather's surgeon's hands: *There's no such thing as a condition. That's just an excuse, our contemporary way of evoking demons—the addiction made me do it.*

If I lie to you now, it's because I'm a liar.

3 Leonard

It's almost six by the time I walk up the driveway. The house is dark except for the third-floor bedroom. Through the window, I can see the glow of the television. I unlock the kitchen door and turn on the light. The note I left is crumpled in a ball. The coffeemaker is still on, and the room smells acrid with burnt coffee.

People other than us—you, Marc, Susan, me—can't understand the situation with your mother. Even Rena, I think, doesn't get it. Or perhaps, unlike Susan, she has refused to involve herself enough to try and make sense of the contradictions: how someone can live like an invalid and then, in January and July, make her annual trips to Palm Beach and Lake Placid. By now, Stone no longer orders blood tests and CAT scans. Anyone who spends most days in bed, he tells me over the phone when I call to convey some new development, is going to get headaches and backaches and bowels that don't do their job. Ten days in bed can be followed by a morning when I'll bring your mother her eleven o'clock breakfast, always the same (a freezer croissant with hotel butter, two soft-boiled eggs in an egg cup with a dollop of strawberry jam, orange juice, coffee with three teaspoons of sugar and a good dousing of cream), and she'll look up from the bed tray with a girlish smile. *I was thinking,* she'll say, *maybe I could manage the itsiest-bitsiest trip to the Short Hills Saks to get a new lipstick. An early dinner at Dantelli's, the calamari with red sauce and a nice lamb chop*. She'll bathe and carry her Hermès bag. If the weather is nice, I might even take the 1962 Mercedes we inherited from her father out of the garage and drive it to the shopping mall.

I turn off the coffeemaker and pour the burnt liquid down the drain. I run warm sudsy water in the pot, letting the bubbles overflow into the sink. I drink a glass of water and climb the stairs to the third floor.

Klara ignores me and I think maybe she's angry that I wasn't there to make her breakfast. She's dressed in a peach bed jacket, and her hair, last Friday's outing, is newly permed. Next to her on the bed is the box of Perugina's your brother sent for Valentine's Day. She's watching a French film with subtitles. She's always had this odd combination of refined taste and an utterly banal sensibility. Impressed as I was at first by her background, it took me a while to be able to discern the latter, to recognize that when she reads the classics—Hardy, the Russians, Flaubert—it's to find out what happens. In thirty-seven years of marriage, we've never discussed a book, a political event, a movie or even a piece of human interaction in anything other than a concrete way.

"How are you?" I ask.

She puts a forefinger to her mouth. "Shhh. There's only fifteen minutes left."

I sit in the armchair by the window. Even after all these years, I can't fully fathom how we got here, continue to live as though this is a temporary condition that at some point I'm going to rally myself to end. Your brother, I know, blames me for having let it happen: "She *obviously* went into a depression after Poppy died." The *obviously* is obviously lobbed in my direction, since he was ten and you were eight at the time. Other times, I think your brother's accusation is really a displacement (forgive me for being so technical, but you know I talk so little with colleagues, it being so unclear in what discipline I now belong, that it gives me pleasure to not have to translate into lay language), the accusation really about his conception, which anyone who can add and subtract can discern was three months before your mother and I married. Characteristically, your brother has never discussed it. You, however, childhood lover of lists—planetary distances and geological stages and Olympic long-distance gold medalists—placed before me, you were perhaps fourteen, a sheet of paper with two lines:

> May 17, 1955 Mom and Dad married
> December 12, 1955 Marc born

Underneath, you'd written the following equation: $^{12}/_{12} - ^{5}/_{17} = 6.83$ months. "What do you conclude?" I asked, and you said the expected.

Your brother's accusations aside, it was not, in fact, so obvious at first that your mother's reactions after your grandfather died were more than grief. Yes, she was a wreck. She required tranquilizers. She tried to throw herself on top of the casket as it was lowered into the ground. The night after the funeral, she hurled Marc's dinner plate onto the floor when he mumbled that the lima beans tasted like worms. But it was, after all, a shock. Your grandfather was in his early sixties. He'd performed three operations the morning he had the heart attack. A first heart attack and dead on the spot. And it was not a normal funeral, but rather a public spectacle what with all the pomp and circumstance of the medical school and the newspapers being there because he was a local celebrity and your mother's two doctor brothers, including her eldest brother, my medical school classmate who'd not spoken with me in over ten years.

Your mother idolized her father: the head of neurosurgery at Johns Hopkins, an editor of *The New England Journal of Medicine*. "You can quote me," she said the night we met at her brother's birthday party. "Daddy will be dean of the medical school one day." She was twenty-two and about to graduate from Wellesley with a C average maintained with the help of tutors who'd written her term papers. The C average, to be fair, was due not to a lack of smarts but rather to a basic laziness. Besides, she was too busy with parties every weekend at Harvard and Tufts and trips home for cousins' baby showers and bridesmaid dress fittings to go to a library. And, I knew from her brother, there were the occasional weekends when she and her girlfriends went to New York, weekends hidden from parents when three or four of them would pool allowances and take a room at the Gramercy Park Hotel. They'd paint black moons over their eyes, curling the line up at the corners, and tease their usually silky hair into poufs and wear their tightest cashmere sweaters and slimmest pencil skirts and go to the bars in the Village, giggling when men would approach. None of them, I'm certain, ever went home with any of these men, but it was a release and a titillation for them to pretend they were free girls, even for just a night, after which they'd return to Wellesley, content to don again their cardigans and saddle shoes.

The night I met your mother (a parent-sponsored weekend with a room at the Sherry Netherland, where her mother would join her the following afternoon for consolation shopping), she was at her brother's party drinking herself blotto because she'd just been dumped by her fiancé after he'd fallen in love with a scrub nurse. The ex-fiancé was a tennis player who'd grown up in her set. His sister had kept her horse at the same stable where your mother kept hers. He'd attended Princeton and then, with the help of your grandfather, medical school at Hopkins. Your mother sized me up: a garment worker's son who'd become a psychiatrist and had just quit his job. "I like surgeons," she informed me, her eyes sweeping the room for men after her brother, a fifth-year surgical resident, introduced us. And, although she was too well bred to say it, it was clear that she wasn't too crazy about Jews, either. Certain she would have no interest in me, her brother entrusted me to walk her, by then three hours more inebriated, back to her hotel.

It was your grandfather who gave me the news. He took the train to New York and invited me to lunch at the University Club. It never occurred to me that the invitation had to do with your mother, to whom I'd not spoken since the unfortunate incident. Naïvely, I assumed he was taking an interest in me, that her brother had told him that my career was foundering, how, after being chief resident and, everyone thought, a shoo-in at the psychoanalytic institutes where I'd applied, I'd quit my hospital job and tabled my applications. How I'd been working nights and weekends as a sub in emergency rooms. Not that sleeping with drunken girls (you'll have to forgive my speaking this way about your mother, I'm just trying to convey my state of mind at the time) was such a common occurrence for me that I'd forgotten it; rather, I'd so immediately known it was a stupid and caddish thing to do, a desperate attempt to exorcise Maria, that I'd put it aside as a mistake I'd not repeat. That next morning, waking on the enormous hotel bed, both of us embarrassed and eager to part, was perhaps the only time your mother and I have had a true meeting of minds.

Her father came armed with a plan. We would have a civil marriage at the end of the week. This was the first mention that your mother had accompanied him to New York. He would stay to witness it. The civil marriage was because she was Episcopal and I was Jewish. I could see he was using all his willpower to put aside the Jewish issue. His only mention of it was to say—and here, he gave me a searing look—he had to insist the child be christened by the minister at their church.

"Klara is not religious, either," he informed me. "The two of you will have to work out the religious issues as you see fit. But her mother will not be able to rest if the child is not baptized. I'm sure you understand," he said, signaling the close of that topic.

He'd heard that I was unemployed. That was the word he used, *unemployed,* and it left me feeling ashamed, dirty. I tried to defend myself, that I was working, just not at a regular job.

"Given the current situation, you must have regular employment." His former mentor was a dean at the newly opened New Jersey College of Medicine and Dentistry. He'd spoken yesterday with him. They could use me to teach the history of psychiatry. "That would suit you," he announced, "with your interest in Freudian analysis." After the baby was born, he would discuss with me starting a private practice.

I must have looked stunned. He offered me a cigarette, and even though I didn't smoke, I took it.

"I'm sorry for both of you, that things happened this way. Klara's mother and I are not people who hold grudges. Once you're married, we will put all this behind us." He lit my cigarette and then his own. "Klara is a complicated girl," he said confidentially. "Perhaps, being in your profession, you will understand her better than her mother or I have been able to."

Your mother assumed that I would proceed exactly as her father had outlined. She had terrible morning sickness that left her eyes ringed with broken capillaries, and on the way to City Hall she had to ask the cab-driver to pull over. Your grandfather and I stood by her at the curb, each holding an elbow. I'd not noticed before how tall she was, how substantial were her wrists and hips. She got a spot on her linen suit and spent the rest of the ride dabbing at it with her father's handkerchief. And I did proceed as her father had outlined, up until the part that had to do with returning to practicing psychiatry. I'm not sure if my break from the designated program at that point was due to its being far enough down the line that I was able by then to reassert something of my own will, or if this—more than the marriage or the christening or the move to New Jersey—was something I simply could not bring myself to do. What I do know, though, is that she hated me for not practicing. Psychiatry was in her mind low enough, for those too squeamish or weak to do real medicine. But to not even practice was to move off the map.

Writing books struck your mother as shabby. Not to mention, not very lucrative. Her incantations about her father and the number of operations he did in a week and the kinds of tools he used to saw open a skull and the eminent people—a Kuwaiti prince, the wife of the former Italian president—who traveled to be operated on by him became her way of expressing her bitterness, which it took me years to see was, at heart, not about what I did for a living but rather about how our coitus that night at the Sherry Netherland had ruined everything for her. Everything being a life like her parents' with the opening of the season in October at the Hunt Dance, and six weeks of holiday parties and debutante balls between Thanksgiving and New Year's when all the houses in Roland Park would be adorned with fresh wreaths on the doors and candles in the windows, their living room rearranged to fit the ten-foot fir her father would cut himself from the back of their property. The cruise wear—tennis whites, striped boating sweaters, lemon evening dresses—purchased each January for the two weeks in the Bahamas, the night of love arias performed for the opera donors' inner circle on Valentine's Day, the Easter baskets her mother made every year for the hospital's children's wing, each with green tinsel and hand-painted eggs and a chocolate bunny and a terry-cloth duck that squeaked and two daffodils from their garden laid on top. The languid summers that began with the Memorial Day barbecue at the country club three miles from their home: a club, mind you, at which members telephoned in the full names of their guests two days in advance so as to make certain that never again would a Jewish guest be discovered in the steam room wrapped in one of the club's monogrammed towels, the offending member having sworn he'd thought that his accountant, Mr. Schulman, was of *pure* German descent.

YOUR MOTHER LIFTS the remote control and aims it at the television set. There's a sound like air being sucked through a pneumatic tube and then it's silent. "You weren't even watching, were you," she says.

"No." For a fleeting moment, the directness of her tone leads me to imagine that I'm going to be able to talk with her about what has happened, that we will be able to face together what needs to be done.

"Klara," I say. Her face contorts and a hand moves to her mouth. "Klara," I repeat.

"No," she whimpers. "Don't tell me." She starts to cry. "Don't tell me. Don't you tell me."

It's hard to hear her with her hand covering her mouth. It sounds like she's saying her head hurts too much. Or is it her heart? She clamps her palms over her ears.

I move to the edge of the bed and pry her fingers from her hair. "Stop it," I say. "Stop." I consider slapping her, which sometimes stems the tide of hysteria but other times only escalates it. I hold her hands between my two. "Listen to me. You have to listen."

She's sobbing. She flails on the bed and twists so her face is buried in the pillow.

"Jesus Christ." I throw the other pillow against the wall and walk down to the second floor. Opening the medicine cabinet, I take out a bottle of Valium. I put two pills in my shirt pocket and go down to the kitchen, where I pour myself a scotch. I get a glass of water for your mother and sit waiting at the kitchen table.

Twenty minutes later, she arrives. She's put on the slippers that match her peach bed jacket. I hand her the two Valium, which she downs with the glass of water. She sits opposite me and closes her eyes. Five minutes pass and then, calmly, she says, "All right, Leonard, I'm ready to listen."

I WAKE IN THE middle of the night thinking about the dream of the burning child in *The Interpretation of Dreams*. A father has spent the past week nursing his dying child. When the child finally dies, the exhausted father goes to rest in an adjacent room, leaving the boy's body under the care of an old man who will pray by candlelight over the corpse. He keeps the door ajar so he can see into the room where the body lies. He dreams that the boy comes to him and says, "Father, don't you see I'm burning?" Awakened by a glare of light, he discovers that the old man has fallen asleep and that the shroud and the arm of his child have been singed by a toppled candle.

When I first read the dream, I railed that such a tragic story had interested Freud mostly in its technical sense: as an exemplar for his theory of dreams as wish fulfillments. By dreaming that the child has come to the father's bedside to report that he is burning, Freud argues, the father fulfills both the wish that his child were still alive and the wish to remain asleep. Now, lying next to your snoring mother, I begin to cry. Where are the father's crimes addressed? A father who left his dead child in the care of a dotty old man. A father who slept while his child's corpse caught fire.

Unable to sleep, I pray. I am a nonbeliever, but still I pray that you are sleeping soundly, that you are not huddling cold and frightened in your cell.

• • •

At five, I go downstairs. I make the coffee, eat my toast over the sink, gaze through the mist at the outlines of trees. With the Valium, your mother remained calm while I told her about your arrest. She asked only two questions: Would your name be in the newspapers? Had Rena been arrested, too? Then she said she wanted to talk with Marc. It was nearly ten when I dialed the number for her. She seemed reassured by his anger at you. Perhaps it made it all seem more like a childhood incident. After a while, Marc asked to speak with me, and although he hadn't changed his mind about helping you, he did inquire if we'd found a lawyer and then volunteered to take your mother. "I guess you'll be out a lot," he said. "Maybe she'd do better being here." Your mother immediately agreed. Before swallowing two more pills and going back upstairs, she dictated a list of what to pack for her. She was already asleep when Susan called to tell me she'd booked a morning flight.

At quarter to seven, I place the two suitcases I've packed for your mother by the front door and go to make her breakfast tray. Between the Valium and the fact that she hasn't been up this early in years, it's hard to rouse her. I peel back the covers and shake vigorously. She looks at me with confused distress, and for a moment I think she is going to burst into tears the way you would as a baby if you were wakened before you were ready. Next to her orange juice I've placed one more Valium, which she takes after eating her eggs and jam.

She dozes in the car on the way to the airport. Guiltily, I wonder if she'll be able to manage alone on the plane. As we pull into short-term parking, she asks if I remembered to pack the belt to her orange dress and I tell her I did.

"The belt that goes with it, not the sash I sometimes wear with it?"

"The belt."

I tell the stewardess that she's not feeling well, and they let me take her to her seat and promise to escort her off the plane in Atlanta and deliver her to Marc. She closes her eyes as soon as she sits down. I lean over to peck her cheek.

Her lids rise and I see a look of terror. "Marc will meet me, won't he?"

I pet her shoulder. "Yes, dear."

It's ten-thirty when I enter the city through the Holland Tunnel. I park the car at Astor Place and walk south, debating what to do with the next three and a half hours until we're supposed to meet Morton. What I'm debating is whether to go, despite Morton's advice to the contrary, to your preliminary hearing.

I raise my hand and a cab veers toward me. Decided.

At the courthouse entrance, I ask a guard where the courtrooms are.

"Information booth end of lobby," he says without moving a muscle.

I point to the long queue. "I just need to know the floor."

"Information booth end of lobby."

It takes twenty minutes to reach the head of the line, after which I wait another five while a huge girl with crimson lips and hoop earrings moves papers from one pile to another. She hoists herself from her stool to get her purse, and I watch while she unwraps a hard candy.

"Spell that again," she says when I give your name.

Slowly, she runs a finger down a column of names, stopping at yours. At ours. She writes a number on a paper and hands it to me. "Second floor."

I take the elevator to the second floor, push open a heavy door to a cavernous room with wooden pews. I sit in back and slouch so my face is obstructed by the man in front of me. I spot you immediately, your black hair curling over the collar of a tweed jacket. Last year, I'd noticed a few wiry white strands over your ears. They were coiled tightly like cartoon character hair and I'd had the urge to yank them out, as if with their disappearance I could arrest time, wrest you from the mechanism that rotates beneath both our lives, leading you to walk at precisely the same fifteen months I did, marching you forward to a head of gray at the same forty-two that both my father and I lost the black color of ours.

You're in the front row with a dozen or so other people, all seated in pairs. The lawyers are showered and freshly shaved; like you, the defendants are in clothes they appear to have slept in overnight. Everyone's whispering, the voices gathering into a drone that seems to be gaining velocity. There's an ominous feel in the overheated room: a mixture of deceit and despair and cynicism and, underneath it all, fear.

Two lawyers are arguing about the parole status of a kid with a shaved head. He's dressed in a camouflage outfit and enormous black boots. An armed policeman stands beside him. When the kid lowers his head, I can see something that looks like a swastika but with an extra leg or two tattooed on his albumen scalp. My mouth tastes like copper pennies, and I am suddenly very scared for you.

They've moved on to another case, something about the fraudulent sale of public telephones to restaurants. The defendant is a man my age. He's sweating profusely. His collar is too tight and the judge keeps glancing at him, afraid, it seems, that he'll have a coronary right here in her courtroom. "Does your client need a recess?" she asks his lawyer. The lawyer confers with the sweating man. My mind drifts—an afternoon some sixty years ago, sitting at my Uncle Jack's dining room table, doing my homework. I could see across West End Avenue to the opposite building. An animal was crawling on one of the window ledges. At first I thought it was a pigeon. Then I thought it was a kitten that had climbed outside. Suddenly, the animal dropped from the ledge. It passed through the square of sky I could see from my chair. I rushed to the window to look below, but there were people on the sidewalk and cars going north and south and I'd been unable to detect anything.

I hear your name being called. You sit in the same chair as the boy with the swastika on his scalp and the guy who looked like he was having a heart attack. The same armed police officer stands beside you. Morton is dressed in a brown suit, hair slicked back from his face. That confidence we invest in strangers on whom we need to depend dissolves and I stare at this simian-shaped man, jumping now from place to place with a yellow pad in hand. You look paler and thinner than the last time I saw you. I count back eight weeks to the day I handed you my credit card. Your eyes and nose appear to be running, and I think I can see the tremor in your hands. Despite Morton's reassurances that the jail doctors will stay on top of detoxing you from the barbiturates, I'm afraid that your fine brain is going to seize.

The other lawyer, the federal prosecutor, has the appearance of someone who has resigned himself to being fat. When he stands, his sport coat hikes over the waistband of his pants, elasticized in back. He reads the charges in a singsong voice: conspiracy to commit burglary, conspiracy to distribute controlled substances. He clears his throat. "In addition, we have been advised by representatives of the State of New York that they will be independently pursuing their own investigation through the Manhattan district attorney's office and will be presenting a case to a state's grand jury to secure an indictment of Mr. Dubinsky on manslaughter charges."

"What?" Morton says. "The weapon was never employed."

"The pharmacist, Mrs. Kim Sun, miscarried from the shock of the experience."

Morton stands. The back of his neck is red. "What's going on here?"

"The miscarriage just took place this weekend. Mrs. Sun's gynecologist is prepared to testify to this court that the pregnancy was well established prior to the burglary and that the trauma of the event was a precipitating factor."

The judge looks over at you. You are staring at the federal prosecutor. She beckons for the two lawyers to approach her. Afterwards, Morton goes to talk with you. The room is getting hotter and hotter, and I can hear the heat blasting in the radiators under windows the guards have pushed open. The judge bangs her gavel and Morton addresses her. "Your Honor, I would like, despite this new information which I do not believe further incriminates my client, to request that my client be released on his own recognizance. He is an employed physician. His wife, father and brother are also professionals. He has strong roots in the community and poses no risk to the court to fail to appear throughout these proceedings."

The judge writes some notes. Then she turns to the federal prosecutor. He twists in his seat to look at you as if to accentuate your utter depravity. "We are recommending no bail option. The defendant is an active substance abuser. As the court may recall, we have data showing the extremely high percentage of nonappearances by substance abusers. Moreover"—here, the federal prosecutor raises his hands, as though to ward off a pending attack—"the government believes that the defendant is at particularly high risk to flee the jurisdiction of this court. The individual suspected to be his coconspirator, Mr. Reed Michaelson, has, we believe, already fled to the Canary Islands. Mr.—excuse me, Dr. Dubinsky is undoubtedly aware that his career as a physician is severely threatened by these proceedings and may well be motivated to join Mr. Michaelson wherever he may be."

Morton bangs the table where the federal prosecutor has spread his papers. Coffee from a styrofoam cup sloshes onto the surface. "This is garbage. No one informed us of this information."

"Counselor," the judge says. "I must request that you maintain decorum in my courtroom."

Morton leans over you. You shake your head, and then I see you starting to turn. I duck as though picking up a dropped piece of paper. The drone filters down to the floor. Crouched over, I make my way to the door.

MORTON'S HANDS ARE frozen in fists, fighter's fists with the thumb pressed on top of the forefinger. Rena sits motionless. She's wearing pleated black pants with gold knots in her earlobes and a pale green jacket. Her face looks fragile and bony, all cheekbones and eye sockets. Her lips are parted as if she needs extra air.

Morton has told us the bail decision. "Two hundred and fifty thousand, no noncash alternative." He explains that this is because of Michaelson's disappearance. He doesn't say anything about the pharmacist having miscarried and the second-degree manslaughter charge, and I don't know if this is because he doesn't see this as the relevant factor or if this is so serious he doesn't want to break it to us now.

"What does that mean?" Rena asks.

"Usually they accept ten percent cash and the rest of the bail as a note—a commitment from the bail bondsman to pay if your boy skips town. With no noncash alternative, it's got to be all cash. That means you're going to have to come up with two hundred and fifty thousand dollars in cash. No notes."

Rena looks at me. "How would we do that?"

"Assuming you don't keep that kind of dough sitting in the bank and you don't have a cousin who's a banker waiting to put that kind of loan through for you, the only way it can be done is with a bail bondsman who might take a risk on you for a hefty charge. I've got one guy in mind, Charlie Green, but he's not someone I play games with. If I tell him he can put money on my man, he counts on me to mean that one hundred and fifty percent."

Morton squirms in his seat. He stretches a rubber band between his forefingers and snaps at it with his thumbs.

"Fatso, the feds' prosecutor, is right. Your boy's a risk. He's strung out. He's got the means to get out of here. Sticking around is not going to look so good. When Green asks me what I think, I'm going to have to say so."

"That will nix it from the start, won't it?" I say.

Morton leans back in his chair. He looks over the door frame at a hoop mounted there. Your brother has the same thing in his office, this club of men for whom twelve was the apex of pleasure. When he loses a case, he can cover the floor with wads of paper tossed through the hoop. "These guys make money by purchasing risk. Green makes his own decisions. Sometimes he does these things as a gamble. Sometimes he'll do it if he can structure the deal so he wins no matter what. Nothing lost by giving him a try."

CHARLIE GREEN MOVES his fingers in and out. He's a tall man with thick black hair receding at the temples and a nose with a prominent bump. Last year's calendar is taped to the wall, and there's a stained coffeemaker on top of the file cabinet. In the background is the rumble of what sounds like a police radio. Rena has taken off her jacket, the curve of her breasts and her narrow waist now revealed through her blouse. She seems more alert, and I can't help wondering if she's taken off her jacket on purpose.

"Do you own your apartment?" Green asks her.

"No, we rent."

"Car, boat, stocks, bonds, artwork, jewelry, anything of significant value?"

"We each have an IRA. Saul has his stereo and record collection. We have a few paintings, pieces we bought from a young artist, nothing that we could get any real money for."

"How about you, Pops?"

I freeze. No one has ever called me Pops. An old, horrid feeling surfaces from when I was a kid and someone would yell *Hey, Jewboy* and I would die a thousand deaths, afraid to fight, humiliated to just walk by, praying they would think I hadn't heard.

"I own my house. An IRA. Some stocks and bonds."

"Car?"

"A Honda Accord. My deceased father-in-law's Mercedes-Benz."

"What's the house valued at?"

"I couldn't say. We've never had it appraised."

"Three hundred grand?"

"More. At least four."

"What year's the Benz?"

"1962."

Green jots numbers on his desk blotter pad. He rubs the bump on his nose, which looks from this angle like it's been broken.

"How much you got liquid?"

I add in my head. Bank accounts. Credit lines. "Maybe thirty-seven thousand."

"You put the house up as collateral and the first twenty-five K, I'll post the bond."

I think about it. So, if you skip town, I've sold my house for two hundred and twenty-five thousand dollars. No. Wrong. If you skip town, I've sold my house for zero dollars since there won't be any money or any house.

Rena touches my arm. "We should talk about this." She looks at the clock on Green's desk. It's nearly four-thirty. "How late are you here?" she asks Green.

"Sweetheart, this ain't a nine-to-five business. I'm here when I'm here. Could be eleven tonight. Could be three in the morning."

"I'll need to discuss this with my wife," I say. "The house is in her name, too."

"You talk about it with whoever you want, Pops. You can talk about it with the mayor, as far as I'm concerned. Only, those are my conditions and you might as well know, I don't negotiate. I go with my first instinct, and it's a superstition of mine not to tamper with that."

RENA SUGGESTS I STAY over rather than drive back and forth again from New Jersey. I accept, letting myself entertain the idea that she'd prefer not to be alone, a delusion that fades in the face of her careful politeness beneath which I can see what a strain she finds even simple conversation, how inconceivable it is to her that I or, I suppose at this point, anyone, might be a comfort to her.

We walk in silence. She pulls a beret out of her coat pocket and stuffs her hair inside. The sky is muddy, neither black nor blue, and there's a messy half-moon hanging low. The temperature has risen as it does on those days when nightfall draws a curtain on the wind. When we get to Franklin Street, she says, "I guess we should get the subway here." On the platform, a toothless woman in a flowered skirt is singing in Portuguese. During the chorus, she claps her hands and moves in small circles, first one direction, then the other. She shifts from side to side and I remember when you were first learning to walk how, when you heard music, a record I was playing or a phrase on television, you would stop and stare as if trying to find the instrument. Planting your feet wide apart, you'd sway back and forth.

A young ponytailed man stops before the singer. He's carrying yellow roses wrapped in white butcher's paper. He hands her one. She makes an ironic little curtsy and sticks the stem through her matted hair. The words are close enough to Spanish that I can catch the gist: a mother lamenting her son's death at war.

Rena orders Chinese food, setting out place mats on your coffee table. I sit on the couch and she sits on the floor in gray sweatpants, burying her nose in a mug of the steamy soup. She barely touches anything else. Miserably, I eat too much, drugging myself with food. She puts down her mug and stretches her legs out under the coffee table. I cannot think of you. I cannot think of you and think about what to do for you at the same time.

"I just want you to know that I don't expect you to do it, to sign over your house. Morton's right. He could run. He tried to run when the police came."

"I don't think he would if he knew his mother and I would lose our house."

The words sound false before they finish on my lips. I feel terribly lonely, as though you have traveled to a place so foreign I can no longer even imagine you in your surrounds. "I can't not do it. I couldn't live with myself if I didn't."

Rena looks at me curiously and I think, well, she's not a parent, she doesn't know how it is with children, how, when you have children, there are no heroic acts. What's hard are the small things, the things we excuse ourselves for overlooking or turning from. For years, I operated under a haze of guilt: the dozen little betrayals perpetrated toward you and your brother every day. Whereas at first I thought that my attention toward the two of you increased after your mother abdicated out of necessity—a sort of zero-sum game, if she wasn't going to do it, I had to—it was such a relief to have the guilt of small neglects lifted that even had your mother recovered, I could not have returned to tuning you out. Like one of those feedback loops, Darwinian in its effects, the more I put your needs first, the happier and less demanding the two of you became, which then inspired more in kind on my part. I remember once foolishly trying to explain this cycle to your mother, but she was already too far gone, too lost in herself, to be able to think about anything she couldn't touch with her hands. "Leonard," she said in her high, tight voice, "surely even you can see that I have a headache?"

I look at my watch. It's nearly nine. Time for Klara's tranquilizers. Now or never. "I guess I better call Klara."

I start clearing the dishes, but Rena waves a hand. "Go. I'll do it. There's a phone in there." She points to the room with the futon. I pull the door shut behind me, embarrassed to have her hear the way I talk to your mother.

Susan answers. She gives me the outlines of Klara's arrival. How she was taken in a wheelchair off the plane because she'd told the stewardess she felt dizzy. How the stewardess whispered to Marc that Klara had fallen ill so suddenly; she'd chatted with the person next to her for the entire flight and eaten all of the lunch. "She perked up," Susan says, "once she got to the house. I set her up on the chaise longue with a glass of lemonade and some pecan sandies. Marc grilled steaks for dinner and miraculously, she said, her appetite returned. She and Marc are sitting on the patio having their coffee."

Susan doesn't ask about you. With your brother I would assume this to be deliberate, but with Susan it seems possible that it is genuinely oversight, that your mother's arrival, has, in fact, occluded everything else. She brings the portable phone outside and I listen while your mother recounts the heart palpitations she felt during the landing, the near fainting as she tried to get out of the seat. "I sat there thinking, oh, my goodness, what am I going to do, I can't even get off the plane. I was so upset, thinking about Marc standing there waiting, but luckily there was this nice stewardess, a black girl, who helped me. They had to call for a wheelchair, and I felt so badly holding her up like that . . ."

I study my watch. After five minutes, I say, "Klara." She halts, my interjection sharper than I'd intended. "I need to talk with you about Saul." I imagine your mother shutting her eyes, remember reading back when Marc was a baby that shutting the eyes is the earliest of the defense mechanisms. He'd shut his eyes tight, screw up his face and scream.

"Are you listening?"

A long, languorous sigh followed by short, staccato gasps float over the line.

"Rena and I went to see a bail bondsman. The only way we might get Saul out on bail is by putting up the house as collateral. I've thought about it. There's obviously some risk, but I think we should do it."

"I can't bear it," your mother says. There's sobbing and then a banging sound, the phone, it seems, dropped to the ground.

"What did you say to her?" Marc asks. "Hold on." I hear Marc yelling, "Susan, come here," and then Susan's voice rising over your mother's cacophony: "Mother, Mother, calm down. Now, you have to stay calm." The line goes static and then clear again, and I surmise that Marc has walked back into the house.

I tell him Charlie Green's proposal.

"Look," Marc says, "if the judge set the bail without a noncash alternative, that means she thinks there's a good chance he'll skip town. She has no other motivation for keeping him in jail. Take your lead from her. You don't want to lose the house."

"Saul wouldn't do that."

"Don't be a fool. He's a drug addict. It looks like he was an accomplice in an armed robbery. He'll probably lose his medical license. You think he's worrying about your house?"

I want to chastise your brother for calling me a fool, but I force myself to stay focused. "I've made up my mind. I'm going to do it. But I can't go forward without your mother's agreement."

"Well, I can't advise Mom to do that. I have to advise her against it."

We continue a few minutes longer under the guise of furious politeness. I tell Marc I'll call tomorrow, first thing, to talk with your mother.

Rena helps me unfold the futon in your study. She brings me sheets and towels and a pair of your pajamas. Your pajamas are too small. I lie on the futon in my underwear still fuming at your brother, imagining calling him back to say, *I don't give a goddamn what you think about this, I expect you to do as I say.*

I pull the shade up and stare out the window at the postage stamp garden. A trash can lid bangs. A cat darts toward the easement between the buildings. It occurs to me that maybe I've inadvertently set you up by sending your mother to Atlanta, where she can be pulled into Marc's sphere of influence. I meditate on that word, *inadvertently,* and how the notion of the unconscious wipes out its meaning. Your mother's not going to do it. And even if she were, your brother would do anything in his power to prevent it.

• • •

At eight, a locksmith arrives to drill a hole in the metal door and install a new cylinder. It's Ruth who has insisted this must be done, Maggie who has arranged for the man to come.

Your mother calls while the locksmith is still at work. Her tone is firm but friendly. What a businesswoman she could have been had her feelings about her father not felled her so early on. A Leona Helmsley in a sharp red suit.

She sighs. "I didn't sleep a wink, up all night thinking about this." For once, I believe her. "We cannot risk our house, where would we live, and besides that would be unfair to Marc since the house is our largest asset and will someday be half his. But I'll put up my jewelry. The pearls, the diamond earrings, the pieces I inherited from my mother. And there's our silverware, too."

She's a card player. She knows these items all together aren't worth fifty grand. At Wellesley, there'd been a set of them who played poker with some dissolute Harvard boys. The loser supplied the next game's bottle of bourbon. After we moved to New Jersey, she'd given it up because in our neighborhood men and women didn't play together. The women played bridge in a way that lacked cunning. They drank coffee and ate pineapple upside-down cake.

I don't have the heart to dig at her. The locksmith is sweeping up. I follow Rena into the kitchen while she makes a pot of tea and cuts up fruit. I tell her your mother's proposal. She responds with a series of quick, sharp chops.

We reach Green late morning. First Rena, then I, try to get him to accept what we can come up with, but we both know that we're just going through the motions: he's not going to change his initial offer and we cannot meet it. At noon, Rena calls Morton to tell him we've reached an impasse with Green. I listen on the extension.

"Sorry," Morton says. "But it was a long shot. Look, he's lucky these are federal charges. As I told you before, the MCC is a hell of a lot better than Rikers."

"Is there anyone else?"

"If Green won't do it, no one will."

Morton pauses to allow Rena a decent amount of time to take this in. "I just came from seeing Saul."

"How is he?"

"He's struggling with the detox. Sometimes it's just as well for them to have something else to think about."

"Can we visit him?"

"Well, we'll have to talk about that. Right now, he says he doesn't want any visitors. You don't have too many rights inside, but you can refuse visitors."

A silence falls and for a split second I think maybe the line has gone dead. I jump in. "It's me, Leonard," I say. "I'm on the extension. Why is that?"

"He says he feels too awful."

"Physically or mentally?"

"He didn't say. I'd guess both."

Rena stays quiet for the rest of the phone call. I talk with Morton about what will happen next. He tells us that they've set the state prosecutor's presentation of the manslaughter case against you before the grand jury for the ninth of March. I count days on my fingers: nineteen. Neither you nor Morton is permitted to attend.

"I'll stop by to see him every day," Morton says. "Depending on how the evidence shakes out, we'll most likely keep the not-guilty plea, which means we'll then have to prepare for trial." He sniffs. He's a sniffer, one of those people always fighting some kind of upper respiratory thing. I wonder if like Green he, too, had a broken nose. "Don't worry about this not wanting visitors thing. It'll pass. A lot of them feel that way for the first week or so."

Rena and I convene in the living room. We go over the conversation. We're not talking about anything, just talking to ward off a tide of emptiness.

At the door, I hug her loosely. There's a little heave in her chest. I tighten my grip and she stays still that second longer that transforms what was ceremonial into something else. Quickly, she straightens and her face rearranges itself.

It takes over an hour to walk to Penn Station, by the end of which I've decided that your wife's eyes were, indeed, damp. The idea that as much of a strain as my presence was for her, she might feel worse once I left, hadn't occurred to me any more than it probably had to her. Standing at a bank of phones, I call her. I reach your machine with your voice, then stumble over sentences about how she should call me if there's anything she needs, even just to talk. I purchase my ticket and board the train.

On the ticket stub, I write a shopping list. Milk, fruit, stamps. I cannot think of anything else to buy. I cannot imagine what I will do once I get back to the house.

Sometime after Newark, I doze off. When I wake, you are in my mind's eye: a crescent moon on a thin mattress on the floor of your cell. Your eyes are open and there are water bugs and I worry that you are cold. That old feeling from when you and Marc were babies and I would spend the nights in and out of my bed going to lift one or the other of you crying from your crib. That anxious sleepy look on your face as you stood clutching the bars. Maybe that's it. The bars. Are you clutching the bars?

I WRITE YOU EVERY DAY. Long, struggling letters, some of which I know better than to mail. After a week, I see that they could be titled like country-and-western songs: How Could I Have Failed to See Your Pain, What Have You Done to Yourself, What Have I Done to You, You Must Be Strong: The Travails of Life Are the Iron in the Steel (this one I don't send), I Will Stand by You Through Thick and Thin.

You don't respond. Morton reassures me that you're receiving the letters, that you're doing well with the barbiturate detox and that you've told him to tell me you will write when you feel able. I don't believe you've sent such a message, particularly in the middle of the night when I lie in the dark, my routine now shattered so that like your mother I am up until three and asleep half the morning.

In the middle of your second week in jail, Morton calls to tell me that the grand jury date has been changed to Friday, March 13.

"Great. Friday the thirteenth."

Morton doesn't respond. As always, I am surprised that other people are not superstitious the way I am, that they don't walk around saying touch wood and reaching down to tap the leg of a chair. Superstition has always struck me as not what it seems, not a belief in magic, but rather a belief that it is beneficial to be on guard. If you worry about even implying something might go well, you're less likely to overlook that your wings are attached with beeswax that will melt in the sun.

I hear Morton swallow. "There's something else. If they return an indictment, which they're going to do ninety-nine percent chance, I'm going to recommend he enter a guilty plea."

"A guilty plea?"

"Most of them, by this time, are so eager to get out, they'd sell their mother. Saul, though, doesn't have the heart to defend himself. But even if he did, I'd still say it's the way we got to go. These guys have a rock-solid case. It's like telling a terminal cancer patient to plan for a cruise next winter. Don't make any sense."

I don't like the analogy. Morton senses this immediately. He's careless in certain ways, and then can turn around and be exquisitely perceptive.

"Okay, bad metaphor, simile, whatever the hell you call it, but you get the point. If we give them a guilty, we can work on cutting a deal: they drop the state's manslaughter two, we take burglary and conspiracy to distribute controlled substances. Judges go a lot lighter on a guilty plea than a guilty verdict at trial."

"If he pleads guilty, what happens after that?"

"He stays where he is another couple of weeks while they do the presentencing investigation. That's the report the federal probation department writes recommending sentencing parameters to the judge. They'd probably interview you, Rena, some people from the hospital. We'd have a good chance of painting him as a good guy gone astray. Then there's another hearing when the sentencing is done."

Hearing *probation,* my hopes soar. "You mean he might get probation?"

"No. I'm sorry, Leonard." It's the first time he's used my name. "That's just the department that does the report. These are federal charges, and they have mandatory minimums."

I didn't touch wood. All along, I've been putting one foot in front of another by focusing on how this is temporary: until the trial, until you got out to do public service or a drug rehabilitation program or something. Suspension of your license. Anything other than staying where you are.

"What sort of minimums?" My voice is almost a groan.

"With these charges, we're talking forty-eight months with fifty-some days off a year for good behavior."

I put the phone down on the desk and cradle my face in my hands. I can hear Morton talking and talking and then my name, *Leonard, Leonard.*

Forty-eight months.

There's silence, then the high-pitched screech of a receiver off the hook, then a woman's whine, over and over, *If you'd like to make a call, please hang up.*

Four years.

4 Rena

She senses Leonard's caution, the care he takes not to call her more than every few days. An outsider might say that it's impossible to tell from which of them the distance originates—whether he's stepped back and she has in that inchoate way people gauge closeness and distance shifted in kind or vice versa—but she knows it's her. Mostly they talk about the case, the newest updates they've each received from Morton.

When she calls Morton today, he suggests that a certain amount hinges on whether they can apprehend Reed. If so, Morton says, they might let Saul cut a deal by supplying information on Reed.

"Do you think he'd do that?" she asks.

"Hard to say. Every day's a different story the first month with them. On the one hand, Saul tells me this Reed character sacrificed him—left knowing Saul would get caught. Then he turns around and says it's irrelevant, he still did what he did."

A disturbing protectiveness toward Reed surfaces in Rena at Morton's reference to him as this character, disturbing because to anyone looking at Saul and Reed together, as she does often in the one photo she has of the two of them, Reed seems so clearly in control. It's one of those photographs composed by convention: a stranger walks over to two people taking pictures of each other and says, "I'll snap you guys together," and one guy throws an arm across the other and both mug smiles for the camera. They're in a box at Madison Square Garden and it's Reed's arm over Saul—a thick, muscular arm sheathed in the sleeve of an expensive-looking black suit. Blond hair frames a face as perfectly chiseled as a Greek statue.

Still, she thinks Saul is wrong. Although she's hardly seen Reed these past ten years, really only a few times after she and Saul had bumped into him at the Whitney, it's inconceivable to her that Reed, who believed in the karma of everyday life, who'd taken her camping in the Sierras, taught her the Eagle Scout method for making a fire, carting out not only his own garbage but litter collected along the trail, had left knowing Saul would get caught.

WHEN LEONARD COMES to visit, it's clear that his goal is to try and figure out Reed. It strikes her as unseemly to make Leonard fish. She shows him the photograph.

"I'd pictured beady eyes, a little goatee. Not a California All-American boy."

"That's exactly what he was. His father owned an engineering firm in Palo Alto, made a lot of money in the sixties and seventies on radar systems for airplanes." Spook stuff, he'd called it, none of it used for any good. He'd taken the football scholarship at Stanford, he told her, even though he'd already lost interest in the game, rather than coming east to Harvard, where there would have been no sports scholarship, because he hadn't wanted to take his father's dirty money.

"You said he had a drug problem back when he was your roommate?"

"Before. Basically marijuana, some hallucinogens. He'd dropped out of Stanford and was working for a moving company, smoking pot every day with the guys on the truck. Then he got busted with some marijuana he'd brought down to the city from Mendocino. His mother was devastated. He'd been her golden child. Star athlete, president of the student council, the most popular girls for his girlfriends. His father got the charges dropped in exchange for his going to a drug clinic."

She sees Leonard's consternation. Despite Klara, Leonard had managed to bump along through his boys' teenage years with Marc a beer-guzzling frat boy and Saul never even touching coffee.

"By the time I met Reed, he was on a macrobiotic diet. He drank wheat grass juice and ate mostly Japanese food. His friends called him Seaweed. That's why it was so hard for me, at first, to believe he'd gotten back into drugs."

Leonard holds the picture close to his face. "Why did he come to New York?"

"To finish college. His parents hated New York, but Columbia was the only place he'd go. It was the same year I started Yale. He was the only person I knew from California, and I sort of clung to him. I'd come down on weekends, and he'd take me around."

She knows Leonard must be thinking that Reed was a boyfriend. That it would be hard for Leonard, knowing her now, to imagine how Reed, with his exotic girlfriends and ease everywhere, had seemed back then out of her league.

"After he graduated, he bought a van he drove to Peru. We lost touch. It was just luck"—she pauses on this word—"bumping into him that day at the Whitney. He'd gone to law school and got a job working for a top firm. He hated it, said it was like hazing, seventy hours a week working on some glitch involving the intersection of American and French tax law."

Leonard hands the photo back to Rena. She can see on his face that he's wondering if she's holding something back. If so, it's more about Saul than Reed: how, to Saul, Reed had seemed like a benign version of Marc. A breath of fresh air in the claustrophobia of medicine, someone who didn't regard Hispanics as poor people who are more inconvenient than other poor people because they don't speak English and have their own healing practices. As for her relationship with Reed, Saul had commented on it only once. It saddened him, he said, that Reed, not he, had known her as a girl—*as a girl,* Saul's euphemism for when her life was scrappy and sordid, every corner filled with shame.

Morton gives her the lowdown he's heard from the lawyer for Reed's girlfriend, Bria, a twenty-three-year-old Brazilian divorcée with platinum hair and a Spanish passport that lists her address as her family's compound in the Tenerife district of the Canary Islands: that Reed quit his job in lieu of being fired, that he'd been doing what Morton called "some private work for a Eurotrash crowd."

Bria, Morton says, is the one who was busted at Kennedy three days before Saul's arrest. "Dumb," Morton says over the phone. "Telling the customs agent the stuffed panda she was carrying was a Valentine's Day present for her mother. Too cute. The agents get suspicious with cute. Especially the female ones."

What the agent on the four-to-twelve shift saw before her was a girl with white hair dark at the roots, an armful of silver bracelets and a purple suede jacket. Her nostrils looked raw. Slitting the lining of the Louis Vuitton suitcases, the agent found a pharmacy of pills.

"That, too, the Vuitton, was dumb. The sharp smugglers know you're better off with Amelia Earhart."

With her one phone call, Bria called her lawyer—Reed. When no lawyer arrived, the Treasury guys realized the call had been a tip-off. By then, Reed was on a plane from Hartford to Madrid. Bria waited forty-eight hours before telling them she'd been headed to Tenerife to greet a package Reed had mailed there a few days before—just enough time, DEA agents suspected, for Reed to get the package and disappear.

"That's why," Morton says, "they did Saul's arrest with so much pyrotechnics. Usually, this kind of thing, with a professional involved, would be a Monday-to-Friday, nine-to-five job. Lots of times they would even have a voluntary surrender, the suspect bringing himself in with his attorney for the booking. They were pissed that Reed had left the country, that this dumb chick had been stringing them along."

The way Bria's lawyer tells it, when Saul asked Reed to sell him some Quaaludes, some Valium, anything to help him sleep now that Arlen, the doctor who'd been treating Saul, was holding his triplicate prescription pads, Reed refused. Saul had gone then to Bobby, someone he'd met through Reed. Bobby brought him to Fabio, a guy from Washington

Heights, one of the new breed of Dominican dealers who don't use drugs themselves but keep a neighborhood and select downtown trade.

With Fabio, Saul has told Morton, it was the same story as before Saul had gone to Arlen; unable to sleep, Saul took Fabio's barbs, little pink pills made in a bootleg lab outside Santa Fe. When they left him groggy, he asked Fabio for something to help with that. Fabio gave Saul a vial of cocaine. He rolled a hundred-dollar bill to show Saul how to inhale. The first vial was on Fabio. After that, it was ninety dollars a gram. By December, Saul owed Fabio over three thousand dollars. Fabio refused to give Saul anything more until he settled his tab. It was only then, Bria's lawyer says, that Saul had gone back to Reed. Begging this time.

Bria's lawyer concedes that it was Reed who came up with the hospital pharmacy robbery scheme, but he adds that it was Reed's attempt to help Saul get out of hock with Fabio. Fabio supplied the robber, a guy who worked as a night security guard in a midtown office building. Fabio took his cut immediately—a quarter of the take in exchange for wiping clean Saul's tab. The rest went to Reed, who gave Saul a small personal stash, just enough to detox himself. Reed mailed three-fourths of his share to Bria's address in Tenerife; she was to bring the rest in the Louis Vuitton.

Bria, her lawyer claims, did all this out of love. She believed, he claims, that once Reed cleared his debts he'd clean up and they would get married and buy a starter Tudor in Westchester and he'd go back to working as a lawyer and she'd have a baby and stay home baking cookies and sewing curtains.

"Why don't you tell the DA what Bria's lawyer told you about Fabio and the other guy?" Rena asks Morton. "Wouldn't that help things for Saul?"

"Can't. Forget about what is and isn't admissible, though we got to assume some of this story is being fed to us. We all rely on each other to try and piece things together."

"Couldn't Saul do it himself? Tell the police what he knows about them?"

"He could, but he won't. Even if he were in the frame of mind where he'd be looking to offload some of the blame, he'd be too scared about what those characters would do to retaliate."

Saul's job, Bria's lawyer says, was to provide a typed list of the generic and commercial names of the drugs worth taking, a map showing where the pharmacy is in the basement corridor and the dates when Kim Sun, the barely five-foot pharmacist, would be working the night shift.

No one had known that Kim Sun was nine weeks pregnant.

No one had known that after the burglar handed Kim Sun the list of drugs Saul had typed—codeine, Darvon, Nembutal, Seconal, phenobarbital, Tuinal, Dalmane, Valium, Librium, Demerol, Dilaudid, Percodan, benzadrine, dexadrine, methedrine, Ritalin, Ativan, cough medication—and she filled the duffel bag, he would say, "My old lady, she gets cramps with her monthly. What do you got for that?"

Kim Sun was so frightened, her voice was inaudible.

The burglar, thinking Kim Sun was tooling with him, pointed his gun at her head.

"Midol," she croaked before passing out.

THE DAY AFTER the grand jury returns an indictment, Saul writes her for the first time. She can visit. If she wants. Would she bring him books? His father has promised to mail Freud's Standard Edition. Could she bring *Eros and Civilization, Ulysses*, *Anna Karenina*? He encloses a little drawing like the ones he used to leave on her pillow: a stick figure with a headful of ringlets and two shopping bags overflowing with books approaching a wrought-iron gate. Men in striped pajamas stick big noses through the spaces in the fence.

If she wants. That first day, in Morton's office, when he'd still been in her mind's eye naked and scared, surrounded by boots and guns, then she'd wanted. But now, a month later, there's only dread at the thought of sitting face to face. A carnage of her neglect and his deceit.

She takes the bus from Port Authority. It's early Sunday morning, the only other passengers a mother with a sad little boy and two elderly women hovering over hard-boiled eggs wrapped in foil and squares of crumbly cake.

For Saul, she carries his mail, a Walkman with a selection of his jazz tapes, the requested books. In her pocket, Saul's letter stamped with the number of his cell block. Everything important that has happened between Saul and her, it occurs to her now, has been heralded by a letter from him, starting with the one to her five years ago care of the *New York Times*. She'd submitted the piece anonymously, so Saul hadn't known he was writing to a woman. That, more than anything, was what drew her to him in the first place. Years later, reading Ruth's work on women living outside of marriage and their use of the idea of celibacy as the equivalent of purity, it came as a slow, needling awareness that this had been part of her attraction to Saul. On the one hand, there was purity: a man who wrote you to discuss your ideas. On the other hand, there was what Sammy and the others at Alil's Adult Showcase & Lounge had called "doing cage": dancing topless in the glass enclosures in the back room.

Saul's second letter had been written a year later on her mother's fiftieth birthday, written in what had once been Rena's room. It was the first time he'd met either her mother or her brother, and so much had changed by then for the better that Rena had feared he would think she'd fabricated or at best exaggerated her stories about Eleanor: her mother kowtowing to fat Nick of Nick's Ristorante, letting him shoo Rena downstairs to wait in the kitchen while he had his *little visits,* how Eleanor had fallen apart after the birth of the twins, the girl stillborn, Eleanor bingeing and crying and sleeping, unable to care for Gene so that the job had fallen to Rena, then fifteen. The crazed state Eleanor sank into when Joe, Gene's father, died of a heart attack in the cab of his truck while having sex with an underage girl he'd picked up hitchhiking south of Santa Cruz. Eleanor sleeping with any man who would participate, letting Rena bring Gene, then nine, back east.

It had taken her mother two years and Rena would not hazard to guess how many men before she'd come to her senses, the rage either siphoned off or tucked into some other place. Arriving with Saul on her first visit since Gene's return to live with their mother, she'd found the house unrecognizable: her room, Joe's storage room before she and Eleanor moved in, with the gun cabinet by the door and the rifle mounted on the wall, now freshly painted with a tatami mat on the floor and a meditation altar beneath the window; the living room, where once there'd been a deer's head over the couch and Joe's enormous television always blaring, now quiet and light with a breeze from the garden and a vase holding daffodils.

"She seems so peaceful," Saul commented that first night. Sensing Rena's fear, he wrote at dawn, placing the letter in her hands as she opened her eyes: "I know things are rarely as they seem—that your mother's serene demeanor does not mean she has always been this way or even is so now."

Rena's eyes dampened. "It's not that I want you to vilify my mother. I just can't bear it if you think I'm crazy."

He nodded, and later, when she decided without regrets to marry him, she would pinpoint the start of loving him to reading that letter in which she'd seen so clearly the intrepidness of his orderly mind, his refusal to turn a blind eye—unlike her, she thinks now in the hum of the bus—to other people's distress.

Saul's third letter came last year after the disastrous trip to visit Sylvia in Montauk when she'd found the camera bag filled with vials of sleeping pills, stimulants, painkillers and tranquilizers. Then, she'd been too shocked and angry to turn away. He'd acted as though she was making a big deal out of nothing. "You know I can't stand that," she screamed when Sylvia left to buy groceries. She'd never yelled at anyone before. "Being told something real is all in my head." They drove the four hours back to Manhattan in silence. She dumped her sandy clothes in a pile on the apartment floor and, while he was in the shower, repacked her suitcase. On the bedroom mirror, she wrote with lipstick: "Not coming back until you agree to get help."

At the end of the week, Saul's letter arrived at her job: *Okay.*

One typed word.

Now, with his latest letter, he is prodding her to smile. It's like being on Novocain. She can sense the pressure without feeling the touch. Unless she's been smiling in her sleep, she does not believe she has smiled since his arrest.

THE VISITORS' REGISTRATION area is thick with waiting. The purposeless waiting she remembers as a child, sitting with her mother in rooms filled with people holding numbers that won't be called for hours. Her first month at Yale, she'd been amazed to see how efficiently everything ran, how her classmates complained if they had to wait half an hour to get registration forms signed. How a person's time was assumed to have value.

There are a dozen or so others. Mostly women, the younger ones in jeans and ankle boots and oversize sweatshirts with glittery logos across the chests, the older ones in cotton skirts and layers of sweaters and snow boots over feet swollen, she imagines, from working in hospital laundries or cleaning offices at night. She feels unnerved. Not for herself. To her, it all seems unwelcomingly familiar. For Saul.

An hour passes before the clerk calls Rena's name. "Sign here, here and here."

Rena signs at the three X's.

"Packages."

A female guard empties the shopping bag. She flips through the books, opens the Walkman. "Gotta check you, too. Arms up."

Rena lifts her hands over her head. The guard pats her sides, under her breasts, between her legs. *It's nothing, it's nothing,* she repeats to herself, the silent mantra lurching to a stop with the disposable gloves the guard puts on before inspecting her hair.

There's a long green hall and then a double gate where Rena is handed over to a second guard. A group of prisoners, their heads individualized with berets and bandannas and T-shirts tied into kaffiyehs, files past flanked by corrections officers front and back. Someone whistles. A sound like a cat's hiss passes up and down the row. The corrections officer in front does an about-face. He looks at her, his eyes narrowing, before turning to someone at the front of the line. "Cut the shit. Morris, I know that's you. It's absolute silence, I mean so I can hear a pin drop, or your ass is going back in lockup so fast you ain't going to have time to wipe."

The guard leads her into a small room. There's a table with two chairs and a buzzer on top. The glass in the door is reinforced by wire. "Remember, no physical contact, nothing goes to the prisoner except what's in the bag I checked. You need assistance, hit the buzzer."

She'd expected to talk to Saul through a window. She'd never thought they'd be alone together in a room. Her mouth turns to cotton. Her head throbs.

The door opens: Saul followed by a different guard. For a moment, there's the distraction of the new guard. He points to the clock on the wall. "You got forty-five minutes. That's till five past two." He checks the buzzer, looks at Rena. "That chair you're in, it's got to stay center and the bag's got to be on the table."

Rena moves her chair in closer and places the shopping bag on the table. The door bangs closed.

To her surprise, he looks better, the wells under his eyes less prominent, his hair, cut shorter than before, less unruly. He slides a hand under the bag and touches her arm. She freezes, expecting the guard to rush in. He runs a finger up and down the skin between her wrist and the cuff of her sweater.

"I'm sorry." His voice seems too loud. She has to force herself to keep looking at him. He pulls his hand out from under the bag and touches his lips with the finger that had been on her wrist and then slides it back. A speck of saliva from his mouth moistens her skin.

"I love you." She can feel his desperation to sink an anchor in her. His gaze is unbearable. She lowers her eyes. Thankfully, he knows to withdraw his finger.

"Rena." His eyes are wet. He is a beautiful man. Beautiful in the way a woman is with high cheekbones and a peaked upper lip. "I just wanted to tell you that. That's all."

She leans forward on the table so her head rests on one arm.

"You look awful," he says.

"You look terrific."

"It had been a while since I'd had three squares and gone to the gym regularly."

A stab of guilt. Rarely home before nine, she'd hardly cooked so they'd lived on takeout and omelettes and tuna salad. Every night, she'd prettily set the table as though the napkins folded in triangles would make up for the inadequate fare.

"That's the best of it. Sharing an eight-by-ten cell with another man is no picnic. The worst part is the noise. There's always noise. Men yelling to each other, the loudspeaker day and night. I'd kill for an hour of complete silence."

He leans back in his chair. "Still, the truth is, it's better than being strung out. Those last weeks, scrambling to get money, worrying at every corner I turned that a hired thug was going to knock out my teeth, that was the real hell."

"The truth?" She immediately regrets the jab.

"I've got some work to do on that score."

The lies had been the hardest thing, the endless lies, all the more unnerving because she'd always thought of Saul as an earnest, guileless man who never knew when a woman was looking at him, who would leave his wallet in restaurants and his credit card on department store counters, so that even now she can't help but feel that this, too, is some sort of scam.

"I'll have a long time to work on it here."

She glances at the clock. Unbelievably, only seven minutes have passed. She does not think she will be able to manage another thirty-eight. She prays, her version of praying, that he will not say, I'm going to make it up to you, because then she'll have to say I'm sorry, I'm going to have to leave now.

He senses it. She can see him trying to shift gears.

"How's work? What's happening with the Braner campaign?"

Her eyes narrow.

"I didn't have a lobotomy."

She refrains from saying that it would be easier if he had, if she could reclaim what he knows about her. It's not that he knows firsthand (not like Reed, who'd known her while she worked at Alil's, while she was the then congressional candidate Ascher Malone's hidden white girl), but he'd probed, gently, really, she thinks now, in his own way, relentlessly, for the details. How the first time she and Ascher had stopped seeing each other, he had turned her over to Rebecca, his teacher at the San Francisco Socialist School, who'd taken Rena under her wing, encouraging Rena to take the SATs (something Rena had never thought to do) and, after seeing Rena's scores, pressing her to apply to Yale where Rebecca's graduate school roommate, then an assistant dean, helped Rena get a little-known grant designated for women of Italian-American descent. How, about to graduate with Gene to support, she'd asked Ascher to help her get a job, the only time she let him help her: a simple calculation—no job, no Gene.

"The one thing there's plenty of here is newspapers. I've been reading about what's going on with Braner in Colorado. Cassen and Silvano are right-wing functionaries, but you can say this for them: at least they work only for people they believe in. If you think about it, it's got more integrity than what Kerrigan and Muskowitz were into these last couple years, making candidates the Democratic party could sell."

She sees it: he's trying to seduce her with his thoughts. She feels thrown by how chipper he sounds. From what Monk had said, she'd expected to find him listless and demoralized. Has something happened since he's been here? Or is he feigning a false optimism for her benefit?

The guard presses his forehead to the glass. She waits for him to leave.

"You decided to plead guilty."

"I am guilty."

Saul watches her eyes land on his trembling wrist. He steadies his wrist by lacing his fingers together. "I've got three more days on the barb detox. It's a lot better than it was."

"You pled guilty because you *feel* guilty?"

"I pled guilty because my lawyer told me it was the smartest thing to do—given that Reed seems to have left me holding the bag. But I'm relieved to do so."

For a moment, she feels tempted to challenge Saul's belief that Reed abandoned him, but with *relieved* a bubble of distress rises in her, bursting against her anesthetized demeanor so that she imagines crying out, *How did this all happen?* By then, though, Saul has launched a description of the prison routine. He will not be assigned a job until after his sentencing. For the interim, they've put him on pots detail.

"You should see the pots they use for the soups and stews. It takes two of us to lift one from the stove."

Three times a week, his cell block goes to the gym. Someone has shown him how to use the barbells. He flexes an arm, stroking a small ball of muscle in mock vanity. "Biceps, triceps, deltoids, pectorals. These guys know more anatomy than I did my first year of medical school."

Visions of a horde of men, thighs thick as tree trunks, and she has to ask, "Is it safe—is it safe here?"

His jaw twitches. "The double whiteys—the white guys here on white-collar crimes—live in constant fear. Pharmacy robbery has cachet. One of the lifers, they call him one of the big ten because he still runs a street gang out of Brooklyn, adopted me as his secretary. I write his letters for him. He likes having me sign them Dr. Dubinsky, Secretary for Marsden Stem, Grand Marshal of the Blackjacks. As long as I do his letters, word's out that anyone who harasses me is dead meat."

For the first time during the visit, she detects fear in him. She can smell it, his breath acrid like the scent of iron tools left overnight on wet grass. His face collapses and his entire visage shifts so she can see the bruised skin under his eyes, the despair leaching out like rust seeping into the aquifer.

SHE TAKES THE BUS back to Port Authority. She knows that she should call Leonard, that he won't call to inquire, at least not today, but that he'll be waiting. When she gets back to Ninety-Fifth Street, though, it's all she can do to pull the blinds and stand in the galley kitchen and eat some cereal out of the box, then bring a glass of milk, the Sunday paper and her briefcase with her calendar for work into bed.

She sleeps with the light on, the milk souring on the bedside stand, her calendar on her chest, the papers spread out where Saul used to be. At four, she is awakened by a sharp sound somewhere between a clang and a screech. A cat vaulting between the trash cans. Her feet are very cold. She clears the bed and wraps the blankets around her ankles as though these lower extremities are a baby she is swaddling. She can see Saul smiling as he talked about scrubbing crusted macaroni and cheese from the bottom of a thirty-six-inch pot. Again she wonders, is his good cheer a pretense? He must know that there are mandatory sentences for federal drug convictions, that he is going to be locked up, Monk said, somewhere on the order of forty-eight months. At the very least, he must know that he is going to lose his license.

Her feet will not warm. She tucks them under her. The despair shifts, one of those figure-ground illusions where the vase becomes a face, and her eyes well with tears that flow in the darkness as she sees that it is not only he who has lost her, but she who has lost him.

SHE WAKES THINKING of Reed. In the shower, it occurs to her that Saul must have had a phone number and address for Reed. Never a snoop (her stepfather, Joe, whose suspicions of Eleanor had extended to Rena as if they were collaborators in a scheme against him, had so routinely searched her drawers and backpack she'd told her mother they should leave him notes tucked between her underwear), she'd not thought to pick the lock on Saul's rolltop desk.

She snaps the lock with a metal nail file. It appalls her how easily it comes to her. Behind the rolltop, she finds scraps of paper with scrawled telephone numbers. The abbreviated pocket version of the *Diagnostic and Statistical Manual*. Saul's address book. Under M, Reed's address, no longer on John Street where she'd left the messages last year for him but on East Eighty-Eighth.

She calls her job to say she'll be late, takes the Ninety-Sixth Street crosstown bus to Second Avenue and walks the eight blocks south. The building has a frayed green awning and no doorman. Next to 6E, she sees Bria's name. Bria Estefan. She rings the bell and waits.

A man in a maintenance shirt enters the lobby with a bucket on wheels and a spaghetti string mop. Rena taps on the glass. He opens the door.

"I'm looking for Bria Estefan."

"She's gone. Been gone a month, maybe more."

"Did she leave a forwarding address?"

"You go talk to the super, Rafael. He's in the office downstairs."

Rena takes the stairs to the basement. In the office, Rafael is drinking coffee and reading the *Post*. He peers at her over the top of his paper.

"I'm looking for Bria Estefan. Actually, I'm looking for her boyfriend, Reed Michaelson."

"You, darlin', and everyone else in this city. She went back to Brazil, someone said."

"For good?"

"One of the cops who was around here said she'd been deported, but then she paid rent for April. You figure."

"I'm Reed's sister. There are some papers I need for the family."

Rafael takes a loose cigarette from his pocket and lights up. Clumsily, remembering Ascher when he'd needed things done, she pulls out two twenties from her wallet and lays them on the desk. Rafael exhales a plume of smoke. The twenties disappear under the *Post*.

"The cops took a couple garbage bags of stuff, but you can pick through the rest. Tell the guy cleaning the floor I said to open 6E for you."

Six E stinks of cigarettes and cat piss. A partially eaten jelly doughnut sits on the kitchen counter, a roach expired on the red center. Long black hairs festoon the bathroom sink. Women's clothes are strewn over the unmade bed. Rena picks up a snakeskin print dress. Victoria's Secret, size 2.

She opens the closets and drawers. Either the police have taken most everything belonging to Reed or he had been only temporarily parked here. Under the bed, she finds a pair of men's running shoes and a set of barbells. In the kitchen cabinet, a can of the loose green tea Reed drank by the potful when they'd roomed together. There's no desk, no bookshelves, just a pile of fashion magazines and paperbacks, mostly romances in Portuguese it seems from the covers, on a table pushed against the living room wall. Only one book jumps out at her as Reed's: the *Michelin Atlas Routier*.

She carries the atlas to the couch. It's a spiral-bound collection of detailed maps of France chopped into a hundred-some sections, either, she imagines, a souvenir from his last job when he'd worked on Franco-American trading agreements or something collected during his Columbia years when he'd gone through a Francophile period in which he'd revered Godard and slept with the French 101 teaching assistant, a girl with beaded cornrows from Port-au-Prince.

Camping in the Sierras, Reed had shown her how to read a topographical map, how to imagine a landscape from the shadings of brown and green and the density of the switchback squiggles.

The couch reeks of perfume. She puts the *Atlas Routier* in her tote. It's hard to imagine Saul in this room with Reed and Bria, how he found his way here.

She covers her face. The answer is obvious. Through her.

5 Leonard

The morning we're scheduled to be visited by Ms. Sandra Wright, the probation officer doing the presentencing investigation, your mother announces the worst sinus infection she's had in ten years.

Ten years, I think. Not eight? Not twelve? I pull out the legs on her bed tray and set it across her lap.

"After you've eaten, we'll see how you feel."

Your mother turns her face to the wall, though not before, I notice, stealing a glance at the croissant.

I call Morton, who reassures me that I can do the interview on my own. Although he doesn't come out and say so, his tone suggests that Ms. Wright's visit is a formality, that nothing could incriminate you further. Still, I cannot help feeling it's important, if for no other reason than it's the only thing at this stage I can do.

At three, a taxi stops in front of our house. I cannot recall having ever seen a cab in our neighborhood. A young black woman carrying a raincoat and a briefcase gets out of the back. I wait for her to ring the bell before going to the door.

I take her coat, ask if she had trouble finding the house.

"No. Piece of cake. I don't get out of the city too often doing these things. Unless you count going up to the Bronx." She smiles. My heart sinks. "Sure is pretty."

I ask if she'd like some coffee.

"Love it. That afternoon slump."

I settle Ms. Wright in the living room while I start the coffee and put cookies on a plate. The tray is still upstairs with your mother, so I end up shuttling what seems like a ridiculous number of times back and forth from the kitchen to get everything onto the coffee table.

Ms. Wright eats two cookies and puts three spoons of sugar in her coffee. I cross my fingers and hope this bodes well for you. She takes a clipboard with a stapled form that looks like a medical history from her briefcase. "Well, I suppose we should get going."

She reads from the form. "The purpose of this interview is to assist the probation department in making its recommendations to the judge for the sentencing of . . ." She looks at a sheet of paper at her side. "Mr. Dubinovsky."

"Dubinsky."

"Sorry about that," she says sotto voce, as if there is an official exchange between us and then some other parenthetical, more human one. "I'm batting oh-for-eight this week."

She finishes reading the bureaucratese, then hands me something to sign: paragraph after paragraph of informed consent. I skim the words. Foolishly, I'd imagined that the people going over your case would find you so anomalous, such an interesting case, that everything would be handled delicately. If Morton and the penal officers have found anything curious about a shy, intellectual psychiatrist being held for conspiracy to commit armed robbery, they have given no sign. As for this Ms. Wright, there seems to be nothing new under the sun, life a series of daytime talk shows—transvestite lesbian nuns, men who love women with bad skin, people who believe vegetables have a soul.

She asks me to describe you in my own words, and I have to refrain from a nasty quip about who else's words could I use. Spurred by Ms. Wright's friendly lack of curiosity, I permit myself a touch of florid overstatement. I describe you as the dreamy grandchild of a socialist grandfather, as having grown up with a mother who was bedridden. I lower my voice and point upstairs. A pacifist who refused to fight the boys on the school bus who would stick their legs out to trip you. How you'd chosen Swarthmore because of its Quaker affiliations, been a student volunteer at a prison where you first became interested in the interface between social disintegration and deviant behavior. I watch Ms. Wright, amazed that she sees no irony in this.

My anxiety ratchets up a notch as I see that Ms. Wright is taking only the most occasional notes on the clipboard. Worried how the judge will piece your story together, I add more and more details, hoping that if I say more, Ms. Wright will have to convey more. I describe your medical school years, how you always selected the rotations in the city hospitals rather than the private suburban ones, how you went into psychiatry thinking it would provide more of a home for a social analysis of illness.

Ms. Wright leans forward, and for a moment my heart leaps as I think it's to ask a question. She takes another cookie.

I tell her how demoralized you felt during your residency by the focus on the biological aspects of psychiatric difficulties and the perfunctory hand-waving toward the social underpinnings. I describe your reasons for taking your first job at a hospital in the Bronx, thinking surely Ms. Wright will admire you for this. You'd come to feel that there was something wrong, intellectually and morally, I tell Ms. Wright, with treating patients who came to your clinic with depressions related to the depressing aspects of their lives as though their fundamentally economic problems were psychiatric disorders. For those patients with what you thought of as real psychiatric problems, you felt even worse —that the best you could do given your enormous caseload was a patch-up job.

She runs her tongue over her teeth as if checking for bits of chocolate.

Afterwards, though, after Ms. Wright puts her clipboard back in her briefcase and we call the cab to return her to the train station and she thanks me for the coffee and cookies, afterwards when I'm shuttling everything back into the kitchen and starting dinner for your mother, I realize that the judge will have no problem piecing my story together because he'll never hear it. Too much to write, too much even to take notes on. The whole thing will, undoubtedly, be condensed into a paragraph or two, something like *accused has long history of unrealistic expectations and disappointments in vocational sphere.*

WHEN WE CAME BACK from your grandfather's funeral in that tenth year of our marriage, your mother took to her bed. It was May and, as I said, I believed her fatigue to be simple grief. In June, I enrolled the two of you in a day camp, thinking that she needed a quiet summer. A bus would come for you before eight and deliver you tired and dirty at five. After dinner, we would climb the stairs and the two of you would visit with your mother until I'd see her pressing her fingers to her temples, when quietly I would suggest that you say your good nights. She'd smile feebly at me and I'd smile back. For the first time, her complaints about me had ceased. Briefly, I felt cheered by this turn of events, but when the headaches escalated from evenings to all day—headaches that sent her to our bedroom by eleven in the morning where she would lie with a cold washcloth covering her forehead—I had to acknowledge that it was not a good sign, that it was as though with her father's death, her whole system of resentment had lost its ballast and she'd collapsed en suite.

Stone did bloodwork. We went to see one of her father's colleagues, who did an EEG and talked with her about stress. Tactfully, he suggested she might see a therapist to discuss this. Trying too hard to be offhand, I mentioned someone she'd once met, but she caught the scent of my growing suspicions, indignant that no one believed her. "No one's saying that you don't really have headaches," I explained. "Rather, we're wondering if they're brought on by something of a psychological nature." Your mother looked at me with disdain. She switched from washcloths to an ice pack on top of her head.

By July, your mother was convinced that the headaches were the result of allergies, and we installed an air conditioner in the bedroom so she could keep the windows closed. By fall, she was complaining of dizziness, which she stated was worsened by noise. In November, we moved our bedroom up to the third floor of the house so she could be away from your after-school horseplay. The dizziness became pain in her back for which no orthopedist could identify the source. Conversation, never abundant, shrank to discussions of her symptoms: how the headache might one day be better but the dizziness worse; how she thought the houseplants were irritating her sinuses. From backaches, we moved to heart palpitations, and from there to nausea. This time not asking, I scheduled an appointment for her with a psychiatrist who specialized in psychosomatics. She went once and then canceled the next three appointments, claiming that the nausea prevented her from leaving her bed.

On the first anniversary of your grandfather's death, I hired Mrs. Smiley. She toured the house: the linen closets your mother had never bothered to put in order and that had further deteriorated this past year as you boys fetched your own sheets and towels, the basement piled with laundry I tried to do in the evenings, the dusty living room, the oven I'd never thought to clean. "I have my pattern," Mrs. Smiley said. "Mondays I do laundry. Tuesdays I clean bathrooms and the kitchen. Wednesdays I vacuum and dust. Thursdays I shop. Fridays I bake and cook for the weekend. There's a story I watch every day at noon while I eat my lunch. I have a coffee and piece of cake at four. I don't use the telephone. I'll need a car to do the shopping and a shelf to keep my things because I don't work in my street clothes."

Within a month, the house was spotless and we had all fallen into Mrs. Smiley's routine. Your mother's ailments didn't abate, but they ceased their previous expansion. I was certain this improvement, if you could call it such, was due to Mrs. Smiley, the only person I've ever known your mother to feel intimidated by. If your mother wanted something from Mrs. Smiley, she'd instruct me to convey the message: *Perhaps you could ask Mrs. Smiley to give me a little more orange juice; this sinus condition leaves me so dehydrated. Tell Mrs. Smiley to make more of that applesauce cake. When I'm nauseous, it's the one thing that goes down easily.* As for Mrs. Smiley, she seemed to have a precise instinct as to how much she could push your mother. Slowly, she laid down her rules. "If she's going to stay in bed," Mrs. Smiley informed me, "the sheets have to be changed every day. I do beds at ten." So every day your mother had to move downstairs while Mrs. Smiley tidied our room. A week later, holding at arm's length a soiled dinner plate that had been left on the bedside stand, Mrs. Smiley announced that her pot roast could not be eaten lying down. Obediently, your mother took to joining us for twenty minutes each evening at the table.

I knew that it was a devil's pact. You boys got fried chicken and mashed potatoes and fresh vegetables every night and I got starched shirts and an immaculate porcelain tub and all the free time I needed and your mother got her retreat from us all. I taught two mornings a week, had office hours one afternoon. Other than that, I spent the days at home, behind the closed door of the study I set up in what had been our bedroom. I began my second book on the historical precursors of the psychoanalytic unconscious: a radical departure from my first book on the history of the asylum in nineteenth-century America, which had been about the history of a "thing," involving what I thought of as "proper" research including, one summer, what your mother called the loony bin tour—the three of you splashing in Howard Johnson swimming pools while I rummaged through hospital storage rooms inspecting old hydrotherapy tubs and primitive electroshock machines.

Your mother's retreat suited me in another way, as well. It gave me the two of you. Not that she'd ever been possessive of you; rather, her focus had been on efficiency, and for that reason she'd left little room for my involvement. When you were babies, this had taken me by surprise because she was in other ways impulsive and disorganized. She'd prided herself on what she seemed to think of as the tricks of the trade: preserving her own sleep by leaving bottles hidden in the corners of your crib for you to grope for in the dark, toilet-training Marc before you were born so there'd be only one child in diapers, putting the two of you on the same schedule so she'd have her evenings free. You both seemed reasonably happy, so it was hard for me to put my finger on what bothered me. All I knew was that there were times when we'd be around other families and I would sense something different in the way things worked, a back-and-forth flow between the children's needs and the parents' attempts to bring the children into the world, something like the way waters of different temperatures mix together.

Don't misunderstand me. It's not that you and your brother weren't attached to your mother. You'd run crying to her when something happened, when Marc's shove as you reached for the toy he had in his hand would result in your chin hitting the bookshelf, and she'd pick you up and put you on her hip. But it was always pat-pat and a brusque, or so it sounded to me, *come, come, forget about it, let's find a different toy for you.* It was not until after your mother took to her bed that I came to understand her approach—the very one I found myself using with her. Drawing you out to discuss how you felt must have seemed to her too dangerous. *If possible, do not operate on an impaired system,* I recalled learning during the first year of medical school. *Even a tooth extraction should be delayed if the patient has an infection.* That's how at first I rationalized my approach with your mother. I was waiting for the infection to pass.

Still, I could not overlook that your mother's retirement had a greater effect on you than on your brother. For a year already, he had begun to have a separate life centered on his sports teams and the friends he had through these teams. You would come home to the Saran-covered slice of applesauce cake Mrs. Smiley left on the kitchen table. Through the basement door, you'd hear the German radio station she listened to as she ironed or folded laundry. Upstairs would be silent.

The first time I saw you sitting by yourself at the kitchen table with your plate of cake, your skinny eight-year-old legs still silky and hairless, your head resting on one arm, I nearly wept. Unable to bear the image of your loneliness, I took to breaking from my work when I heard you at the back door. After a week, I ceased working altogether after three, saving my day's walk for your return from school. Together we'd walk the half-mile to the lake, where we'd circle the perimeter, watching out for our fowled friends: the family of magenta-headed ducks, the three white swans, the black male that appeared only on rainy days. Sometimes I'd bring along a blanket that we'd spread in autumn over crackly brown leaves, in spring over damp green shoots, both of us stretching out to stare at the sky or read the books we'd carry in our backpacks. When the weather was inclement, we'd walk to the public library, each of us disappearing into the stacks to rejoin with armloads of books. Sometimes you'd come find me to show me something you'd discovered (a chart of the evolutionary path from tyrannosaurus to iguana, a book listing the largest one hundred rivers in order of length and volume), and sometimes I'd help you look up something that interested you that day in the adult encyclopedias.

Now, thinking back, I can't recall when we stopped those afternoons, probably by the time you reached junior high school and I could sense your embarrassment at being seen palling around with your dad, but I do know there were times before then, walking home with you, talking about the things we'd seen at the lake or discovered at the library, when it would seem that the planets had fallen strangely into order, your mother's neurasthenia having bequeathed us this time together.

MORTON TELEPHONES TO say that the sentencing hearing took place and there'd been no surprises; it had all gone as expected, the forty-eight months with the fifty days a year off for good behavior. I call Rena to tell her.

"Morton said it's good news when it goes as expected. Sometimes it goes worse."

"Yes, I can see that," she says, like me, I suspect, not seeing it at all but somehow thinking it important that the sentencing be interpreted as having been in your favor.

"He'll be staying where he is. That makes it easier than being moved somewhere else."

"Right. Of course."

In the background, I hear what sounds like the tub running. She's told me that in the morning she'll fly to Denver, where she'll be for the rest of the week.

"Thanks for letting me know," she says. "I'll go see him when I get back."

"I can drive you. I'm going to try to go every Sunday."

"The bus is fine. I actually like it." She pauses, taken aback, I imagine, by the gracelessness of her own response. "That's very kind of you. Can we play it by ear?"

I hear the creak of the faucets turning, then the quiet of the water no longer running. I chastise myself for wondering if she's wrapped in a towel.

We say our careful good-byes, both of us knowing there's no way she'll let me drive her. She couldn't bear it, two hours in a car obliged to converse with me.

THERE ARE TIMES when I no longer know if I am talking with you or talking with the you that lives in my head or writing to you in my mind or rehearsing what it is I will say when I next see you. This last week, what I keep going over is Mitch and how I could have acted like you'd moved on. Of course, we'd talked about it a lot at the beginning when it was in all the papers. Then you stopped bringing it up. I stopped asking. Behaved as if it was not on your mind while knowing all the while that it was. Did I think that by asking I would be encouraging you to remain bound up with the boy and that by not asking I was in some way spurring you to let go? Or did I make what you would call the physicalist assumption: assuming that mental life operates on the same principles as the body—that an emotional wound, like a cut to the skin, should be left after a point to heal on its own?

The day after your sentencing hearing, I attempt to resume my work. There's a pencil lodged in the album of newspaper clippings at the page where I was reading the morning Rena called to tell me about your arrest. I reread an article from a Mexico City paper that describes Carmelita as a seventeen-year-old girl from a pueblo outside Oaxaca who claimed to have conceived, like Our Blessed Virgin, without sexual relations. The article is dated February 21, 1955—a few days after the drowned baby was found by a group of women scrubbing their wash on the flat rocks at the edge of the stream. Carmelita, wakened in her hut, said the devil had killed her Jesus.

I flip forward to the account of the trial in the Oaxaca daily. A priest was called to testify on the religious validity of Carmelita's statements that God had spoken to her, telling her that the devil had murdered her baby. In the transcript of the trial, there'd been nothing short of a philosophical debate about the meaning of the concept of religious validity until the judge called a halt to the exchange, stating that in his courtroom all that was to be determined was whether other Catholics would believe that God might speak to a girl of seventeen about why her baby was dead—not whether there is a God or such a God speaks or whether there is a devil and such a devil could sink a baby to a bottom of a stream. A psychiatrist came from Veracruz to report on an outbreak of religious hallucinations among girls in rural areas. Asking for a blackboard, he drew a diagram of the brain to show the sector where hallucinations originate. What the jurors thought of all of this, it was impossible to say, since not a one of them was interviewed and they all disappeared within hours of the end of the trial back to their plots of rocky land, but we can conclude not much since Carmelita was convicted of infanticide. Twelve days later she was found dead. A suicide, the authorities stated, despite the absence of rope burns on her neck and her sisters having declared it impossible, *Carmelita loved life too dearly.*

I review my introduction in which I outline three frames through which the case can be viewed: the psychopathological—the girl as psychotic, perhaps even a postpartum psychosis on top of an already existing delusion about the conception; the cultural-relativist—why would we accept the story of Mary's virginal pregnancy but not a modern-day story of miracles?; the sociological—the disruption of traditional family life by the opening of an American-owned copper mine outside the town. Reading over what I've written, I see that I've given extra weight to the third explanation, the shift from families working side by side to the creation of public and private spheres, the separation of fathers from children, the unspoken humiliations of the male workers, having to ask permission to use the toilet, the men responding with a denigration of their wives, the wives retaliating by an assertion of their own power via the virgin birth fantasy.

I have no idea if this materialist lens is right or any more right than the other interpretations. As a child, I didn't know it was a lens; it seemed natural that everything would be seen as a piece of politics, as part of the inexorable struggle between workers and owners. Now it seems uncomfortably close to my own father's situation, to Merckin's harping from his throne behind the couch about the triumph I'd felt watching my father crushed by the capitalist machine.

Usually, I determine the truth value of my ideas by visceral conviction —are they tepid or insistently, heart-poundingly "right"?—but today everything seems flat and two-dimensional, my inner sense turned tin. Asked today, I could not say if a painting is banal or luminous, if a piece of music is clichéd or haunting, if Morton is leveling with me or sugar-coating the facts.

If you are a soul turned evil or a person traumatized by life's tragedies.

If my ministrations toward your wife are for my benefit or yours.

6 Rena

On the plane to Denver, Rena sits next to a plump woman in a yellow jogging suit and white sneakers who is headed out to help her third daughter after the birth of her second child.

"She had an awful time of it, upchucking everything, and I mean everything, those first twelve weeks. She was so tiny to start with and she lost so much weight, they thought they'd have to put her in the hospital. But the baby was nine pounds! So the Lord has his miracles. And you, dear? Are you married?"

"Yes."

"What does your husband do?"

For a split second, Rena imagines saying, *He's an inmate at a federal prison.* "He's a doctor."

"Well, isn't that nice. Lucky you." She pokes Rena in the ribs. "You probably have a real nice house with a pool. My oldest boy, Joey, we always thought he'd be a doctor, but those chemistry courses killed him. Do you have children? Don't tell me, I know, not yet, but you want them, right?"

"I suppose."

"See, I can tell. You have that look. Just don't wait too long. My middle daughter waited till thirty-eight and she had a dickens of a time."

"If you'll excuse me." Rena takes her tote bag and heads toward the back of the half-empty plane. Spotting an open pair of seats, she sits in the one next to the window. She leans against the glass, staring out at the spidery haze.

After her visit in March, Saul had written that she could visit as often as she wished but he wouldn't harangue her to come. That was the word he had used: *harangue*. She spent a long time on the word, first because it was impossible to imagine Saul haranguing anyone, but also because it has always fascinated her the way he slides up and down within the language, adjusting his vocabulary to the listener, not in a way that seems condescending, but rather a kind of transposition, more like moving from A minor back to C major. On the surface, his letter suggested self-possession; he would allow her to work out her own feelings and visit or not visit as she wished. Beneath (though there was nothing she could point to in the sentences, not even after many readings), there was panic, his awareness that in the realm of the emotions, repairs are few and far between.

Not until the pilot announces their approach to Denver and she returns to her own seat does she realize that it's not the busybody she's angry with, but Saul. Saul for ruining everything. Saul for making her hide again.

HER FIRST NIGHT in Denver, she cannot sleep. At three in the morning, she gives up and runs a tub: the soak she'd abandoned yesterday after Leonard's call. Watching the water rise, she wonders if Leonard's tone, the implication that the sentencing was a victory, that there was nothing for them to discuss about it, had been affected for her benefit—she who couldn't even manage a car trip with him. It occurs to her that her remark about taking the bus had been not only hurtful but also unfair. Certainly, Saul never expected idle chitchat. He was the one who'd taught her the many moods of silence: the enraged homicidal mood that afternoon driving back from Sylvia's but, more often, the companionable possibilities, reading together in bed, walking with their feet in the surf. It had been a revelation after Ascher, who'd never left room for silence, who, having seen her at Alil's serving drinks in the front room while Sammy and the other girls danced in the back, the men's lips flattened like fish mugs against the glass, had left her with no self to protect.

She lowers herself into the water, sinking down so she has to lift her chin to keep her mouth from being submerged. The first night she spent with Ascher, in a motel outside Monterey, they talked until the sky turned silver. Ascher told her how his green eyes were the heritage of a white horse trader who'd raped his great-grandmother, the thirteen-year-old house slave of a Louisiana farmer who'd taken one of the trader's horses as payment for touching "one of my niggers." He told her about his father, who'd been in the black infantry that crossed from Calais to Normandy, and what it was like when the Panthers first came to Oakland and he'd been faced with trying to square the ethos of *dignity within* he'd learned from his father (forty years working for the Pacific Railroad, never challenging a system in which all the conductors were white and all the porters were black but never, either, letting anyone call him *boy*) with the ideas of black separatism and *smash whitey and their liberal do-goodism.*

He told her about his wife, Delia, with the face of a Nubian princess, the first black graduate of her pharmacy school, her voice a balm to the elderly customers whose prescriptions she filled, some of whom she called daily to check that they'd taken their pills—the woman from whose bed Rena, nineteen, had taken him. How he could not remember Delia ever losing her temper with either of their boys or ever going to bed with the dishes not dried and put away or without a scarf wrapped around her processed hair, how she seemed never to age so that at thirty-five she looked little different than she had at twenty and would, he imagined, remain so until she tumbled down the precipice to the frailty of real old age.

Rena lets the water out, climbs shivering from the tub, remembering how at dawn Ascher turned his face to the wall and whispered that Delia was a saint and he couldn't make love to a saint, and then told her how ashamed he'd felt when a bachelor party brought him to Alil's and he'd first seen her in a black cocktail waitress uniform, the tops of her breasts visible over the neckline, her eyes fixed straight ahead like a mannequin staring out from a department store window. He couldn't get her face out of his mind, he told her, like a song that goes round and round in your head until you want to shoot your own ears, an obsession leading him to lie for the first time in his fourteen years of marriage to Delia about where he'd been the night he went back to Alil's.

She gets into bed with a towel still wrapped around her wet hair. She pulls the blankets up to her eyes. Two good men brought to their knees.

RETURNING AFTER COLORADO to the apartment, she feels oppressed by the magnitude of Saul's things: the books overflowing the shelves, the framed posters covering the walls, the file folders, records, tapes and CDs crammed everywhere.

When she first moved in, she'd urged Saul to undertake a purging and reorganization, but she'd given up after seeing how painful it would be for him to devote the precious little time he had after his seventy-plus hours a week of residency to sorting and weeding, tasks that seemed to him unnecessary given that he could always, well, nearly always, find what he needed. She'd comforted herself by undertaking a judicious pruning of Saul's ragtag furniture, keeping the better pieces he'd taken from Klara's basement collection of discards and replacing the shabbier items with the few warehouse sale purchases she'd made during her early years at Muskowitz & Kerrigan. Only now does it strike her as odd that she'd never thought to hang any of her own things, so that the two watercolors she'd inherited from Rebecca and the black-and-white city photos she'd bought after Gene moved back west (when, for the first time, she'd had a little extra money) had remained all these years wrapped in brown paper under the bed.

Her first morning back, she recalls her first dream since Saul's arrest. She's in a cage, like the glass enclosures at Alil's, and she and Braner are dancing together. Cassen stands by the door collecting money. She wakes with the thought *I have to quit*. All week, the idea grows. When she goes to Ruth and Maggie's for dinner, she talks to them about it.

Maggie gets a pad of paper, insists they write out a budget. Surveying the list of numbers, she circles the huge rent payment.

"You could move," Maggie says, placing an asterisk next to the circle.

Rena must look startled, because she can feel Ruth studying her face.

Maggie takes her hand. "Four years is a long time." Had it been Ruth who'd spoken, Rena knows she would have said something like *Christ Almighty, no one expects you to pay the rent for a two-bedroom apartment out of loyalty.*

She takes a cab home, the driver heading south on Riverside Drive. Frederick Law Olmsted, Saul once told her, had designed the drive to follow the shoreline. A piece of frozen choreography along the riverbank. She remembers, now, that she'd been thinking about this the evening before Saul's arrest, how the drive does not so much mirror the shoreline as suggest the movement of the water in the river below. Then, too, she'd gone to dinner at Ruth and Maggie's, taking the bus that night north along this same arbored sweep of road. Between the apartment buildings with their limestone façades and the street stretched a sloping field covered with snow that after two days of freezing rain had turned to a slick of ice. The hillside was cast pale blue from the streetlights and etched with the shadows of the branches above. Before coming east, she'd never seen frozen earth. In San Francisco, there'd been cold snaps —damp and chill, an occasional sleet storm. In the Sierras, there'd been heavy snowfalls in late winter. But never had she seen the ground crusted with ice. It had struck her as something horrific, like a frozen finger or a charred piece of flesh.

Eerie—the massive trees rising from the frozen slope, the grand apartment buildings like sentry guards at the edge of the city, the empty drive—and she recalls now, a season later, the sense of foreboding, prescience of the bang on the door to come.

AT NIGHT, SHE STILL hears the echo of the police bullhorn coming from the garden, thinks how relieved she would feel to move.

She yearns to be Klara, to do what she wants without concern for what it means. When she tells this to Ruth the following Sunday while they bike in the park, Ruth laughs and says, "Yes, in my next life, I'm hoping to come back as one of these trees." She points up at an oak overhanging the walkway. "Waving my branches in the breeze, looking out at the river."

Rena cannot help feeling slightly chastised.

Ruth reaches out to touch Rena's handlebar. "You don't have to quit in order to move if moving is what you really want. As I tell my students with their mangled term papers, S.I.S: keep separate ideas separate."

"He has so much stuff. I don't think I could even fit into a smaller place."

"Put his stuff in storage."

"Oh my God, how could I do that? It seems so brutal. Besides, if I move anything, he'll never be able to find it again."

"Don't be ridiculous. Finding his college notes about Hegel or his Louis Armstrong recording will be the least of his problems four years from now."

Once Ruth has planted the idea of storing Saul's things, of living without his possessions, Rena's mind keeps coming back to it. When she first got to know Ruth, shortly after she and Gene moved to the city, she was struck by how streamlined Ruth keeps her affairs. While Rena routinely donates her old clothing out of fear of appearing shabby (her preference to make do with two new sweaters rather than a drawerful with stretched-out necklines and little stains, the kind she'd worn as a child), Ruth does so due to her belief that it's a drain to have more than one needs. While Rena usually feels as though the weekends are barely long enough to do the food shopping and the laundry and clean the apartment and write the bills, Ruth has an abundance of time. Every day, she works, she bicycles, she reads, she spends time with friends.

"When do you clean your tub, when do you wash your stockings, when do you do your taxes?" Rena once lamented.

"Look at our tub," Ruth said. "There's primordial soup creeping up the edges. Housework is the real cancer. You scrub the tub and two days later it's dirty all over again. My mother has a mop squeegee permanently attached to her hand. All her life, she's been trying to get caught up, to reach that mythical moment when the housework will all be done and she can do what she *really* wants. Only now, if she does have a free half-hour, her nervous system is so shot she can't concentrate or think about anything other than the next thing she has to do. Once you opt out of the American antiseptic ideal, you have loads of time. By not making the bed, you gain two and a half hours a month. Think what you can do in two and a half hours. You can read half a book. You can see an exhibit. You can have a love affair."

Like Ruth's mother, Rena has lived with the illusion that after she "gets through" the next thing, then she'll be able to do what she wants. Only there's been an endless progression of things to get through: her mother's pregnancy, her mother's depression after Gene's birth, the breakup with Ascher. Joe's death, settling Gene first in New Haven and then in New York, adjusting to Muskowitz & Kerrigan, adjusting to Gene moving back west, adjusting to living with Saul. Adjusting, adjusting, adjusting. Her marriage, the merger with Cassen & Silvano. Now, Saul's arrest. Twenty years. It could go on and on until her death, past that, until her funeral and the headstone were set.

SHE GIVES NOTICE at her job that she will be leaving at the end of the month and to her landlord that she will stay through June. A farewell party is planned for the evening after her last day at work. A couple of people give her little winks and her secretary whispers that the office rumor is that she is leaving because she's pregnant.

Cassen arranges for Rena's farewell party to be held in a private room at a restaurant where reservations are usually required months in advance. Men in tuxedo shirts announce the hors d'oeuvres as though they're special guests: prawns infused with vanilla bean oil, carpaccio stuffed with red caviar. As Cassen supervises the uncorking of the wine, it dawns on Rena that he's treating her departure as a grand celebration, the removal from his life of a source of frustration.

Throughout the cocktail hour, Cassen watches her. Her neck bristles from his gaze. When, right before the dinner is served, she goes to the rest room, he follows her downstairs. She turns, her back to the ladies' room door. He stops so close she can smell the Macallan on his breath. In the flats she is wearing with her gray silk pants, they are exactly the same height. Knowing that this is the last time she will have to see him, that she will no longer have to manage him, she does not avert her eyes: a body shaped by boyhood games, college athletics, a social life centered on tennis and skiing and sailing—the sort of physique that will turn, perhaps in fifteen years, perhaps, if time treats him well, in twenty, from lithe to scrawn. A face etched with the marks of a million deceptions.

"I want to thank you," he says, "for all your hard work."

Her muscles tighten like a dog detecting an intruder.

"I know the transition to the new partnership was difficult for you—with your political affiliations." He says the words *political affiliations* slowly, as though they are slightly unsavory. "I appreciate your professionalism in all of this."

She listens carefully. She thinks, he is going to let it go with everything smoothed over.

"If you need any recommendations, I would be happy to provide them for you."

"Thank you."

He reaches out a hand as though to shake hers. Their fingers touch and then quickly he pulls her toward him, squeezing her hand so hard in his that she feels a sharp crushing pain. She gasps, and he pushes his tongue into her mouth. Across her front teeth and then deep inside. She digs the nails of the hand he's squeezing into his palm. There are voices and then footsteps at the top of the stairs. He releases her and smiles.

A man passes by them into the men's room. Rena waits until Cassen is gone from the stairwell before entering the ladies' room. She locks the door and runs the cold water. Pulling back her lower lip, she leans under the faucet so the water bathes her mouth.

She swishes and spits. *Bastard,* swish. He must have calculated that now, after her last day at work, he'd be safe from a harassment charge. *Bastard,* spit.

She puts on fresh lipstick, recomposes her face and heads back upstairs. An oversized white plate with a piece of seared tuna has been set at her place. She's seated between Cassen and Muskowitz.

"Rena looks a little shook up, doesn't she, Harold," Cassen says to Muskowitz.

"Maybe she's having second thoughts about leaving us."

"Let me open your tuna for you, my dear," Cassen says. "One has to cut seared tuna the correct way or the juices seep out."

He reaches over and swiftly cuts the piece of fish in half. A drop of pink liquid slides between the halves.

"Perfectly done," Cassen proclaims. "Absolutely perfect."

SHE CANNOT SLEEP. Unwilling to draw attention to herself, she'd eaten half the tuna even though the sight of it and Cassen's thinly disguised smirk had made her ill. *Got you,* she imagines Cassen thinking, as though it had been a game of tennis between them and he'd beaten her in the final match.

She'd had the same feeling ten years ago with her stepfather, Joe: that he'd timed his heart attack to coincide with her Christmas break, when she'd come west to care for Rebecca; timed it so as to sabotage her opportunity to help Rebecca, who'd helped her to leave Joe and Novato behind. At the police station, they had Eleanor sit in a chair and grip the arms before they would tell her about the girl who'd made the report: a sixteen-year-old hitchhiker who told the detective interviewing her that she'd gone in the back of the truck with Joe willingly, he hadn't forced her or anything, and how she'd thought his groan was—and here she had to look at the floor—*well, you know what.*

At first, Rena had planned to stay only a few days past Joe's funeral, but then Eleanor disappeared to track down the girl and Gene stopped eating or talking. Waking one night to check on Gene, she found his bed empty and then heard a whimper from the closet where he crouched inside. In the morning, she called the dean's office and arranged to take incompletes in her courses and, since they wouldn't grant less than a year's absence, a leave for the following year.

"I'll stay," she told Eleanor, "but I can't live with the deer and the guns."

Eleanor nodded. Usually not a drinker, Eleanor had been intoxicated since the funeral. Rena bartered with the guy across the street, Russell, a contractor with a side yard filled with tires. He'd haul out the deer's head and the boxes of girlie magazines in exchange for one of the guns, the rest of which he helped her sell to a pawnshop in San Rafael.

In February, after the electricity was turned off because Eleanor had failed to pay the bill, Rena began taking the seven A.M. shift at the diner where Eleanor worked three to eleven. Rena would ride her bike there and then drive Eleanor's car back, the bike hanging out of the trunk, five minutes to spare before Gene got home from school. Afternoons she and Gene would play catch in the yard or board games on the floor, and she'd make them dinners of soup and burgers or casseroles of macaroni and cheese. Every day she'd tell her mother, "Call if you need a lift home," and Eleanor would nod, but she never called, never made it back before three in the morning, after the bars had closed when someone, maybe the bartender, would drive her home. Every night Rena would do the dishes, help Gene with his homework, pack his lunch, forcing herself to go to bed with pillows over her ears so she would not listen for the sounds of her mother coming in. Sometimes six would roll around and there'd still be no Eleanor and Rena would be sitting in her waitress uniform at the kitchen table drinking tea, Gene's breakfast set up, and she'd have to call the hostess and say, "I'm going to be a little late, Gene's bus comes at half past seven," and she could hear Sheila sighing because they'd have to juggle for an hour with two girls and everyone impatient to get served right away.

Saturdays she'd take Gene and they'd go to stay with Rebecca for the weekend. Rebecca seemed cheered to have a child around, and while she and Gene sat on the couch reading together, Rena would do the housework. It was a beautiful house, a Victorian that Rebecca had bought before the Mission District became popular, with a carved banister, picture rail moldings and Romanesque friezes over the two fireplaces. When Rena was done with the cleaning, she and Gene would walk to Twenty-Fourth Street to do the week's food shopping and buy burritos for dinner. They'd eat at the round oak table overlooking the walled garden, where a fir and palm tree grew side by side. Rebecca would retire early, and Gene would draw or read or build things with the pulleys and springs and wires they'd recovered from a wooden trunk in what had once been Rebecca's son, Max's, room.

For three months, Ascher stayed away while Rena was there. He would come during the week to visit Rebecca (even from her sickbed, still his teacher) and to cook for her. He did Rebecca's banking, left the crisp twenty-dollar bills Rena used to do the shopping in a carved box on the foyer table. Sometimes, rounding a corner in the house, she'd think she detected his smell—sharp like the scent of wet moss under a rock. On a few occasions, he left her coded messages: papayas, a fruit he had introduced to her and she loved, set on the kitchen counter; the week of her birthday, calla lilies placed by the bed where she slept.

Then, in April, he came. It was a warm afternoon, and she'd dug out a pair of Max's gym shorts and an old T-shirt she'd tied at her waist. In the upstairs bathroom she bent over the tub, the window open, the radio up high, vigorously scrubbing, as if success in removing the stains from the hundred-year-old porcelain would translate into a victory over the cancer and its relentless march through Rebecca's lymph nodes. Superstitiously, she scrubbed and scrubbed, so that she did not know how long Ascher stood watching her backside, only that when she turned to get more cleanser there was a shadow cutting the tiles. She looked up into his face. Slowly, she raised herself so she was seated on her knees. She wiped her hands on the T-shirt as he moved in from the doorway, closing the door behind him and then reaching down to pull her up from the wet floor. "Your hair," he murmured, his thick fingers moving over her scalp.

And so they resumed, this second try, four years since the Democratic party Brahmins had told Ascher he had a choice: the girl or your place on the ticket. Every night he would drive his Jaguar, the car the firm had leased him after he lost—*my consolation prize,* he joked to Rena—over the Golden Gate Bridge. Arriving after Gene went to bed, he would leave before Eleanor returned. All spring, they'd gone on this way, lucky, Gene never waking to discover them, Eleanor never surprising them. An extended parenthesis with the poignancy of something that will not last—a casaba so sweet and ripe it's almost a juice, a triangle of sunlight on a polished oak floor. It didn't matter that she didn't let him help her in any practical way, that Eleanor and Gene had never heard her so much as mention his name. She was leaning on him inside. He was the one she talked to in her head at the diner as she carried platters of sunny-side-up eggs and hash browns, as she prepared meals for Gene, coaxing him to eat. It was a marvelous trick, this narration of all the day's events to Ascher, first in her head, then later, lying in the crook of his arm: it made the days unreal, like a bad movie that can be flipped on and off.

It was all stolen time, the nights ticking off—one month, two months, three—until the point when someone would inevitably find out. Last time, it had been Mano, Ascher's driver. This time, they never figured out who. It could have been anyone: the toll clerk at the bridge, the attendant at the garage where he parked. A dick a corporate client had put on his tail. Someone from the community who felt betrayed that he'd disappeared from politics into his work at the firm. A white racist furious that he was with a white woman. Someone who knew how to type a note with gloves on his hands. Who knew to speak through a wad of tissues. One sentence: *I'm onto you, nigger*. Then, a few days later, a call, a muffled voice: *The girl, we know who she is*. Click.

SHE HEADS INTO the kitchen to turn on the kettle. It's a Saturday morning, but without the prospect of work on Monday she feels at sea. The answering machine blinks with last night's messages. She listens as she waits for the water to boil.

"Hi. It's Maggie. Calling to see how you made out on your last day. Hope the party was fun. Give us a call."

Another beep. "Rena," Saul says. "I wanted to hear your voice. But all I hear is my own voice still on the message tape." A pause. A sigh. "Well, there's not much to say. I had to wait an hour and a quarter to make this call, so it'll probably be a while before I try again. My father says it's impossible to get through to me here, so maybe that's why I haven't heard from you. Or maybe you've needed some space."

Saul laughs. It's a forced laugh, more anxiety than amusement. Rena stands rooted to the kitchen floor.

"Space. What does that mean? Space in your head? What do I have, fifteen seconds left? Well, I finished *Ulysses*. All the way through to Algeciras. Algeciras. I'm working in the metal shop now. Not license plates. Brackets for shelving. Oh, and you probably heard, the sentence was set. What can—" and then he is cut off.

SHE SITS AT THE BACK of the bus with her sweater draped over her chest, the shopping bag with more magazines, books and tapes on the adjacent seat. It's been nearly two months since she last visited, a spur-of-the-moment decision after hearing Saul's spooky message which left her feeling both ashamed that she hadn't gone and afraid of what she might see.

At the visitation center, the clerk, a doe-eyed girl with straightened hair, takes Rena's name and Saul's ID number.

"You okay?" She smiles, revealing a gold front tooth.

"I'm fine. Just a little carsick from the bus."

"That happens to me, too. There's a cafeteria over in Building Ten for staff and visitors. Visiting hours aren't until one. You can get something to drink there while you wait." The girl glances behind her, then reaches into the pocket of her uniform shirt. "Here, have a piece of gum. It'll settle your stomach."

Rena takes the stick of gum, mumbles her thanks.

"Your old man?"

Rena nods.

"How long?"

"Four years."

"That's not too bad. My brother's in for twenty. You want another piece?"

"No, thanks. I'm fine now."

"I always keep something on me. People come here looking kind of ragged."

Rena heads over to Building Ten, more out of fear of disappointing the girl than out of any desire for food. She walks through the cafeteria line, taking a saucer with a spotted banana and a styrofoam cup of tea. The room smells of ground meat: sloppy joes, meat loaf, hamburgers with gravy. She sits as far as possible from the food line.

At one, she returns to the reception area. She steels herself for the pat-down, empties out the shopping bag. A second guard leads her down the long hall and through the double gates to a room identical to the one where she saw Saul last time. She sits at the table and puts the bag in the middle.

A few minutes later, a third guard escorts Saul into the room. Rena senses it immediately: the sunken chest, the brightness drained from the eyes, the smell the skin gets when a person has collapsed, thoughts slowed to an excruciating crawl.

The guard repeats the directions about the buzzer and no physical contact. She fights the urge to grab the guard's sleeve and plead, *Don't leave me alone here with him.*

"You don't look so good."

"I've been kind of down." Saul shifts his gaze to the back wall.

"When did this happen?"

"A little after the sentencing. It hit me then. That I'm here for a long time. A tenth of the rest of my life."

"It's a long time."

"And it seems even longer when you can't sleep. At least if you can sleep, you have a third of the time off."

"Maybe they can give you something." She's appalled at her words—the same ones that had started this whole thing. She watches his reaction, his inability to muster the energy to pull off the kind of snappy rejoinder he would have in the past about no one wanting to fix a plumber's leaky faucet.

"Dealing with the medical staff here is enough to turn anyone into a bigot. Not one of them speaks fluent English. They're all afraid of me. Afraid I'll report them to the medical board for some piece of sloppiness and threaten their immigration status."

"That's absurd. Did you talk to Morton about it?"

"No. That's the point. That's what they expect me to do."

Saul pulls on a cuticle, the surrounding area inflamed and red. He puts the injured finger to his mouth. "What I can't figure out is your old buddy. Why he chose me to be the sacrificial lamb."

When Morton had told her Saul believed Reed had left knowing Saul would be arrested, she'd assumed, wrongly, she sees now, it was something that would pass. "What makes you think that?"

"Oh, come on, Rena. They must have worked it all out. If Bria got caught, she'd make a deal by telling them about me."

What she wants to say is, *I don't believe that, I don't believe Reed would ever do that to you, to me,* but she feels Saul's deadness washing against her, is afraid that anything she says now will only make it seem that her loyalty lies with Reed, not him.

"Are you still the secretary for that guy, the gang leader?"

"Marsden Stem, Grand Marshal of the Blackjacks. Yes." Saul closes his eyes. "I have to do that. If I stop doing that, it's all over for me."

She squeezes her hands together. It's a familiar feeling, one she knew with Eleanor: the wish to run, to leave the other person to rot by the side of the road, to find air free of depression's stench.

"I brought you some books."

"I can't read. Next to not sleeping, that's the worst part. By the time I get to the fourth line, my concentration's shot. Sometimes at night it's a little better, but then the noise is so bad—everyone jerking off and hooting and cursing."

Silence gathers between them, Saul in that state where even if it occurred to him to ask about her, he would not be able to feign interest. Although he does not know why she's come—an impulse this morning to tell him that she'd finally quit her job—she feels foolish for having thought it would matter to him.

They remain in silence. She cannot say if it is two minutes or ten. Then, searching for something to say, she asks about his prison job.

"Same. Making brackets for state shelving. Three hundred a day."

"And your parents?"

He stares at her. It's the first time she has ever seen him look at her with disdain, disdain for filling time, for retreating from him.

"They're okay. My father comes every Sunday."

Abruptly, Saul pushes back his chair and stands. "Tell Santiago. Tell him about me."

The guard opens the door and before Rena can say *the magazines, the books,* Saul is gone.

THE SECOND TIME with Ascher, she'd said it first. There was no choice but to stop. It would destroy him. He couldn't bear to humiliate his wife, Delia, that way. So they stopped as suddenly as they'd started. The first time, the hard, heavy feeling in her chest had slowly slid down toward her abdomen, letting her breathe again; this time, the weight grew day by day, like rocks one on top of another.

In August she slept with Russell, the guy across the street who'd carted out Joe's deer head. Like mother (Eleanor had gone on a crash diet and taken to wearing tighter blouses and shorter skirts and screwing everyone in sight), like daughter, she thought. Russell was perfect—physically gorgeous and spiritually bankrupt. Answering the door barechested and barefoot, the snap of his blue jeans would still be open. He lied about everything. It got his goat that she didn't care who else he slept with. He fucked more and more vigorously, banging into her, throwing her around, until one morning, catching a glimpse of herself in the mirror, she saw her tailbone black and blue. Horrified, she left him a note: "This is getting out of hand. Count me out."

A few days later, sitting on the front steps waiting for Eleanor to come in from the night so she could leave for work, Rena watched Russell, a towel wrapped around his middle, open his front door and her mother walk out onto the porch. Her mother's head tipped backwards, inviting a kiss. Russell waved at Rena before bending over Eleanor. Rena felt sick. She was twenty-five. Eleanor was forty-four. Russell was right in the middle. The peanut butter and jelly.

In the evening, Rena banged on Russell's door. He laughed as she pushed past him.

"Lay off my mother. You don't give a damn about anyone, do you?"

He moved toward her, his hands reaching for her breasts. "She's not bad, your mother. But she ain't got these."

Everything went static, the electrical circuits that usually keep thought and action in separate channels suddenly blown, and the next thing she knew she was punching him. She'd never hit another human being, but she pummeled him: on the nose, at his ears, on his chest. A trickle of blood ran over his top lip onto his chin. Then he pushed her. Hard. Her knee slammed against the floor. Everything rocked and she saw black. He stood over her, his stunned expression turned stone. His mouth moved as if he were chewing. "You want to get rough with me, we can get rough."

For a week, she hobbled around the diner with a knee brace. Nights, she lay with her leg propped on pillows, her mother out at the bars or perhaps across the street with Russell, Gene asleep down the hall. It was then that she really hit bottom about Ascher. The first time they'd separated, he'd given her Rebecca. This time, it was as though all the losses of her life had been piled together and she found herself sinking to a place she'd never visited before, beyond sadness, beyond grief, where the body gives out and there is no more sleep or appetite.

She saw Ascher only one more time, in May, when Rebecca died. He stood two people away from her at the gravesite and she'd not let him catch her eye, afraid he would see that her tears were as much for him as for Rebecca.

BACK IN NEW YORK, she calls Monk and Leonard. Monk curses. "Assholes. I told them two weeks ago to have the shrink there look Saul over. Half the time you can't tell if they're not doing something deliberately or they're just so inept and disorganized they don't even know they haven't done it."

Leonard is not surprised. "It's been coming," he says. Rather, he seems more surprised to hear from her. Nearly a month has passed since they last spoke, the drift apart, it seems to her now, coinciding with Saul's letter that he was not going to "harangue" her to visit. Had Saul and Leonard planned together to leave her alone?

Cautiously, Leonard asks how she's been.

"Well," she says, "I quit my job. Finally."

Leonard pauses, his consternation a live thing between them. "I knew you were upset with the changes there, but I hadn't realized you were thinking of leaving."

For the rest of the night, she can't stop going over the conversation with Leonard. She can't say what it is, but something strikes her as wrong. She takes a silver cloth to her earrings, pays the basket of bills. It's after two before she pinpoints what it was: talking about Saul, she'd sounded so distant, her efforts on his behalf a set of willed actions—do this, do this, do this—like the movements of a limb that's fallen asleep. None of the agitated intensity she'd felt so often with Gene, that reserve of energy that allows some mothers to stay up night after night with a newborn, some fathers—here, she imagines Ascher and Leonard—to lift a car off a trapped child.

MONDAY MORNING, SHE wakes with the realization that this is the first time since before Gene was born that she does not have a job or a fixed set of obligations. She unplugs the phone, closes the shades, spends the morning in bed. In her waking moments, she remembers the weeks Eleanor lay unbathed on the couch, rising only to use the toilet. Candy wrappers littering the floor. Joe: *You fat pig. You lazy fat pig.* Eleanor unable even to cry. Unable to do anything other than stare at the ceiling and eat.

By noon, she's scared out of her lassitude. She showers, dresses, sits down at the kitchen table with the want ads, mostly temporary agencies looking for word processors. Why not, she thinks. She's an excellent typist. At Muskowitz & Kerrigan, they'd hired temps to do the overnight typing. There'd been a guy who'd worked on her projects for nearly a year. Once, working late, she'd met him, surprised to see that he was not a kid but a gentle, portly man with a gray goatee. They'd spoken for only two, three minutes—long enough for her to see that people were painful for him. Working nights, he had only to nod at the guard in the lobby.

She calls one of the numbers from the paper. Someone tells her to come in at three.

She deletes the four years at Yale and the seven years at Muskowitz & Kerrigan from the application she fills out before taking the typing and spelling tests. Afterwards, she's interviewed by a woman dressed in a suit closer to what a soap opera star in the role of a businesswoman would wear than the attire of any professional she's known. The interviewer looks up questioningly from the spare application.

"My husband and I recently separated. I need a job."

A sympathetic look, a glance at the test scores. "My goodness. I've never seen anyone get a hundred on the spelling test. Aren't we smart? And your typing is very good. Let me see here . . ." She flips through a directory of their current openings. "You said you prefer nights?"

Rena nods.

"This might be perfect. A large law firm, one of our regular clients. The lawyers mark up the last drafts of the day and want a clean copy for the morning. They need someone who's very careful, very meticulous. You might work out well there. The only thing is, they don't like to change girls, so you'd need to make a commitment to stay for at least two months. Can you do that?"

July, August. Suddenly, Rena feels completely exhausted and entirely alone, as though only now, in this air-conditioned midtown office with this paper doll woman, has the magnitude of Saul's arrest taken hold. Had the woman said six months, she probably would have said yes to that, too, the months stretching forward without demarcation.

Forty-eight moons lined up in a row.

FOR A WEEK, she tells herself that she can call Santiago Domengo and let him know over the phone about Saul's arrest, and that will be that, obligation fulfilled, no more required, but all the while she knows that she cannot do it, that no one she has ever respected, Rebecca, Ruth, Saul, would drop a bomb and run.

In the end, she does not call at all but instead goes to the address she finds in Saul's book, a building on Riverside Drive a few blocks north of where she'd lived with Gene—not far, from what her mother has told her, from where they'd lived with her father after she was born. Assuming that Santiago wouldn't recognize her last name, she has the doorman announce her as Saul's wife. She takes the elevator to the eleventh floor and rings the bell.

An old man with dark glasses and a black beret opens the door. His skin is dotted with liver spots and his fine lips are almost white. He's frailer than she'd expected, the vast store of knowledge Saul had described hard to place in this slight, stooped form. With one veined hand, he balances on a cane, seemingly unsurprised at her presence at his door, so that it passes fleetingly, absurdly she decides, through her mind that he already knows about Saul. He extends the other hand.

"Mrs. Dubinsky, what an honor to meet you. So many times I have said to Saul you must bring your bride to meet me. Come in, come in."

The foyer is filled floor to ceiling with dark bookshelves, now empty of books. On a few of the lower shelves are piles of clothing: sweaters, socks, pants. She follows Santiago into the living room, frozen in fifties modern, the furniture worn beyond repair. Through the scrim of grime on the windows, closed despite the warm weather, she can see the Hudson, this afternoon a sailor's blue. Santiago motions for her to sit in a low armchair. A puff of dust rises when she touches the seat. He lowers himself onto a couch covered with a flowered sheet.

"How is Saul? I have been worried, it's so unlike him to not come." Santiago cups his knees with his hands. "He must be very busy with his job."

Disappointment washes over her, the fantasy that the blind can see what's invisible to the rest of us, that he would explain what happened, punctured.

"We were in the middle of reading *Moby-Dick*. Have you read it? Your American genius, Mr. Melville."

"It's been a long time. Fifteen years ago. More."

"Saul is a marvelous reader." Santiago points to the bookshelves, where Rena now sees a tape recorder and a pile of audiotapes. "The social worker from the Guild for the Blind sent me a copy on Books on Tape so I could hear the rest."

The apartment has a funny smell: mothballs, wet wool, chili peppers. Other than the one visit she'd made with her mother and Gene to see her grandfather, she's never really had occasion to spend time with anyone old.

She'd promised nothing to Saul. He'd bolted from the room before she could respond. She could make small talk and leave.

Santiago tilts an ear in her direction.

She could.

She could not.

"Mr. Domengo, I came because of Saul."

"Please call me Santiago. All these years, everyone calling me Professor Domengo, I'm too old for it now."

"Santiago. I'm afraid it's not good news."

"He is sick?"

"No. He's well. Physically, that is. He's been arrested."

"Arrested?" Santiago puts a hand on his chest. "For what? Some kind of political protest?"

"He was implicated in a pharmacy burglary. He'd become addicted to prescription drugs. Perhaps Saul told you about his patient who'd lost his legs? It was after that, when he couldn't sleep."

Santiago lets out a faint whistle of air. He leans against the flowered sheet. She cannot see his eyes, hidden behind the dark glasses.

"I'm sorry to have to tell you."

"Saul has been like a son to me." His voice shakes.

She waits for him to regain his composure. Behind him, an oil tanker creeps south toward the harbor.

"How long will he be in the prison?"

"Four years. More or less. He asked me to tell you. I think he was feeling badly that he'd let you down."

"It is true that I was worried about him. But I never thought drugs. All these years that I've known him, since he was a university student, Saul was such a responsible boy. More realistic than my son, Bernardo, who was so naïve."

"Did you suspect anything?"

"His mother, she begged him not to go. She knew. She was a very intelligent woman. Here I was the professor of political science, but it was she who really kept up with what went on in the world."

Rena raises an eyebrow, but of course Santiago cannot see her confusion.

"She knew it was very dangerous then. A guerrilla war. Later, when we went down to try and find him, we heard about whole families who'd been murdered for having an uncle who was part of the resistance movement. Terrible, terrible things, we heard. Whole villages where every man and male child had been shot."

"Saul told me about your son."

"He organized a fund at Swarthmore to help us with the search. He was a very kind boy. Too kind, I used to tell him. Too much compassion, I used to tell him, can lead you astray. The good comes from the balance of the hard and the soft."

Santiago takes off his glasses. His lids are puffy, almost purple, and he keeps them shut as he wipes his sightless eyes.

After he puts his dark glasses back on, she tells him she has to go. He insists on escorting her to the lobby. In the elevator, he flattens the palm of his hand against the paneling, remarks that he still remembers the grain of the teak, a tree found in the forests near where he was born.

"You lost your sight since you've been here?"

"In 1979. First I lost my son. Then, two years later, my sight. My wife got rid of my books the next year. Four thousand three hundred and sixty-three volumes donated to the City University library. She said the dust bothered her, but I knew it was really that she could not bear to see them because she thought they, my work, were why we'd lost our son."

He falters, the grief so close to the surface that she fears he will break down again, but like music moving from sadness to sweetness, he recovers. "She was a wonderful woman. She read to me every day, wrote all my correspondence. You would be amazed at how much mail still comes from people who want to discuss articles I wrote forty years ago."

The door opens onto the lobby and Rena holds a hand against the sensor while Santiago enters, his cane tap-tapping ahead. "But I cannot complain. I am ninety-three and I still manage on my own. And the people here are very good to me. Since my wife died, Pedro, the day doorman, takes me every morning to the corner to buy whatever I need for the day. A very generous man."

"Perhaps I could come to read to you."

"What a pleasure that would be."

The doorman approaches. He waits for Santiago to finish speaking before touching his shoulder.

"I have just had the honor of making the acquaintance of Señora Dubinsky, the wife of my good young friend."

Pedro smiles shyly at her. Santiago removes his beret and places it over his heart. He bows slightly. "Good day, señora. *Hasta martes*." Until Tuesday.

SHE'S NO MORE than halfway up the block before she regrets the offer, misconstrued by Santiago since she'd meant on occasion, not every week and certainly not this Tuesday. Tomorrow she'll call, she'll clarify, tactfully extricate herself, but by the time she reaches Broadway, she can hear Saul's gentle chide: *And what else do you have to do that's so pressing? Polish your earrings again?*

She stops to buy fruit and milk. Afterwards, crossing Broadway, it occurs to her that her one memory of her father—a blurred still, a father and child marooned on an island in the middle of a wide boulevard waiting for the light to change, the father's long arm reaching down, the child's short one stretching up—probably took place nearby. It has always disturbed her that her memories of the braggadocio Johnny Campanella, the man her mother ran away with, Rena, age two, in tow, are more vivid: leaning against the side of Johnny's red Ford while she ate a strawberry ice-cream cone, the fat drips rolling down the brown wafer, the sudden idea to turn the cone over to let the drips fall onto the ground. When the pink ball fell, splat, she must have started to cry because the next thing she remembers is Johnny slapping her hand and her mother swooping her up, yelling, "Don't you ever touch her, she's not your child," and then Johnny throwing something, maybe the map, against the side of the car and her mother carrying her to the rest room, where the two of them stayed locked inside until someone started banging on the door.

Johnny Campanella hadn't lasted long. A week after they reached San Francisco, he turned the Ford back around and headed for Brooklyn, leaving Eleanor and Rena in their North Beach hotel room. For a day, Eleanor was nervous: there was enough money for a couple of cartons of milk, some bread, a jar of peanut butter. By nightfall, though, she was smiling. "Just as well, big stupid creep. He got us here, didn't he, baby?" And by the next day she'd found the job at Nick's Ristorante, where the cook let Rena play in the corner of the kitchen while the waitresses fed her the tastiest morsels from the untouched food on the customers' plates.

INSTEAD OF CALLING SANTIAGO, she calls Leonard to tell him that she's taken a job as a temp and is going to start looking for a smaller apartment. Plunging forward, she asks if she could store some of Saul's things in his attic.

"With a one-bedroom, I won't be able to fit all his books and records and files."

Leonard pauses just long enough for Rena to notice the questions he doesn't ask. He offers to come with a U-Haul before she moves.

The new job suits Rena. She leaves the house at eight in the evening, just as the summer heat begins to lift, walking the three miles south and east to the law firm's office at Thirty-Ninth and Park. She stops at the Zaro's in Grand Central for a sandwich and water and then sits on the steps of the law firm's building, reading and nibbling. At quarter to ten, she feeds the crusts to the pigeons and heads inside, showing her identification card to the security guard and then riding the elevator up to the twenty-sixth floor. Unlike Muskowitz & Kerrigan, where there would rarely be anyone in the office at this hour, here there are always a couple of the first- or second-year associates wandering around, the women with their shoes kicked off, the men with their ties askew, sometimes one of the regular secretaries coerced into staying late.

It takes Rena a few days to adjust to her new status as support staff, to give a little wave to the secretary and save the small nods of the head for the young associates. It surprises her how liberating it feels to no longer be one of the professionals mired with anxieties about what the senior partner thinks that lead them to leave their written work until the eleventh hour and then fuel themselves with candy bars and coffee in order to get it done. Each night, she heads to the cubicle set aside for the temp, reads over the list of projects the office manager, Sari, has left her, the diskettes clipped to the marked-up pages. The tasks are complicated enough not to be tedious but simple enough to do without strain. By one, she is usually alone and can turn on the radio she keeps in her drawer and listen to the chamber music the classical station plays at this hour. She works until six and then walks home in the cool morning air. At home, she bathes and puts in earplugs before climbing into bed.

There is something delicious about it all: the walks at dusk and daybreak, the long, quiet hours spent midtown, the deep sleep so much easier for her to come by in the light of day.

WHAT SANTIAGO WANTS her to read to him is John Rawls' *A Theory of Justice*.

"I taught this book the year I had Saul in class," he says. "But I haven't read it since. Saul brought me his copy. We were going to read it after Mr. Melville."

On the inside cover, Rena sees Saul's signature from a decade before they met. The same crooked scrawl, alternatingly too much and too little pressure applied to the pen. Letters formed by someone at risk of tripping over his own feet.

"If you would start, please, with Chapter Six. Duty and Obligation." Santiago's voice is surprisingly strong today, the Rawls having revived his habitual teacherly projection.

She reads slowly and loudly. While she can imagine Saul being riveted by the words, she reads with little attention to what she's saying until the passage on mutual aid pulls her back into focus. " 'Consider, for example,' " she reads, " 'the duty of mutual aid. Kant suggests, and others have followed him here, that the ground for proposing this duty is that situations may arise in which we will need the help of others, and not to acknowledge this principle is to deprive ourselves of their assistance.' "

Santiago nods vigorously.

" 'But this is not the only argument for the duty of mutual aid,' " Rena continues, " 'or even the most important one. A sufficient ground for adopting this duty is its pervasive effect on the quality of everyday life. The public knowledge that we are living in a society in which we can depend upon others to come to our assistance in difficult circumstances is itself of great value.' "

"These are the most important sentences in the book," Santiago says. "Here, in your country, self-sufficiency is idealized. Receiving help, people think it is demeaning. After Bernardo disappeared, people became embarrassed around us. They pitied us because we needed so much help to continue our search."

"But what if a person refuses help?" She is thinking of Saul, how he'd never told her about the pills.

Santiago takes so long to respond, she wonders if he has not heard her. Or is he thinking that if Saul rejected her help, it was never truly offered?

He clears his throat, lifts his chin. "In a capitalist society, money becomes the metaphor for everything. People believe that help is a limited resource, that they've spent their ration. They don't understand that love is like air. We can take as much as we need."

ON HER THIRD VISIT to Santiago, she tells him she's been apartment hunting, looking, in fact, for something here on Riverside Drive.

"But my neighbors just told me they are moving! Of course, I have not seen the apartment in years, but it has the same view as mine. Before they moved in, my daughter and her husband were going to take it, but then they moved to Saudi Arabia."

"I didn't know you had a daughter."

"By my first marriage. Flora's mother died in the childbirth, so she was raised by her mother's mother, a good woman but very cold to me. She blamed me for her daughter's death. Then she blamed me when Flora eloped at fifteen with an older cousin."

Behind Santiago, the river shimmies in the wind. "A disaster. He was a philanderer and a gambler. My daughter followed him to Caracas, where he lost both of their allowances. It took her grandmother three years to get the marriage annulled."

"She's remarried now?"

"The year Bernardo disappeared."

Santiago leans forward on his white-tipped cane. With the mention of his son, the room fills with silence. Rena places the Rawls on the coffee table. She forces herself to ask. "What happened—with your son?"

"If only I could answer that question. He'd gone with his tape recorder to visit a man who lived about three kilometers outside the town. He must have been kidnapped on the way. That's all we really know."

Only Santiago's lips move—movements so small it seems no voice could emerge. "We took out ads in the newspapers saying we would pay fifty thousand dollars American to anyone who could return our son or lead us to him. I did not say this to my Helen, but I knew when we had no response, we would not find him."

Santiago lowers his head. His shoulders heave and the cane wobbles. Rena raises herself from her chair, goes to sit at his side. She wonders if Santiago was like this with Saul: his grief infiltrating everything. She places a hand on his back, so thin she can feel his spine.

He takes a handkerchief from his shirt pocket. "No one would tell me who killed my son. The army, someone paid by the local police . . ."

It is the first time he has used that word: *killed*.

"It used to matter to me who it was. Now—it doesn't seem to matter."

"You're certain he was killed?"

"For many years, I thought there was a chance he was in prison. Sometimes, at night, I would imagine it was like one of those romance stories where the hero gets amnesia. That he'd been in an accident and lost his memory but was living in good health somewhere. Other times, I would imagine things much worse. The imagination is crueler than a torturer. Not seeing the body, I was left with no limit of possibilities. I am an atheist. But still, I have never been able to get over feeling that it is a break, a breach—is that the word, my English in these matters, it still fails me—not to bury your kin."

Santiago wipes his dripping nose with the handkerchief and blows.

"It is a basic law. We must consecrate our dead. It goes through all civilizations."

His shoulders heave again. "That is the worst part for me. That I could not even bury my child."

THE SUPER shows her the apartment. A kitchen with the original paned cabinets and room for a table. A small living room with a long hallway leading back to a bedroom and an enormous bath, both facing west so that she can see over the treetops to the river. In the bath, a clawfoot tub and a huge window filled after dark with the sparkling of the lights from the Jersey shoreline. She imagines a pale yellow kitchen with geraniums in the window, a bedroom all in white. She hesitates, wary of living next door to Santiago, afraid not that Santiago will in any real way intrude on her but that she will be unable to maintain a wall between her wishes and his, his sadness and hers. In the end, though, the apartment is too wonderful to pass up.

Ruth and Maggie volunteer to help paint. At first, it is going to be just the three of them, but then Leonard calls to say he can come that same morning to take Saul's things and insists on staying to give a hand.

"It will be like an old-fashioned barn raising," Leonard says over the phone. There's an unfamiliar touch of joviality in his voice, as if painting her apartment will be the most congenial thing he's done in months. "Where is it?"

"Actually, it's in Santiago Domengo's building." She doesn't say the apartment next door.

"I remember that building. There's a marble bench in the lobby. Saul took me there once. Years ago, before Santiago's wife died."

After they hang up, she can't shake an uneasy feeling—a reluctance to let Leonard see her, her empty walls, up close. The first time she met Leonard, she'd felt this same uneasiness. Seated in a Chinese restaurant on Columbus Avenue, dawdling over the last few Hunan shrimp and the remaining broccoli with garlic, Saul and Leonard had discussed biography and the nature of memory while Klara made a show of some kind of advancing malaise, a transparent display of displeasure at the déclassé restaurant and the quiet new girlfriend, pretty enough but dressed in clothes that looked like they came from a catalog.

What had set it off—this uneasy feeling—was a single sentence of Leonard's. *Our personal history begins with the memories of our grandparents.* In her mind's eye, she'd seen the photographs Saul had shown her of his grandparents: his maternal grandfather elegantly arranged in his Johns Hopkins office (a man with memories stretching back to his own grandparents and the china they brought from Edinburgh to the United States the year Andrew Jackson became president); Leonard's mother, the perky little Rita who had left a village in the Ukraine in 1909, never again to see her babushka'd grandmother plucking chickens or her white-bearded grandfather bowed over a religious book.

Leonard, of course, had not known that Rena could remember only one of her grandparents, her mother's father, who by then had lost his own memories, unable to recognize even his daughter, and that for the other three, she could not even imagine their memories. As though with Eleanor's run to the west coast, a bag hastily packed for Rena and her, not a photograph, not a dish, not even a toy taken along, history had been leveled, a city brought to rubble, and it would take generations—Rena's children's children—before there would be relics again.

7 Leonard

I've not held a paintbrush since before I met your mother, when I lived in a studio apartment in Hell's Kitchen and painted the walls sunflower yellow and cobalt blue thinking it would make me feel like I was in Provence rather than the basement of a cigar shop where you could hear the rats chasing each other between the walls. Not that I'd ever been in Provence, but I'd seen the paintings collected by the Cone sisters, Dr. Claribel and Etta, and had imagined myself belonging somewhere near the Mediterranean Sea: at one moment, an arid rust vista, at the next, ochre cliffs aglow with the pink of a setting sun. In Provence, I imagined Nature showing herself with full abandon, like a young girl with her lover—the peaches paler and softer, the olives almost navy in their delicious saltiness. Everywhere the hint of the sea: the anchovies in the bread, the white of fishbones. A more pleasing picture than the small dusty city in the Ukraine, the color of mud, where my mother, in fact, spent her first fourteen years—her first sight of the sea, the icy waves at Antwerp where she embarked for New York, everyone except herself (*a stomach of iron,* she proudly proclaimed) vomiting five, six times a day on the weeklong crossing.

I remember the envy I felt at your semester abroad, eight weeks of study in Aix-en-Provence and then a long, rambling journey. I followed your trip in my atlas as deduced from your postcards. You clung to the

Mediterranean, traveling from Málaga to Naples, and then across Italy and the Adriatic Sea to Athens and on to Crete. I located Aghios Nikolais, where you wrote that you'd found a room in a house above the port.

I wished for you a little Cretan friend, a girl with black hair that touched her waist and brows like friendly caterpillars. A girl with a black mole on the inside of her thigh who pulled the sheets over her breasts only when she felt cold. I castigated myself for having given you my bookish legacy, that amalgam of too much seriousness and a passive reserve that made it likely your bed partners would remain the journal and paperbacks you carted around in your rucksack. So you can see why I was so surprised when you introduced us to Rena, not that she looks like the little Greek friend I wished for you, but rather that she has, despite her skittish veneer, an elusive but nonetheless undeniable beauty. Not the easy American cover-girl beauty that your brother saw in Susan but something more interesting that comes from the Old World, where things are not prized for being shiny and bright: long legs caught in the corner of an eye on a stone-laid street, thick hair pushed back from a face absorbed in thought, an aquiline nose suggesting an ancient hieroglyph.

I'm embarrassed, an old man, talking like this. It's been too many years living with your mother, the celibacy a disease. Twenty-six years of it, since I was forty-one, since the spring her father died. The suburban house, our few vacations spent in wall-to-wall carpeted resorts with life-size sculptures of tennis pros perched on a weedless lawn. The body—something to be sanitized and controlled.

So why did you go along with it? I hear you asking. *Why did you let her dictate everything?*

What makes you think it was her?

MAGGIE, WHO TELLS ME she worked for two years in a feminist painters' collective in Santa Fe, lays out the game plan: we'll spend today covering the floors with drop cloths, taping the trim and prepping the walls. Our goal will be to roll one coat of primer and the first coat of paint. Tomorrow, we'll do the second coat of paint and the trim.

Rena looks at me. "Don't feel that you have to do this all weekend."

"Count me in, soup to nuts." The words are still stiff in my mouth when I remember that tomorrow is Sunday, the day I visit you.

Isn't that interesting, I imagine you saying. *You forgot you were coming to see me.*

Overdetermination doesn't negate coincidence, I rejoin—but this is all fantasy because you have lost the energy for snappy remarks and it is apparent even to me that I forgot because I wanted to forget, because I am scared to see you in your current state of mind.

"I'll take the boxes home tonight and come back tomorrow by noon."

Maggie divides us into work teams: Ruth and Rena, she and I. We begin the prep work on the bedroom. Maggie raises the blinds and it is stunning, the view of the river and park—the green treetops, the wide swatch of blue, the sailboats headed downstream, a tug and a barge moving north. I can see the spray from the prow of the barge and the gulls circling over the water, and for the first time I see that Rena is leaving you, that she is making a life on her own.

IT'S ELEVEN AT NIGHT by the time I haul your things up to the attic, your young man artifacts now stored in a space not much smaller than the five-by-eight cell you share with a twenty-four-year-old kid on his third mail fraud conviction.

I begin at six in the morning trying to call you at the pay phone on your floor. For the first hour there's no answer, and then, starting at seven, the phone is ceaselessly busy. I leave a message for you at the warden's office that I can't come today, that I'll be there Tuesday morning. The clerk answering the phone doesn't want to take the message—"We're not an answering service," she says nastily, "we don't take messages"—but I pull doctor's rank (something I've always hated, the New Jersey cardiologists with their BMWs with the MD plates double-parked outside Le Cirque), saying this is Dr. Dubinsky, and she reluctantly agrees to have the message passed on to you. Afterwards, I feel miserable, and it's hard to know how much is guilt for postponing my visit to you and how much is guilt that I'm posing as a physician—I who have not seen a patient in nearly four decades, unless you count your mother as a practice unto herself.

I spend the rest of the morning doing penance for leaving your mother untended for two afternoons in a row. I put chicken pieces in the oven for her dinner, take a croissant out of the freezer, go to the store for milk, fresh orange juice and a pint of her favorite black cherry chocolate-chip ice cream. At ten, I soft-boil her eggs and fetch the strawberry jam.

She stirs as I come in with her breakfast tray. "You're early."

"I need to leave in half an hour. I'm going to help Rena finish painting her apartment."

She asks no questions about the new apartment. "I slept terribly. I feel so *weak*." She stretches out *weak* over several seconds and then, as if forgetting the whole thing, swirls the strawberry jam into the yellows of her soft-boiled eggs. A fleck of croissant falls onto her neck and I reach over to wipe it off with the pink cloth napkin she likes on her tray.

She picks up the Sunday paper I've put by her side, reading as always the wedding announcements first.

"Deborah Gibbons. I wonder if that's Edward Gibbons' daughter."

I try to recall who Edward Gibbons is, but it is irrelevant since I am not expected to respond.

"She married the son of the president of one of the Sony divisions. He's an investment banker at Goldman Sachs." She laughs, a bitter laugh intended to imply how much richer and better everyone else is than us and ours. I feel terrible for you, that your mother has never been able to be proud of you, to view you as doing something important and worthy of respect. Not that she'd ever had any respect for psychiatry, but when we were first married she'd still held medicine in awe and this had extended in some feeble way to me. With her father's death, the pedestal had cracked, as though if her father were no longer a doctor, there could be, at least in the way she'd always thought of them, no more doctors. She'd purse her lips when someone referred to doctors, once remarking to a neighbor, "Well, really, if you think about it, it's very much like being a manicurist or an appliance repair person—just another service job."

"Let me help you move to the armchair to finish your coffee. Then I can change the sheets."

Obediently, she inches her legs over the side of the bed. Her ankles are swollen, her feet puffy on top. For twenty-some years, Stone has told us she will keep retaining water until she changes her diet and starts getting daily exercise.

"I used to have such lovely feet. So smooth and slender."

"Yes, you did, dear." I take her hand and guide her to the armchair.

"Amy Loodis, she was my roommate my first year at Wellesley, she used to say she'd die three times over to have my feet. She had these awful size nine and a halfs."

I put fresh sheets on the bed, plump up the pillows: everything done the way Mrs. Smiley used to do. With two college tuitions to pay, I'd had to let Mrs. Smiley go the year you began Swarthmore. Or rather, good soul that she is, she'd sensed the financial strain and found herself another position. "You can manage fine now, Dr. D, with a girl who comes in once a week to do your cleaning and laundry. That is, if you don't mind doing the shopping and taking Mrs. D her trays."

It took me a few days after you and Marc left for college to understand that the irritation I felt at both of you was resentment that you still needed me to keep the household running. I fought the idea; after all, you were eighteen and twenty, gone most of the year. But the bottom line was if I didn't maintain a household, you had none. Different as my circumstances had been—there'd been no money for me to go away to college; I'd felt lucky that my mother had a steady job and could give me room and board and I could make enough to cover my City College tuition and incidentals by working summers for my uncle—my mother had always kept house with grace and good cheer. She'd never missed a beat, not after my father and Eunice died, not after Lil and Rose got married, not when it was just the two of us and me hardly ever home in the Pelham Parkway flat. Always, she stocked the icebox, cooked for the holidays, put the blankets in mothballs, vacuumed under the beds. (Merckin, my analyst until I quit my job and had no money to see him anymore, made a quizzical grunt when I described my mother this way, insinuating an unmetabolized oedipal complex. During the two years I lay five times a week on his couch, I argued with him about his spurious logic: if I hated my mother, it would be a defense against the incestual wishes; if I loved her, it was evidence thereof.) It frightened me that your well-being still depended so centrally on me.

For six months after Mrs. Smiley left, I felt nothing but distraction when I entered my study. Seated at my desk, my mind would race to review the day's chores. I'd jump up to look in the phone book for a store that stocked the bulb for the freezer. I explained the anxiety that I wouldn't be able to work again (by work, I meant my books; the teaching, from which I was planning to retire once you finished college, was by then so automatic, my lectures all written a decade before, it didn't even enter into the equation) as a postpartum reaction to the completion of my second book, the last year of Mrs. Smiley's employ. Five hundred pages on the literary, scientific and philosophical precursors of the idea of the unconscious. It would be absurd, I told myself, to think that one could complete a project of that magnitude and not have a period of rebound. By the time summer rolled around, though, I had to acknowledge that the problem was deeper than needing breathing room at the end of a project, deeper than not knowing how to do two things at once. For the first time since I'd abandoned the practice of psychiatry for the contemplation of its concepts, I'd run aground onto a shore with no ideas. No seaweed, no shells, no jellyfish, no sand diggers, only the white white sand and hot hot sun.

MAGGIE REORGANIZES THE TEAMS, so I'm working with Ruth today. Ruth rolls the walls and I keep the paint tray filled, moving it and the stepladder for her.

"How's your book coming?" Ruth asks.

I pause long enough that she glances over her shoulder to check my face. There's a white splotch on her nose like the marking on a horse.

"It's not."

Ruth dips the roller in the paint tray. "What's the problem?"

I don't know how to respond. It's been so long since anyone asked me this kind of question, I feel rusty. I'm not saying that we, you and I, didn't talk. We talked a lot before that thing with the boy and the subway train. But we talked about the ideas I was struggling with, not the work itself: an entirely different beast.

"I'm lost. I don't know how to tell the story of this girl, Carmelita. Whether to tell it as I've reconstructed it chronologically or to tell it as the pieces unfolded through my research or to tell it as it was told by all these people who used it to fight various battles. I keep circling around. I can't get any momentum going."

I feel self-conscious talking this way to your wife's friend, someone younger even than you. Like me, she has two published books under her belt. Unlike me, for whom everything about writing continues to feel chaotic, without principles or methodology, I feel certain that she has by now learned how to construct a book: a master builder, in control of her work, not wandering around like I do staring perplexed at the tools.

"Every book is like that," she says. "You think you know what you're saying when you start out and then you find there's a softness, something not thought through, at its center. It's so painful to see that what you thought would carry itself has these thin, slushy patches. A lot of the time, the writer is facile enough to skate right over what's missing. That's the paradox of language: it's what we need to think, but it can also provide a beautiful subterfuge for not thinking."

"I'm not poetic enough to do that. I wish I were."

"You're lucky. My grandmother used to say to me, it's a great fortune, Ruthie, not to be beautiful. That means whoever falls in love with you has really fallen in love with *you*. Of course, she meant a man, but that's beside the point. I've reached that slushy place with both of my books. And I see it coming with my current work. Only now, I understand that the way to move through that space is to figure out why you've chosen this project. What it's about for you."

I know I'm the psychiatrist and she's the historian, but this idea gives me the willies. Why I've chosen the Carmelita story? What the story of a murdered or suicided girl and her dead baby means to me?

"It's true with everything," she says. "With all your projects. With the people in your life. Once you know what you're aiming for, you can get under the muddy swamp into the bedrock and really lay down a foundation."

I look at this short, squat woman, a painter's cap covering her ear-length black hair, her chin pointed skyward as she rolls the upper parts of your wife's bedroom wall. Either I'm hearing a distillation of some piece of wisdom dearly earned or a gussied-up version of an Ann Landers column.

"Sorry to wax so philosophic," she says. "Only I've been struggling with this myself these past few weeks." She leans down and carefully places the roller in the pan I've brought over to her side. I look up at a perfectly painted white wall.

AT FIVE, I HEAD out with Rena to fetch sandwiches for everyone. In the hall, an old man fumbles to lock the door next to Rena's. Not until he turns his head toward us and I see his dark glasses and the white tip of his cane do I realize it's Santiago Domengo.

Rena touches his arm. "It's me, Rena." She kisses his cheek. A wave of jealousy passes over me.

"But I did not think you were moving in until next week! I would have greeted you."

"I'm not. They let me come in early to paint. Saul's father is here helping me."

I extend a hand to Santiago, but instead of shaking it, he strokes my palm, the way my mother would do when I was too old to crawl into her lap but too young to bear an injury without her comforting me.

"Padre Dubinsky," he says. "Padre Dubinsky."

DRIVING TO SEE you two days later, I realize that I've put myself in a situation where I don't know what I can or should tell you. I know that you know Rena is moving into Santiago's building. But do you know that your things now reside in my attic?

I'd like to think that this has never happened before, that our relationship has up until now always been marked by candor, but here on this empty road, in the dull light of the interstate, in the beige interior of this mediocre car, too new to engender the carefree feeling of an old jalopy, too cheap to emanate even a hint of glamour, the whole thing feels uncomfortably familiar: what to say or not say about your mother, about psychiatry, about why I practiced for only a year. After your mother fell ill (see, even then, when you were eight, it was unclear to me if you understood this, that *fell ill* was a shortcut, an abbreviation for something else), you became my companion. At the time, I thought I was doing it for you, but now, I see, you were also doing it for me. Our afternoon walks. Our language games. Our philosophical explorations. And although your marriage attenuated this, things didn't really change, did they, until that boy jumped in front of the subway train and the you who had always left room to keep up this patter with me was crushed.

Yesterday, I was remembering taking you into Manhattan to see the building where I lived those three years with my Uncle Jack and Aunt Mindyl. You were young enough to still hold my hand in a dimly lit place. A Saturday morning, your mother in bed, your brother at one of his team practices. A flush in your cheeks, crisp air, fallen leaves in the tree pits. Pointing up to the eighth floor, I told you about the Depression and what that had meant and how my three sisters and I had slept in the dining room, our parents in the maid's room, all of us sharing the tiny maid's bath, this while Jack and Mindyl each kept their own bedroom and bath in the rest of the sprawling apartment, their attitude toward us a mixture of self-congratulation at their generosity in taking in poor relations and superiority that they could live in the equivalent of staterooms while my parents had to make do with steerage. We stood in front of the building, the Orthodox Jews from the neighborhood exiting the synagogue on the corner, the women in their Saturday finery, the men in their black hats, and I was proud that you knew not to point at the boys with the tefillin sticking out of their pants. Afterwards, I took you to the store where my Uncle Jack used to go Sunday mornings, the old man slicing the nova familiar enough for me to imagine he'd been the young man who had always taken my uncle's orders for creamed herring, knishes and whitefish. I could see you struggling to put it all together, this world in which your father once lived, and how it fit with your bedroom in a New Jersey colonial acquired with a down payment given to us by your mother's parents or with their enormous Roland Park home where you'd gone for Christmas every year until your grandfather's death.

Walking with me to get sandwiches, Rena asked if I'd ever considered divorce. My surprise must have shown, because she reached out and lightly touched my arm, this in the middle of Broadway, on the island where we'd been caught when the light turned red mid-crossing. "I'm sorry," she said, "that was an intrusive question."

"No. It's a reasonable question for anyone who sees how Klara and I live."

My first thought was that the question had something to do with the encounter with Santiago Domengo, who you once told me still carries on about his wife like a newlywed. My second thought was your wife is a shiksa, that's why she doesn't understand. The men of my father's generation didn't divorce their wives. My Uncle Jack lived the last thirty years of his life on a different coast from Mindyl, unable to stand any longer her endless harping. But divorce her? Never. He was her husband. He'd made a vow to be her husband. She needed a husband. It was oddly liberating, this view of marriage: you didn't have to love each other or "work on the relationship." All you had to do was fulfill your responsibilities. Impossible as Jack found Mindyl to talk to, to live with, he never questioned giving her money. He arranged doctors for her. He made sure that food was delivered to the apartment where she lived and that, at the end, a nurse was at her side.

I live in a world in between. As a youth, we all talked about love marriages, as though this were something quite revolutionary. Of my set, I was the only one who married out of obligation. I am sure that there are men my age who still talk in hushed voices with their wives under the covers at night. Legs looped together like noodles in a pot. Sagging bellies pressed against one another.

For a moment, eyes on the pavement, I feel a need to cry, but I am so out of practice—other than the night after your arrest, I cannot recall the last time I cried, perhaps at my mother's funeral—my tear ducts seem not to know what to do. This happens, I know, throughout the body: the brain needs stimulation, the muscles have to move or they atrophy. The less a person has sex, I once read, the less they want it. Believe me, no one had to tell me that.

"ARE YOU SURE?" I ask the guard sent from the lockup.

"That's what he say."

"I just drove two and a half hours to see him." And then, in a lower voice, "I'm his father."

"Sorry. Prisoner's right to decline a visitation."

"Could you ask him to come for just five minutes?"

The guard hooks his thumbs under the waistband of his pants. A gun dangles on a leather holster. "Can't do that." He sniffs, twists his face as though adjusting his sinuses. "Next visitation's Thursday night. Five to eight. You can come back then. Lots of times they change their minds."

I drive to a diner just outside the prison gates and order coffee and a cherry Danish. I don't need coffee. I don't eat pastries. Thinking maybe there's something Morton can do, I call his office but all I get is his answering machine. I leave the number of the pay phone and move to a booth where I can hear it ring.

I drink coffee and stare at the black hairs on my fingers. When we first got married, your mother was horrified to see that I had hair on my back. Her brother's pale torso had been smooth as a chicken's. Apparently, the night we'd conceived Marc, she hadn't been looking at my back. Your brother inherited my hairiness. Like the men on your mother's side, you have tame sprays of hair on your chest, forearms and legs.

Again, I see you curled like a shrimp on your mattress.

In my residency, it was in vogue to talk about something called projective identification—a way that one person could be made to feel what was experienced but disowned by the other. Particularly, it was thought, this occurred between patients and therapists, with patients depositing pods of their own feelings into their therapist's consciousness. My fellow residents would smugly bandy the term about, either in their discussions of their own cases, where they would glibly admit to having been aware of a harshly critical attitude toward a patient, or in their Monday morning quarterbacking about other therapists' cases. I'd been the skeptic in the class. It seemed too magical to me, this notion of feelings floating between people. And how exactly are these feelings transmitted, I would demand. What is the mechanism?

With Maria, though, I'd become a believer. Not only had I become a believer, but I'd grown convinced that it worked both ways: the therapist could feel things that originated in the patient, but just as easily the patient could feel things that originated in the therapist. Or, even worse, what if it was impossible to know what originated where?

By then, I was a year out of residency and there were no case seminars where I had to present. My classmates, those of us who'd stayed in New York, that being mostly the Jews who worried about getting a job anywhere else, continued to convene, but our gatherings grew increasingly social in character. None of us talked about our cases except in cursory ways. Not wanting to eat my hat, I was content to stick with the Chinese food and the banter about hospital politics. At my job, they'd assigned me a supervisor, Dr. Herbert Nettles, an analyst who worked two days a week at the hospital so he could get health insurance and a retirement plan to augment his Fifth Avenue practice. Tentatively, I broached my ideas to him.

"Yes, Dr. Dubinsky, this is logically possible. But you are overlooking the major force, the raison d'être, behind projective identification—the ego weaknesses that necessitate the use of this maladaptive, primitive defense mechanism. Remember, except in cases of psychic arrest, we give up the primitive defenses for those that are more advanced."

I hadn't dared to push it further. Hadn't dared to tell Dr. Herbert Nettles of Fifth Avenue that I'd had a dream of holding Maria's buttocks like two ripe pears in my hands, her skirt hiked high on the plump thighs which I could see in the tighter and tighter skirts she'd taken to wearing to our sessions. That I'd been so aroused when I woke, I'd had to lie on top of my hands, unable to bear the thought of relieving myself with the image of those thighs. If Maria's increasingly hysterical behavior with me (in one session, a button had popped off her blouse; when I passed on the ward, she would begin to cough uncontrollably) was the consequence of my own disowned erotic feelings toward her, then I was the one who'd failed to give up the primitive for the advanced.

It was on the occasion of reporting this dream to my own analyst, Merckin, along with my conclusion that I was the one with Nettles' psychic arrest, that Merckin interpreted my immaculate conception fantasy: "You hold on to the idea that like Mary, you should be pure as the driven snow, free of your sexual desires which you think will poison others. You cling to your belief in an age of innocence, before Eve bit into the apple, because it allows you to deny the sexual feelings you harbored as a little boy for your mother, the murder in your heart for your father."

"Aren't you mixing up the Old and New Testaments?"

"More of your intellectual shenanigans. You refuse to hear me."

The waitress brings more coffee. I watch her filling salt shakers and sugar dispensers, a blank expression on her face as if she doesn't quite take anything in, as if, were she asked to describe who'd been sitting this morning at my table, all she'd be able to say is a man, older, I don't know, a man, kind of older.

Maria. Why today has she inserted herself back in my thoughts?

Is it that I'd let my eyes linger on your wife's hips, slim as a boy's, as she bent over the paint cans, a hammer in hand to pound the lids back on? That I'd imagined handling her breasts from behind and pressing myself against her hard coccyx bone?

I listen for the phone. For a split second, I get confused and think I am waiting for you, not Morton, to call.

Is it that I'd not wanted to see you, afraid to meet your eyes, and you'd caught it, this affliction of mine, and then not wanted to see me?

Part Two

POTIONS

8 Rena

By the end of her first month on the job, she's met all the first-year associates except Beersden—heard them talk about him with a mix of resentment and admiration that he not only earns their same salary working from nine-thirty in the morning after he drops his twin daughters off at their preschool to six at night when he invariably leaves, but seems to get more done than anyone else in two-thirds the time.

In late July, Hornby, a short balding man the first-years call *le petit Napoléon,* is promoted to junior partner in the litigation department, where Beersden works. His first night in his new position, Hornby schedules an eleven o'clock meeting for the lawyers he supervises. When Rena arrives, the women have their shoes on and the men's ties are tightened. Hornby storms out of the conference room, slamming the door.

"Telephone that asshole Beersden," he barks at Rena.

"Excuse me?"

"I said telephone Beersden. Donald Beersden."

"I am the temporary word processor, not the secretary, but if you delete the expletives and give me a clue as to how to reach him, I will try to help you."

Hornby blushes. "Look in my Rolodex. Please."

Rena goes into Hornby's office. Behind his desk is a row of shoes; his dry cleaning hangs on the back of the door. She finds the number and dials. A woman groggily answers.

"I'm sorry to wake you," Rena says. "I need to speak with Mr. Beersden."

"He's not here at the moment."

"I'm calling for Mr. Hornby."

The woman hesitates. "I can probably reach him. I'll try and have him call you."

Rena leaves the number at her desk. Ten minutes later, the phone rings.

"Hornby. He called me."

Behind the low, gravelly voice, she can hear a rumble of conversation and music playing. "He asked me to let you know that he's having a meeting with the associates."

"When?"

"Now."

Beersden snorts. "Are we supposed to lick his shoes, too?"

"I'm just relaying the message, Mr. Beersden."

"Tell him I have a previous engagement."

Two nights later, a guy with thick bristly hair, prematurely gray, follows her onto the elevator. She's listening on her Walkman to a tape of Billie Holiday songs Saul once made her. He leans against the wall, a motorcycle helmet under his arm. At the end of "God Bless the Child," she stops the tape. He gets off with her at the twenty-sixth floor and waits for her to unlock the door.

"Can I help you?" Rena asks.

"Yeah, let me in." She recognizes the voice—a night voice, whiskey, cigarettes. "Beersden. I'm one of the lawyers here."

"I talked to you on the phone."

She can feel him looking her over, appraising the pieces: the tailored slacks from one of her former work suits, the walking shoes, her hair, uncut since she left Muskowitz & Kerrigan, a mop of curls.

"Sorry about that. I realized after I hung up that I'd given you a hard time—the thing about killing the messenger." Beersden intertwines his long fingers. There's a tightness in her chest. He looks at her throat as she swallows. "So here I am. Spoon-feeding *le Napoléon* a tidbit for his pint-size ego: one night meeting a week, ten to twelve."

A week later, she sees him standing by the elevator bank. She watches the elevator come and go before realizing that he's waiting for her.

"I brought you something." He hands her a cassette. "A German woman doing Billie Holiday—a very silky rendition."

She flushes. Had her Walkman been turned up so high he'd heard the music or had he looked at it sitting on her desk?

Upstairs, he disappears into Hornby's office. Alone in her cubicle, Rena unfolds the notes that accompany the cassette. Among the performers' names, she sees Beersden listed as the pianist for five of the cuts.

At quarter to twelve, she takes her break. She sits in the chair in the ladies' room listening to the German singer, not wanting to see Beersden as he comes out of the conference room. But the next night, when she arrives at the building, he's on the steps, his motorcycle helmet at his side.

"How'd you like the tape?"

"I liked it a lot. You're very good." Her fingertips are tingling, and she feels separate from herself—perched atop a boa tree looking down at the wildebeests beginning a mating dance. "They have you here two nights in a row?"

"No." He pauses. "I'm on my way downtown to practice with my band. We have a gig Thursdays through Sundays, and we practice Wednesdays."

It's simply sexual energy, she tries to reassure herself. You've just forgotten.

"So they think it's because of your family that you're not here nights, but really its because of your music."

"Even if I weren't also a musician, I wouldn't put in more hours. Lawyering is a job, not a life."

"Still, you stay incognito?"

"Yes." He looks her straight in the eyes, a look during which she has the uncomfortable feeling that he knows everything, about Saul, about Ascher, about her lost father. "Just like you."

She stares at her shoes.

"When do you take your break?"

She can see it already, what will come. I'm not ready for this, she thinks. She counts the months since Saul's arrest on her fingers. Six.

"They give you a break, don't they?"

"At two."

"I'll take you out to breakfast. Meet me here."

By one-thirty, the last of the associates has left the office. In the ladies' room, she washes her face, brushes her teeth with the toothbrush she keeps in her cubby. She studies her face in the mirror: her mother's heavy-lidded eyes, the Italianate mouth. Until Ascher, she'd always thought of herself as odd-looking—scrawny with big breasts, pale skin, and unruly hair too dark for a blonde and too light for a brunette. Ascher, though, had found her beautiful. He would push her hair off her forehead and stare at her face. To him, it was all the same, beauty and goodness. What was beautiful must be good, and although she'd later come to see this as a dangerous idea, with Ascher it was a belief that went back to fairy tales, to maidens in gardens and princesses in towers and girls bathing in a sun-dappled stream. He'd seen her face in the flashing lights of the front room at Alil's with the pounding beat of the music coming from the room in back, where men pressed their crotches to the glass cages inside which Sammy and the other girls danced, and he'd been unable to think of anything else until he had her out of there.

With Saul, she has never felt that her face or for that matter any other part of her body particularly moves him. At first, she'd thought it's because they're too similar, eight long, thin limbs, two curly heads, as though the same cast were used to create them both with her breasts and his genitals added on afterwards. Not that Saul has not desired her. But what he desires is to commune with her desire. Once, she'd tried to tell him that if he were less concerned with her, if she didn't feel him watching her so closely, it would be easier. "Did you ever have sex just to have sex?" she asked. He looked at her curiously. She could feel him trying to understand her question. What she was trying to understand in him. What she was trying to tell him about herself. "The first time. To get rid of the burden of virginity. My brother gave me the girl. She really wanted him, but she was willing to settle for me."

In truth, what Saul wants is her mind. To think with her. To watch her think. To see her spirit. Perhaps that's it. He's seen her spirit as beautiful. Her face, her body, have been largely irrelevant. It's very noble. If it isn't very exciting, whose problem is that?

She takes the elevator downstairs, passes the guard and walks out into the August night. The air is hot and moist like the inside of a mouth. Beersden is standing in front of his motorcycle with an extra helmet under his arm.

"Here," he says. He places the helmet on her head and buckles the strap under her chin. He looks at her sleeveless dress and then takes off his denim jacket. "Wear this. It's cooler when you ride." She puts on the jacket. She can smell him in the denim. He climbs on the bike and she gets on behind. She holds on to two fistfuls of his T-shirt.

At Eighteenth Street, he turns west. He stops in front of one of the retro diners that now dot the city: Hopper with cappuccino machines. She's relieved that he knows not to bring her to a bar or a dark, smoky place. Inside, there are hanging lights and emerald green booths. He orders a hamburger and a beer. She feels too nervous to eat, her stomach hard and heavy as if she'd swallowed a river rock; afraid of exposing this, she orders iced tea and a turkey club.

When the sandwich comes, it's a many-layered thing with red-flagged toothpicks holding the stacks together. Bacon peeks out from one section, slices of turkey and avocado from another. She picks up a piece and tries to bite but can't get her mouth around it.

He pulls her plate toward him and takes the stacks apart, reconfiguring them into smaller sandwiches. "When you have kids, you spend half your time in restaurants fixing the food."

"How old are your children?"

"Four. Identical twins." He opens his wallet: two little girls crouched back to back on a shaggy green rug, two blond heads bent over two identical baby dolls.

"Is your wife home full time with them?"

"She's a freelance writer. Now that they're in school, she actually has some time to work."

"And she doesn't mind your going out to breakfast or lunch or whatever you call this with other women?"

He looks down at his burger. The muscles in his face seem to collapse and she sees that she has hurt him. Half an hour alone and already she has hurt him.

She puts down the mini sandwich he's made for her. "I'm sorry. That was crude of me."

"It's warranted." He closes his eyes and presses his fingertips against the lids. She sees that she's had him all wrong—a rebel without a cause, an artist who lives by his feelings, something out of late-night television. Something that has nothing to do with him.

"I've never done this before." He jerks sideways so his legs are freed from the booth. She can see the outline of his thighs under his jeans. "I love my wife. I love my children. I don't know why I'm here."

SATURDAY NIGHT, HE CALLS her from a phone booth on West End Avenue. It's three in the morning and she's undressed, reading in bed. "I'm on the way home from my gig. Can you give a guy a cup of coffee?"

"I don't drink coffee."

"A beer?"

"No beer."

"Can I slurp from your sink?"

"You're driving from the Village to Brooklyn through the Upper West Side?"

"I'll explain when I get there. What's your address?"

She gives it to him and he hangs up quickly, as though if he lingers one of them will change their minds. She puts on shorts and a T-shirt, runs damp fingers through her hair. Outside, she hears a motorcycle turn the corner and stop in front. The night doorman buzzes. "A Mr. Beersden here to see you."

She had not thought about this part. About the doorman as witness. About Santiago next door.

She opens the door before the bell rings. He's carrying his helmet. He looks first at her solemn expression and then over her shoulder at the long hall lined with her black-and-white city photographs, at the vase filled with calla lilies on her coffee table, at the doorway to her bedroom and the lights from across the river shining beyond. He sighs as if something is now confirmed. He pauses for a second to look in her eyes, to be certain of her consent before kissing her, and she feels startled by her own response: her muscles tightening, her inner sensations gone liquid. She leads him back to her room, onto the bed with the sheets still warm from her body. She peels off his leather vest and he moves on top of her, his belt pressing into her stomach. He pushes her hair back from her eyes. "Now I can see you," he whispers. He kisses her again, and again she is startled because for so long what she had felt with men was revulsion, every mouth her stepfather's reeking of halitosis and beer, so that only now does she see that what she had thought of as desire with Ascher and then with Saul was simply the absence of revulsion: that this, this craving of her own mouth for his, this way that her hands work to get off his jeans and T-shirt, this arching of her hips into his, is something else.

She feels embarrassed by her own activity, as though she is the man and he the woman, but her body and her breath have a mind of their own, her movements toward him matched by his so that he grows ever more intent on her, and for a moment she fears she will dissolve in sorrow as she sees that she has never understood bodies or sex and that it is only by chance, the chance of Hornby's temper tantrum, that this has come to pass. Together, their skins feel satiny, without temperature, neither warm nor cool, and she thinks, how could I not have known this before, that a man and a woman can pull one another into each other.

Afterwards, he lies propped on pillows watching the night river, the lights of the boats moving like constellations at the horizon, while she fetches iced glasses of juice. She sits cross-legged at the foot of the bed in one of Saul's undershirts, only he doesn't know yet about Saul. He sweeps an arm around at her Florentine sheets and the Persian rug that had come from Saul's grandparents' house and the set of perfume bottles she'd inherited from Rebecca, neither of them wearing perfume but both enchanted by the glass, and the Victorian fainting couch Saul had purchased in anticipation of one day becoming an analyst. "These are not a secretary's digs," he says, reaching out a hand to stroke her ankle.

She tells him about Muskowitz & Kerrigan and about the merger with Cassen & Silvano, about quitting in June, about taking the job at the law firm as a holding position while she thinks through what to do next. He finishes his juice and moves toward her, his mouth tasting of fermented fruit, and she inhales his breath and lets him draw her up to the pillows and then down on the sheets where he puts his hands under her buttocks and lifts her legs up around his waist and whispers, "You haven't told me a thing, I'll have to discover it all for myself," and her hands move down his back and her pelvis up to meet his and again she thinks, how can it be that only now, at thirty-four, I am learning that my body can want like this?

She thinks about the two men she has loved, and how with each there'd been this great wall in their sexual life. Ascher had overpowered her with his obsession for her, his passion leaving no room for her own timid wishes to emerge. At eighteen, starved for love as she'd been, it had been impossible to untangle what she felt for him from what she felt about being so loved. With Saul, there was the relief of his lightness: the lightness of his slender torso atop her, the lightness of his desire, the corpus a vestigial inconvenience, a leftover from animal ancestry, sex, at base, an epiphenomenon. Their sexual encounters had struck her as almost technical exercises, like Hannon piano scales, Saul's vast concentration brought to bear on catalyzing her responsiveness. Patiently, he persisted, both of them declaring his efforts a success, so that only now does she see what a limited success it had been.

Beersden curls around her, his hands cupped over her breasts. He talks, whispering in her ear. He tells her how he's never so much as flirted with another woman in eight years of marriage to Sherry. Not while she was pregnant and blew up like a balloon. Not while he struggled with his terrible resentment that with the news of twins, it was clear that Sherry would not be able to go back to full-time work anytime soon, a fact that had prompted the two sets of parents (her father a prominent lawyer, his father a banker) to come together to devise the plan of his going to law school. It was Sherry who wept at his having to give up living in music. She kissed each of his fingers. She looked with horror at her huge belly, inside of which two little mouths were already making sucking motions. Comforting her, he lied that it would be an adjustment, not a change. He regaled her with stories of musicians who were doctors by day. Painters who taught elementary school. And, in fact, it had worked out. Yes, for the first two years of law school, while the girls were babies and the household a circus of diapers and bottles and pacifiers and toys and laundry, he was unable to play music with other people. But, even then, he put fingers to keys every day. He rocked bouncy seats with his left foot while he played Chopin mazurkas, Debussy nocturnes, Scarlatti sonatas, gave bottles while listening to Artur Rubinstein, to McCoy Tyner, to the tapes of African bands the percussion player from his old group sent in the mail. Day and night, the apartment was bathed in music, which the girls called alternatively *mukey* and *mucus* and *pano* and *sinning* as they made their first attempts at speech.

Santiago's toilet flushes. Rena's neck tightens. Sherry. Delia. Two madonnas. Beersden smells her hair and nuzzles her scalp.

"Do they know at the firm that you play in a band?"

"They know I'm a musician. They know I'm not going to give them eighty hours a week. We discussed that at the outset on account of the twins. But I'm a very fast writer. It's like playing jazz: being able to improvise on a theme. So the trade-off for them is they can't pad their billables with me but they get a lot of bang for their buck. And then, my father shifted just enough of his bank's legal work to the firm to make it worth their while to keep me around even if I'm just a break-even deal."

Santiago's apartment is quiet again. Has he gone back to sleep? And Saul—is he asleep? On his stomach, his head turned to the outside?

Beersden laces his hands over her stomach. His thumbs press her ribs. "I never lost my music. What I lost was my lust for my wife. Not my love for her. Not even my attraction to her. I just don't have any sexual feelings for her anymore. She thinks it's because of the changes after the pregnancy—that she never got her little waistline back and now has flesh in new places. She thinks if she could just get enough willpower to jog every day, things would be like before."

He shifts onto his back, folding his arms under his head. Rena turns so she can see his face. "When I see her dragging herself out of bed at six in the morning on a January day to put on sweatpants and run through the streets, I know there is no God because if he existed, he would strike me dead on the spot. Here is this beautiful woman, this devoted mother who put her career on the back burner to raise our daughters, who's always supported my music. Who loves that I'm a musician. But when I look at her, what I think about is having to leave my piano in the mornings to face an office of people biting their cuticles over how a senior partner who lives on a five-million-dollar estate in Connecticut and gets chauffeured into the city will respond to their late legal briefs."

His eyes are slits of anguish. Ascher, too, had loved his wife, but with Ascher the anguish had been at the thought of hurting Delia were she to find out. That, he could not bear. Having sex with Rena had never troubled him.

She wants to say, don't do this, let's stop now, but she sees that it is futile: he'd still not want his wife.

"I'm so sorry," she whispers, drawing him into her arms and then further.

AT FOUR-THIRTY, HE gets up and pulls on his jeans. "I have to go. My girls are up by six, and I take them so Sherry can go jogging and get organized for the day."

She watches him tuck his T-shirt into his pants, put on the leather vest. "Won't she wonder where you were?"

"Lots of nights I stay out after our gigs. Sometimes we get inspired and jam for a couple of hours after the club closes down."

For a moment, she wonders if he's been lying, if he's done this before. No. She'd sense it in his body. Nothing about him felt that way.

"What do you do with your girls at six in the morning?"

"We have our little routine. First we go in and wake their mother and fool around on what they call the big bed for a while. Once their mother's up, we play three-handed piano. Then we have breakfast, which is a whole production unto itself involving four different kinds of cereal and Becky who likes hers with the milk on the side and Rachel who will cry if there's not enough milk."

He smiles, thinking about his daughters, and Rena imagines him with the two little girls from the photograph and then his wife as a larger version of the girls, all of them pajamaed and laughing on a king-size bed. "They can play the piano?"

"Ditties. 'Itsy-Bitsy Spider.' 'Twinkle, Twinkle, Little Star.' Things like that."

Beersden pulls on his boots. He leans over the bed and kisses her on the cheek and then the mouth. She resists the impulse to reach out to him, is relieved that he knows not to say anything as he turns to leave.

BEFORE BEERSDEN, RENA had tried to resume a normal schedule on the weekends. But it had been impossible to engineer. She'd get home from work at eight in the morning on Saturdays from her Friday shift and need to sleep. Having slept all day, she'd be unable to get to bed until early Sunday morning. The whole thing would replay itself on Sunday, and then Monday would roll around and she'd need to sleep anyway before heading off to work that night.

With Beersden, she gives up entirely since it's after his gigs on Saturday and Sunday nights that he comes over. Two in the morning, he arrives with bags of food: bagels and lox, souvlaki, pastrami on rye. He stocks her refrigerator with dark beer, and they have a picnic on the floor of her bedroom with a sheet spread out to catch the crumbs and pillows to prop themselves on so they can watch the night river traffic:

the barges lit with only one red flare on bow and stern guided by perky tugs bedecked in green lights. On moonless nights, the water invisible, the tugs appear to be sailing through the sky with sparkling rubies in their wake. The gourmand's gourmand, Beersden calls himself, arching back his neck to open his jaw for the enormous sandwiches, dangling a slice of shiny red onion under his nose before tossing it onto the discarded wrapping paper. "Oh, what lust will do to a man—to give up raw onion!"

At first, she thinks that their affair is based on his taste for the night scene: that Beersden has spent so much time in clubs, he can sense her time at Alil's. He scrutinizes the selection of Saul's CDs and tapes she's kept, picking pieces they can dance to. "Usually guys take their music," he says, but does not question her further when she tells him that Saul's new quarters are too cramped. Saul had been a listener, not a dancer; other than the obligatory slow dance at a wedding, they'd never danced together. Beersden holds her hips. He sings the lyrics like Bob Dylan gone jazzy. One night, they roll up the rug in the foyer and he teaches her how to samba to a recording he's brought of the Johnny Colon Orchestra.

"Hey, babe," he teases, "we could run away to the Catskills and do a dance act. You've definitely got rhythm in your blood." Walking to work the next evening, she can't get the phrase out of her mind: *rhythm in your blood*. Something in her blood. A link to her father.

She turns south on Columbus Avenue. It's early September, the week after Labor Day, and the restaurants are filled with people back in the city after the summer respite. Tanned faces sip Campari and white wine on the skimpy outdoor terraces. Everywhere, grilled meats, curlicue greens, baskets filled with herbed rolls. In fact, she really hasn't thought about her father in years. As a girl, she'd gone through phases when she would ask her mother the same questions over and over: how her mother had met her father, what he'd looked like, the things he'd done with Rena. "He used to sing to you," her mother would say. "Sing and play his saxophone. He bought you a toy saxophone, but of course you only wanted his."

In all the years that she's been here in New York, it has never occurred to her that perhaps he is still here. She adds numbers in her head. Her mother nineteen when Rena was born; her father three years older. Fifty-six.

She doesn't even know his last name. Sam. That's all she knows.

SHE WAITS FOR the office to empty before calling Eleanor. As always, there's the surprise at how well her mother sounds—no hint of the leaden depression after Gene's birth, of the monumental frenzy after Joe's death. And yet, despite the changes, the years that have passed since the very bad times, she's not been able to bring herself to tell Eleanor about Saul's arrest.

"ESP," Eleanor says. "Gene and I were just talking about you. He's been thinking about driving cross-country once he saves up enough money. He'd come visit you and Saul and then head down to see a friend who's living in Georgia."

The low point between them had come shortly after she and Gene moved to New York when Eleanor, living in Eureka with a roll-towel salesman she'd met in a bar, accused her of stealing Gene. At the time, Rena had brushed it off as the alcohol talking, but later, after her mother pulled herself together and Gene returned to California, she found herself cautious with him, afraid of doing anything that would make it look like she was trying to usurp her mother's role. "When would that be?"

"Oh, don't hold your breath. His car needs a lot of work and he owes me five hundred dollars for his insurance. No trip, I've told him, until I'm paid."

Rena lurches forward. "I know this is weird to ask now, only I just realized that I don't know my father's last name."

Eleanor doesn't answer immediately. Then, slowly, she says the name. "Freedman. Freed with two e's."

"Did he stay in the city?"

"I don't know. I haven't heard from him since you were three."

"I thought I was two when we moved."

"You were. For the first year, I kept a post-office box. He would write these letters about not knowing if he should get a private detective to find us and get custody of you or if he should just let me go and let us make our own life. I guess in the end that's what he did."

"I've never even seen a picture of him."

"I don't have any. When you leave the way I did, packing up in an hour, you don't bring the photo albums. Not that we had photo albums. We didn't live that way."

"Did you know his parents?"

"I never met them. They lived in Riverdale. I don't think his mother ever knew about us. His father was a fancy lawyer. He knew, but he wouldn't visit."

"Because you weren't married?"

"Because I wasn't Jewish." Eleanor sighs. "It was a different time. Your father, they hardly left him room to breathe with all their demands. When I walked out that front door, or rather snuck out, I thought I was in love with that dumbo Johnny Campanella. If it was love, though, it was the quickest case to hit New York, since it disappeared by the time we reached Pennsylvania. I think maybe on some level I was trying to save your father. We were just barely scraping by. He was driving a cab during the day and playing his music at night. I couldn't control myself. I was complaining all the time that there wasn't enough money for diapers, for meat, for new shoes for you. He was starting to talk about maybe he should get a real job, maybe we should get married. I felt like I was destroying him."

Rena feels everything moving in blurred, undulating patterns, Beersden's story, her father's story, as if she needs to clear her head, get fresh air, but all the windows are sealed, the temperature controlled from a box twenty-six floors below. After they hang up, she goes to the copy room and pulls down the Manhattan and Bronx phone books. In Manhattan there are three Samuel Freedmans and another five S. Freedmans. In the Bronx there are four Samuel Freedmans and another three with the initial S. She tries to imagine telephoning all these numbers. What would she say? I'm Rena Peretti? I'm wondering if you're my father?

FOR SEVERAL DAYS, it's cold and damp, never raining but always on the verge. Walking home in the gray mornings, she fantasizes about going back to California, about a path Reed once showed her south of Mill Valley that leads out to the beach, the long grasses yielding first to a warm lagoon before being overpowered by the huge rocks and the cold spray of the Pacific. She wonders if this is where Reed has gone, perhaps somewhere farther north, a bit inland, where countless people who, like Reed, have abandoned the lives their parents imagined for them scrape by doing a little this and that.

On a couple of occasions, Reed had driven her to visit Eleanor and Gene, the visits always timed with one of Joe's out-of-state hauls. Eleanor was still on medication then—not as much as when Rena had been in high school, but enough to keep her bloated and tired all the time. She and Rena would sit on the steps, not saying much, watching Reed teach Gene to throw and catch one or another kind of ball. After one of the visits, Reed said to her, "It's a question of the glass half empty, half full. In a way, you're free with your mother. Nothing you do is going to disappoint her."

At the end of the week, what Rena thinks of as an Eleanor-letter arrives. Her mother began writing letters after she had left the roll-towel salesman and moved back to Novato to try and stitch together a life, the early letters page after page of uncontrolled thoughts, a great gush of language addressed to both Rena and Gene, oblivious, it had seemed, to either of her readers. Two or three would arrive each week, the pace slowing as Eleanor settled into her new pursuits: the bookkeeping course, the garden she planted in the yard where Joe's junked cars had once been berthed, the yoga classes she began attending. "Never again will I serve pancakes," she wrote, "never again will I fill a ketchup bottle, count change from my apron pocket, argue with a cook about whose hair landed in the sunny-side-up eggs." Then, later, after she ripped up the mildewed wall-to-wall carpet and bartered with Russell (the junked cars, Joe's monster television set and old couch in exchange for Russell painting the walls, upstairs and down, a butter frosting), Rena amazed not only by the deal her mother had struck but by the fact that Eleanor had been able to see Russell for the two-bit philanderer but decent painter he was, *Never again will I live with a man.*

Those letters were handwritten on the crosshatched ledger pads Eleanor had received as part of her bookkeeping course. Since she got her job and Gene returned to live with her, the letters have been printed on shiny copy paper.

Dear Rena,

After our phone call, I called my sister Betty. I asked her if she had any photographs of your father. We used to go to her house a lot when you were a baby what with my father being as he was and all of us scared of ruffling his feathers. That was where my mother would see you, at Betty's. Once, I told my mother that I was sick of it and I was going to tell my father about you. She looked me smack in the eye and said, I wouldn't do that, Elly. That's what she called me, Elly. I think she was afraid he'd kill you due to some crazed idea that a child with a Jew for a father was the devil. As if I'd had a baby with a goat.

Betty said she never throws anything out, just stores it in the attic, and she'll get Donny to bring down the boxes of photos she keeps up there and she'll look through to see what she has. I gave her your address and she said she'd send you whatever she finds.

I have a new boss—a woman! She has a little boy, five years old, and she's always asking me questions about did this happen or that happen with you or Gene. It's so strange, I tell her, but I can hardly remember what it was like then. It seems like such a long time ago.

You should see my garden. I've added some fancy stuff—pineapple lilies and this vine called Spanish flag. There's a Chinese man across the street who planted his entire backyard with snow peas. Everyone talked behind his back about what a stupid thing that was. Yesterday, he told me he's made four thousand dollars so far this summer selling snow peas to restaurants in Chinatown!

It was good to talk with you. Are you making any progress figuring out what you want to do now that you've left your political consulting job?

Love to Saul.

A string of X's and O's follows, and then her mother's loose, loopy *Eleanor/Mom.*

During Eleanor's only trip east, when she'd come to take Gene back to California after his three years with Rena, they'd gone to Staten Island to visit Betty and Donny. It was the first time Rena or Gene had met their grandfather, living by then with Betty and Donny, too ill with Alzheimer's for there really to be anyone to meet. On the ferry ride over, Eleanor had tried to prepare Rena: "Your aunt, she's very dramatic. Sarah Bernhardt, my mother used to call her. When we were girls, she would attract busloads of boys with her gorgeous red hair and her tight sweaters. Donny was the sexiest boy in the neighborhood. After they got married, he went to work in my father and uncle's fish market on Fulton Street. Betty couldn't bear staying home alone with the baby, so she'd bring him into the store and she and my mother would trade off watching him. Really, my mother would mostly watch him. Betty would be out front in the store, flirting madly with anyone who had hair on his chin. Then she'd see Donny smile at a female customer and she'd go nuts. Twice she chased him out onto the street with a fish knife, threatening to cut off his you-know-what."

Donny, a big man with a full head of unnaturally black hair and a friendly, impersonal smile (the same display of bleached teeth directed at the other descending passengers as at his sister-in-law), met them at the ferry. He surveyed Eleanor—slender and pert in her navy slacks and taupe blouse, her hair cut in a way that accentuated her round brown eyes—and grinned. "My God, El, you look like the day you left. Now don't let your jaw fall out of your face when you see Betty." He rearranged the chains on his neck and made a whistling sound. "She's gotten pretty big."

They drove in Donny's maroon Ford down streets of clapboard houses, each with a porch and a driveway and a large tree and a flower bed in front. "Betty's been cooking and cleaning up a storm, waiting for you to come. She still had her manicotti on the stove's why she sent me to get you."

Donny pulled up at a house with a cupid fountain set in the lawn. "We got a pool, an above-ground back from when the kids still lived home. And a barbecue pit, we call it Donny's kitchen." He led them inside to a room with a white shag rug and white leather couches covered with plastic and a wall hung with pieces of mirrors mounted in a diamond pattern. Betty appeared in a haze of red: red hair, red lips, red nails. A pink apron swaddled her girth. Flowered leggings covered legs as thick as telephone poles.

Donny videotaped Betty hugging Eleanor, narrating all the while that this was the historic meeting of the Peretti girls. Betty kept putting her hand out to block the camera, which she addressed in a stage whisper: "I'm not really this fat, it's just the video that makes me look this way."

Betty showed them the backyard, where an old man in a ratty blue cardigan sat slumped in a lawn chair. Saliva ran down a gully etched between the corner of his mouth and the bottom of his chin. Gene splashed around in the pool while Betty tried to get her father to recall his youngest daughter: "You remember, Dad. Eleanor, Elly, the one who moved out west."

The old man kept his eyes on the lawn, Betty repeating herself more and more loudly as though the problem were one of audition until finally Donny, grilling clams on the barbecue, called out, "Christ Almighty, Bet. Give it up. He clearly don't remember."

Rena helped Betty bring the food out to the picnic table while her mother sat quietly stroking the old man's hand, her face set in a way that made it impossible to guess what she was feeling. The old man refused to touch the clams but ate some of the manicotti after Betty leaned over and cut it into small pieces. Then, in the middle of dessert, he looked up at Eleanor. "You're that actress, the one in that movie."

Betty started to cry. "Look at this hair," she said, pulling at the top. "Every week, I sit in that goddamn beauty parlor under that burning dryer. Look at these nails." She thrust her long red nails, each with a gold stripe running diagonally across, toward Eleanor. "I wash him, I do his stinking laundry, I clip his toenails, and you're the one he thinks looks like a movie star."

Mascara ran down Betty's cheeks. The old man kept his eyes fixed on Eleanor. Gene stared at Betty.

"Goddamnit, Betty," Donny hollered, "you start in on this jealousy shit and I'm out the door," and Eleanor looked horrified and then helplessly at Rena, who quickly gathered up Gene's wet clothes and their bags and sweaters, mumbling all the while, no, no, they really had to go.

THE LAST WEEKEND in September, Beersden and his band have a gig in the Hamptons. He books a room at a motel in Montauk, far enough away that it's unlikely he'll bump into anyone he knows. On Thursday, it turns hot. Against her better judgment, Rena agrees to come. She leaves work early, takes a cab home and sleeps for a few hours before getting up to pack an overnight bag.

At noon, an hour late, he calls. There's a tension in his voice she's not heard before. "Sorry. I'm just walking to the garage. I had some things I had to deal with before I could leave."

It's nearly one when Pedro buzzes to say that Mr. Beersden is here. Downstairs, she looks for him; she's not seen his car before. Across the street is a blue station wagon. He's leaning back with his eyes closed. Behind him are two children's car seats.

Rena opens the rear door and puts her bag at the foot of one of the seats. He opens the passenger door. It's daylight. They've never been out in daylight. He reaches a hand across the front seat, out of sight from the street, to touch her leg.

"Sorry," he says again. "Sherry threw a fit about having the twins to herself this weekend even though her parents are coming in." Rena watches the contortions in his face: the wish to reassure her that he wants to be here with her. The inability to rid himself of his concern for his wife.

They drive largely in silence. She imagines Sherry on her hands and knees with the minivac cleaning up crumbs, the girls hot and whiny in the cramped, toy-strewn apartment.

As they reach the Long Island Expressway, her lids grow heavy. She yawns.

"Get some sleep."

She rests her head against the door and dozes. When he pulls off the highway for gas, she keeps her eyes closed.

He parks behind the motel. "I'll register," he says, and she knows to let him carry their bags up the outside stairs and to wait until he's drawn the drapes across the sliding doors with their view of the parking lot before going up the stairs herself.

She lets herself in. He's lying on the bed, surveying the orange and brown room. Using the bedside switch, he flips the lights on and then off. "Pretty awful," he says.

"It's fine." She sits next to him. "The beach is right across the street."

He doubles a pillow under his neck and strokes her knee. Don't worry, she wants to say, ashamed that her days with Ascher have left her a pro. I know how to do this. You just stay out of restaurants, go to the 7-Eleven for breakfast, take sandwiches to the beach for lunch, have a picnic on the floor for dinner.

She changes into a bathing suit and packs her tote. Beersden has crawled under the covers, the bedspread pulled to his chin.

"I'm going to the beach," she whispers.

He nods. "Twenty minutes' shut-eye and I'll be fine."

She crosses the road and climbs down the wooden ramp that leads over the dunes. The sun is hidden under the clouds, turning sea, driftwood and sand all the same dove. She spreads out the towel and slathers herself with sunblock. Like an eerie déjà vu, not of a scene but of a mood, she recalls the last time she was at a beach with Saul. Then, too, she'd walked alone to the water's edge, his teacher Sylvia's house hovering above.

She spots Beersden crossing the sand, a beach chair under each arm. From a distance, with his gray hair and his torso contracted to balance the weight of his load, he looks like an old man. He sets the chairs side by side so they both face the water. She's relieved not to sit face to face. She stares at the ocean, an oil tanker at the horizon, the pleasure boats. He flips through the paper, turning the pages at a rate that betrays that he's not really reading. He glances at her periodically in a humorless, forlorn way as if he knows she's counting the minutes until he'll leave to get ready for his gig and she can then be alone. She imagines staying until dark: reading her book in the canvas chair, swimming at the warm hour when the sun is low over the water, lying at the ocean's edge and watching the little holes that appear in the smooth wet sand with the retreat of each wave. Pulling on a sweatshirt as the air grows cool and letting her hair dry wild and salty.

When she was fifteen, she'd had her first boyfriend, a sixteen-year-old boy named Rusty who was in love with surfing. Every morning before school she'd driven with him to Stinson Beach. She'd sit wrapped in a blanket while Rusty put on his wet suit and carried his surfboard down to the breaking waves. Entering the water, he'd slip in sideways, his front arm petting the froth, the board lodged under the pit of his back arm. Had she been closer, she was certain, she would have heard him talking to the sea in a low steady voice, the way a person who knows dogs will approach a growling German shepherd. Never—not even the following spring after Gene was born and she missed five weeks of school and her best friend, Cheryl, told her that Rusty had twice been seen driving with MaryAnn, a cheerleader with auburn hair that fell in sleek bunches over her shoulders—had she regretted that Rusty had been the first person, the only person before Ascher, with whom she'd taken off her clothes. A Sunday afternoon, his parents gone to a wedding, his first time, too, the awe of the moment expanded by his telling her so. They'd undressed each other, he her, then she him, talking and stroking one another's arms, and she'd thought as he moved closer and closer of the way he approached the water, so gradually you couldn't tell where his body cut the surface of the sea.

"What are you thinking about?" Beersden asks.

"Nothing much."

He cocks his head, a careful gesture behind which she can sense his broiling hurt that she has closed herself with her response.

"Saul?"

"No. Actually, I was thinking about a beach I used to go to when I was in high school."

She avoids his gaze. We're both just tired, she says to herself. The cheerless weather. Having not yet told Beersden about Saul's arrest, it hardly feels like the time to do so now. What she has told him is that they separated in February, that they talk every few weeks. That she is uncertain what will happen between them. Not a lie in it all, but not a piece of truth, either.

With Saul, she'd agreed that honesty in their marriage required what he called no untruths. After that, though, they had diverged, Saul arguing that withholding was itself a kind of lying. For years—that is, until Mitch, when everything fell apart—they'd debated what constituted withholding. Was there anything one could keep to oneself and not have it become a destructive kernel, a thing that grew fat on secrecy?

"How about if you're pleased as punch about a new tie you've bought and I think it's hideous?" Rena had asked. "Do I need to tell you that?"

"You don't like my new tie?"

"I didn't say that."

"You didn't say otherwise."

He tickled her until she said, "Well, the tie is okay, it was the shirt you wore with it. Green-and-yellow paisley with a blue striped shirt?"

"You see. My point exactly. Had you not revealed your disapproval, our marriage could have foundered over a fashion faux pas."

"How about if you think a woman who's sitting across from us on the subway is gorgeous and you have a sexual fantasy about her? Are you going to share that with me?"

"I've never had such a thought."

"Bullshit," and then it was she who pounced on him, tickling him in the tender spot just south of his armpits, and he said, "I confess, I confess. Last week at the movies there was a girl sitting next to me who had these plump legs and I had the thought of touching her thighs."

"You louse. You held my hand while you were fantasizing about some girl's thighs?"

"Yes."

"You watched that Lotte whatever her name is, up there on the screen unlacing whatever that thing was to wash her breasts, and all the while you were thinking about the girl sitting next to you?"

"Don't tell me you've not had fantasies about other men since we've been married."

"You're evading my question."

Saul raised a hand in mock solemnity. "I plead the Fifth."

"Ditto."

His tone shifted. "Rena, kidding aside, you can't claim to have never had sexual fantasies about anyone else since we've been together?"

She grew serious thinking about it. "No, I really haven't. I mean, I've noticed men the way you notice a garden or a piece of furniture and I've thought what a handsome face or whatever. But I can't say that my mind has gone further than that."

The way Saul looked at her left her wondering if there was something wrong with her. But it was true. Not that she wasn't acutely conscious of bodies. All day long, it was the central piece of her work, analyzing bodies and how and what they convey. Their balance of perfection and imperfection. But she no more thought about touching them than she did the façades of the buildings she studied as she walked home each night.

Beersden raises the back of his chair. He buries a foot in the sand. "You must be relieved that you didn't have children. That makes it so much harder to split up."

"No," she says slowly. "It makes it harder for me. It makes it unlikely that I'll ever have a child. Given my age, I'd have to get divorced, meet the right person, get married and then get pregnant all in the next five years."

She sees how foreign this is to him. He has children. They are what keep him from even considering divorce. For a moment, the emotional situation between them seems to her like a physics diagram with vectors shooting off in different directions. If she continues to not tell Beersden about Saul, it will be, as Saul had in fact finally convinced her, an expulsive force between them. If she tells him, it will draw them together. Drawn closer together, a conflict would be introduced: Beersden would then be pulled between the pact this would entail with her and the pact he made long ago with his wife.

After he leaves, she walks along the water's edge until the soreness in her legs and the sounds of the surf finally lull her into a state in which she can concentrate on what had bothered her this afternoon. It was not simply Beersden's anxiety about their being seen. It was not even primarily his feeling guilty about betraying his wife. It was more basic yet. It was his feelings for her. Falling in love doesn't capture it. That suggests something more joyous and also more ephemeral. No, this was an entirely sober matter tinged with grief. Before, they had shared being smitten with one another—a loose feeling, garments easily put on, easily taken off. Now everything feels cold and waterlogged. Already, she imagines, he is anguishing about the moment Monday morning when he will drop her at her door and they will again be apart.

She wants to flee. It's a hateful feeling, wanting to flee from someone's need.

This was not the bargain, she imagines protesting.

The bargain, she can hear him slowly repeating.

It's dusk, the dark wet sand packed so hard that only her large toe leaves an impression. *Yes, the bargain.*

WHEN SHE GETS BACK, she goes biking with Ruth.

"I hate this time of year," Ruth laments. "Leaving the country, closing up the cabin. Then there are the students. They go nuts the first six weeks of classes. Obsessing about whether to keep their courses or use the drop option. One kid told me last week that she had never written more than fifteen pages and didn't think there would be any topic on which she'd be able to write more. When I tried to explain to her that the page specifications were simply guidelines to suggest the scope for the paper, she insisted that she had to know how much she'd be docked if the paper was less than twenty pages. Well, I said, if you've fully reviewed the literature and thoughtfully addressed the topic, I don't really care if it's ten. She almost had a nervous breakdown right there in my office. I finally suggested that this might not be the course for her, after which she got furious and complained to the dean."

They're carrying their bikes down the stairs to one of the lower levels of Riverside Park, a gracefully proportioned stretch of promenade but a place where a person can easily feel trapped with no steps up to street level for blocks on end. More than once, Rena has stopped to assist a frightened baby-sitter who's wandered with baby and stroller down to the promenade only to realize there's no upward path in sight.

"Then there are the Jewish holidays. Every year, I remind myself that no one is making me go to my parents' house. Every year, I arrive and it's the same thing: the dining room table set for twenty-two with the special china and my mother in the kitchen frenetically instructing her cleaning woman on how to put the carrot slice on top of the gefilte fish. My sisters all dolled up in these dresses the likes of which I swear I never even see here in the city, chartreuse and lime green, fitted like a glove with big buttons everywhere, going on and on about the name of the designer, it could be Donald Duck for all I know, and what a steal they got it for at Loehmann's and, I'm not kidding, they can spend half an hour debating the virtues of the Long Island Loehmann's versus the one in Paramus. All the while, my mother giving me this sourpuss designed to convey, Ruthie, you're breaking my heart, here I am letting your girlfriend come to my holiday table and you can't just for your mother wear a little dress?"

Ruth sets her bike on the walkway and climbs on. "I feel like I'm in a *Saturday Night Live* skit: Weirdo Lesbo Daughter Goes Home to Huntington. Maggie says I should count my lucky stars. In Randallstown, Mississippi, where she grew up, she swears nine out of ten people don't know what the word *lesbian* means. Her mother, she says, once gave her a piece of paper with six words on it—words like *sodomy* and *fellatio* and *labia*—and asked her if she could explain what they meant."

"What did she say?"

"She says she looked at the list and at her mother, who's never even been to Biloxi, and then folded the paper in quarters, put it in her pocket and said, 'Mom, there are some words you're better off not fussing with.' My mother likes to tell Maggie and me how she consulted with the rabbi in their synagogue. 'Now, of course,' she told Maggie, 'we are Reform so they're more open-minded there, but that's why Ruthie's father and I joined. Our rabbi explained that love is love in God's eyes, he doesn't stop to check the anatomy. Isn't that a cute line? Doesn't stop to check the anatomy.' That, I have to give my mother credit for. She never hides what she calls *you girls' relationship*. Not wearing panty hose, though, that's a serious matter."

"Does Maggie wear a dress?"

"Maggie doesn't have to wear a dress. She's got eight inches on any of the women in my family and that white Swedish hair and those watery blue eyes. She sticks on a pair of silver earrings or wraps a scarf around her waist, and my sisters go nuts trying to figure out if this is Soho chic or street vendor junk. It drives them crazy that Maggie walks around with twenty pounds of meat on her bones, perfectly comfortable to have hips and thighs. In their eyes, this is a tragedy, like defacing Michelangelo's David."

They cross Ninety-Sixth Street and head south another five blocks to the hippo park, a children's playground where plasticine hippos wallow in imaginary rubberized mud. Children crawl in and out of the hippos' mouths and pet the iron turtles perched on top. Toward the river, there are beds of flowers and people walking their city dogs: teacup schnauzers and golden terriers and beauty parlor poodles. Everywhere there is squealing and the insistent voices of parents alternately cajoling and prohibiting.

They park their bikes and sit on two of the empty swings. Ruth pushes herself off and pumps her legs until she attains a goodly height. Rena rocks back and forth, her toes in the dirt. She watches as Ruth stops pumping and the swing shortens its arc.

"I've been blathering on," Ruth says, "and I haven't heard anything about you."

"Well . . ." Rena kicks the dirt, uncertain why she is hesitating.

Ruth brings her swing to a halt.

"I've been having an affair."

Ruth looks Rena squarely in the face. It's a look that Rena knows others find disarming but that she has always found reassuring: an availability to hear the truth, a refusal to respond with anything less than frankness.

"Someone I met where I'm working. One of the lawyers there. A musician who went to law school after his wife had twins."

"He's married?"

"Yes. I feel terrible about that, about his wife. And for him, it makes the whole thing have too much weight."

She's aware that she's not even getting at the half of it. "I don't know. When I was young, I thought sex was sex. If you were two consenting adults and no one got a disease and no babies were made, it seemed like it was no big deal. Now I find myself thinking that sex must be like one of those Kantian imperatives that Leonard and Saul are always talking about. Something that in its nature is fundamentally different."

Outside the gate surrounding the swings, two toddlers tussle over who is going to climb onto a tricycle. "You have to share," a woman says in a singsong mother's voice.

"Maybe human beings are just not cut out to have sexual relations recreationally," Rena continues. "Maybe we've evolved to have emotions that won't let it work. Someone inevitably falls in love. Unless you couple permanently, someone inevitably gets hurt. I know this sounds like one of those reactionary sociobiologists, but I can't get it out of my mind that I'm doing something that's wrong to the bones."

"Because he's married?"

"More than that. Because he needs to be with his girls. Not just for them—for himself, too."

Ruth twists her swing like a corkscrew and then lifts her feet until she winds back to center. "You're leaving something out."

"What's that?"

She looks at Rena with pained bemusement. "Your husband. Saul."

When she leaves work the following morning, it's drizzling. A cold mist creeps into her hair and under her collar. She walks west to Sixth Avenue and waits for the Riverside Drive bus. Once on Riverside, the bus picks up speed. They pass the majestic firemen's monument, the wind caught in the ever-flying flag, the park gleaming in the rain. Shortly after her move, mimeographed sheets from the Landmark Preservation Society, ordered by Leonard, had arrived in the mail describing the history of her block: a pasture until late in the last century, the white five-story townhouses designed to emulate a certain Parisian Beaux-Arts district where ladies kept their own coaches and there were special cabinets to store eighteen-inch gloves.

It's nearly seven when Rena gets off the bus. She thinks of Beersden in Brooklyn pouring cereal for his twins. Rachel's the purple girl, he'd told her, Becky the pink one. Rachel gets the purple bowl, Becky the pink. All day long they follow this dictum, Rachel with her purple lunch box, Becky with her pink backpack; Rachel with her purple washcloth, Becky with her pink pajamas.

During the first few weeks with Beersden, she'd entertained the idea that the rules of sex—yes if you're married, no if you're not—were equally childish and arbitrary. Not that her mother had discussed any of this with her; it would have seemed preposterous given Eleanor's own life. Still, the rules had been as omnipresent as in any family where they were preached. They were the principles that Eleanor had violated, the reason she and Rena lived in two rooms over Nick's Ristorante, the reason Nick could throw Eleanor's underwear and Rena's dolls out the window and then padlock the door. The reason Ascher had been told by the party organization after someone had found out about them that he had to choose between the campaign and her. They were the principles that not only Beersden but, as Ruth had pointed out, she too had broken.

It has come as a surprise and, Rena has to admit, a bit of a disappointment to see that Ruth has no more of a solution to this dilemma of the deeper ethics of sex than she does. If you overlook that she sleeps with a woman instead of a man and that all of this occurs without a wedding band, her sexual dicta are basically conventional: you sleep with and only with the one person you have committed to love.

Rena exchanges hellos with Pedro, just arriving for the day, and presses the elevator button. With Beersden, she'd dumbly thought that sex would be the alchemy through which loneliness could be transformed into comfort, but incompetent witch that she is, she's created only a pot of misery.

The white tip of a cane pokes out from the elevator door. Her heart sinks. Although she's continued their Tuesday reading sessions, other than the day painting with Leonard she has not bumped into Santiago in the building.

"Good morning." She pauses, then adds, "It's me, Rena."

"What a pleasure to see you! Well, of course, I cannot see you, but to hear your voice."

"You're out early."

"My daughter woke me. She called at four-thirty."

Reluctantly—because all she wants is to get into her bed with a book, to not think about Beersden and his daughters, but afraid of falling further out of grace with what she thinks of loosely as the cosmos, of letting selfishness prevail—she guides Santiago to the lobby love seat.

"Is there a problem with your daughter?"

"With her, it is always the same. She needs more money."

For the first time, Rena feels flummoxed by Santiago's blindness, which does not allow the usual vague facial expressions of sympathy to speak for themselves. "That must be hard."

"No. It is not hard. What use do I have for money? It just makes me sad that at forty-six she still lives like this. Not that my Bernardo was so much more practical."

"Saul, too. Before the drugs, he never got into trouble with money only because he was never interested in buying anything. When I first moved in with him, there was mayonnaise in the refrigerator two years past the toss date. The sheets were like cheesecloth."

"My Helen used to say the life of the mind is no virtue. It's the life of a child. Sometimes, now, I think she was right." Santiago sets his lips. With nowhere to look, he has only silence to damper his words.

Pedro approaches. He touches Santiago's shoulder. "It's stopped raining. If we go now, you won't get wet."

Santiago places his cane on the floor and leans forward to raise himself from the love seat. Pedro helps him up.

"Oh, old age," Santiago says cheerfully. "What it does to the body."

His skin crumples as he smiles, and Rena thinks that if she were to touch his cheek with a finger or a kiss, it would break into tiny pieces. He balances on Pedro's arm and, as he did the first time they met, removes his beret and makes a little bow with the top of his liver-spotted head.

SUNDAY MORNING, BEERSDEN arrives as usual a little after three. He carries two bags out of which stick tinfoil caps, his motorcycle helmet hanging from an arm. He grins ear to ear.

"Our bass player took me to this place on Second Avenue. There must have been fifteen cabs double-parked in front. You should see it! It's like Damascus inside. All these Arab men bent over plates of grilled lamb and tabouli. Piles of pita, I'm not exaggerating, three feet high."

She takes the bags and he follows her into the kitchen, where she puts the food on plates. He gets a beer from the refrigerator and picks up the plates to take them back to the bedroom.

"Let's eat here," Rena says, pointing at the kitchen table.

Beersden's mood, revved up from the night's performance and the motorcycle ride uptown and his excitement to see her, ratchets down a notch in response. She sets out forks and knives and glasses. He pours the beer he usually drinks from the bottle into a glass. The kitchen lights glare like operating room spots.

Beersden bites into his falafel. She watches his attempt to transport the pita to his mouth without losing half to his chin. After three bites, he pushes back the plate. "Okay, Rena, why don't you tell me what's up."

She has not rehearsed her words. She does not know what words to use. He refuses to break his gaze. "I need to stop. Us. This."

"Why is that?"

"It feels wrong. It's not going to work. This is not going to go anywhere. You're not going to leave your wife."

His eyes narrow and his cheeks droop.

"And I wouldn't want you to. That would be terrible. Your girls are so young."

He picks up his glass as though to drink and then bangs it on the table. She freezes. "Bullshit, Rena. You're not leveling with me."

There's a screech of wood on tile as he pushes back his chair. "Is it your husband? Are you going back to your shrink husband?"

"No."

"Come on, Rena. You can't tell me you're going to live like this too much longer. A Yale grad typing nights. You've got to be thinking that whatever happened with your doctor hubby can be patched up."

"No, I'm not." She can feel the agitation rising inside her, and she fears that she will do something stupid and cheap like blurt out that Saul is in jail.

"I don't believe you."

"It has nothing to do with Saul."

He stands up suddenly. Her heart pounds violently against her ribs. He strides past her and then down the hall. She hears the hard stream of his urine hitting the water.

When he returns, his hair is damp from the water he's splashed on his face, now more composed. He reaches out a hand to pull her up from the chair. "Let's go talk in the back."

His voice has softened and she follows him to her room, where he lies on the bed with his head and shoulders propped against the pillows. She sits cross-legged beside him.

"Just level with me, Rena."

She closes her eyes and tries to think what is the truth and whether he really wants to hear it. "The truth is I don't love you."

He laughs. "What, you think because I'm in love with you, you're supposed to reciprocate? Very polite of you, sweetheart."

He moves his hand to his mouth in mock horror. "Oh, I get it, you're not supposed to have sex if you don't love the guy."

"Yes."

He looks at her curiously.

"Yes, I am coming to believe that. It feels wrong to go on without love." And then to her dismay she starts to cry. She buries her face in her hands and keeps it there until long after she hears him gathering his things from the heap in the hall and closing the front door behind him.

MAGGIE INSISTS ON making what she calls her love-affair consolation meal. "You have to come," she urges Rena over the phone. "It's a guaranteed cure."

"I'm not the forlorn one. I'm the guilty, confused one."

"It works for both the rejected and the rejecter. You eat these foods and three hours later the bad feelings are at least half gone."

When Rena arrives, the apartment smells of roast chicken and caramelized onions. Maggie hands her hot cider with a cinnamon stick. While they eat, she tells stories about the shelter. The woman who snuck out to call the husband who'd broken her arm and then gave him the wrong address so the police arrested him trying to climb in the basement window of the brownstone across the street. The shelter manager who lost it when she found her vacuum cleaner jammed with cotton balls and two of her pots scorched with burnt milk and started screaming that she was going to beat the shit out of whoever did this.

"Then Donna, our director—she's one of those people born without the irony appreciation cells—sends out a memo saying there will be no physical violence in the battered women's shelter."

"You're being kind," Ruth says. "Donna is missing more than that. All that healthy Kansas air stopped at her lungs."

"She's from Lawrence, Kansas. Where, come to think of it, I just read there's a huge concentration of DDT in the ecosystem."

"See," Ruth says. "It's probably that."

Rena lets Maggie give her more chicken, more scalloped potatoes, lets Ruth refill her glass with wine. She takes a few more bites, then puts down her fork. "All I feel is warm and sleepy and filled with wonderful foods."

"I told you," Maggie says. "It always works. Medieval white magic."

"Chicken fat and heavy cream," Ruth sings.

"Now you have to take a nap before dessert. That's part of the regime."

"You cooked. I'm going to do the dishes."

"Absolutely not. You've taken the medicine. You need to let it take effect."

Rena lets Maggie take her hand and lead her into the living room. She lies down on the couch where she'd slept the week after discovering Saul's pills, and Maggie covers her with an afghan Ruth's mother crocheted for them one Hanukkah. Rena closes her eyes and thinks this must be what it's like to be a child with one of those mothers who makes soup when you're sick and brings you trays in bed, and then she thinks about trays and the wooden trays she'd brought to Rebecca and the napkin-covered trays Leonard fixes for Klara and the orange plastic trays in the prison cafeteria.

When she wakes, Maggie is in the armchair with her feet up on an ottoman, doing the crossword puzzle. Her long earrings catch the lamplight. Ruth is lying on her stomach, reading the Sunday book review with her unlaced work boots next to her on the floor.

"How do you feel?" Maggie asks.

Rena stretches her arms over her head. "Good. Rested. How long did I sleep?"

Maggie looks at the clock on the coffee table. "An hour and a half."

"I don't think I've ever taken a nap like that before."

"It's the food."

"And I had the weirdest dream."

"That always happens. You dream about the one you're grieving over."

Rena's first instinct is to say nothing, to not tell them that Beersden was only a bit player, the opening jester in the dream. But she feels the warm fullness in her stomach and smells the sweet residues of the meal, and she thinks, *these are my friends, my friends who love me*. She sits up and draws her knees to her chest. "Only it was Saul I dreamt about."

She covers her face. Maggie and Ruth move beside her. Ruth puts an arm around her and Maggie smooths her hair, incanting, "Of course, of course, it's about time."

THEY WALK HER HOME, the three of them arm in arm on Riverside Drive. There's a lopped-off moon, like a sad tilted face surrounded by a pale halo. The trees have begun to turn, and in the moonlight the leaves glow the musky yellow of fall things: squash and hay and skin still holding its tan.

"I think I need to tell him," Rena says. "I think I haven't been going to see him because I can't handle faking it."

"Tell him?"

It takes Rena a moment to understand Maggie's question, to see that she hasn't been able, even here in the dark, with her friends, to say it out loud.

"That I want a divorce."

They walk in silence the rest of the way to Rena's building. Maggie opens her arms wide and then wraps them around Rena. It's a hug with no holding back, not one of the skittish little hugs Eleanor or for that matter she herself tends to give.

In her dark kitchen, the answering machine blinks. Pushing PLAY, she hears a high voice with a little gurgle at the bottom. "Rena? Is this Rena? There's no name, just a phone number. This is Betty, your Aunt Betty. Can you come for Thanksgiving at my house? Don't ask me why this year. I guess because your mother sent that letter saying you want to see pictures of your father, and I went through all these boxes in the attic and it made me remember you as a baby. Very serious with these big eyes. I said to Donny, how come we never invite her to any of our family things and I said I would invite you for Thanksgiving. Donny and the boys sit around all afternoon watching football, so after we eat we'll have lots of time to look through everything. Okay? You just call us when you get to the ferry terminal and Donny will come get you. Come early. You know, two or three." A beep, and then Betty's voice again. "I forgot, my brains, they get fried in that beauty parlor. Bring . . ." She pauses and then rescues herself. "Bring your husband. I hung up and Donny says you didn't even invite her husband. Of course, bring him. Just tell him that we're simple people. Nothing fancy."

Betty's laugh echoes in Rena's kitchen, the horrid ashamed laugh of people who think of themselves as unimportant, shut out from some larger, more elegant world.

ON THE BUS to the prison, Rena counts the months since Saul's arrest: nearly nine. We could have had a baby, she thinks. I could have grown a pumpkin belly. I could be decorating a nursery.

She hasn't seen him since June. He looks remarkably better. Heavier, the yellow cast to his skin now gone. She inhales. He smiles as he catches her doing this, *the smellomaniac,* he'd teased about her belief that she can detect people's states of health by their scent. With her mother, the way her scent had changed as she sank into melancholy: a sharp mildewed smell like a pillow gone damp inside. With Gene, the way she'd been able to track the waxing and waning of colds and viruses, constipation, toothache from the sour smell of his breath.

"Not depressed," she announces.

"No, not depressed."

They sit across from each other at the metal table, Rena facing the door. "So how are you?" she asks.

"Better. It was a long summer. I understand now why they take inmates' belts and don't allow bedsheets. There were days when the only thing that held me back was my father. Knowing that he believes suicide is revenge on the living. He would spend the rest of his days trying to ferret out his crimes." Saul folds his arms. Beneath his khaki shirtsleeves, she can see the movement of the new ridge of muscles. "Actually, it's a relief to be here. Awful as this is, the constant noise, the constant bickering, having to sleep with one eye open, living with the cesspool of human actions—don't think I don't include myself—it's a relief to be off the drugs. I've seen people watch themselves deteriorate physically and mentally. Watching myself deteriorate morally, the deceptions and oversights that became habitual lying and outright neglect and maltreatment of my patients that became, in the end, stealing . . . murder." Saul shudders. "That was hell."

"The pharmacist didn't die."

"The fetus did." He grips his elbows. "It's like having your soul chewed on by rats."

The guard peers through the wired window. Seeing Rena glance up, Saul looks over his shoulder.

"That's Richardson. He's been working here eighteen years. Three years older than I am and he's got a twenty-two-year-old son. He just asked me to write his kid a letter of recommendation for medical school."

"Did you do it?"

"Sure. Why not? It's not as though they check the credentials of the people who write these letters. The crazy thing is, I lost my license but not my job. Technically, I'm suspended. Once the suspension expires, the personnel people wrote me, they'll convert it to a personal leave. It's a moot point, since without a license I can't practice medicine." He leans back in his chair, tipping it onto the rear legs. "So, pray tell, to what do I owe this visit?"

She falls silent. How can I do this, she thinks. Ruin the equanimity he's managed to acquire. And yet what are the alternatives? Wait for him to get depressed again? Forget the whole thing?

Saul rubs his eyes as though tiring of the visit, which suddenly seems like a charade, as if he already knows.

"I . . ." She hesitates, looks into his chocolate eyes. "I want a divorce."

Saul drops the chair back to an upright position. He puts his fingertips together like a church steeple.

She'd planned on saying so much more. About how she does not believe that she could trust him again, cannot imagine being able to share a bed. Make a life. Have a child.

"That's it? You traveled all the way up here to tell me that?"

Her cheeks turn hot. Is he making fun of her? "What do you mean?"

He looks at her levelly and then raises an eyebrow.

THERE ARE FOUR DOORS TO be locked and unlocked. Free again, she does not want to leave. She feels like one big ball of failure. First the marriage, now even the ending.

Back in the prison lobby, she lifts the receiver for the automatic line installed by the local cab company. Waiting, her jaw trembles. This cannot be it, she thinks. That raised eyebrow. No more words. No meaning squeezed out of it all.

By the time the cab arrives, she has decided to return in the morning.

"Is there a motel nearby?" she asks the driver.

"Depends on what you want."

"Something not too expensive. Close by."

"Sounds like the Motel Six. Not that they're still six dollars, but prices aren't too bad, people say." He yanks his cap so it's pulled low on his head, turns left at the end of the prison driveway. They pass a stretch of scrappy woods and then a strip mall with a pet store, bakery and sewing supplies outlet tucked amid boarded-up fronts. At the light, Rena watches a group of teenagers in the parking lot, the girls with long, stringy hair and tight jeans, the boys in bowling jackets, the slouchy boredom of nowhere to go other than the Taco Bell.

Five minutes later, the driver stops in front of a motel with a sign flashing VACANCY. A kid, sullen with acne, leads Rena to a room with two twin beds and laminate furniture. He flips on the lights, shows her where she can adjust the heat, lingering at the door until she realizes—she'd not thought of it, having no luggage—that he's waiting for a tip. She finds two dollars in her wallet and then asks if there's anywhere to eat within walking distance.

"Mildred's Ice Cream Parlor. Make a right, maybe a quarter-mile. They got sandwiches, things like that."

She washes her hands and face. In the mirror, she examines her face. She looks gaunt. Her jeans, well-fitting last fall, hang from her hipbones. Outside, she walks opposite the traffic so the headlights shine on her, the cars and the drivers' faces looming large on the approach and then disappearing in an instant. Mildred's Ice Cream Parlor has red-and-white striped curtains and pictures of men with big waxed mustaches. She orders soup and a dish of chocolate ice cream. After fifteen mintutes, the food is gone and she feels like she should leave. It's only seven-thirty when she gets back to the motel. She draws the drapes and locks the door. The sheets are thin and slightly sticky, the residue of soap not fully rinsed.

Once, early in the morning, her eyes open and she sees a sliver of light that has slipped in through the crack between the drapes. The sheets, the smells, like any of the dozen motels where she and Ascher had stayed. The early morning light, his fingers roaming her hair, his words at this parting hour, always the same: *I love you more than the moon, the earth and the stars.* Syllables more hypnotic than any drug.

Not until they were married did Rena recognize Saul's kind of danger—the risk he posed to her self. Although Saul had never said it, he'd wanted her to be the doctor's wife to his doctor. Not in the silly Junior League way in which Klara had been raised where the doctor's wife and the minister's wife were expected to lead the other women in their seasonal projects: the Sadie Hawkins Dance, the Chrysanthemum Fest, the midnight hayride, the canned goods drive. What Saul had wanted was more demanding. He'd wanted her to enter into his world of ideas, to read with him, to be his helpmeet in thinking through the endless vine of questions and paradoxes and dilemmas his work posed every day. But she hadn't wanted to do it, to be his intellectual handmaiden.

Of course, she'd never said this; instead, what she said was, "You're lucky, you have your father to talk with about these things." A look of pain darted across Saul's face. He'd taken her remark to be the barometer she could now see it, in fact, to have been: that never had she wanted to fully immerse herself in him.

IN THE MORNING, she returns to Mildred's Ice Cream Parlor for tea and a roll. She has the same waitress: LINDA HERE TO SERVE YOU. Thin arms and legs, a little potbelly below her flat chest.

Linda looks at her curiously. "You were here last night. Chicken rice soup, one scoop chocolate in a dish."

"Good memory."

"A curse. Someone who hasn't been here in eight months, I'd still remember what they ordered the last time." She opens the napkin dispenser and puts a wad of napkins inside. "You staying at the motel?"

"Just last night."

"A war bride, huh? You got an old man up there in the dungeon on the hill?"

"How did you know?"

"Takes one to know one."

The woman reminds her of Sammy—the way she lets people feel she's making room for them. "Your husband's there, too?"

"Four years in January. Two more to go. After a year of dragging my baby back and forth on the bus, I said screw this and we moved here. It turned out just fine. My little girl's in school now, and she likes it a lot." She tops off Rena's water glass. "I'd eat more than that," she says. "The food in that cafeteria is foul. You got kids?"

"No."

"Most of the wives who don't have kids are goners after the first year."

Rena puts down her cup. She's had enough. She could leave now, gather her things, head to the register, but, in fact, it's a comfort to talk without a cost. Even with Ruth and Maggie, the confidences threaten a balance between them in which at bottom they each aim to keep their troubles in their own corral.

What she wants to ask Linda is: Did your husband lie to you? Over and over again? Were you able to forgive him? Will you ever be able to trust him again? Instead, she says, "I came here to tell him I want a divorce."

Linda whistles. "I can see why you're not up for eating."

"Actually, I already told him. I wanted to have some more time to talk with him."

"Well, good for you, honey. A lot of them don't even show up to deliver the news."

"I thought about it. Sending a letter. Only I thought it would haunt me, not knowing how he reacted."

"How'd he take it?"

"It's hard to say. He didn't really say anything."

"He must've known."

"What do you mean?"

"They know. It's amazing what these guys know. It's like there's a brotherhood among them. There was a customer here, about a year back, a little guy with a squeaky voice, pushing forty and still living with his mother. Talking about her, too, all the time. He was sweet on me in this harmless way, giving me moonie eyes, always asking to be seated at my station, leaving a dollar tip on a cup of coffee. Probably just needed somebody to think about when he jerked off in the shower. Sorry, don't mean to be rude, but you know what I mean. Nothing more than that. Never so much as asked me for my phone number. Somehow my old man, he knew."

"You're kidding."

"I swear to God. One week I notice I haven't seen Squeaky here in a couple of days, and next thing I know, someone tells me he got beat up in the driveway of his house. A stocking face came after him with a crowbar and broke his nose. Told him this was just the hors d'oeuvre to what would happen if he showed up here again." She wipes her hands on her apron. "I felt awful. I wanted to go visit him, but I was afraid it would make it worse."

Rena picks at her roll. She thinks about Saul's raised eyebrow. "How did your husband find out?"

"Beats me. Maybe someone who used to be up there was in here and saw Squeaky staring at me. My old man wouldn't say. That's the other thing. They're close-lipped as the Masons."

"DID YOU KNOW?" she asks after Saul sits down. They're in a different room today. There's a larger table with a heart etched into the surface: RICKY AND JONI FUCKIN FOREVER.

"Know what?"

She's not sure what she means—did he know about Beersden or did he know that she'd decided to ask him for a divorce. If he knows about Beersden, she wants to reassure him that it's over, that Beersden has nothing to do with it. But if he doesn't know, she doesn't want to tell him.

He looks at her frankly and she sees he is shedding his boyish dreaminess, his love affair with ideas. It's the first time she has ever felt a sharpness to him, a challenging edge, and it embarrasses her to discover that she finds it exciting.

"That you were planning to ditch me?" he says.

She starts to cry. It appalls her that it is she, not he, with the tears.

"I'm sorry. That was uncalled for." He reaches out and wipes her eyes with his sleeve. "Listen to me. It's my fault. I'm not saying that masochistically. Just realistically. I betrayed you. You have every right to leave now."

Her chest feels unbearably heavy, as if an enormous piece of furniture—an armoire or a breakfront, something laden with silver and crystal and years of use—has been set on top. For the first time in a long while, she feels the stirrings of the love she'd had for him. Not in a way that suggests she's making a mistake but rather to remind her of the life that has passed between them.

She fights the temptation to erase what she's said. To go back to the pretenses of the past months: things will change, time will heal what has happened if only she will endure. In his frank gaze, she detects his plea that she speak honestly with him, that if he is to survive the years here it must be without artifice. She gropes to gather her thoughts, to say what is most true. "It's not that, really. It's not that I want to be rid of you or to stop being involved with you."

He is watching her intently.

"I can't sleep with you again. I can't carry on as though we're going to live together again and go forward and do all the things married people do."

There is a slight tremor in his bottom lip. "So what do you want?"

"I don't know. Remember when we first met? That first afternoon at Cafe Vivaldi, when you came with a copy of the op-ed piece I'd written all marked up with your questions and comments and we just talked? No flirting, no seduction games. Just talked. I was so exhilarated. I'd never talked with a man like that. I'd talked with Rebecca, but she was always so far ahead of me. With you, it was the pure pleasure of sharing ideas and spurring each other to think more."

She traces the graffiti heart with a finger. "Please don't be hurt by this. But I think that's what we did best."

"You mean sex was a bust."

"Not a bust. You were the first man I ever really felt anything with. I can't call that a bust. But I realize now that it was because it was like sex without being sex."

"You seemed so fragile. I held myself back. It was as much for me as for you."

"What do you mean?"

"It was a convenient way not to face certain troubling parts of myself. I've been thinking a lot about it since I've been here. The way Marc and I divvied up the world. Or rather, being the older one, he grabbed certain things for himself and I was left to pick among the remains. He took all the machismo stuff: sports, girls, the aggressive career. I got the Talmudic approach, androgyny, these impossible ideals. He screwed fifteen girls in high school and collected football trophies. I spent the afternoons debating the philosphical underpinnings of psychoanalysis with my father."

"Poor Saul. Then you get me, whom you have to treat like a convalescent. What you needed was a lusty girl with a nice bottom who would let you enjoy yourself."

"You've got a nice bottom."

"Too bony."

"But nice."

They gaze at each other, and Rena feels astonished that this is happening, this warmth between them. "I just want to talk with you. I guess that's what it boils down to," she says.

His eyes dampen. "That was the worst part about the drugs. Words became sounds employed for deceptions." He pushes his hair off his forehead and she sees the fine physiognomy of his oval face, remembers a conversation once, shortly after they became lovers, when he'd talked about language as the most profound achievement of humanity, the ability to use the tongue and the palate to create a bridge between two minds. His voice softens, thins like a stream running into a silt plateau. "It's a relief for me, too."

"How so?"

"Less pressure. Less guilt. I can't promise how I'll react if you say there's another man. I guess I'll have to handle that as it comes."

"There's not another man."

He looks at her steadily. This is the watershed, she thinks: if she can tell him about Beersden.

"There was for a few months, but it's over."

Briefly, he covers his face.

"I'm sorry. Should I have not told you?"

"No. This won't work if you have to hide things."

"Do you want to know more?"

"Do you want to tell me more?"

"He was married with two daughters. It was a built-in limit. Not that I was in love with him. I never fell in love with him." She pauses. He's asking for the truth, she reminds herself. "The most significant thing was it made me realize I'd stopped feeling married. I felt like he was married, but not me."

A tear cascades off Saul's cheek. She watches his chest rise and fall.

"It's amazing, isn't it," he says, "that there's no ceremonial way of dissolving a marriage. No reverse marriage rites. At least we're not Catholic. To end the marriage, we'd have to declare it had never existed."

"This existed. I would never want to say our marriage did not exist."

Saul takes her hands in his and, despite the prison injunctions, holds them—gently, like two injured birds. She closes her eyes to keep from weeping. She feels certain that their minds are on the same thing: how much simpler it would be to mourn a love destroyed than this, a love never fully formed. She feels his thumbs tracing the bones in her fingers, one by one, until they both startle with the rap of the guard on the glass.

9 Leonard

I plan to call her on Thanksgiving Day. My mother always called me on Thanksgiving Day. My Uncle Jack, who devoted himself to Americanisms, who took the turkeys and firecrackers and little red, white and blue flags as seriously as his father had the unfurling and furling of the Torah each Yom Kippur, always called my mother on Thanksgiving. The bigger the turkey, the more American. Jack pronounced *big* the way you and Marc did as toddlers: *bee-ig*. One year he claimed that my Aunt Mindyl had roasted a thirty-three-pound bird. My mother laughed and laughed: "The butcher, knowing Jack, stuffed the neck with stones."

After Marc moved to Atlanta and you missed two Thanksgivings due to being on call, I gave up on preparing a holiday meal. If I'm willing to participate in your mother's dance about not feeling well enough, she is perfectly happy to go to the Ramada Inn where they do the entire spread, pumpkin soup to pumpkin pie. No matter the weather, she wears her full-length mink, the last present from her father. Thinking about it now, I don't know why you and Rena have never joined us. Did we ask and you declined or did I assume it would be too bizarre a grouping, the four of us seated in the windowless mirrored dining room of a motel whose main attraction is its proximity to the parkway?

Thanksgiving morning, I rise as always at five. Making coffee, I watch the birds pecking for seeds. Never, it occurs to me, have we had a bird feeder. All these years watching them scavenge for food, and never once have I taken the hour to go to the garden supply store and buy a feeder. Shtetl mentality. Jews from the Bronx don't go to garden nurseries. It's Italian men who plant yellow rosebushes and blue hydrangeas, who keep basement workshops where they probably make their own bird feeders.

I take a box of bread crumbs from the cabinet and open the kitchen door. In my slippers and pajamas, I step into the cold morning air. It takes a moment for the dampness to seep through the flannel. I sprinkle the patch of grass just beyond the patio. Back inside, I watch a flock of sparrows descend. They peck for the crumbs, their beaks tiny jackhammers.

I wonder if you are still sleeping. Rather, I wonder if you have slept at all. This last month, you have reassured me that Rena's announcement that she wants a divorce has been a strange relief. At first, I wondered if this was just more of your masochism. Like when you were first arrested and Morton told us you wanted to plead guilty. That in your perverse logic, it is a good thing for you to suffer so therefore you feel less depressed. When I asked you about this, you looked perplexed and then amused: "It's nowhere near that elegant. Once I got over the self-pity about Rena leaving me and the anxiety about living alone after I get out of here, I had to admit how impossible marriage is for me now. About as likely as someone who's just had open-heart surgery going mountain climbing."

The question I want to ask you but cannot is: *Was it sex? Was sex the problem?* I feel certain that the answer is yes but that you would not be able to say so. Not out of prudery but rather out of ignorance. Perhaps this is my arrogance to think of you as a sexual innocent. Still, I imagine you and Rena as twin flamingos, your spindly legs planted in watery marshland, your delicate necks caressed by the balmy breezes. Your fussy sleep. Your non-appetites. No alchemy, no fire in two such similar creatures. I believe this. I do. That we are built to desire the dissimilar. That we cannot rely on morality alone to ward off incest but need to have lust itself most inflamed by what is different.

Seeing you without the cloak of lethargy, I actually felt alarmed. Were they giving you an experimental mood elevator? Something that would burn out your serotonin circuits? I was relieved when you said your sleep remained poor—that whatever shift taking place in you was at least in this way proceeding gradually. Ever since you could get out of your crib on your own, I recall your episodes of sleeplessness. At two, when you still slept in pajamas with feet, I would hear you padding out of your bedroom, your eyes bloodshot with fatigue, dragging your blanket, tearful that you couldn't fall asleep. Your mother had no patience for this. She'd grown up in a household where there were clear and abundant rules for children. "Never would I dare get out of my bed without my parents' permission. It was the same with food. I never even opened the icebox until my thirteenth birthday." No wonder, I thought, she'd been so intemperate once given the opportunity. Hell, if they'd let her get her own juice, maybe she wouldn't have gotten drunk and gone to bed with me and maybe we wouldn't be so miserably here.

Now I know that your sleeplessness was our fault, your mother's and mine. You couldn't sleep because we never helped you learn how. Even when we lived in Jack's dining room, my mother always made bedtime a thing so sweet it is painful to recollect. We would lie on our cots while she read to us in her hushed alto voice: first picture books for Lil and me, then a chapter from a girl's adventure story for Rose and Eunice. She'd close the book and come to each of us, one at a time—Rose, then Eunice, then Lil, then me—kissing our cheek, stroking our hair, whispering, *I love you, I love you, my child*. Solemnly, my father would follow behind, awed by this piece of beauty my mother created in our cramped quarters.

In my study, I close the scrapbook left open on my desk and turn on the computer. I stare at the screen and the words stare back, white and inert. My lids are heavy. Already, at six in the morning, it seems too late.

I lay my head on the desk, close my eyes, slip into sleep as quickly as a stone dropped into a cold clear quarry. Twenty minutes later, I wake and immediately begin:

On March 18, the day after the baby was found drowned, Carmelita woke to the sound of banging. The village women had come to exorcise the devil from her. With Carmelita still on her mat, they dismantled the hut piece by piece. She lay motionless on the dirt floor during the hour it took them to tear the straw from the wood frame and then hack the frame to bits. When they were finished, they poured goat urine over her garments, rubbed chicken blood in her hair and left her lying bare to the elements in the midst of the rubble.

AT ELEVEN, I STOP to prepare your mother's breakfast. I make a fresh pot of coffee and scramble eggs with salami, a dish she wrinkled her nose at the first time I cooked it for her but devoured after tasting it and then began to request. Although I'm the one who comes from the peasant stock (you cannot imagine how intimidated we immigrant Ukrainians were of the second-generation German Jews with their heritage of professorships at the university in Frankfurt and diamond stores in Berlin, how often your mother in the first years of our marriage would remind me of these differences between my family and the Jewish colleagues her father had known), your mother is the one who possesses the peasant's appetite and body, too: the broad hips, the round belly, the square face, all exaggerated now by a quarter-century on the horizontal.

Your mother is unusually cheerful. She slathers the eggs and salami with strawberry jam, makes a tiny belch when she's done. "Excuse me," she giggles, putting her hand over her mouth, her gestures more girlish now at fifty-nine than they were at twenty. After these rare warm moments, I tell myself that I was right to stay with her all these years, that love flourishes in the caring for others. It's not a sentiment I am able to sustain—either that familiarity breeds affection breeds love or that anything so elevated as love has motivated me with your mother in any way.

While she bathes, I change the sheets on her bed and bring her the *tiny piece of cookie* and the television guide she has requested. Dressed in her peach bed jacket, she sits in the armchair and flips through the pages. "Leonard," she says, looking up at me with alarm, "you didn't tell me today is Thanksgiving."

"Yes, dear," I say, surprised because she usually tracks the calendar like a hawk.

She slumps in the chair. "My sinuses. They've been awful."

We go on about her sinuses and the headaches they cause. The outing to the Ramada Inn, I cajole, will do her good. I help her back into bed.

"Maybe if I rest awhile."

I adjust the shades, switch off the light, turn to leave.

"My mink . . ."

I CALL MARC FIRST. The conversation is defined by his not asking about you. He talks about his law practice, his golf game, Susan's job teaching sign language. It was you who first pointed out the peculiar nature of these conversations. At the time, you were upset and railing a bit: "These phone calls, they're not about trying to communicate anything. They're rituals. Incantations employed to reassure himself that what seems empty makes sense: *I know it's ridiculous hours. Half the time, I think I should sell the house and we should move to Wyoming and I'll work digging ditches. But, look, I guess you have to make these sacrifices at this time of life. No one who bills under twenty-five hundred hours in a year is going to make partner.*" You sighed with exasperation. "It's false consciousness," you concluded, the harshest condemnation you can level.

What I want to ask your brother but don't is how he's feeling now that he and Susan are no longer trying to have a baby. Six years of ovulation kits, hormone injections, egg extractions yielding three conceptions and three miscarriages. The last at eighteen weeks, after the sonogram, after seeing the baby curled knees to chest in the amniotic balloon. Susan, grief-struck, too afraid to try again. At the time, I'd wanted to call her, to comfort her by reminding her that one out of four conceptions miscarry, Nature's way of weeding its garden; my grandmother, your great-grandmother, had six miscarriages and sixteen live births, only ten of which lived beyond childhood. But I hadn't called. Marc said she didn't want to talk about it. Instead, as always, it was you and I who discussed it: how these extraordinary efforts to boost fertility leave no room for the early losses, the medical interventions making each conception too precious, the loss of the fetus (for my grandmother, as expected as not) a devastation.

With you, it takes over an hour to get through the busy signal. I keep hitting redial until I'm lucky and get a free line in the split second between someone hanging up and someone else dropping their quarters in the slot. "Shit," I hear someone say. "Fifteen minutes, I'm standing here for this phone and that motherfuck Dubinsky gets a call. Dubinsky," he yells. "It's your boyfriend. Get your whiteboy ass over here."

I wait three, maybe four minutes. "Fuck 'em, fuck 'em," someone mutters before the line goes dead.

Rena is my last call. She answers slightly out of breath.

"Happy Thanksgiving," I say.

"Oh, Leonard, it's good to hear your voice. I just walked in the door."

I hold while she takes off her coat, a jealous interlude during which I'm convinced that she's coming in from the night.

She's good enough to puncture my fantasies. "I walked up to Riverside Church. I've never seen it so bright inside. It must be the angle of the sun." This information is meant, I can see, as a hand reaching out to pat my arm. This place you and I have passed countless times on our walks to Grant's Tomb.

I do something impulsive. It's because, I tell myself, I cannot reach you. "Are you free Saturday? For coffee, dinner?"

She pauses. I am flooded with anxiety. Anxiety that she will say no. Anxiety that she will say yes.

"That would be really nice. It's sweet of you to ask me."

I am surprised that she seems touched. I always think of her as inaccessible, surrounded by the flurry of her glamorous job, well, her old glamorous job, her lesbian friends, her idiosyncratic beauty. She suggests the Alice in Wonderland statue in the park, near the model boat basin, half past four, sufficient light for a brisk stroll before an early dinner, and it is not until I am at the sink washing your mother's breakfast dishes that it occurs to me I have not asked her what she is doing today, with whom she will spend her Thanksgiving.

I ARRIVE TWENTY MINUTES early and sit at Alice's feet, watching the pigeons skirt the steps that lead down to the basin. The sky is all whites and fading blues, a cold light that erases the yellow and red undertones that lift an ordinary spirit. There are no children, the promise of chill and dark too close, only two men, both mustached, both wearing brimmed caps. They stare at their toy boats, maneuvering them with remote controls, adult men frozen in eternal boyhood.

She arrives exactly on time. Approaching from a distance, her hair covered by the hood of her parka, she could be you, twenty years ago, loping up the hill in front of the house. She kisses me on the cheek, her hood falling back over her shoulders, her hair ringleted from the damp, a haze around her pale, angled face. Ivory soap, lemon from her shampoo.

"You look well, Leonard." She smiles, a mouth of perfect gapless teeth.

"It's been a long time. Since the end of June when you moved." Immediately, I regret saying this, afraid of sounding like one of the guilt vampires, those old people whom you've hardly greeted before they ask when they'll see you again.

She takes my arm, something I can't recall her having ever done before, and we descend the steps to the terrace around the boat basin, the café closed for the winter. "This is one of my favorite places," she says. "I come here in the summer to eat ice cream and watch the children with their boats." She points at the boarded-up building. "Strawberry ice cream in a paper cup."

"I used to take Saul here."

"He told me. Your New York afternoons. The Forty-Second Street library, dim sum in Chinatown. He said you told him this was like a little piece of Paris in New York, how there's a place like this in the Luxembourg Gardens."

"You've been there?"

"No. I've been all over this country, including Hawaii and St. John, but never abroad. We were going to, we were just starting to plan a trip for the fall . . ." She sighs and then smiles, a weary ironic smile that suggests what choice but to make mincemeat tarts of our miseries and serve them up with sweetened tea. "I've promised myself a trip before my fortieth birthday. The classic tour that you read about in Henry James and Edith Wharton. Paris to Baden-Baden to Venice to Rome."

She stops ten feet north of one of the mustached boy-men. He keeps his eyes fixed on the sailboat, its leeward side tilted into the wind. "The truth is, if you don't travel when you're young, you feel intimidated. I'd be scared to go anyplace I don't speak the language."

We walk north through the park and then out onto Fifth Avenue. I let her lead, uncertain where she is headed. When I ask about her Thanksgiving, she tells me how she'd been lured to Staten Island, to her mother's sister's house, with the promise of photos of her father.

"There was my Aunt Betty, dressed in exactly the same clothes I'd seen her in eight years ago. Flowered leggings and a pink apron. Her husband picked me up at the ferry, but once we got to the house I don't think he said a dozen more words to me. He and their two sons sat glued to the television. They didn't even leave the set to eat, just filled their plates and brought them into the family room. My aunt and I ate alone at the kitchen table. It was really sad."

I glance at Rena, refrain from placing my hand on her back. "My aunt spent the whole meal talking about how fat she is and all these diet centers she's tried, Jenny Craig, Weight Watchers, Living Lady, Gorgeous Gals, and all the while she's heaping more and more food onto her plate. Eating and complaining about my mother and how she never calls and how my grandfather, who's now in a VA home, is all her responsibility. I kept waiting for her to show me the photos, but we got all the dishes washed and the floor wiped down and still no mention of them. When I finally asked her, she looked at me with this tormented expression, like how could I even dream of asking for pictures after she's been up since three in the morning cooking."

We are nearing the Metropolitan museum, announced by the convocation of Senegalese men, heads covered by brilliant tightly woven caps, selling knockoffs of Cartier watches and Ferragamo bags. The first time you went on your own to the city, you brought back one of those watches for your mother. This was before it became chic to sport the fake items, when the vendors still claimed they were genuine goods rather than trinkets manufactured in a Hong Kong sweatshop. Fifteen dollars for a Rolex, you proudly reported. You were devastated when Marc snickered, *sucker*. How I'd wished your mother would just put on the damn thing and say, what do I care, it's a lovely watch and I'll love wearing it, but instead she sank back onto her pillows and repeated the story about the time her mother had taken her pearls to be cleaned. The jeweler had replaced one of the pearls, mind you, your mother said, just one, with a fake pearl, but she knew, your mother's mother, she knew her pearls, she knew to examine her jewelry anytime it went out of her sight and she had discovered it. When she threatened to call the police, the jeweler broke down and wept. Never before, he told your grandmother, had he done such a thing. Never had he so much as fudged on one one-hundredth of a carat when weighing a diamond. Only he had an ailing sister and your grandmother's pearls were so fine that one, simply one, would pay for two months of doctor's visits. Your grandmother had held firm, your mother enjoyed recounting, held firm that the pearl be replaced and had then, with the strand restored and securely clasped to her warbly neck (well, perhaps it was not warbly then) told the man (in, I'm sure, her haughtiest tone) to bring his sister the next day to your grandfather's clinic.

I tell Rena about the fifteen-dollar Rolex.

"Not the tale of a budding criminal mind," she says.

"If you'd told me thirty years ago that Saul would end up in prison,

I'd have said you were crazy. Saul was the kid whose ball was always grabbed at the playground, who would leave his Halloween candy out in the open for his brother to rifle through."

"Well, maybe it's not inconsistent. I don't mean to paint him as a victim, but I think he fell into drugs with that kind of innocence." It's touching to hear her defend you. "At first, he was just desperate to sleep. He was so afraid he'd make another mistake if he couldn't clear his head."

We've passed the museum with the circus of tourists and children and students climbing or sitting or pausing on the steps. We walk on the park side, the crowd thinning north of Eighty-Sixth Street. Your wife's face grows dimmer and dimmer as dusk falls, and then suddenly the streetlights turn on and gold darts off her hair like a halo in a Florentine oil.

"It's really my fault," she says matter-of-factly, not in a browbeating manner or a way intended to invoke reassurances and the putrid psychobabble of not blaming oneself. "He was impaired. I should have insisted then, at the beginning, that he see someone. You know the old adage that a doctor who treats himself has a fool for a patient. Saul certainly did. At the beginning, I thought it was just a few sleeping pills, but still, the fact that he was prescribing for himself at all should have told me his judgment was gone." She hugs her arms. "If it had been something practical—getting the air conditioners installed, making airline reservations—I would have taken care of it. But I was so used to Saul being the expert on things emotional, I deferred."

"A professional hazard," I say. "Everyone assumes shrinks can handle their own problems."

She stares at me. Something between disappointment and despair at my generic explanation passes over her face. Ahead of us, the Guggenheim looms like a crustacean deposited from the sea.

"He found my blind spot."

She looks lost. I am reminded how little I know about her, afraid if I ask, *what do you mean, your blind spot,* it will sound accusatory and she will bolt on her long, slender legs, a gazelle slipping into the park. I point to the bench ahead. "Let's sit."

If there is a center point to the Guggenheim, it seems that this bench is directly across from it. The problem with sleeping pills is they don't work. Yes, they may deliver sleep for a while, but they are no balm for the mind. "There are three potions to soothe an ailing spirit," I recall a teacher of mine once saying. A small beatific man whom the other psychiatry professors tolerated as representative of a fringe point of view. "Love, nature and art. We offer love, adult love purified of sexual intent, and in so doing we hope to unlock the natural appreciation for nature and art." Love and nature have always seemed too daunting to me. But I exposed you and your brother from an early age to art, hoping it would be this balm for you.

Right, I hear my old professors, the analysts, sneering. *Right,* I hear the new generation, your peers, the pill pushers, mocking. *You would have prescribed an hour of Ravel and a walk through that unearthly building across the street.*

"Look," Rena says. She touches my arm and points northward. There's a tall woman with a scarf tied over her thick black hair. A long camel hair coat swings slightly as she walks. Loose pants skirt the tops of suede flats. She looks straight ahead, her gait a tincture of supreme confidence and nervousness. I know her. I know I know her.

The woman passes right in front of us. A face that's familiar in the way that even the strangers in your dreams always seem.

"It's Jackie Onassis," Rena whispers. "She lives in one of these buildings. I heard that she walks in the park every day, but I've never seen her before."

I stare at the back of Jackie's coat. At the way her trousers swoosh against her shoes. Your mother was obsessed with Jackie. You were born the same year as Caroline, and your mother felt that this gave her and Jackie a special connection.

When Kennedy was shot, your mother wept not for the loss of our president but for the tragedy this meant for Jackie.

• • •

WE EAT IN ONE of those restaurants that looks like it's been put together from a hodgepodge of Hollywood sets: a bar from an Irish pub, the starched tablecloths of a Parisian bistro, the terra-cotta planters of a Tuscan trattoria. I order what's on tap and the grilled tuna, and Rena orders a hot mulled cider and a pasta dish from the chalkboard specials. She keeps her hands over the top of the mug, letting the steam warm her palms. The beer has given me a warm, satisfied feeling. I push out of mind the thought of you eating sloppy joes served with canned peas and carrots, forty institution-size cans to fill three pots, each pot large enough, you've told me, for a man to sit inside.

Rena bites into one of the puffy cheese straws the waiter has left in a basket. "What kind of dog do you think it was?" she asks.

"What dog?"

She giggles. Your wife is not a giggler. She flicks a fleck of pastry off her bottom lip. "The one Jackie was walking."

"I didn't see a dog."

I glance to my right. Do people think she's my daughter? My secretary? A May-to-December marriage? Could anyone mistake me for one of those men with their ramrod postures and gleaming white hair? Or does anyone, in these days of men walking hand in hand and high school girls with rings in their noses, even bother to speculate?

Three-plus decades in the New Jersey suburbs and I've become a greenhorn.

"You didn't see the dog?"

"No." I don't know why this seems so funny, but we're both laughing now. "Jackie wouldn't walk the dog."

I've never seen Rena really laugh before. She laughs so hard, her eyes water. "That's what she was doing. Walking the dog."

When the waiter comes with our food, he has a bemused expression. We both struggle to control our faces while he lays an oversize white plate before Rena, fat fettuccine noodles under glistening vegetables, and a stainless-steel platter before me, the fish still sizzling on the metal.

Rena twists a noodle around her fork, then looks up at me, the laden fork still in her hand. "I've asked Saul for a divorce."

I finish chewing. I have an abhorrence of people talking with their mouths full, have never really understood how a person is supposed to converse over dinner. Even rushing the food down, it takes half a minute before my mouth is empty and wiped. "He told me."

We look directly at each other, as though everything that has taken place during the two hours up to now has been a kind of ceremony.

"I feel like a louse, of course. But I can't imagine ever being able to trust him again. Certain things don't go backwards." She lays down her fork. "Frogs can't become tadpoles again."

I think of those conundrums you used to love about the identity of objects. At what point is a machine whose every part has been changed no longer the same machine? That's what it must seem like to Rena. That nothing about you resembles the person she married.

"You don't have to apologize to me."

"I can't help feeling I need to. Now all he has is you."

"Marriage isn't the same as parenthood." I wonder why I am condoning her actions, what is going on here.

"You never left Klara."

"No, but not because of any great nobility on my part."

The waiter approaches. He refills our water glasses. I ask for another lemon even though I don't really need any more. Afterwards, the conversation shifts—away from your mother tucked in her bed, away from you locked in your cell.

SHE REFUSES MY OFFER to escort her home.

"Don't be silly. It's completely out of your way. I'll walk up to Ninety-Sixth and take the crosstown bus."

She kisses me on the cheek, leaves me waiting for a cab. After she turns her back, I lower my hand. I'm tempted to follow her, a careful ten paces behind. Instead, I remain rooted on the corner of Madison Avenue, watching her slim receding form.

What was it I said when she told me she'd overlooked your being impaired?

A professional hazard—as though the two of you were case examples in a textbook.

She must have felt I was pushing her away. Only now do I see that I didn't ask what she meant by her blind spot, not because I feared she would bolt, but rather because I was afraid to hear what she might say.

The same way, she was trying to tell me, she'd felt with you.

10 Rena

Lying in bed the day after seeing Leonard, she watches the river, this afternoon a choppy slate, the high-rises and abandoned piers hugging the Jersey shoreline. A handful of birds swoop in frenzied arcs over the water, perhaps stragglers lost from their migratory flock.

The birds vanish from sight. Living with Gene a decade ago on the sixteenth floor, she'd learned how to translate this vertiginous landscape into an understanding of weather. How sun in cold air refracts differently on the surface of water than sun in warm air. How to detect the velocity of the wind from the wave patterns. She's been surprised at how quickly the discernments return, like a mother who can hear in her baby's cries the difference between hunger and anger. Her own mother had taught her this when Gene was a newborn and Eleanor was too depressed to rouse herself to tend to his nighttime needs. Instead, she would call out to Rena, then fifteen: he wants a bottle, pick him up, he needs to be changed.

Once Rena no longer needed Eleanor to interpret Gene's cries, she'd taken to rolling the bassinet into her room at night. Secretly, she'd been relieved to sleep with the baby so near. When they'd lived over Nick's restaurant, before Gene was born, she and her mother had shared the room's one bed. On the nights following Nick's visits, she could smell his cologne, the acrid dank scent (had she known at the time or is this a retrospective recognition?) of his semen on the sheets. After the scurry through the parking lot of Nick's restaurant to retrieve as many of their things as could be stuffed into the trunk of Joe's car, neither she nor Eleanor had dared to object when Joe led Rena into the storage room that would become her bedroom for the next eight years. The first night, she'd slept on two blankets on the floor with the overhead light glaring above. Waking from the cold, she'd seen the rifle hanging on the wall, the pistols gleaming behind the gun cabinet's glass doors.

EVENINGS, WHEN SHE leaves for work, she stands outside Santiago's apartment door waiting for the elevator, listening to the faint strains of a Cuban guitar and thinking how she should knock on his door and invite him for tea. She is home all day. He is home all the time. She cannot explain her refusal, the way she holds to the Tuesday reading sessions, not allowing anything more.

Then, in early December, an evening passes when she hears no music. In the morning, Pedro tells her that Santiago is in the hospital.

"The girl who comes to clean, she found Mr. Domengo on the living room floor. She told me Mr. Domengo, he was conscious, but with one eye rolled up. Mrs. Lehrman, the lady in 7C, said it was a stroke."

Pedro shakes his head back and forth. "Twenty-four years, ever since I came to work here, he's been my friend. Before he lost his son, there was always a smile on his face. But after that, he was broken. When he went blind, the doctors said it was something medical, but to me it seems he just didn't want to see no more."

Had Santiago called out, hoping she'd hear him?

"The daughter, she is very cold. Never once do I see a letter from her. Every few years she comes to visit, but all she does is shop when she's here. She doesn't even take him out. Always asking me to do things for her. Once she gave me this bag of dresses and asked if I could get a box and pack them in it for her. When I told her I don't have no box, she said things to me, you would have thought she came from a different kind of family."

She thinks about calling Grita Lehrman, but then, at the end of the week, she sees her in the elevator, bundled in hat and scarf with a stack of oversize envelopes pressed to her chest.

"Off to the post office," Grita announces. "To beat the morning rush."

"I was going to call you to ask for Santiago's hospital address."

Grita Lehrman sighs. She straightens the pile of envelopes. "Save your stamp, dear. He's passed the point of 'get well' wishes."

STANDING OUTSIDE THE law firm's glass doors, she hears the din of voices and then recalls the memo in her cubby about the office Christmas party. She considers simply turning around, but before she can make up her mind, one of the associates spots her and waves. She looks down at her jeans and work boots and thinks, oh, what the hell.

Inside, the women are spruced up for evening: a jacket removed at the end of the workday to reveal a chiffon blouse or sheath dress, extra-high heels, freshly applied lipstick. The associate who'd waved approaches, his face flushed.

"A gate-crasher!" he says, raising a plastic champagne glass as she realizes the wave was not recognition but rather compulsive flirtation directed at any female face. "I love it!"

He places a hand on Rena's shoulder and leads her to the large conference room, where a bar is being run by two young women in black tuxedos. There's a table laid with a half-devoured spread of food. He spears a shrimp with a toothpick and points dolefully at an empty silver tray at the end of the table. "But you're late. There was Alaskan king crab earlier."

She recognizes him as Kyle Stuart, the enfant terrible of the firm, his antics—two fails on the bar exam, a handful of indiscretions with various secretaries—buffered by his managing partner uncle. Sari, the office manager who hired Rena, hurries over. She takes Rends hand. "I'm so glad you came. I haven't laid eyes on you in ages."

"Well, by accident. I thought I was coming to work. Otherwise I would have dressed for the occasion."

"Ladies, champagne across the board," Kyle announces. At the bar, he pulls one bartender's ponytail, pokes at the other's bow tie.

"Let's make our escape before the menace returns," Sari whispers. Rena follows her to the atrium in the middle of the office. The secretaries' cubicles have been pushed back to make room for dancing. At the rear, Beersden sits behind an electronic keyboard. Rena sees the drummer and bass player from his band. A woman with hair fried from too many perms is singing a jazzy rendition of "Rudolph the Red-Nosed Reindeer." A few people are self-consciously dancing: a senior partner with a first-year associate, some of the younger lawyers with the paralegals.

Rena watches Beersden, who is bent over the keyboard. She feels her body stirring, the memory of her legs wrapped around his waist. At the end of the piece, he looks up. She watches him squint, bringing her face into focus, listens as he announces a break. Someone turns on a tape of sixties music, and a few more people, including Sari, are cajoled into dancing. Beersden makes his way toward her, his progress halted by various back-thumpers.

"Beersden, you son of a gun."

"Hey, Beersden, next time we get across the table from one of those stick-up-their-rear-ends from Cravath, we'll send you in with your keys to lighten things up."

She squeezes past the group of people lingering in the atrium archway and heads down the long hall to the secretaries' lounge, uncertain if what she's fleeing is Beersden, the way he'd stopped the music on seeing her, or the feeling of temptation: the wind on her cheeks as they'd ride uptown on his motorcycle, her hands on his shoulders as he'd unlace her boots.

She closes the door behind her and looks in her cubby, where each night she finds her graveyard assignments—empty tonight save for a note from Sari. "Revel and enjoy." See, she says to herself. Permission. A night off.

Wrong, the little priestess in her, that amalgam of her best self and Rebecca, rejoins. There are no nights off. You sleep with him tonight and Monday he'll be here waiting for you.

The door opens wide enough for Beersden to come inside. He places a finger over his lips. They stand in silence while a group of people passes in the corridor outside. He leans against the row of cubbies. "For someone who used to advise politicians on how to put themselves together, you look like you could use some help yourself."

"I didn't realize tonight was the party."

She sees that her words have stung him, that he's been harboring the idea that she'd come to see him.

"So I must be an unpleasant surprise." He moves closer. She can smell the beer on his breath.

"You're not doing anything to make it pleasant."

"Oh, I see. I'm supposed to get down on my hands and knees and beg you to fuck me again?"

Her heart pounds. She remembers the bang of his glass on the table two months ago. Does he know he'd scared her? Unsure what she is doing, she crosses the room, relieved when she sees the coffeemaker. She rips open a packet of coffee, fills the pot from the watercooler. Beersden sinks into the couch.

"I thought you didn't want people to know about your music."

"It got to be too much of a burden. I couldn't concentrate on my playing. All night, I'd be peering into the audience, worrying that someone I knew was going to show up. Besides, there's a long tradition of lawyers who are also musicians. Now that I've let people know, I'm Mister Popularity around here." He kicks his legs out in front of him, crossing his feet. "These guys bring their wives and college kids down to the club, make a big show of coming up to talk to me at the breaks. I'm a piece of exotica they can append to their lapel."

"My mother knew a lawyer who was a jazz saxophonist."

"Who's that?"

She hesitates before saying his name. "Freedman."

"There's a family of lawyers by that name. A guy I knew in law school clerked for the old man, Ben Freedman. Two of his brothers and one son were lawyers, too."

Her ears ring. All these years in the city and she's never let herself wonder if any of the faces around her belong to her father's family.

The door swings open. "No work!" Sari sings out. "Work is banned tonight. You tell her, Mr. Beersden."

"Donald."

"You tell her, Donald. Too serious, this one. You need to get her out of here and onto the dance floor."

"Righto," Beersden says, lifting himself up from the couch.

Rena holds up two cups. "These need to be washed." Out in the corridor, she moves quickly to the reception area. She throws her coat over an arm and pushes the door open. Not until she is in the elevator, dropping down the twenty-six floors, does it register that the dirty cups are still in her hands.

PEDRO GIVES HER a package sent to her old apartment and forwarded on to the new.

She reads the return address: Por Juguete, Rambla de Cataluna, Barcelona, España.

"*Por Juguete,*" Pedro says, leaning over her shoulder. "That means for fun. Maybe a toy store?"

Inside her apartment, Rena places the package on her desk. She cuts the string and tape, pulls out the pink and blue tissue paper. Underneath is a soft purple giraffe with yellow spots and a black felt nose.

She holds the giraffe to her cheek. Feeling strangely nervous, as though someone is watching her, she stares out at the river and then down at the street, where a man with a briefcase is waiting at the bus stop. She lowers the shades and then empties everything out of the box. Nothing but tissue. She rips the packing label off, but there is no other paper beneath.

She takes off her clothes and puts on Saul's pajamas. From the bed, she stares at the giraffe on her desk. *Giraffe.* That's what Reed had called her when they first met. Because she'd been so skinny and frightened-looking. She gets out of bed and examines the giraffe under her desk light. The button eyes. The braided yarn tail. She examines the seams, behind the stiff ears, along the neck, on the back. She examines a part of the seam on the belly that looks slightly puckered.

She takes the giraffe into the bathroom, locking the door behind her. Sitting on the lid of the toilet seat, she holds a nail scissors in one hand and the giraffe in the other. Carefully, she cuts the seam in the spot where there's a pucker. She cuts about two inches and then pushes two fingers inside. There's the foam stuffing and then something different, like a piece of plastic. She pulls out some of the foam and works an edge of the plastic out to the seam. Slowly, she pulls out a baggie. Opening the bag, she counts one hundred and twenty hundred-dollar bills.

FOR SEVEN DAYS, she leaves the money inside the resewn giraffe while she struggles with the question of whose money it is. Not whose money it was—clearly, it came from the sale of the hospital pharmaceuticals—but whose money it is now. The insurance company that paid the hospital's claim? The government? Money that, were she to report it, would be used to try to trace a path to Reed.

She marvels at Reed's certainty that she wouldn't turn the package over, that she could no more turn over evidence against him than she could with Saul.

On the seventh day, she places the box and the tissue paper in the garbage can in the service entry to her hall. She puts the packing label through the shredder at work. She waits for three days, half expecting each morning as she returns from work to find a DEA agent outside her door, but when nothing happens she takes the nail scissors and for a second time cuts open the giraffe. She puts the baggie in a manila file labeled G in her locked file cabinet and sews up the giraffe's belly again. Dropping the giraffe in a garbage bag, she dumps the contents of her kitchen can on top, and on her way to work tosses it in a trash basket in the park.

She spends the first of the hundred-dollar bills at a post-Christmas sale at Bloomingdale's, where she buys her own pair of pajamas. Slowly, she exits the store, studying the crowd around her for the person who will squeeze her arm, saying, *miss, you need to come with me*. The next day, she cashes a second bill at the health food store, where she buys two bags of organic produce.

She imagines clicking sounds on her telephone line. She rips apart her room looking for a hidden microphone. She waits but nothing happens.

SHE WAKES EARLY on New Year's Day, relieved that the holidays have come to a close. She thinks about calling Saul, but despairs at the thought of the endlessly busy line. Or is the despair about the giraffe, the burden of keeping a secret? Here she'd cleared Beersden, and now this. For the first time, it bothers her that the package was addressed only to her. Does that mean Reed knows about Saul's arrest—that Saul is right that when Reed left, he had known Saul would be caught?

Since her last visit, she and Saul have exchanged short, chatty notes. Saul's—humorous anecdotes about prison life, pithy reflections on the human condition—have echoed her tone, a tone meant to convey that they no longer have a hold on each other, no longer expect the other to take responsibility for their well-being. Only the news about Santiago, that the stroke had been followed by a staph infection that developed into a pneumonia, has introduced a somber note.

When the phone rings a little after nine, she imagines it to be Saul. Dislodged, it takes her a moment to recognize Leonard's voice.

"Happy new year."

"Happy new year to you, too."

"They let them get incoming phone calls between seven and eight on holidays. I had my finger on the phone at six fifty-nine and miraculously got through. I promised Saul I'd call you to wish you a happy new year from him."

Leonard tells her about Saul's three resolutions for the upcoming year: to read all of Shakespeare's plays, to learn how to play chess, to work on his triceps.

Rena laughs at the triceps resolution. "What's that about?"

"I didn't ask. Maybe it's a way of getting respect in there."

"If I know Saul, there's some grander reason."

There's a pause and then Rena continues, blurts out, it seems to her,

"I just want you to know how much your calls have meant to me. I wouldn't have blamed you if you'd decided to have nothing to do with me after I told Saul about wanting the divorce. I hope we'll remain in touch."

She hears the catch in her voice, and then Leonard clearing his throat. "My sentiments exactly."

They hang up and she heads downstairs to get milk, flowers, the newspaper. The lobby is empty except for Pedro, who stands in his gold-trimmed overcoat in the front vestibule.

"Happy new year, Pedro."

Pedro takes off his cap and holds it over his heart. "Not a good day." His eyes fill with tears.

Rena leads Pedro to the marble bench by the door. Seated, Pedro bows his head and dabs at his face with a pressed white handkerchief.

Five minutes, maybe more, go by before Pedro speaks.

"Mr. Domengo. He passed last night."

THE PRISON WARDEN allows Saul to come to the phone.

"Is it my father?"

"Santiago."

Saul exhales loudly.

"He was still in the hospital. A woman here in the building who was close with him said he went in his sleep."

She can hear Saul crying.

"I'm sorry, honey." The honey surprises her.

"I kept thinking that at some point I'd write him, give you a letter to read him. It's just that everything I have to say seems hackneyed. I couldn't bear to be hackneyed with him."

"I think he understood."

"I never thought he'd die while I was here."

PEDRO TELLS HER that Santiago's daughter, Flora, has arrived and has said nothing to him other than to ask for the key. Coming in from work, Rena slips a condolence card under Santiago's door. All morning she sleeps deeply, no dreams, only snatches of images, like scenery whizzing past on a highway, so that when she wakes to a ringing, it takes her a moment to discern that the sensation is coming from outside this inner montage—coming from her own front door.

She puts on her robe. Heading to the door, she imagines the giraffe, labeled and tagged on a precinct desk, feels the same beating rush of nearly a year ago, certain they've come now for her.

Lifting the peephole cover, she peers at a female face. She cracks the door, leaving the chain in place. A woman with black hair and skin so devoid of color it looks ghostly holds out a typewriter case.

"The doorman thought maybe you'd want this."

Rena undoes the chain and opens the door. The woman puts the case down at Rena's feet. Despite her ghoulish surface, there's a girlishness about her, a breathiness in her voice or perhaps it's the state of her spine—straight and limber—such that Rena imagines her sitting on the floor to tie the canvas shoes she wears under her loose black pants. She turns to leave.

"Excuse me," Rena says. "Who are you?"

"Flora Fahrsi." She points next door.

"I'm sorry, I didn't put it together. I'm sorry about your father."

"Why? He was an old man." Flora Fahrsi pushes her hair out of her eyes. "There's more stuff inside. I've been telling people to take whatever they want."

Rena takes her keys. Barefoot, still in her robe, she follows Flora next door. It's been over a month since she's been in Santiago's apartment, and the first thing that strikes her is the new smell: something strong and caustic, one of those green cleaning agents in a large plastic bottle. A suitcase sits in the middle of the living room floor.

Flora waves a hand toward the kitchen. "Maybe there's something you can use. There are some lamps in the bedroom."

She's never before been in Santiago's bedroom. The lamps have brown watermarks on the shades and chips on the ceramic bases. Over the dresser is a framed watercolor, poorly matted: three amoeboid shapes in primary colors. It reminds her of early Calders, of a discussion she'd once had about them with Rebecca. What had Rebecca called them? Clever naïfs.

She takes the picture off the wall and carries it into the living room, where Flora is kneeling on the floor folding things into the suitcase.

"If no one wants this, I'll take it."

Flora doesn't look up. "Whatever."

"Do you know who did it?"

Flora glances over. "That's just a kid's painting. Their son did it when he was in kindergarten or something."

She stares at Flora's back. Flora had called Bernardo their son, not her brother or even, as in fact he more precisely would be, her half brother. "Are you certain you don't want it?" she asks softly.

"You've never flown on a Saudi airline. They're Nazis about the weight limits. My husband says they tamper with the scales so that even if you're under the limit, you still come out over. One ounce extra and they make you start throwing things out. Of course, they just keep whatever you have to leave. There . . ."

Flora pushes on the top of the suitcase with one hand while she struggles with the other to close the clasps. Propping the picture against a chair, Rena presses down on the hard suitcase top.

"The real reason, though, is that they let the royalty carry as much as they want. The super rich ones, of course, have their own planes, but the princesses, there must be a thousand of them, the distant cousins of the king, sometimes three of them will book the whole first class. Coming over, I counted. One had twenty-eight suitcases. That's before her shopping trip. It's a miracle we don't all end up in the Mediterranean."

"I think you have to take some things out."

Flora mumbles under her breath. "This always happens." She pulls out two men's sweaters from inside the suitcase. "Here, you want these? I thought my husband might use them if we ever get out of Riyadh."

Rena places the sweaters next to her. One of them is a cardigan with some buttons missing. The other has a hole in the sleeve. "He's Saudi, your husband?"

"Lebanese. He and his brothers run the concession stands outside the embassies. He's the eldest, so he took the best spot, the American embassy."

Rena pushes down again on the suitcase top, and this time Flora succeeds in closing it.

"My husband was a student of your father's. Your father's teaching had a big influence on him."

Flora sits back on her haunches. "Well, I hope all that crap helped him more than it did me."

AT WORK, SHE DRAGS. She'd forgotten to ask Flora about the funeral. When she gets back, Pedro is slumped on the marble bench. If I get right into bed, she thinks, I'll be able to sleep. *Do it,* she orders herself. *Walk by.*

She sits down next to Pedro.

"I feel sick to my heart. Such a cold woman, Mr. Domengo's daughter. Every day, since his wife died, I visited him before I started work. I brought him groceries from my own refrigerator. Sweaters knitted by my own sister. When I told her I wanted to go to the funeral, do you know what she said? No funeral, he's too old." He rubs his chest. "Mrs. Lehrman, she told me the daughter gave his body to medical science. That this is what Mr. Domengo wanted. Still, they should have had a funeral. A great man like that."

Rena watches the entranceway, worried someone will come through and be angry that Pedro is not holding the door.

"A very important person. He went before the Congress when they had those hearings."

"You mean the House Un-American Activities Committee."

Pedro takes out his handkerchief. Ceremoniously, he blows his nose. "And she didn't even say good-bye to me. I didn't know she left until Mrs. Lehrman told me this morning." He points to a pile of mail on the table near the mailroom. "She didn't leave no forwarding address. All this mail and no address to send it."

"I'm sure someone must have Flora's address. I'll ask around."

She stands. When Pedro follows her, she assumes it's to press the elevator button. Instead, he takes the pile of Santiago's mail from the table and thrusts it into her arms with a vehemence that makes it clear that the mere presence of the letters is salt in a wound.

VISITING SAUL, SHE TELLS him that she has inherited Santiago's mail—that Pedro now puts it in her box. "What set Pedro over the top was Flora not having a funeral. He just kept shaking his head and saying, 'a great man like that.' "

"You see it all the time. Old people who sign their bodies over to medical schools because they're afraid no one will bury them."

"I'm going to have to dust off my Nancy Drew and try to find Flora's address."

"Santiago's neighbor, the one who set him up with the Guild for the Blind, you should ask her."

It's the first time in a long while that she's heard Saul's doctorly problem-solving voice. She studies his filled-out face. He appears oddly more prosperous than he did before going to prison.

"Jail suits you."

He looks at her in a way that makes her think he is going to make some sort of sexual innuendo. Please don't, she silently intones. Instead, he pulls out a photograph from his shirt pocket: a plump woman with small eyes and a flattened nose.

"Who's this?"

"Peg. A woman I've been corresponding with."

On second examination, the woman seems older. Something flutters inside her. It's not jealousy but the need to readjust the space between them.

"I met her through a prison correspondence club. Pen pals for convicts. She's one of those women who has the hots for men behind bars."

She's never heard Saul talk like this—with this touch of vulgarity. With her, he'd always been so delicate, talking about sex only in its spiritual and clinical aspects.

"Peg's been married twice to men in prison."

"What happens when they get out?"

"They get divorced, of course."

GRITA LEHRMAN OPENS the door dressed in house slippers and a cardigan sweater that falls off her shoulders as if still on the hanger. Her gray bun is askew in a way that leads Rena to suspect she's aroused Grita from an afternoon snooze.

"Yes, dear," the *dear* and the little smile intended, Rena sees, to hide the forgetting of her name.

"Rena. Your neighbor downstairs."

"Of course. Of course. Come in. I was just preparing my afternoon coffee."

Rena follows Grita into the living room. The apartment is the same line as her own, four stories below. Where in Rena's apartment the light spills in, splashing the walls, here, in the curtained rooms, it is more blue than yellow—muted and somehow sad.

"I'll fetch the coffee. Make yourself at home."

Rena sits on the couch, velvet with rolled arms and an embroidered shawl arranged over the top. The walls are covered with prints hung in stair-step clusters, each print suggesting a story: a painter friend who inhabits the Green Mountains, a watercolor Grita fell in love with at a little shop on Third Avenue bought by her husband as an unexpected gift. On the end tables are pieces of glass, ceramic bowls, a gourd, a sepia-tone family portrait that looks like it made an Atlantic crossing.

It's the kind of room Rena associates with Jewish people of Grita's age who consider themselves part of the broad band of the intelligentsia, who, no longer believing that religion brings meaning to life, have found in culture their organizing principle—the kind of room, Rena imagines, Leonard would have created had Klara not insisted on purchasing sets back in those early years before she'd abdicated as homemaker. Living room sets, a dining set, bedroom sets for themselves and the boys. An era when elegance was equated with achieving perfect matches: a matter of endurance and cunning to have found shoes the exact blue of the dress, wall-to-wall carpet the same pea soup green as the stripe in the sofa and chair. Only in Leonard's study, furnished with remnants from the furniture sets Klara had once replaced every few years, is there any hint of the aesthetics that would have enlivened him.

An ashtray from Peru. A strand of Indonesian paper fish. A photograph of the Mena House Hotel at Giza with the Cheops and Chephren pyramids looming behind.

"Just another minute, dear," Grita calls out.

Studying the Giza photograph on one of her rare visits to Leonard and Klara's house, Rena had remembered a time when she'd been fascinated by the pharaohs and the cities they'd erected for their dead. Young enough to still hold her mother's hand, she and Eleanor had walked in silence through the Egyptology collection of the De Young Museum, as beautiful a building as she'd ever seen, reading how wives, cats, gold and dishes had been buried with the pharaohs for use in the world beyond. It had seemed terrible and wonderful all at once, this life so many millennia ago, these relics now inside locked cases in the windowless room, cool and dark as the insides of the pyramids themselves. Emerging from the museum into the sun of Golden Gate Park and Eleanor's gay *Let's go to the teahouse,* and then, as if vaulting across the Indian Ocean, sitting on cushions on the floor of a pagoda perched by a rippling brook, all polished teak and rice paper dividers, trying to find the least expensive thing to order without letting her mother see that she knew the pot of tea they shared would leave them with little more than the bus fare home. Everything as unreal and distant as the pharaohs themselves or as the day itself, a day without Nick and his belches as he passed on the stairs.

Grita returns with two china cups filled with coffee. She holds the saucer in one hand as she takes hot gulps, gets right to the point about Flora Fahrsi. "She was a pill. I'd lent Santiago my tape player. I told her to keep it while she was there. She never even bothered to return it. Just left it on the floor with the door to the apartment open." She finishes her coffee in one long gulp. "Santiago loved both his wives in a way that would make anyone with an ounce of feeling weep. After the death of his first wife, Flora's mother, he wrote a eulogy for her that he published in an arts magazine in France about how she had danced with the Diaghilev Ballet when she was a girl and how she approached all of life with the same kind of grace. When I told Flora that her father had shown me the article, she shrugged her shoulders and said she'd never read it. The consciousness of a toad, that woman."

"I need to send her Santiago's mail. She didn't leave a forwarding address."

"Pedro told me. Santiago's lawyer, Brenda O'Hare of O'Hare & O'Hare, probably has it. Whether Flora will do anything, that's a different question."

SHE CALLS BRENDA O'HARE and, to her surprise, is put right through.

"The Cuban gentleman. Right, I remember. The blind professor who once taught Castro. Let's see."

Rena hears things being moved around.

"Here it is. An address in Riyadh."

Using Santiago's old typewriter, she writes a letter to Flora: undoubtedly, it has slipped Flora's mind to make arrangements for her father's mail; would she kindly confirm her address so that Rena can send what has collected and arrange for the post office to forward future pieces?

She sends the letter two-day delivery. Twelve days later, Flora calls. It's four in the morning on a Saturday night. She does not identify herself, but instead launches right in.

"I live in a tiny room. I have no space for all that junk, no money for these bills, these lousy leeching doctors. No time to write all his Communist friends. The word will get around soon enough that he is *did*."

"Did?"

"Just throw it all out."

Static fills the line. Either Flora has hung up or the connection has been lost.

In the afternoon, Rena xeroxes a notice stating that Santiago Domengo is deceased and no funds remain for paying his final bills. At first it's simple—bills, flyers from organizations for the blind, junk mail, all of which she clips to the notice and sends to the return address. Then a hand-addressed letter from Havana arrives. For a few days, she debates whether to do the same. The notice, though, seems so impersonal. She imagines the recipient reading the typed lines, leaning against a doorjamb.

She opens the letter. It's in Spanish in the large, loopy hand of a young person. Pedro translates for her. "It is, how do I say this, the godchild of a professor he used to work with in Cuba. She is planning to come here in the summer. She wants to stay with Mr. Domengo." The next day, Rena brings him paper and pen and, while she dictates, he translates her reply into Spanish.

SHE WALKS HOME from work the morning of her birthday. For a week, she's been dreading this day. A year since the bang on the door, since she watched the cops circle Saul. She counts the people who know: Ruth, Maggie, Leonard, Klara, Marc, Susan, Monk. Santiago. As for not telling her mother, it's not so much fear of being disappointed by Eleanor's response, the stretches when she could think of no one but herself long gone, as fear of herself—that buried wish to be someone's child, to be more vital to that someone than they are to themselves.

Like Saul is to Leonard. Like Bernardo was for Santiago.

Unlocking the door, she hears the phone ringing.

"Happy birthday, darling," her mother says.

Rena looks at her watch. It's four-fifteen in the morning California time. "What are you doing up at this hour?"

"Oh, I have all my little things I do before work. Yoga, the garden, writing in my journal."

"You just caught me. I just got home."

"You must be tired. Even when I was waitressing, I was never able to do that graveyard shift."

Her mother's voice is soft and even. Rena closes her eyes. She focuses her mind as though preparing to parachute into something unknown. "There's something I need to tell you," she says.

"Yes, darling."

"Is this an okay time for you? I could call later."

"It's fine. Is something the matter?"

"It's about Saul."

"Yes?"

"He's in prison. He was arrested a year ago." She braces herself for her mother's response. "Actually, it's exactly a year today. Some bad things happened at his job and he started using prescription drugs and it got out of hand. It's a long story. I'll tell you, just not this morning."

Eleanor is silent for a time during which Rena tries to imagine her mother now on the other end of the line, but can instead only see her pretty smile when they'd play cards both cross-legged on the rickety bed they'd shared over Nick's Ristorante, the broken blood vessels in her cheeks after they'd put her on medication and she'd eaten without cease until there'd been nothing she could fit in but an old Hawaiian muumuu, her desperate look when she'd crossed the street from Russell's house in her too-tight miniskirt.

"You should have told me, but I guess I understand why you didn't. Do you need anything?"

"No. I'm okay."

"Money?"

"No, Mom. I'm fine on that front."

"Maybe I could come visit?"

She hears the hesitancy in her mother's voice, and it takes her a moment to recognize that it's not conflicted generosity but a fear—after all these years—of intruding.

"I could come on the weekend."

Despite herself, Rena's eyes flood. She cannot remember when she and her mother were last alone, but then she thinks of the expense, of the months, the year perhaps, it would take her mother to pay off her credit-card bill.

"Thank you. Just knowing you would is a comfort."

AT THE END of the week, she calls Leonard and asks if she can go with him on Sunday when he visits Saul. She detects his surprise, is grateful that he doesn't comment on its being the first time they'll travel together. During the car ride up, she tells him about Flora's refusal to handle her father's mail.

"There's nothing like the wrath of an indignant child," he says. "Marc is more polished, but it's there underneath."

"What's he so angry about?"

"The same thing as Santiago's daughter. He blames me for what happened to his mother."

Rena drinks a cup of tea in the visitors' cafeteria while Leonard visits with Saul. Afterwards, they switch. Saul is chipper, joking about his ex-wife and his father becoming buddies.

"I told my mother about you," Rena says. "Your being here." He looks at her curiously, and she realizes it had not occurred to him that she would not have told Eleanor long before. "She's been very sweet and attentive, calling me every few days. She told Gene, and he called me and we talked about it. When I said I didn't want him worrying about me, he said, look, Sis, I'm not a kid anymore, I'm twenty. Which, of course, I knew, but it still surprised me."

"Ditto with your mother. You've always felt like she was a kid."

"True."

"Nothing like having your husband go to jail to put you on the right track."

As Rena comes in the door, Pedro waves a certified letter addressed to Santiago (for which he unthinkingly signed) under her nose.

She takes the letter to the marble bench, where Santiago used to rest summer evenings in his black glasses and black beret. She studies the envelope and the State Department seal on the front. Carefully, she opens the letter and reads the three typed paragraphs. She feels lightheaded, as if ether is being released from the paper. When she looks up, Pedro is tugging on his jacket sleeve. She reads the letter through again.

"They've found the remains of a body they think is Santiago's son. They say it matches the dental records they have on file. They're writing to say that Mr. Domengo or his delegated representative can claim the body."

Pedro crosses himself. "Fifteen years he waits for this, and then it happens three months after he dies."

She sends a copy of the letter to Flora with a note clipped to the top: "I understand that you have not wanted to be bothered with your father's correspondence, but I thought you would most certainly want to see this. Kindly call me collect to acknowledge receipt."

Two weeks later, Pedro hands the letter back to her. She waits until she's upstairs, seated at her kitchen table with a cup of tea and the phone in front of her, before she examines the envelope. It's covered with Arabic postmarks over which is stamped a red finger and the words MOVED. NO FORWARDING ADDRESS.

She picks up the phone. It takes three operators to reach someone who can give her the number for the American embassy in Riyadh, four transfers to find anyone who knew Flora Fahrsi.

"She never worked for us. Her husband ran a concession stand here up until last month. End of the month, he came in and said he wasn't going to renew."

"Do you know why?"

"Oh, I just assumed he moved on. There's a lot of turnover."

"Is there a forwarding address for him?"

"We don't keep that kind of information on people who have contracts with us."

Rena's eyes feel dry from fatigue. She presses her fingertips against the lids. "It's an urgent family matter. Wouldn't the embassy be able to help in some way?"

"I'm sorry. If she were a tourist here, we'd be able to look into it. Otherwise, no."

"Perhaps there's a number for him in the phone book? Maybe they're still in Riyadh."

"There are thousands of persons with the last name Fahrsi in Saudi Arabia. If you need further assistance, miss, you will need to contact the State Department."

With the *miss,* Rena hears that she has lost the sympathy of this woman six thousand miles away. She looks at her watch. It's almost five o'clock in Riyadh. Closing time.

She reads the letter again: Remains of a person identified from dental records to be Bernardo Domengo . . . found in a formaldehyde vat in the basement of the district morgue for the village of Nebaj and brought to a police morgue in Guatemala City. . . . Since the incident was classified as a hostile action against a United States citizen, the State Department will arrange for the return of the remains following claim in person by the next of kin or their designated representative.

Bernardo, Santiago had told her, had been doing his dissertation research on the atonal music of the Queche people near Nebaj. At first he'd rented a room in the *pensión,* but after his recording equipment was stolen, he moved into the barn of a family of weavers who lived outside the village.

"I was seventy-eight when my son disappeared. The American embassy sent one of their investigators, but he brought back nothing of use. Rumors that the guerrillas killed him because they thought he was a spy, rumors that he used to wander alone in the woods and had been eaten by wolves. They never thought I would go myself to try and find him."

Santiago held his head very still. "I cannot say what happened. Only that I know the army was involved. There was a journalist I met in Guatemala City who told me that the Guatemalan government kept track of every American living there and that the United States government let them see the FBI files. When we came back, we petitioned for Bernardo's FBI file. My son, who was never interested in politics, whose entire life was about music, who loved the music of daily life, songs never notated—the government of the country he was born in was keeping a file on him. Right on the top, first sentence, it said, Father: Cuban Communist. There were lists of the magazines my son subscribed to and the courses he took in college. An entire page on my contacts with Fidel Castro, all of it lies. So it was a farce, my asking the embassy to help me find Bernardo. They were in—how do you call it here—in bed with the killers."

Monk picks up on the first ring. He is silent as she tells him about Santiago and the State Department letter and how she cannot find Flora Fahrsi to let her know about Bernardo's body.

"Okay," he says when she reaches the end. "You're hitting me with a lot at once for nine-fifteen in the morning. The body they found of the boy in Guatemala is the brother of the woman in Saudi Arabia?"

"Yes. Well, actually, it's her half brother."

Monk makes a little whistle. "Let's slow down here. It's very nice of you to try and find this lady, but you don't stand a chance of getting the State Department involved. It would be one thing if she'd said she wanted her father's mail, but she didn't."

"Don't they want someone to claim the body?"

"There's no *they*. It's just one more task some low-level functionary has been assigned. He, or I guess it could be a she, doesn't give a damn about the Domengos. He just wants to be sure that everyone above him thinks he's doing a good job."

"Managing the disposal of dead bodies?"

He sighs. What was it that Ruth's sister had said about Monk's older brother? That he'd gone to Vietnam and come back without an arm? Or was it without his mind? She waits for Monk to say something biting like *Don't go getting sappy and sixtyish on me; go find some deadbeat hippie publication and send them a letter about the inhumanity of the war machine,* but all he says is "Yes. That's about the long and short of it."

"And what if you were to contact the embassy? Maybe they'd be more helpful if they knew a lawyer was involved."

Rena can hear him pushing his chair back from the desk, the squeak of the rollers on the plastic pad. She imagines his wrestler's legs, tendons like cables, being hefted up to the desk. "What makes you think the sister, half sister, whatever the hell she is, wants to claim this decomposed corpse?"

Rena thinks of Santiago and the way the lids were puffy over his eyes. "I'll pay you for your time."

Immediately, she fears that she has insulted him.

"It's not my business to waste people's money."

"For me, it's not a waste."

"I'll give it two days. Call me Thursday."

She recounts the money in the file cabinet: eleven thousand eight hundred dollars. Outside her window someone is doing trick turns in a speedboat, and for a moment she imagines it's Reed sending her a coded message. You're flipping out, she tells herself. Next thing, you'll be thinking the radio is broadcasting special messages to you.

"NO GO," MONK SAYS. "I went through all the brass in Riyadh and then to the State Department. They can't justify a search for Flora Fahrsi since there's no evidence that she's missing. She's what they call *absent*—someone who has removed themselves from communication."

"You told them why? About Bernardo's body needing to be claimed?"

"I tried the 'one hand washing the other' routine—that this was their affair in Guatemala that they could clean up if they'd put in the legwork in Riyadh, but they didn't bite. The only thing they said they could do was to allow an exception to the rules of claim."

"What does that mean?"

"If it could be documented that Flora Fahrsi is the sole living relative and that she cannot be reached, friends of the deceased or of the family would be permitted to claim the body." Monk snorts. "After a truckload of notarized triple-stamped paperwork."

She pulls a chair out from the kitchen table, holds herself back from saying she's glad he is getting such a chuckle out of all this.

"How's your little boy?" she asks.

"He's fine. About to finish his first year of preschool."

"How old is he now?"

"Four. Going on sixteen." He laughs the laugh of parents dying to tell the cute stories about their kids they know better than to tell.

"Bernardo was his only son." It's a low blow and she knows it.

Monk makes chewing sounds. Or are they spitting sounds? Something with his mouth.

"Who do I contact?" she asks.

"For what?"

"To get permission to claim the body." She looks down at her hands. They're shaking. This is just a piece of theater, she thinks. I'm just trying this out on Monk.

"Christ, Rena, don't go cracking up on me here. How many months has it been? February, March, April. Fourteen months. Look, you come down tomorrow and we'll have lunch, okay? I'll take you out for Irish corned beef and cabbage, and we'll talk it over."

His voice has turned soft and pillowy, and she thinks how nice it would be to sit with him in a dark wood-paneled bar, drinking and saying nothing.

"Meet me here at one."

She's seen only one picture of Bernardo. Santiago had extracted a dog-eared photograph from his wallet. A thin face framed with glossy black hair. Brown eyes. A cleft in the chin. At the time, she'd wondered if Santiago had ever seen the photograph—if the little tears and creases, the scratch that ran diagonally across the face, were from his pressing it to his cheek as he did that day.

"I have to do it," she says. "I have no choice."

11 Leonard

I believe that every life has a navel, a center point from which everything else evolves. As a teenager, you were fascinated by those fringes of physics where time is viewed as a Möbius strip curving back on itself. How can this be, I imagine you asking, that what comes after could determine what comes before? This is not, though, what I mean. Nothing mechanical, no crystal balls. Rather, we organize the stories we tell about ourselves around that navel so that what came before is seen in relation to that point as much as what comes after.

For me, that navel is Maria. You would be confused, I know, to hear me say this—a name you have never heard me speak. But how could I have told you about her? Besides, even I can see that she is irrelevant. By this, I mean it is not the she whom I knew for only nine months and haven't seen in thirty years—I don't even know if she's still alive—but the she who lived then and lives now in my mind.

I practice this speech as I prepare for my trip to see you tomorrow, an unscheduled visit prompted by Monk's call yesterday afternoon. "She's losing it," Monk said. "Your daughter-in-law. This happens. They hold on tight while it's an emergency, and then they fall apart. She wants to claim a body from a morgue in Guatemala City. A graduate student murdered in the seventies."

"They found the son?"

"You knew the neighbor?"

"He was a teacher of Saul's. I met him once."

"Right, right. I forgot about that part. Well, I thought you'd want to know."

For a few moments after I put the phone down, I imagine myself as the protagonist of a Mexican melodrama. Rescuing the beautiful widow of my dead younger brother. Murdered, aren't they usually murdered? Murdered younger brother. Not imprisoned son. Then I called her. Listened while she told me about the letter from the State Department, the failed attempt to contact the ghoulish daughter.

"I know this sounds like I'm trying to be Mother Teresa or some such thing," she says, "but you tell me, what would you do in my shoes?"

Nothing. Goddamn nothing.

You will be surprised, I know, to see me on a Thursday. I'm not sure if the visit will please you. "It's an odd kind of loneliness, here," you've told me. "Surrounded always by people, so that I would give any sum of money for an hour a day of solitude, and yet completely alone." Uncertain, I make only a cursory attempt to call you first, giving up after ten minutes of pressing the redial button. Instead, I prepare for tomorrow's absence from your mother. Put on my old corduroy coat and drive to the A & P to buy a chicken and lettuce. Roast the chicken the way my mother did with cut-up potatoes and onions in the pan and a piece of cooking string tied in a bow around the legs. Wash the lettuce—half for tonight's meal, half for tomorrow's—add the garlic croutons your mother likes. Fix her dinner tray. Help her into her armchair, set up the lap desk I bought for her birthday, place the tray on top.

"Aren't you going to eat?" she asks.

I shake my head no, grateful that she is not one of those women who cannot bear to eat unless there is someone with them eating more heartily than they.

She is watching a magazine show, an exposé of a car company that knew two years before five people died from locked brake rotors that there was a defect. I wait for the commercial.

"I'm going to go see Saul tomorrow."

Her mouth tautens, mid-chew. Fleetingly, I entertain the idea that it is feeling for you, that she will say, *I'll come, I want to see him,* but then she lifts the thighbone to her mouth and arranges it so her tongue can reach the fatty morsel wedged behind the cartilage and I know that what she is thinking about is who will make her meals and the unease that overtakes her on being alone in the house.

"I'll cut up the rest of the chicken so all you have to do is warm it in the microwave. And there's washed lettuce in the vegetable crisper. I'll be back by eight."

She glares at me, the thighbone midair between her glistening mouth and the plate.

"I can ask Mrs. Smiley to come for the day."

She wipes her mouth with the pink cloth napkin, shakes her head with a violence intended to communicate that she'd starve to death before submitting again to Mrs. Smiley. She turns back to the television screen and for the first time in the more than twenty years since she assumed this invalid role, it strikes me as having a kind of backbone to it, some principle to which your mother is sacrificing herself, and I have to refrain from smiling at the old girl.

YOU'RE CLEANLY SHAVEN, and there's something different, more erect, about your posture. You stick a hand in your pocket and pull out a candy wrapped in silver foil. A chocolate toffee, the same kind I buy your mother by the bagful every week at the grocery store.

"Here," you say. "Mom sends them to me."

I look at the silver foil, confused, trying to imagine how she even got your address or the envelope or the stamps. "She's been writing you?"

"I guess you could call it that. She tapes the candies, two or three at a time, to a piece of pink stationery and sticks them in an envelope. They used to open each one to check if they were drugs, but the guards now know they're the toffees from Mom. I don't eat them. Just carry them around to give the guys when they look like they're going over the edge."

You hold the toffee between your thumb and forefinger. I watch you slip into your middle gaze, an expression that used to disarm your grade school teachers, who mistook it for insouciance.

"It's odd, when you think about it, how arbitrary what we call a drug is. Mom is as addicted to these candies as I ever was to my pills. The pharmacologists have all these criteria about tolerance and withdrawal that they get around when they need to by allowing for psychological dependence. But in the end what we call a drug boils down to money. Half the countries in South America, if we didn't threaten to cut off aid, would have long ago legalized marijuana and cocaine. And their governments would be a lot better off, not just because of the tax dollars but also because of all the money lost on enforcement, all the corruption illegality breeds."

You tap the table and I study your hands, the way they've roughened from manual work. "Still working in the kitchen?" I ask, not in the mood to debate the legalization of drugs or the social structure of prohibitions.

You look at me.

Sorry, I want to say. I just can't do it today.

I think of all the betrayals we foist on those we love—of the way trust deteriorates, tooth by tooth, joint by joint. For years, I couldn't forgive your mother for crying the day my mother died: for crying for herself and the way my mother's death revived her feelings about her father's death five years before, for forcing me to attend to her grief over mine. "I just can't handle it," she said, and I thought, no, you just *won't* handle it—the perversity of our therapeutic culture where the awareness of self wipes away common decency so that your mother no longer felt obliged, even ceremonially, even on the day of my mother's death, to let my emotions be in the foreground. I know you would consider it foolish denial to not allow that the self is the vortex of each of our universes. *Isn't that what ultimately allows for personal freedom?* you would say. *By placing the self center stage, we are forced to acknowledge that we are masters of our own destinies.* Yes, I would counter. But does that not mean that we have the will to yield that center at times to another?

"I'm rising through the ranks. Off pots and onto dishes. There are dishwashers for the plates and flatware so it's a lot easier. If I stay long enough, I'll get to be a cook."

My jaw locks. What was it Monk said about days off for good behavior? Some kind of formula. What I can't remember is if the opposite is true—days added for bad.

"Just kidding." Oh, I see. A little revenge for throwing water on your sociology of drugs dissertation.

"I'm a model inmate. An exemplar of penal rehabilitation. Now that I've earned C-level privileges, I can go to the library on my own. Most of the white-collars end up in Danbury, but there are a couple others here. A chiropractor in for insurance fraud, an accountant for embezzling, an engineer convicted on a manslaughter charge. We've formed a club: The Fallen. Prisoners need an officially declared and approved reason to convene, so we've constituted ourselves as a reading group. The only thing we could get four copies of here is the Bible, so that's what we're reading."

The guard presses his nose against the wired glass. He holds up five fingers. I wonder if they hate you white-collar guys more than the others or if it's like in school where the teachers seemed to be in awe of the rich kids, as though wealth were a special talent.

"Rena told you about wanting to go to Guatemala," you say.

"Actually, Morton's the one who told me. I called her after that."

You look me in the eye, the way you did as a very young child when you'd say things that at the time seemed preternaturally true. "You should go with her."

I gape at you, rooted in that swampy place of understanding but not understanding what you mean.

"To Guatemala. You speak Spanish. It would help her to have someone along who knows the language."

There's a jangle of keys as the guard opens the door. You twist around to look.

"Time, Dubinsky."

"Two minutes," you say.

"One. And that's my watch that's ticking."

You stand. "I would feel better if you went."

I, who've never left this country, who, for that matter, rarely leaves the eastern seaboard, feel too stunned to respond. That it's absurd for Rena to go? That it's even more absurd for me?

"Trust me," you say, and then, glancing down at your inmate's uniform, you smile bemusedly. "It's the right thing to do."

Out in the hallway, the guard is whistling. "I could never leave your mother for that long."

"Mrs. Smiley could stay with her."

"Now that I've spoiled her, she'd never accept going back to Mrs. Smiley's regimen."

"I'll handle Mom." You pause. "If I handle her, you'll go?"

I laugh. "Sure."

The guard pokes his head in. "Okay, Dubinsky. None of your dawdling." He pulls the metal door open. We exit, first you, then me, in accord with the visitation rules. In the second while he circles behind us, you hold out your pinkie finger. Quickly, I crook my own in yours.

"Deal," you say, as it dawns on me that this is not a philosophical debate. You've ambushed me.

IN THE MIDDLE of the night, I wake with my sister Lil on my mind. I cannot remember when we last spoke. Years. Shortly after you were married, when I called to tell her the news. Now I remember. She asked questions about Rena that I couldn't answer. She the film producer, me the psychiatrist, and yet it was she who put into focus how little I knew: the father, the route from waitress's daughter to Yale.

How can it be that four years have passed since we've spoken? Weeks, months, years gone by without my making a phone call. For a long time, I thought the distance between all of us was a thick hide acquired after my sister Eunice's death. None of us grown: Rose just twenty-one, Lil only eighteen, me barely fourteen. Eunice, a tall nineteen-year-old with round everything and red hair gathered into a ponytail. It was summer, and Rose had taught Eunice how to trick the maître d' at the Catskills hotel where they both worked into thinking she'd complied with the stockings requirement by using an eyebrow pencil to draw a line up the back of each leg to look like a seam. A boy, a place one drove to for drinking and dancing, a car crash.

For the next year, Rose could not sleep and Lil could not eat. My mother ran herself to distraction trying to engineer things so Rose might sleep: dinner early, but not too early; plenty of exercise but not overexertion. For Lil, schmaltz drizzled on her potatoes and cream mixed into her milk. I tried to stay out of the way, feeling that it was not my right to grieve as openly as my sisters. They'd been *the girls*. Three of them in the span of three years. I was the son, born four years later. They belonged to each other whereas I belonged to Lil alone, who, when I was a baby, would stick out her arms if Eunice or Rose would approach me and yell, *no, he's mine*. She'd taught me to walk, taught me my letters, my numbers, how to hit a baseball, tie a tie, kiss a girl, write a love letter.

On the first anniversary of Eunice's death, we traveled to the cemetery for the unveiling of her headstone. It was the same design my mother had selected for my father, only smaller. Afterwards, my mother caused a scandal among the aunts and uncles and cousins by not inviting anyone to the house. Poor Uncle Jack had probably spent the trip out to Queens consoling himself with thoughts of the creamed herring and nova to come. "I need to talk with my children," my mother announced.

Back in the apartment, my mother called us into the living room. Holding her back straight, she assumed her position on the sofa. Only the tips of her shoes reached the floor. She patted the worn mustard cushion at her side, motioning for me to sit beside her. Rose sat in the green wing chair. With her permed hair and bloodred lipstick and fake beauty mark, she looked more like the matriarch than our diminutive mother. Lil lowered herself onto the rug, her long legs curled under her emaciated frame. It was July, and a fan whirred on the table where my father's picture was displayed. My mother held my hand. "The one blessing in all of this," she said, "is that your father died first. Every day

I thank God that he did not have to endure the loss of a child." Her eyes pooled and her voice grew hoarse, and for the first time since Eunice's death I feared she might break into inconsolable sobs. But she did not. Instead, she opened the top button on her navy crepe dress. There was a lace-edged collar and pearl buttons that rose up from a cloth-covered belt. "Now, children," she said, "it is time for us to move on. I do not want to see any more long faces. No more tears. We cannot all six of us die."

By the end of the year, Lil was married to Moishe, a gawky thirty-year-old who would in the next few years make a fortune by convincing his father to convert their drapery factory to the wartime production of parachutes. She was so thin that no matter how many times my mother took in her wedding gown, she looked like a kid playing dress-up. Desperate to flee the constant talk in our household about what was happening in Poland and Germany, Rose took a job, room and board provided, at a girls' day school in Connecticut, and only my mother and I were left in the apartment.

For ten years, my mother and I lived, just the two of us, in that apartment: three years I spent at the Bronx High School of Science, three years I raced through City College, four years of medical school. Although when Jack had promised to pay my tuition for medical school, he'd never said it was contingent on my living at home, my living at home allowed his daily visits to remain safely sanctioned under the guise of a brother-in-law who'd assumed responsibility for a widowed sister-in-law's family. Countless nights, I pecked my mother's cheek as she headed off on Jack's arm, my Aunt Mindyl, by then so fat and diabetic she rarely left the house, happy to have her younger sister accompany her still healthy husband to the opera and theater and symphony.

("It is your fear of discovering your identification with your Uncle Jack that is leading you to quit your analysis," Merckin later proclaimed. "The way that you both triumphed over your father when his death left you the men of the household." As for my claim that without my job, which I quit following Maria's suicide attempt, I could no longer afford Merckin's fee at five times per week, he swatted it away like a pesky fly. Furious, I refused to admit that he was in his clumsy way close to the mark, that I felt with Maria like Jack putting on his thin show of propriety.)

My sisters came home for holidays and birthdays and occasional Saturday afternoons, but there was a cautiousness between us. Lil's husband was taciturn. Rose's goyim boyfriends before she married your Uncle Syd were all boys who'd ended up as teachers at her school by default, too dissolute or dull to manage in the worlds of commerce and law where their brothers and college classmates now worked, saved from the war by flat feet or myopic eyes. And, jumping ahead, neither of my sisters ever liked your mother. How could they, the way she talked incessantly about the way *she'd* grown up, *unlike Leonard,* she'd say right to their faces as though that didn't mean unlike them too.

Still, I was devastated when Lil and her husband moved to San Diego shortly before Marc was born. Moishe, who had by then inherited his father's business, had the wherewithal not to talk about it in front of us, but it was clear that the move was a way to avoid the unions. In San Diego, there was cheap Mexican labor and, Lil wrote, gorgeous light. She took up painting, set up a studio in what had been the guest cottage of the La Jolla property they bought. A year later, Moishe died. She was thirty-five and he left everything to her. Before this, your mother had been able to think of Lil as the poor wife of a rich man, but once the money was Lil's alone your mother grew green with envy. Shamelessly, she courted Lil, to whom she'd barely spoken before. Every few weeks, she would make a trip to the post office to send off a missive: cards and books and toffees. A nightgown purchased at the local lingerie store. An invitation to join us for the holidays. Lil never responded due, I was certain, to her distaste for the evident falseness. For my part, I was mortified that she might think I was somehow involved.

My mother began spending the winters in San Diego with Lil. Through her, I learned that Lil's hair had gone gray early and that she'd taken to wearing beautiful trousers that suited her slender form. She took a course in set design, went to work for one of the studios that was still using painted backdrops in its films, and moved to Venice, the artists' enclave in Los Angeles, where she could run her dachshund on the beach. In her forties, she sold Moishe's business and opened a production company that made documentary films.

One of Lil's first films was about Japanese families, laborers living since the turn of the century in the San Joaquin valley. Perhaps you remember the afternoon we took the copy she'd sent us to the public library, where we watched it on a projector set up in a room in the basement. What I remember is sitting in the dark, trying to untangle how your entire lifetime had passed with Lil and I having hardly anything to do with each other. Yes, there was your mother's condition, but why had I not taken you boys there over the summers? The best I'd been able to come up with was an odd resentment that had developed between Lil and me such that it was unclear who had abandoned whom. The silences had become our communication: a ringing accusation. On my part, too, there was an illusion, as if time did not exist, as though all of this were happening in some interlude outside of real life. Lil and I, who had loved each other as children, who had shared a cot when we'd lived in Jack and Mindyl's dining room, were not *really* estranged. Our lives were not *really* passing with nothing to do with one another.

After this, I wrote her, telling her how much I'd admired the film and how badly I felt that we had drifted so far apart. She wrote back thanking me for my kind words and indicating a reciprocity of sentiments. But neither of us had possessed the wisdom to see that extra effort would be needed. Again, foolishly, we acted as if it were only practicalities that kept us from talking with each other—time differences that interfered with phone calls. At my mother's funeral, Lil and Rose and I hugged and vowed to stay in closer touch now. Afterwards, we all went to Rose's house in White Plains. Even though we lived less than fifty miles away, you and Marc had been there on only a couple of occasions. You'd forgotten the feline decor. Cat wallpaper in the bathroom. Coffee served out of mugs painted with pictures of cats. A cabinet filled with porcelain cats. Sitting with my plate of food, I watched the relatives studying Lil with begrudging admiration: her black pantsuit and expensive flats. Her gray hair cut in a way that made the face below appear unexpectedly young. Later, scrutinizing Lil in the photographs taken that day, your mother declared, "She's a lesbian, you can tell, from the way she holds her cigarette. And why is there no man? A woman as good-looking as that?"

I get out of bed and go downstairs to my study. I look up Lil's number. Outside, I can see the outlines of the Japanese maple, just starting to bud. I push the buttons.

It's the voice of an old woman on the other end of the line.

"Lil?"

There's a pause. Not more than a few seconds, but the sign of a lifetime passed since each other's voice and smell were as familiar to us as our own. "Lenny?" A space just long enough to allow this to serve as a question. "Lenny, is everything all right?"

"No, I mean yes. No, there's not a problem. Yes, everything is all right." Idiot. How could I have not realized that it would scare her to have me call at this hour?

"You frightened me. I thought . . ."

"Someone had croaked."

She laughs. "Well, if you have to put it that way. Still, we are getting to that age."

"I just wanted to talk with you."

"It must be two in the morning your time."

"I couldn't sleep. I was thinking about all of us, when we lived with Jack and Mindyl."

There's a moment's silence during which I fear that I've offended her by assuming too intimate a tone or hurt her by pressing against something she'd rather not touch.

"You know what I remember the most about that room?" she says. "The way there were four layers of molding. I used to lie awake studying the design. I can still remember the sequence."

"How's everything? How are you?"

"Oh, I'm getting old. It's been a winter of the flesh giving out on me.

Arthritis in my hands. Cataracts in my eyes. Now they say my hip is going." She laughs again. It's eerie. The same laugh as our mother. The refusal to take oneself too seriously. "I figure we don't have longevity in our genes. Papa died when he was forty-three. Mama made it to seventy-six. I think I'm hitting that obsolete stage."

"It was the times. Today they would have resuscitated him, done a bypass and put him on medication."

"How's Rose?"

"I haven't talked with her in a while. She calls Klara every month or so, but I only hear about it afterwards."

Lil sighs. "Who would have ever thunk?"

"Yeah, who would have ever thunk." My breathing feels labored, as if the lost decades have lodged in the bottom of my lungs. I long to put my arms around Lil, for us to hold each other the way we did when we were kids. "Lil, how has this happened? That we've grown so apart?"

"I don't know. Sometimes I blame myself for having moved out here."

"It's no more your fault than mine."

"Rose . . . well, you know Rose. I wouldn't see her other than holidays even if I'd stayed back east. Those cats, that kitsch, kitsch, kitsch. But us, do you think we would be close?"

I can imagine Lil living in an apartment in the Village, going out for early dinners with her. Maybe having a Philharmonic subscription together.

"I worry about you. The situation with Klara. How hard that must be."

"I worry about you."

"Why?"

"Living alone. Out there in wild Califor-nee."

"People always think there's something hard about living alone. But it's so much easier than living with someone. I just read a proposal for a documentary on these highly developed monkeys from an island near Bali. They go back and forth between living in multigenerational groups where the babies are raised and being what the filmmaker calls free agents. Existing independently on the periphery of these groups. That's what I am. A free agent."

Another pause. "So tell me, how are the boys?"

I stare at the photograph of the pyramids at Giza that hangs over my desk. Clearly, I knew when I telephoned her that she would ask this question and I see now that this is why I have called her: to tell her about you.

So I tell her. It might as well be the first telling, since other than your mother and brother I have not told anyone. And she's wonderful. She grasps immediately what I can only call the sweep of it all. The tragic quality—a good boy gone wrong without ever going bad.

"He's like you, Lenny. One of those sweet souls who attract bees like honey. Your thing was Klara, getting tangled up with her."

"And now there's something else. Rena has got herself involved in a situation with an old professor of Saul's, a blind guy whose son disappeared fifteen years ago in Guatemala. The old guy died, and now they've found the son's body and she wants to bring it back and bury it."

"You're not talking about Santiago Domengo?"

"You knew him?"

"I knew the son's girlfriend—well, it wasn't even clear that she'd been his girlfriend, only that she'd been in love with him. She wanted to make a film about what happened. About the father and his relationship with Castro and whether the CIA was involved. It was fascinating. She wanted to include these tapes the son had made of the indigenous music in the area he'd been studying. Letters he'd sent her. Reports from the private detectives the parents had hired to try and find out what happened. Only she was so addled about the whole thing, there was no way to figure out what was fact and what was fantasy. This was maybe ten years ago. More. My lawyer said it was a landmine for lawsuits. She showed me a videotaped interview she did with the parents. The father had just gone blind and the mother, if I remember correctly, was an opera singer."

"Something like that."

"That story has bothered me ever since. The idea that certain people are too emotional to be heard. I've always thought it was a failure of nerve on my part not to do it."

"Not only is Saul not discouraging Rena, he wants me to go with her. To help out since I speak Spanish."

I laugh. I wait for Lil to join me. There's a tapping sound. Her fingers on the bedside table?

My sister clears her throat. I clutch the receiver.

"Do it, Lenny. You should do it."

Part Three

EL HOYO

12 Rena

Driving north from La Aurora, the airport set smack in the center of the city, past the BEBA COCA-COLA billboards, past the workers' residences built after the 1976 earthquake, the sun beating like Hades on the black roof of the taxi, her nostrils inflamed from the smell of garbage, Rena thinks: it's like walking into someone else's nightmare.

At the airport information center, she'd heard Leonard's careful Spanish, the *r*'s rolling cautiously off his tongue, as he talked with a woman in a plum blouse under whose unbreathing fabric the skin must be hot and wet as spilt tea. Slowly, the woman telephoned hotels in search of a room, finding two, she said, *imposible*. Rena had held herself back from insisting that a shared room was out of the question, afraid of both insulting Leonard and dissolving the already feeble commitment the woman had to assisting them, her anxiety not so much about physical privacy (Leonard had spent the night at her apartment, seen her in pajamas) but about how she would manage without a respite from conversation.

The rearview mirror rattles with dangling crosses, miniature dolls, Christmas tinsel. At the *posada* on the outskirts of Zona Uno, Leonard pays the driver from the wad of quetzals she handed him after exchanging money at the airport, a compromise, Leonard having wanted to pay his own way and Rena having wanted to pay for them both: he would handle his airline ticket, she would do the rest. ("Are you sure you can manage?" he'd asked, tempting her to reveal the money from Reed, but she'd held firm to her resolve that if she were going to keep it, she could not put anyone in the position of knowing about it.)

The driver hands Leonard their bags, one filled with papers from the State Department documenting her designation as guardian of Bernardo's remains. Dressed in his khaki fisherman's vest and leather sandals, Leonard looks younger and somehow taller, as if leaving New Jersey has let him finally stretch his limbs. Rena raps the brass knocker on the door of the *posada* and turns the handle. They enter a dark anteroom with a mahogany counter and a row of plastic chairs. An archway leads to a corridor opening into the courtyard. On the wall, there's a bulletin board with photos of Anglo couples holding Indian babies. A notice covered with cellophane describes in English the *posada* policies:

1. Every room with crib and baby bathtub.
2. Stove in kitchen for warming bottles.
3. Use bins in refrigerator. Each one marked with room number.

DO NOT KEEP FOODS IN ROOM.

While Leonard fills out their registration forms, Rena investigates the courtyard. Chipped bricks, a dilapidated palm tree, a fountain drizzling green water, but also a wall brilliant with bougainvillea, beds of geraniums, a miniature orange tree. In the distance, she can see the tops of a few higher buildings. Her throat is scratchy and her eyes burn. Ozone? "Guatemala City is the ozone capital of Central America," Saul had written in the notebook, *One Hundred Facts about Guatemala, Useful and Otherwise,* he'd sent her before she left.

A white woman with frizzy black hair and a long cotton skirt steps out from a room across the courtyard. She's holding a brown baby dressed in a diaper and pink top. She squints in the sunlight. A balding man follows with a baby carrier strapped around his middle. He pulls a key from a pocket in the hem of his shorts and begins to do battle with the lock.

The woman spots Rena. As she approaches, the gray at her temples becomes visible and Rena can hear the baby's whimpering. Cover her head, Rena wants to say. The midday sun, the heat.

"Hi. I'm Sonia. And that's Hank over there, trying to lock that damn door." The baby kicks the hot air, attempting to move from the squished position in which it's stuck. Sonia makes clucking sounds. "Poor thing. I know your tummy hurts. A parasite. They finally diagnosed it, thank God, but the medicine makes it hurt even more for the first week or two. You're not here for a baby, are you?"

Rena's head throbs from the heat. "Excuse me?"

"We saw you get out of the cab. You can tell by the number of suitcases. You should have seen us. What with the diapers and the clothes and the bottles and the formula, we had nine bags."

Leonard comes into the courtyard as Hank turns from the door. Hank's T-shirt clings to his stomach in a large, wet oval. He pulls at the waistband of the baby carrier.

"Great vest," Hank says to Leonard. "A thief would need a crowbar to get into that."

"Thanks. My wife found it in a catalog."

"Maybe you could give me the name," Hank says to Rena.

Rena glances at Leonard, who looks at his feet. "This is my father-in-law, Leonard, Dr. Dubinsky." She pauses, afraid the *Dr.* sounds pompous.

"And you're . . ."

"Rena. I'm sorry, I'm confused. What kind of hotel is this?"

Sonia laughs. "It's what they call an adoption hotel—for people who come to spend the six weeks you need to stay in the country before you can take a baby back. The agencies all know about this place. There's a second one, too, run by the owner's sister in Zona Nueve. That one's really nice, but expensive. We've been here four weeks. We timed it for the summer so Hank, he's a university professor, could come."

The baby's fussing escalates to a cry. "Time for el snuggly," Sonia says.

Rena imagines the baby sunk inside the pouch and then strapped against Hank's hot chest. She reaches out her arms. "Can I hold her?"

"Him. The pink shirt is a hand-me-down from my sister." Sonia gives Rena the baby. "For how many hours? This kid needs to be held round the clock. I'm not joking. He must sleep with one eye open, because he starts to scream if we even *try* to put him down."

Rena lifts the baby onto her shoulder. He molds himself against her breastbone and breathes into the hollow in her neck. "How old is he?"

"Eight weeks. Well, he was three weeks premature, so he's really like five weeks old."

Rena makes little circles on the baby's back. Slowly his breathing steadies and his cries abate. He burps. "Oh, you needed a little burpy, huh?" she coos.

"You look like you have kids," Sonia says.

"No. But I helped raise my half brother. I was fifteen when he was born."

"It's great to have a doctor in the house," Sonia says, touching Leonard's arm. "You can tell us what this medicine is they have us giving him. He screams bloody murder for an hour afterwards. I keep thinking it's turpentine or something barbaric like that."

"You're probably more up to date than I am. I teach the history of medicine and haven't seen patients in almost forty years. But you can sign me up for the baby-holding brigade. That, I remember."

The baby's limbs grow limp and heavy. Twisting her head, Rena sees his eyes beginning to close. She inhales the baby smell: potpourri of sour milk, talcum powder and perspiration. "What's his name?"

"Carlos," Sonia says. "After William Carlos Williams."

"He's so precious," Rena says.

Sonia's eyes fill with tears. "You think so? When you're down here with no one else to fuss over the baby, you can't help wondering. I know it's awful to say, but you don't think his nose is too wide, do you?"

"No, he's sweet sweet sweet." Rena kisses the top of the baby's head. It scratches as though his hair had been shaved.

"Sweet sweet sweet," Sonia echoes. She reaches out her arms for the sleeping baby. "Like Williams' plums."

THEY EAT IN A little restaurant with oilcloth on the tables and the owners' children playing in the corner. Rena studies the menu, settling finally on eggs and beans. When the eggs come, they're too runny, the yolks like melted sherbet. The juice is so thick with sugar, it's almost gritty. She eats the tortillas, drinks some bottled water.

It's a relief to find that Leonard is at ease with silence. The human voice, Saul told her a supervisor of his had once admonished, is a musical instrument, not a noisemaker. With Beersden, she'd incorrectly assumed that as a musician he would naturally understand that silences are simply part of the flow of being with someone else. "The rest in music," Beersden countered, "is the most meaningful part of the phrase, where the tension resides." Indeed, his own sullen silences had been downright noisy in their accusation of her distance and slights.

To Rena's surprise, no one but Monk had tried to dissuade her from making the trip. But then, with Monk, there'd been something sexual mixed up with it, so palpable sitting across from him in the pub where he took her for corned beef and cabbage that the butterflies went berserk in her stomach and she was unable to do anything more with the fatty food than push it around on the plate. Other than his thick hand grazing her shoulder as he reached over her to push open the door, they neither touched nor talked about anything except Saul and what Monk called *this dead body insanity*. Repeating Santiago's words about a body needing a resting place, she tried to explain what she needed to do. Monk leaned back, his shoulders splayed across the cracked red leather of the booth. She could feel him studying her: her hair then in that awkward in-between stage so that she had to keep pushing it out of her eyes, the points of her clavicle evident beneath her sweater. In bed, their toes would brush if their tongues were locked. Nearly the same height, but he with twice her breadth. Inside, she laughed at the bittersweet paradox. What attracted her was the strength of Monk's convictions. Never would he breach his relationship with Saul by sleeping with her.

"Look," he said, "I'm a Catholic. And not totally lapsed, either. We believe in last rites. No one I knew had parents who even thought about college money. But we all had our plots paid for before we finished catechism classes. The way I look at it, there's a statute of limitations on burial obligations. That corpse is fifteen years cold now. Trust me, God has moved on to other things."

Now what she thinks about is not the need to bury Bernardo but Santiago's grief. She'd never seen grief like that. Not Ascher's grief when they had to call it quits. That had been a sweet, almost sexual pain. Not Max when Rebecca died. That had been a deep but anticipated loss. Not Eleanor when Joe died. That had been pure rage and fear. Not Saul after Mitch jumped in front of a train. That had been the endless reverberations of guilt. No, Santiago's grief belonged to the world of begats, to the world where hair can whiten in an instant and sinners are turned to salt. A father blinded, a mother's heart stopped.

Leonard wipes his mouth with a napkin from the metal dispenser. A scrawny chicken leg and thigh float before him in a bowl of greasy broth. She notices how beautiful his table manners are, the way he navigates his knife and fork in the slippery bowl. Who taught him this? His mother? Klara? He looks at her inquisitively, as though sensing her unvoiced question. She lowers her eyes to the congealed yellow pool on her plate.

SHE WAKES TO the sound of a baby screaming. Short, high cries. She sits upright, her feet moving to the floor, that automatic gesture from Gene's infancy when she had started with every noise. Her thoughts gyrate, a needle wildly searching for its groove, as she tries to orient herself. *La Posada de las Madres*. Yesterday she had not understood the meaning. *Zona Uno, Guate*. There's a note propped on Leonard's bed: "Went to get coffee." She'd not thought she'd be able to sleep in the same room as Leonard, but she has no recollections beyond the moment when she lifted from her pillow to turn off the bedside lamp.

She showers under a trickle of lukewarm water, surveying the care Leonard has taken with his things, nothing left out except for his toothbrush and toothpaste set neatly on the rickety wooden table. Shannon,

ate, would on occasion take the train to New York
at the Plaza with her father, in the city on business.
had imagined these visits: Shannon and her father each
own queen-size beds, Shannon talking to her father
d at the extravagantly lit mirror.

s her tote bag with the State Department papers, a map
nd a guidebook, and steps into the courtyard to wait for
blond couple passes a diaper bag, baby carrier and baby be-
m. The screams have stopped, but all around her she can hear
mpers, the sounds of newborns who no more know what they
need than the anxious parents hovering over them.

THEY SIT IN THE annex to the American embassy, a concrete
ker built after the earthquake, across from the assistant to the as-
tant ambassador. Drops of perspiration roll down his pockmarked
row—the fact that he was appointed to this position evidence enough, Rena thinks, of what an unimportant outpost it is deemed. Alternately, he smiles and frowns as he flips through the papers she has given him. He sorts them into stacks that he then reshuffles. She tries to discern a rationale for what he is doing, but in the end all the papers end up in one pile, only out of order. He leans back in his chair to open the middle desk drawer and pulls out an ink stamp with which he smears each page. He then pushes a buzzer and speaks in Spanish over the intercom. A few minutes later, a young woman appears with a piece of paper pinched between her forefinger and thumb. He reads it slowly before handing it to Rena.

"You go next to see the minister of police of Zona Cuatro. Señor Perez. You should have no trouble with him. He studied at the Officers' Academy in the States. He is very cooperative with us. The body is in the morgue there. This paper states that you have been designated as custodian of the remains. So it's now between you and Señor Perez as to how they will be released to you. As a courtesy to an American citizen, we can provide transport of the body on a military flight. The private airlines will also do it—for a fee, of course."

"I plan to have the body cremated," Rena says.

She sees that Leonard is taken aback, realizes that they have no fact, discussed the details beyond claiming the body.

"Well, that makes it easy." The assistant to the assistant ambassad reaches a clammy hand across the desk, a silly expectant expression his face as though he is waiting now to be praised.

In the lobby, Leonard asks the guard for directions to the police station. From her rudimentary Spanish, she makes out that they are being told to take the bus north on La Avenida de la Reforma. On the bus, they stand pressed together in the door well. At each stop, they have to step off to let people descend. In between, Leonard reads from the guidebook. "This is their Upper East Side." He points toward luxury apartment buildings and well-appointed store windows. On the streets, she sees Ladinos in clothing that looks like what people wore five years ago in the States. "Where those private museums Sonia and Hank talked about are."

To her surprise, the names slide off her tongue. "The Popol Vuh. And the Ixchel." Leonard's eyebrows are knit together, and she wonders if he is worrying about Bernardo Domengo's body now less than ten blocks away, remembers how Saul once told her that Leonard had been one of those medical students who pass out the first time they see a cadaver. Like his father's mother, Saul had turned out to have a gut made of iron: "Even the instructor was green when it came to dissecting a penis. But I made it through the testicles without losing my lunch."

She thinks about the dead bodies she's seen. A banker who'd had a heart attack in the back room at Alil's and whose body they'd all lugged into the alleyway before calling an ambulance. Rebecca, who'd gone to the next world without either of her breasts. Joe, before she made the decision to have the casket closed so Gene could come to the funeral without seeing his father's waxy face. A politician she'd worked for in Ohio who was killed in an airplane crash, after which the state party officials requested her help with the selection of his burial clothes. As though he were still running for office. As though Peter would open or close the pearly gates depending on whether his suit was navy or brown.

"They seemed pretty negative on the city," Leonard says. "Hank said they were only here because the trips to the Highlands were too hard to manage with the baby. He was amazed that we were planning to stay longer than overnight." He closes the guidebook. "Still, I wouldn't tell them why you're here."

He holds the book against his chest, and for a moment Rena has the thought that he is signaling her. She glances around, but if there's someone tailing them, it's impossible to tell who. She inhales—Ascher's claim that he could always detect the private investigators by their foul breath, all that coffee, all those cigarettes, all that greasy diner food churning around inside.

"We're in Zona Cuatro now. The downtown." Outside, the traffic has increased and there are Indians again on the streets. They pass the bus station, and then a lot filled with rubble. Children, little children without diapers or underwear, no adults anywhere around, squat in the dust with sticks and pieces of metal in their hands. Skinny legs and swollen bellies. The noon sun baking their heads.

"Two more blocks, and we're there."

She wants to take Leonard's hand, she wants to say, *Don't worry, you don't have to come inside the morgue, I don't expect you to do that,* but she can think of no way to say this without implying that she fears his knees or stomach won't endure what hers will.

"PLEASE, PLEASE," MURMURS the minister of police's plump and gleaming undersecretary, Señor Padillo, for whose return they have waited nearly two hours while he completed his lunch and afternoon siesta. They follow him into a small room, where he seats himself behind a metal desk bare except for a cup with three sharpened pencils. He motions them to sit in two folding chairs that appear to have been brought in for the occasion.

Señor Padillo smiles and folds his chubby hands. "How like you our city?"

"Very much, thank you," Rena says slowly.

Señor Padillo beams at her. "My English not good. You pardon me."

Rena catches Leonard's eye. "I speak Spanish," he says. "I could translate if you'd like."

The man gestures to the ceiling, outside, to himself. His cheeks flush. "La señora, it not sad her if yes?"

They wait while he reads the papers Rena has brought from the embassy. His lips form every word. A day in prison, Saul has told her, is a day spent waiting in lines: lines for the toilet, lines for the cafeteria, lines for the telephone. "A prescription for violence. All these hotheaded kids set to simmer hour after hour after hour. A way of telling us over and over that we're just lumps of flesh. You never think about it when you have control over your time, but time, even more than money, is the ultimate status symbol. That's what you buy with money—not having to wait."

"How do you keep from losing it?" she'd asked.

"I'm ruthless about what I'll do to occupy myself. I used to be appalled when I'd see people bend the corner of a page in a book. Now I rip the pages out and clip them into packets I can fold in a pocket. My father sends me foam earplugs, and I keep them in whenever I'm not talking with someone. All day long, I read my way through the lines."

Señor Padillo scratches his chin. His nails are meticulously manicured. Rena pictures a tiny woman with dark lashes applying a silver file to Señor Padillo's broad white nails. He speaks in Spanish to Leonard. The words move back and forth like a shuttlecock over a net.

Eventually, Leonard and Señor Padillo begin making little nodding gestures. "He says it's out of his jurisdiction to release the body," Leonard tells Rena. "Only the minister of police, Señor Perez, can do that, and he's at the coast until Monday."

She sees dark spots before her eyes. The fan overhead pushes the hot air around the room. She cannot imagine spending six more days in this city. She cannot imagine sharing the room at La Posada de las Madres with Leonard for six more nights. "Tell him he has to do something. That we cannot wait that long."

Leonard and the undersecretary resume their volley of words. From Señor Padillo's excessively polite tone, Rena can tell that any attempt to decrease their ration of waiting will be futile. Leonard turns back to her. "He says that if this were a domestic affair, he might be able to handle it himself but not an international matter."

She thinks of Saul's definition of a bureaucracy: actions pronounced as possible or impossible as though they were laws of nature rather than arbitrary rules. "Ask him if he could contact his boss by telephone."

Leonard translates. Señor Padillo laughs and then Leonard smiles. She has the distinct impression that there is some sort of man-to-man banter that Leonard is leaving untranslated, something along the lines of how the undersecretary does not want to lose his balls and that is what would happen were he to disturb the minister of police on his vacation.

Señor Padillo pushes back his chair. Standing, he shakes Leonard's hand, bows slightly to Rena. "*Lunes, a las nueve.*" Monday, nine o'clock.

IT'S PAST FOUR by the time they leave the police station. Leonard takes her arm. "In the morning, we'll go back to the embassy and see what they can do to intervene."

"Yes," Rena says, but already she knows that nothing will happen, that they can spend two days going back and forth between the assistant to the assistant ambassador and the undersecretary to the minister of police, and even if they're able to jump this up to the assistant ambassador himself, all that will happen will be more apologies for their having to wait.

The day feels topsy-turvy. Too late for lunch, too early for dinner—that old unsettled feeling from childhood when there'd never been regular meals or regular bedtimes, when Eleanor, having eaten at work, would forget that Rena had not. In the cab back to the hotel, Leonard rubs his eyes.

"Why don't you lie down when we get back? You could take a nap before we go for dinner."

Leonard covers his mouth as he yawns. "If you don't mind, I think I will."

While he naps, Rena reads in the courtyard on a wobbly wrought-iron chair under a palm tree. It's a pitiful specimen with withered brown leaves that bring to mind a passage Saul had shown her on the occasion of their trip to St. John, a scalding commentary by a heat-addled nineteenth-century traveler on the depravity of the palm tree: "An over-rated atrocity of a weed with revolting leaves and a scaly trunk."

A baby starts to scream. A hunger scream. Although there are five other couples here with infants, she knows it's Carlos. The door to Hank and Sonia's room swings opens, and Hank bolts past her on legs that drop clumsily one in front of another. "The bottle. I have to get the bottle from the kitchen." Sonia follows with the screaming Carlos, his face and neck splotched with red. "All right, all right," Sonia says. "It's coming. Hold your britches."

Rena stands to give Sonia her shaded chair. Sonia flops down. She's barefoot, and one strap of her sundress has fallen off her shoulder. She leans back so her neck rests on the top of the chair and her short freckled legs stretch in front. In the one piece of frivolity Rena can detect about her, her toenails are painted gold.

"Here, I'll take him for you," Rena says, reaching for Carlos.

"Be my guest. It's like holding a car alarm."

Rena presses the baby's abdomen against her chest. She bounces him up and down as she walks back and forth. "Your baba's coming," she whispers. "Yes, yes, you'll get your baba."

Hank returns, face and neck wet with sweat. "I can't get this thing screwed in right."

Sonia examines the nipple and bottle. "This nipple isn't ours. Ours are the clear ones in the Ziploc on the shelf."

"Shit." Hank races back toward the kitchen. Sonia rolls her eyes.

"I can't blame it on his sex. He's equally useless with a car. And don't even think about tools. Thank God he can do theoretical physics. Otherwise, he'd have to be on welfare."

Rena can feel Carlos trying to suck on her neck. As a baby, Gene would make sucking motions while he slept. What are you dreaming about, she'd murmur into his crib. Warm milk going down your gullet?

When the bottle arrives, Sonia takes Carlos. He drinks avidly, his hands lovingly fingering the plastic. As he relaxes, so does Sonia. "Imagine what he'd be like with a boob." She kisses the top of his head. "A little lady-killer."

THE FOUR OF THEM, five including Carlos asleep in the baby carrier, go to a Chinese restaurant Sonia and Hank were told about by the social worker from the adoption agency.

"What a stitch!" Sonia exclaims as they're seated. The room is decorated with red and green Christmas tree lights and yellow paper lanterns, and the menu features *chop sue* and *eg rol*. Sonia orders bottles of the local beer for everyone. "No teetotalers," she announces. As expected, the food is ghastly, with everything sunk in an orange sweet and sour sauce. Sonia, on her third beer, twirls a pineapple chunk on the tip of a chopstick, close, Rena fears, to degenerating to child's food play.

Neither Hank nor Sonia is particularly curious about Leonard and her, or why they are here. They ask no questions beyond where they each live. When Rena says Manhattan, Sonia commences a story about her years at Barnard and the apartment she shared with four other girls above the Chock Full O' Nuts coffee shop. Only on the subject of Leonard and Rena's travel plans do Sonia and Hank seem interested. "You absolutely cannot stay here," Sonia declares. "That would be like coming to the U.S. and visiting only Pittsburgh."

Sonia's voice shifts to a podium register. "This is a land of waterfalls and conifers and wildflowers in lavenders and crimsons you've only seen on silks. There are seventeen languages spoken in the Highlands. The people, despite the massacres they have endured from their government, maintain a way of life that centers on the earth, on what they create with their hands. If there is a God and he respires, the mists that cross the peaks in the early mornings are his breath. Antigua, Atitlán, the ruins at Tikal: these are sites of wonder. This place"—Sonia sweeps a hand over the vinyl booth and the plastic packets of soy sauce—"is a shit hole."

• • •

After dinner, Hank escorts Leonard to the Guatel office so Leonard can telephone Klara. Rena, carrying Carlos (Hank has transferred the baby carrier to her due to Sonia's delicate back), walks with Sonia back to the *posada*. The air has cooled with the setting sun. Rena drapes her cotton sweater over the carrier. Sonia tucks the sweater around Carlos' feet.

"It's like being on a roller coaster," Sonia says. "There are moments of bliss. Then there are times, in the heat of the day, when he cries and cries and I think this is a living hell."

"It gets better. It's all about the digestive system. Once that matures, they settle down."

"I know—the proverbial settled baby. Only I think that assumes a different kind of mother."

Rena feels Carlos stirring from sleep.

"I'm forty-four years old. I've published some two hundred poems. I have a secure teaching position. We tried for two years to conceive—I'll spare you the boring details—until finally an endocrinologist told me she was going to talk straight with me: we could spend fifty thousand dollars we don't have and another two years hyperstimulating my ovaries and our chances would still be only fifteen percent. She said she wouldn't talk to me like this except that she'd read my poems, had her residents read my poem about watching your eggs drop, month after month, an inheritance dwindling. Afterwards, I cried. I cried for most of two days. People read my work and they think I'm a different person than who I am, that I'm some sort of Amazonian. But I knew she was right. Hank knew she was right. She was talking his lingua franca: probability. We can't wager all our money, he said, and one-twentieth of our remaining years on a fifteen-percent shot. We stayed up drinking Dewars straight from the bottle until the newspaper boy came and the dogs started barking. In the morning we called the agency that brought us here. That was last fall."

Rena touches Sonia's elbow. They're at the intersection for the small street that houses the *posada*. Like Saul, Sonia follows her without even looking at the sign.

"What never occurred to me was that we lose our fertility for a reason. That it's not just an artifact of evolution. That we're born with all our eggs and that the time when the good ones run out is not simply random—that it wasn't simply my body that was too old to have a baby." Sonia hugs her arms. In the dusk, she looks younger, her skin airbrushed by the waning light. "No, it's my psyche too. For twenty-five years, I've woken every day to absolute quiet. It's been the foundation of my day. I've lain in bed and thought about my dreams and then padded to the kitchen to turn on the coffee and then to the bathroom to pee and wash my face and brush my teeth and then I've sat down with a pencil and paper. Sometimes, if we've been away or it's a day I have to teach, I may have only twenty minutes, but for me those twenty minutes are the difference between feeling alive or like an automaton."

They're in front of the *posada*. Sonia stops as if what she has to say cannot be said inside. "I don't know what I was thinking. I guess I thought I'd still be able to do that. Get up before the baby. Let Hank get up with him. But I can't. First, I'm so exhausted, I sleep to the very last minute. Then, when Carlos gets up, I can't just leave him to Hank. I feel like I have to check in with him. See how he is. Only that goes on all day. I keep saying, it's just for now, when we get back to Boston I'll be able to have my morning time. But it's been four weeks and I'm going crazy."

The bass has disappeared from Sonia's voice. Tears balance on the rims of her eyes. "I feel like I've lost my mind. I've stopped dreaming. Or when I do, the dreams are wiped out immediately since I wake up all night to Carlos' cries. Only once have I woken on my own, not to his crying. It's the only dream I can recall since we've had him. The only line I've written. Seven syllables."

Sonia reaches out her hands and grasps Rena's arms. She's laughing through her tears, a kind of hysterical hilarity. "Guess what I was dreaming? That Carlos was crying. I was dreaming that he was crying, and when I woke up there was absolute quiet and I took a pen and wrote on my palm: 'Silence, sugar of the soul.' "

• • •

At three, Rena bolts awake. At first, she thinks it's the sound of a baby crying, or parents half asleep, stumbling and muttering as they make bottles, change diapers, but all she hears is the call of an animal, high-pitched and distant.

Afraid of disturbing Leonard, she refrains from turning on the light to read and instead lies listening to his breathing, insufficiently staccato to qualify as a snore but too loud to permit an easy return to sleep. She can detect his scent, heavier and more pungent than Saul's.

Over dinner, she could feel a tension rising between them—the excess politeness, the absence of any joking. She'd been relieved when Hank volunteered to go with Leonard to the Guatel office—relieved to have the time apart.

She turns onto her side and pulls the thin blanket over her shoulders. It doesn't make any sense. Leonard has been nothing but considerate and helpful. So why does she no longer want him here?

"They're right," Rena says over breakfast. "It's absurd to come this far and see only this city. You should go to the Highlands."

Leonard is cutting a tortilla covered with a fried egg. He finishes the incision and places his knife and fork parallel on the plate. "If we persist with the embassy, we might be able to get them to apply pressure and get us earlier access."

"It's not worth it. It's Wednesday already. We could spend two days badgering them and maybe we'd get the body by Friday. And that's only maybe." She feels oddly like Sonia, talking about facing probability and letting it guide your decisions.

"So why don't we both go? We could leave tomorrow morning. Come back on Sunday. That would give us time to visit Lake Atitlán and one or two of the mountain villages."

From the way Leonard has an itinerary mapped out, it's clear that he's already thought this through, perhaps even consulted with Hank.

"I still need to arrange for the cremation, make sure everything is set for us to bring back the ashes."

"Don't you think we could get that all wrapped up today?"

Rena stares at a black hair afloat in her coffee. She fears she will gag. Fears what will happen if she has to putter around with Leonard until Señor Perez's return. That the strain of the togetherness will overtake her and some undigested piece of nastiness will pop out of her mouth. Nor does she want to tell Leonard that she has promised Sonia she will take Carlos for a night, will keep the baby in her room to allow Sonia a morning to wake in silence, or that Sonia wept at the offer, her words—"You'd really do that, oh my God, if I could have one morning, maybe I could feel okay for a couple more weeks"—all a jumble.

Leonard's eyes narrow. He has registered her wish to be alone.

Touching his wrist, she whispers, "I can't."

13 Leonard

I would never have agreed to go had she not made it clear that she wanted me to leave. I want to leave her phone numbers, ways of reaching me, but she waves her hand: "Leonard, I'm a big girl. I'll never forgive myself if your trip to Guatemala is confined to this city."

Oddly enough, other than an initial flinching, I don't feel insulted that she would prefer to remain here where the air is so thick with grime I have to scrub my neck and wrists to remove the accumulated soot. It is so clear (I hope I am not being overly confident here) that it has nothing to do with me that what I feel is sympathy at how hard it is for her to be in someone else's company. Were I not, after thirty-some years of solitude myself, utterly drained of that wish, it strikes me as something I might do myself. What I do feel, though, is indignation on your behalf. She must have done this a thousand times with you. Yes, she insisted you see that detox doctor. Yes, she called him a couple of times after she sensed more trouble. But it didn't go much further than that, did it?

And how was it different for you with Mom? Did you do more than go through the motions?

Of course. It takes one to know one.

Unable to make any definitive travel plans since the guidebooks warn that bus schedules for the Highlands change without notice depending on weather and the military, who have a habit of closing roads, I tell her I will be back, hell or high water, on Sunday.

Hell or high water: who do I think I am?

SHE INSISTS ON COMING with me to the bus depot, making a respectable effort at small talk on the ride there. Once we arrive, it's hard to figure out what needs to be done. Do I buy the ticket at the window or on the bus? What time does the bus depart? All anyone will tell me is the gate number. "*La cuatro. La cuatro*."

We go to the newspaper kiosk so I can get a *Herald-Tribune*.

"We should have asked Hank," Rena says. She's wearing a dress with buttons that go up the front. In the heat of the station, she's taken off her sweater, leaving her thin arms exposed. Ahead of us is another American, purchasing copies of every available newspaper. "Excuse me," I say as he turns to leave. "Do you know how this works? I'm trying to find the bus to Panajachel."

He's tall with brittle brown hair pulled back with a rubber band. I'm certain that he's as flabby as I am, but his head is big and he carries himself in such a way that his girth under the spirit fabric shirt gives the illusion of muscle rather than fat. His eyes settle on the oval of skin between the top of Rena's dress and the hollow of her neck.

"Works? Nothing works here."

"We're trying to find out the schedule. But all anyone will tell me is the gate number."

"That's because each bus has its own contract and each driver keeps his own schedule. But if you go to the gate, there'll be someone who knows when the next one leaves. Which gate did they say?"

"Four."

"That's on the side facing the market. I'll show you."

I can see Rena studying him, trying to figure out who he is.

"Where are you folks from?"

Rena glances at me. She is deferring to me. Whether I'll say New York for the two of us, or let him know about the river between. Don't be ridiculous, I say to myself. He's just trying to help. A Good Samaritan.

Maybe a little crazed from being alone in this unbeguiling city. I remember my old supervisor, Nettles, long dead, I presume, and how he used to say that I didn't distinguish between what was on my mind and what was on the patient's: *Dr. Dubinsky, one must always keep an eye on the impact of the countertransference.* The countertransference. As though it were a thing with a color and smell.

"Rena's from New York City. I'm from New Jersey."

"And you?" Rena asks. Her voice is cool, almost chilly. It's breathtaking, the contrast between those slender arms and the large breasts. A shark, I think. Hidden under the flab is a shark. And sharks like cold water.

You have your directionality confused, Dr. Dubinsky, Nettles would admonish. *What originates within the doctor and what derives from the patient.* That tone. I could hear it being delivered to the Park Avenue matrons lying year after year on his black leather couch. *Mrs. Randall, certainly even you can see how your associations point toward an envy of the male anatomy? Mrs. Randall, you speak constantly of your husband's lack of sexual interest in you, but you grew very embarrassed when you talked about seeing your friend's abundant pubis when you accompanied her to the changing room at Bergdorf's.*

"Here. I've been living here the past year and a half. The Bay Area before that. Tony Prankle with a 'k,' " he says, extending a hand to me.

"Leonard Dubinsky. And this is my daughter-in-law, Rena Peretti." I have to remind myself that this Tony Prankle with a "k"—a stringer for the wire services, he tells us—does not know that Rena is staying.

"I hate to tell you guys, but this is the dog's way to get to Panajachel. These second-class buses are old Canadian school buses. Unless you got calluses on your derriere, they're pretty rough going. And slow. Most people take one of the private coaches that leave from the hotels. Me, I like these babies because you get to see the rural life, not the tourist life, but you definitely have to be up for it. I've seen every animal smaller than a horse be boarded and Indians so dank you'd think they'd self-combust."

There's a yellow bus waiting at the gate. It's jammed with people, mostly Indians but a few straggly-haired backpackers, too. I approach the Ladino man standing guard at the door and ask if there's room for one. *"Lleno,"* he says. Full.

"You have dollars on you?" Prankle asks.

"Five or six in ones."

"Offer him three dollars American for the two of you."

"It's just me going."

Prankle with a "k," I swear to God, moves an inch closer to Rena. "Offer two American."

I pull out two dollars from the inside zipped pouch of my vest. *"Momentico,"* the guy at the door says. He leans inside and points at a man and a woman and two children all crammed into the seat behind the driver. I can't hear what he's saying, but the next thing I know they're trooping off the bus, the kids carrying satchels tied from cloth and the man gesturing toward the roof filled with baskets. The woman herds the children to the wall where the sign for the gate is posted, and they sit silently, the three of them on the ground, while the man climbs up to retrieve their baskets.

Rena kisses me on the cheek. "I'll see you Sunday," she says. I take my seat behind the driver. His dark eyes fill the rearview mirror. I wave to Rena and she waves back. Prankle points to something on the bus and she smiles.

Nettles. All those weeks in his office with him lecturing me about my countertransference. He didn't understand a thing. Not a goddamn thing.

AN ISOSCELES TRIANGLE. You in prison in Connecticut. Rena in Guatemala City. Me headed slowly, two hours out, already three repetitions of the driver's one cassette, songs of lost love crooned by a Spanish Elvis, to Panajachel, a hippie outpost—my blood pressure still elevated from thinking about the way this Tony Prankle will try to put the moves on Rena.

My intestines are burning, the beginning, I fear, of a case of *turista.* I suspect the Chinese food from the night before last. In one of the

Carmelita documents, a sister described how the family had journeyed all the way to Oaxaca on the occasion of Carmelita's sixteenth birthday to go to the first Chinese restaurant to open in their region. I compute years and dates: 1953, two years before her death. Ten months before she got pregnant. The year I finished my residency. Back then, there'd been a hole-in-the-wall Chinese restaurant on Lower Broadway that a group of us had frequented Friday nights, all of us pledging to keep up our gatherings as we dispersed to our hospital jobs. Five Jew boys congratulating ourselves on our boldness in eating shellfish, and on a Friday night to boot. (I was sure I wasn't the only one who added a silent prayer for leniency in case our agnosticism turned out to be wrong.) Decades before people fussed about Hunan and Szechuan, we'd eaten tureens of wonton soup and plates of chow mein. There'd been bowls filled with crispy fried noodles and afterwards litchi nuts speared with toothpicks. Nothing like the places in your (can I still say your, or should I say Rena's) neighborhood with their diet selection banners—NO FAT NO SUGAR NO MSG—emblazoned across the top of the menus.

Two nights ago, listening to Hank's treatise complete with citations from *Nature* on the latest thinking about the molecular structure of the various hepatitis strains, it struck me how similar the food we were eating was to the fifties fare I'd eaten in bucketfuls. What happened to that place? I stopped going there shortly after I met Maria, those first months so arduous with her screaming every time she saw my beard that by the time I finished my charts, I couldn't face a subway ride downtown and an evening of my colleagues' off-color banter.

So, I hear you saying—your landmark syllable, a container for persistence, irony and tenderness. You before the three A's: accident, addiction, arrest. From those gentle years when we'd get together whenever Rena was out of town. Over dinner, you would tell me about your cases. You'd developed that young psychiatrist habit of resting your chin in the sling of your hand: terrible for the back and neck but a way of keeping the head and face very still.

So, I hear you saying, *Are you or are you not going to tell me about this Maria?*

It takes me a moment to recognize that the question is mine. But why now? Why tell you now about Maria? Is it that you're safely locked away so I can see or not see you at will if my cheeks turn an uncontrollable crimson and even my mouth and palate feel mortified? *Se mortifier*, the French call it. *Je me mortifie*. I mortify myself. (*You are trying to throw us off the path again,* Merckin—that oedipal Johnny-one-note, I'd called him—would proclaim after thirty minutes of my Maria lust confessions.) Or is it that Maria is easier to think about than your wife off somewhere with that slick journalist?

SHE WAS WHAT my friend Rosen, the other first-year attending, called a ball-breaker case. Two years, already, on a back ward, but young enough and smart enough and beautiful enough that it was conceivable she might recover before we destroyed her with the treatments we used then: drugs they wouldn't give today to a horse, enough voltage to the brain to electrocute an errant cow, excisions of what we thought of as little pockets of wild emotions. Might. That was the ball-breaker part. "Don't kid yourself, Dubinsky," Rosen would say. "They're all watching you on this one. I got one, too. The test case. Find out if the kid has talent. Can't you see Nettles and the others sitting around the month before we got here making up our caseloads—nineteen hopeless ones and a ball-breaker apiece?"

Maria was twenty-one, though she looked sixteen and acted nine. A long, thick black braid her grandmother used to plait every morning touched her tailbone. On Saturdays, the grandmother had washed Maria's hair in the kitchen sink. When Maria first arrived, the social worker told me, it had been a ward crisis what to do with this hair. In a struggle with the arrogant ward chief, the nurses, usually generous, particularly with childishness such as this, had refused to wash or comb it; things had gotten ugly enough that they'd made veiled references to their union contract and certain clauses therein. Indeed, a decision had been made to have Maria's hair cut when Mrs. Wong—brought to the hospital by her son after she began insisting she'd been the last mistress of the last emperor of China who, disguised now as the greengrocer, the postman, the fishmonger, was still trying to have his way with her—was found early one morning standing in her embroidered slippers behind a chair dragged from the patients' dining hall plaiting Maria's hair.

The family, I learned, had come from Venice in the early years of the war. The grandmother's mother had been born to a Jewish father and, though not technically a Jew herself, had grown up in the Ghetto Nuovo near the Canareggio canal. Maria was eight when her grandmother, terrified their bloodlines would be discovered, sold the two diamond rings she'd inherited from her mother, her only assets other than the domestic items of her household, to purchase passage to New York for her two children, her one grandchild, and herself. No ticket had been bought for Maria's ne'er-do-well father, Giuseppe. Abandoning her husband, Maria's mother, Francesca, took Maria to the harbor at dawn. Maria watched from the ship's deck as the campanile of San Giorgio Maggiore disappeared in the morning haze. In a ten-day journey, they rounded the tip of Italy, passing out the needle hole at Gibraltar into what her bachelor uncle, Carmine, called the great sea.

The foursome landed in New York and then, because a cousin lived there and because they felt more at home by the water, settled in New Rochelle in a house not far from the Long Island Sound. Trained as a stonemason, Carmine got a job working on the construction of the northern apse of the great Cathedral of St. John the Divine. Every morning, he would walk the mile and a half to the train station to catch the commuter line to 125th Street. Maria's mother took a job in one of the many Italian restaurants that dotted the shoreline. The grandmother, after enrolling Maria in elementary school (because Maria didn't speak a word of English, she was placed in the first grade), found a job cleaning the large Tudor house and doing the starching and ironing for a rich Jewish lady in Wykagyl who would send a black driver to pick her up every morning at eight.

Pooling the modest salaries of the three working adults, the family had lived comfortably. Saturdays, Maria's grandmother would make fresh raviolis and lay them out to dry on trays on her bed. Sundays, they attended mass at a Catholic church in Pelham. In the afternoons, while her grandmother rested on the couch listening to opera, Maria and her mother and uncle would, weather permitting, walk over the drawbridge to Glen Island where they'd watch the sculls and the birds and hear the sounds of the big bands floating down from the casino at the northeast point. Sometimes Carmine would carry his fishing pole, and while Maria and her mother played cards on the grass, he would strike up conversations with the other men, all either old or infirm or immigrants like himself, about the progress of the war.

One morning in the fall of 1943, Maria's mother announced that she was leaving by boat that night for Italy. "Are you *matto*?" Carmine said. "There's a war going on now."

"I need to see the child's father," Francesca replied, refusing further explanation. It struck Maria's grandmother and uncle as odd since there had been no letters from Giuseppe to either Maria or her mother, and if letters had been sent eastward, it had been done in secret. Weeping, the grandmother sent the chauffeur back to her employer's house with the message that she was ill. No one thought to get Maria ready for school. Maria watched as her usually taciturn grandmother literally threw herself at Francesca's feet, but in the end her mother left with the promise that she'd be back by the end of the year.

A month later, on the day after Maria's eleventh birthday, a telegram informed them that Francesca had been killed and that Giuseppe was in jail, the suspect. The war and lack of funds precluded Maria or her grandmother traveling to the funeral. Instructions and money were sent for the aunts and cousins to arrange for the burial. Some time later, a letter came from the sister of Giuseppe: "Not to speak ill words of the deceased, nor to defend the ungodly act of my brother, she was a whore. She came here to taunt him. One lunchtime, he comes home to surprise her with panini and she is doing it with another man in his own bed. He did not kill her. She killed him."

Maria never returned to school. At first, it was because of the nightmares. Such bad nightmares that she became terrified of sleeping during the night. Feeling sorry for the motherless girl, her teachers let the absences slide. Carmine took off a morning from his job to meet with the principal, and arrangements were made that Maria would return in the fall to redo the third grade. It was over the summer that Maria began telling people she could talk with her mother. In public, the grandmother dismissed it as nonsense. In private, she inquired about the conversations. "She is wearing her blue silk dress," Maria would say. "The one with the rose-colored petals. She told me that you should braid my hair more tightly. She thinks Uncle Carmine should get a new fishing pole."

I never figured out why a truant officer was not sent when Maria did not return to school in the fall. Perhaps the family had moved. Indeed, there were many moves over the next several years, one of which was to an apartment where they lived next door to three sisters who worked in a dress factory and would bring the lonely girl bags filled with scraps of fabric—pieces of taffeta, strips of velvet, clippings of lace. Maria began making doll clothes, exquisite creations: fur-trimmed skating outfits, gauzy bouffant evening dresses, lacy wedding gowns. Her grandmother brought some of the clothing to show her employer, who showed it to the women she lunched with on Wednesdays at the B'nai Brith Ladies Auxiliary. Soon, mothers as far away as White Plains were bringing their daughters' dolls to the back door of the house where Maria's grandmother worked with instructions for the outfits their princesses desired. *Sì, sì,* Maria's grandmother would say to each request. Sometimes things got lost in translation, like the request for a tennis oufit that became a dentist outfit, but nonetheless the orders grew to where Maria's little business was making a dent in the family's bills.

From what her uncle would later tell me, Maria was happy. Every morning, after her grandmother left for work, she'd clear the kitchen table and begin to sew. As she sewed, she listened to an Italian radio station that featured romantic ballads. At eleven she'd break to take a walk, winding her way through the little cottages that abutted the sound and then over to Glen Island, where she'd feed the gulls scraps of the morning bread. She'd eat a simple lunch and, because she could not sleep at night, nap until five, when she'd rise to prepare the family's meal. "A wonderful cook," her uncle said. "Nothing fancy, but everything fresh and delicate. Like herself." He wiped a tear from his eye. After dinner, while her uncle did the dishes and her grandmother went early to bed, she'd return to her sewing, working through the night with the radio for company.

Then, the spring after she turned sixteen, everything changed. A man with a black beard and eyebrows that ran unbroken across his forehead rang the apartment bell. Instructed by her grandmother to never open the chain, Maria peered through the crack. "Encyclopaedia Britannica," he said. She shook her head no. He smiled, and then slipped a free calendar through the slot between the door and door frame. There were photographs of each month's flowers. January orchids. February roses. March cherry blossoms. She cut out the April tulips and taped the page on the refrigerator door so she could look at it as she worked. The next morning, the man rang the bell again. "Sorry, miss, a mistake," he said. He pointed to the chain and smiled. She smiled back. He offered her a licorice. While she chewed the black rope, he mopped his brow with a handkerchief. "Warm day," he said. "You wouldn't be so kind as to offer me a drink of water?"

She opened the chain. That evening, her grandmother found her huddled in the corner, her clothes ripped. There was dried blood on her thighs. She was whimpering. She would not let her fingers be peeled back from her face. Her grandmother bathed her. Maria was laid in the grandmother's own bed. Every day, until Maria's next period arrived, her grandmother lit a candle, praying for the flow to come.

After that, according to her uncle, Maria stopped sewing. She never left the house unless accompanied by her grandmother or him. He could not say what she did during the hours he and her grandmother were at work. This went on for three years until, when Maria was nineteen, her grandmother died after lifting the mattress from her employer's bed to vacuum the frame underneath. When the driver came to tell Maria that her grandmother had been taken to the hospital, Maria refused to open the door. While her uncle made the funeral arrangements, she kept the sheets over her head. Visitors heard her murmuring as though she were talking to someone. The morning after the funeral, the uncle took her to the emergency room. In the admitting report she was described as semicatatonic and urine-soaked. A month later, she was transferred to the state hospital.

She'd been there two years by the time I met her. "You should have seen her when she first came," the nurses told me proudly. I was standing in the glass-enclosed nursing station. They pointed at a young woman dressed in a tight red skirt with a wide black belt. She was playing cards with two other patients, smoking and laughing. A long braid lay fetchingly over one shoulder. "Frozen like a statue. We had to lift her onto the toilet. And that hair. What a struggle we had with that."

It takes nearly an hour to wind down the mountain to Panajachel. Through the window, I catch glimpses of a royal blue lake with three volcanoes overhead. I keep my forehead pressed to the glass, transfixed for the first time in my sixty-eight years by Nature's glory.

Inside the town, the spell is broken by the primitive tourism. Indians stroll in native dress, their wares spread out on the sides of the dusty streets. Against the background of the shanty bars and the sixties-style shops with names like Yellow Submarine, they appear to be actors in a historical reconstruction rather than the actual residents.

I settle on a hotel with a view of the lake. It's twice the cost of the room at La Posada de las Madres, but with Rena's insistence on paying for everything, I haven't spent more than a few quetzals. I put bathing trunks on under my shorts, stuff one of the towels into my camera bag and head to the hotel dining room, knowing full well that I'm making a poor choice. It's depressing: all German families and businessmen. I watch a woman in her fifties with her poorly preserved septuagenarian husband. Fingers heavy with rings. Unnaturally thin. Unnaturally tanned. A tall, sultry youth brings her an iced drink with a straw and wedges of fruit perched on the rim of the glass. She examines him head to toe. Her husband appears to be dozing. Am I imagining this, twisted as I am after twenty-seven years (*twenty-seven years,* I hear you echoing, your eyes round with amazement) with only my fantasies—Maria's bottom, her swinging braid—or does she press a folded piece of paper into the waiter's palm?

I order a hamburger, spelled *handburger* on the menu. It comes dry atop a tortilla. Afterwards, I walk down to the lake. Up close, it's navy and vast, the far shore beyond sight. The beach is pebbled and half shaded at this hour. Two German girls, towheaded with bouncy breasts, squeal as they wade into the water. For the first time in my married life, it occurs to me that I could take a lover: real flesh and blood rather than the phantom Maria. Could, like my Uncle Jack with my housebound Aunt Mindyl, count infidelity as the cost of loyalty to an invalid wife.

Quickly, I enter the lake. The shock of the cold halts my breath. I swim out twenty yards. The village disappears and the surrounding bowl of mountains appears.

ON THE WAY BACK to the hotel, I pass a *fonda* with a flagstone terrace strung with colored lights and a menu of local fish. Returning a few hours later, I sit at an outdoor table. Most of the other customers are gringos, but with a distinctly hipper and more knowing air than the hotel's luncheon diners.

While I'm having coffee, a man and a woman come out from inside. They take the table next to mine. The man pushes back a chair and stretches out his blue-jeaned legs. Under the colored lights, his beard is almost orange and his boots, intricately tooled in some kind of exotic leather, shine with more luster than the animal whose hide they once were. The woman is tiny with black hair and a short, clingy dress. She pulls out a pack of Gauloises and lights up.

I nod in their direction. They smile back in the way of travelers who, having exhausted each other's company, are eager for distraction. He orders a shot of tequila. She drinks cognac. He points at my beer: "*Uno más para el señor aquí.*"

"*Gracias,*" I say.

"*De dónde eres?*" he asks.

"*De los Estados Unidos.*"

"Australia. Rodney. And this is Maracel. My little froggy."

"Cut it out," she says in accented English, affectionate on the surface but tired, it's clear, of the joke.

"Pull up a chair. Maracel, here, loves Americans. Especially if they're on the telly."

Over the next hour and through two more rounds of drinks, they tell me their story: how, intending to spend a year traveling around the world, he sold his bicycle shop in Melbourne and is now, seven years later, still at it. Indonesia, Thailand, India, Tibet, the Middle East. Six months in Cairo, down the east coast of Africa to the Cape, then back up through Gabon. The usual places in Europe, where three years ago he and Maracel met. She'd left her studies in Aix to follow him north to the fjords. A couple of months in Stockholm while he recovered from malaria caught somewhere along the way. "Not a dime out of my pocket, either, for the treatment. Two weeks in a sanitorium that was more like a spa than a clinic. Maracel tried to fake a malady to get herself in, right, Froggy?"

Ignoring him, she blows smoke over her right shoulder. I watch the cloud enter his beard, the way he recoils without knowing why. She's older than I'd thought at first. Early thirties rather than twenties. I listen to the rest of their journey. The States east to west and then across to Hawaii. From there, a hitch on a freighter six thousand miles south to Argentina. A year coming back north. Chile, Bolivia, Peru.

A lot of travel, I think, on the proceeds of a bike shop.

Here, in Guatemala, they've been everywhere: to the ruins in Tikal, all through the Highlands. "There are places in these mountains as remote as anywhere in the Andes," Rodney says. "You've just got to get away from Disneyland here. Ten minutes out on the mailboat and you're in a different world. We're stuck for two days because there's a German kid here who works on VWs. He's doing a patch job on the cooling system of our van so we can use it to get back to San Diego. Then it's *arrivederci* to that rattletrap."

They tell me where to get the mailboat, and Maracel writes the name of the village I should visit on the back of her matches. I tell the waiter to put their drinks on my bill.

"Thanks, mate," Rodney says.

Maracel reapplies her lipstick. "Remember, Santiago Atitlán."

They leave before the waiter returns with the check. When it comes, I see that the bottle of Chilean wine they consumed before they came out to the terrace has also found its way onto my tab.

IN THE MORNING, I catch the mailboat. I get off at Santiago Atitlán and tour the village, which consists of a white church, a small store and a handful of houses tucked behind low stone walls with flowers growing in beds along the top. Here, the native costume loses its theatrical quality, the women wrapped waist to toe in spirit fabric with elaborately embroidered *huipiles* above, the designs indicating not only region and town, but, in the pattern, family too, the men in red striped pants and wide, colorful sashes. I buy a loaf of bread and a bottle of water and walk out to the beach on the lake. No longer surprised by the cold, I enter the water slowly but steadily. I swim for a long time, my limbs regaining their youth in the water's buoyancy. Always, I'd wanted to take you boys somewhere magical like this for the summer. We could rent a house in the South of France, I'd urged your mother. Always, I'd let inertia and cowardice overtake me: cowardice about setting out on an adventure, about crossing your mother's wishes.

I dry on a flat warm rock, my skin clean and soft from the mountain water. Three women with baskets balanced on their heads cross the beach to a cove where a stream enters the lake. Singing, they lower the baskets from one another's heads, remove the articles of clothing and, kneeling on rocks that jut over the water, scrub with smaller stones the colorful cloth.

My lids grow heavy. This could be Carmelita by the river where every Tuesday she and her sisters did the family wash, where, one Friday, her baby was found floating facedown. A drowning, the coroner announced, refusing to take sides as to whether Carmelita had killed her own baby or the nefarious deed had been done by some other hand, human or not. After Carmelita's death, her sisters had given sworn testimony that Carmelita would never have taken her own life. That she would have wanted to go to heaven to see her baby. That everyone knows suicide *es el camino al infierno*.

I doze. On awaking, I feel as though the sun and sleep have cleared all circuits. Like electroshock therapy, we were told, in my residency. Prone on my hospitable rock, I stare into the cloudless periwinkle sky.

Perhaps Carmelita, shaded by a hospitable tree, did this during the hot afternoon hours when everywhere, except at the mine, work ceased and people returned home for the large meal of the day and the siesta.

I sit up on my rock. A canoe glides halfway between the shore and horizon where a volcano, still snow-peaked, looms. How, I wonder, could Carmelita have been murdered without anyone in the jail hearing her screams?

I open the small notebook I keep in my camera bag. "1955," I write. "Carmelita deemed a prison suicide." I skip down a line. "1955: Maria attempts suicide in the hospital bathroom."

Blood rushes to my face as I look at the two names together. I put down the notebook and grip my thighs, afraid my body will betray my shock to my neighbors, laughing now as they lay the laundry out to dry.

I stare at the page, horrified that I could have worked for twelve years on the Carmelita story without seeing her kinship with Maria.

Kinship, baloney, I hear Merckin sneering. *What about twinship, my dear Dr. Dubinsky?*

I RETURN TO PANAJACHEL in time for lunch at the Karma Kafe, opened, it says in the statement of purpose included with each menu, in 1969 by two women, Alice and Deb, from Santa Cruz who sought a simpler life where the *chi* could flow. I'm partway through my veggie pocket, served with a bowl of yogurt, when Rodney and Maracel walk in. Maracel plunks down next to me. Rodney shrugs his shoulders and settles into the other empty chair. "Did you go to Santiago Atitlán?" Maracel asks.

"This morning. Every bit as unspoiled as you said. There were women washing their clothing by the lake."

"They wash without soap so as not to toxify the lake."

"Pollute," Rodney corrects. "You should know. Your countrymen specialize in that. The Rhône. The Hérault. An abomination. Children swimming in agricultural runoff."

With this second meeting, I can see how wearing their teasing of each other would soon become to anyone in their company, the hostility only thinly disguised. Your mother did that sort of thing the first years of our marriage: little jabs about Leonard, the academic doctor whose inheritance will go to posterity rather than his two sons. Translation: see how he has failed to give me what a doctor's wife should expect—a swimming pool, a Cadillac, a diamond tennis bracelet.

"Our last decent meal until San Diego," Rodney announces. "Eat up, Froggy." Maracel scowls. "She's allergic to health food. Prefers the French breakfast of a demitasse of mud, a couple of cigarettes and a slab of those airy white baguettes, overrated, if you ask me, and no more nutritious than your American, what do you call it, Miracle Bread?"

"Wonder Bread."

"That's it, Wonder Bread. They sold it in Melbourne at three times the price of our local bread. My mum, telly addict she was, God bless her soul, thought it was this laboratory invention that would guarantee her children would grow to be the size of American football players." Rodney points to his short, stocky legs. "You can see how well it worked. Probably stunted my growth."

I finish my veggie pocket and begin the bowl of sour yogurt. Without asking, Maracel spoons some mango and overripe melon from her plate into my bowl.

"Froggies," Rodney says. "You'd think that since it was one of them who discovered microbes, they'd be a bit more mindful. But no, they act as though bacteria doesn't apply to them." Ignoring Rodney, Maracel uses her spoon to stir her fruit into my yogurt. "We're out of here in an hour. Now that the van is fixed, we'll jam straight through to San Diego. Should take us about forty hours."

"You won't stop to sleep?"

"Nah. We switch off. Don't even have to stop driving. One of us slides over, the other slides out. Maracel here does the nights. She smokes the whole way and stops every few hours for coffee. But you're not going to spend any more time here, are you, mate? This is, no offense, rip-off ville for the tourists. A Mayan theme park."

Rodney looks at his watch. "Listen, if I was you, I'd catch a ride with us as far as Huehuetenango. Today's market day and there'll be a late bus going up to Todos Santos. That's the sticks, but not so far out you'll get the willies. Maybe three hours from Huehue. There's a *pensión* on the square. Two quetzals a night and then extra for each blanket. Take three. At night, it's fucking freezing. No running water, just a pump in the courtyard and a dunny out back filled with fleas. Me, I prefer to go native and use the fields. For food, there's a woman who cooks for travelers out of a stall in the market. It's not bad. Just skip the beef, because the way she does it, you risk getting a disease. And bring a couple of bottles of water and a roll of dunny paper."

MERCKIN WOULD HAVE interpreted my letting Rodney make the decision of where and when I'll voyage, the green van idling in front of my hotel where I quickly pack up, as the breakthrough of a buried homosexual wish to submit. Would interpret what transpires three hours later as we near Huehuetenango with Rodney muttering about the red light on the dash and how it has begun to blink on and off as letting myself get screwed.

Rodney pulls into a gas station on the outskirts of town. Maracel stares out the window, apparently indifferent to the plight of the vehicle. A Ladino man wearing a Hard Rock Cafe T-shirt looks under the hood. Rodney follows him inside the garage. After a while, he beckons to Maracel. She gives him her wallet and he begins counting out bills. I climb down from the van and head toward them.

"What's the matter?"

"The water coolant system. Needs two new hoses and a new pan. Asshole kid in Panajachel. The patch job he did is falling apart already. I should go back and wring his scrawny neck, but this guy here says we wouldn't even make it that far. He can do it, but it's a cash situation only." Rodney looks again at his watch. "And too late for the bank. So listen, mate, what we'll do is get someone here to give you a lift into town so you can catch that bus. Otherwise you'll be stuck here with us overnight."

"If you had the cash, they could fix it for you now?"

"A couple of hours, the guy says. But we only have seventy Guatemalan. And to do it as a rush job, he's going to charge two hundred fifty."

"I can lend you the cash. You can send me the money when you get to the States."

"That's bloody decent of you. You sure that won't leave you short?"

I shake my head no. My intestines are doing funny things. I pull open the Velcro on the inside pocket of my vest and take out two hundred quetzals—about two hundred twenty-five dollars. Rodney writes down my address and then goes to talk to the mechanic, who points at a kid sitting on a crate under a tree. The kid gets up and walks toward a beat-up Chevy Nova parked on a patch of grass. Maracel gives me little pecks on both cheeks. Under her perfume, she smells rangy—in need of a bath. Rodney puts my duffel bag in the front seat of the Nova and clumps me on the back a couple of times. He closes the car door for me.

"I'll send that money order to you first thing when we get to San Diego. Should be waiting for you by the time you get home."

Not until I'm on the bus to Todos Santos, seated again behind the driver on a seat that is barely bolted to the floor, the only person other than the driver who has shoes and who is not carrying either animals or large burlap sacks, do I let myself wonder if I'd fallen for a scam with Rodney and Maracel. Ten quetzals passed to the mechanic to go along with the ruse. Did they spot me last night at the restaurant and take me then as their mark? Or did they innocently, if such a word can apply to such weathered souls, befriend me and were then unable to resist acquiring a few quetzals from it all, perhaps not even clear themselves if they intend to return the cash? It's not the money that concerns me, but the question of whether I can still read character or whether I, too, have grown so withered that trust has become charity.

We bump along, first slow turns as we climb into the mountains, and then, as the terrain grows steeper, sharper and sharper switchbacks. They're low mountains, verdant with vines covering the trees and the lushness of something on the edge of being overripe. In the distance is thunder. Hearing the creak of the brakes with each turn and seeing the clench of the driver's jaw as it begins to rain, I recall reading about a bus that tipped over one of these cliffs. I think of Rena awaiting my return and of you who now has only me to love you and of your mother doomed without me to spend the rest of her life with Mrs. Smiley's rules. For a quarter-hour, I gloomily ruminate. Then we round a curve, and suddenly, like the glow in a Renaissance painting that surrounds the spot where the cherubs stand, the sun breaks out, a gold light pouring down the trees so that the rain, still softly falling, looks now like tinsel and the mist like steam rising from the road. Another bend and we are in a clearing, the mountain peaks bathed with rose and the clouds white pillows jostling one another. The trees are a green I've never seen before, bright and shiny, and, for a moment, with the sparkling haze and the pink sky and the twittering of birds as the rain stops and the Indians around me open the windows, I think we've driven right through heaven's gates.

IT'S DUSK BY THE TIME we arrive in Todos Santos. With the color drained from the landscape, the village looks grim and unwelcoming: no lights to lure tourists; in fact, as far as I can see, no tourists at all. I take my duffel and walk toward the sign marked PENSIÓN. The air has turned cool and damp, the dampness of things never fully dry. The Queche proprieter speaks less Spanish than I do, but she points to a pile of army blankets under a sign that says two quetzals. I take two and then, remembering Rodney's warning, a third. She leads me up a wooden staircase to a room with straw on the floor and a metal cot. Next to the cot, there's a table with a candle melted onto a dish. She points to the candle and pantomimes lighting a match, which she then hands me, a single wooden stick, as she leaves. I open the shutters and look out at the outlines of the mountains, a dark beast asleep on its side.

I eat a plate of rice and beans in the marketplace, drink a cup of boiled coffee that I then pay for by spending most of the night tossing and turning, too afraid of fire to light the candle but too cold to get out of bed and search through my duffel for a flashlight so I can read. I hear the church bells toll one, then two, then three. At three, a baby begins to wail—long, high-pitched cries of pain—and I wonder if there is a doctor in this town or if I am it.

I don't recall hearing the bell chime four o'clock, so it must have been somewhere around then that I fell back asleep. I wake with a dream clearly in mind. Your mother and I are at a party, and I have somehow lost one of my shoes. Maria is there too, dressed as I'd first seen her in a tight red skirt and a wide black belt that set off what was above and below. As I stare at Maria's chest, the buttons begin popping off her blouse. She rushes to hold the blouse together, but I can still see the milky tops of her breasts.

More than Maria, what strikes me about the dream is your mother. In the dream, she is as she was when we first met: not Klara with her bunioned toes, but Klara with hair sleek as a ferret's. Four decades later, I can see that it was not simply alcohol that drew me to her that first night. No, there was behind all her arrogance something sexual, a sexual hunger, so that I wonder, now, if it was not only anger and alienation that made me grow averse to touching her but also my fear of her appetites. If, on her part, the hypochondriasis (forgive my waxing a bit clinical here) was her conjuring—the pain my rejection must have caused her moved to stomach and back, the celibacy made her own.

I SPEND THE MORNING WALKING. I'd like to say hiking, but with my lack of equipment or experience I confine myself to well-cleared trails. Around me are green hills: a patchwork of plots that took someone's lifetime to cultivate, and then, farther up, forested land with, at the top, rough white stones poking through like bald spots.

At noon, I stop under a tree enveloped from the lowest branches to the roots with vines. I have my lunch of tortillas and cheese and water. Afterwards, I stretch out with my folded vest as a pillow. A rooster crows to a chorus of birds and insects, and the next thing I know my eyes are opening. I inhale the air spiced with white orchids and wild thyme. All these years of resisting afternoon sleep, of fearing that it would lead me down some slippery slope into a state of complete lassitude when, clearly, it is built into the bones that men of my age who have lost youth's hearty sleep, who sleep more like babies with our early morning risings, need this midday rest to maintain our vigor.

Vigor. A man of vigor. That's how I'd always thought of my Uncle Jack, who my sisters joked would be still *shtupping* when he could no longer walk. His afternoon naps at his dress factory (he confided in me my fourteenth summer when I first worked there, the force of his personality blinding me to the fact that I already towered above him) followed by a press on the buzzer for the red-haired shiksa bookkeeper who, on his instructions, locked the door behind her. "Every day, boy," he told me, "you eat, you sleep, you crap, you fuck. This is what the body requires. This is how we are made." My cheeks turned red. That's if you are an animal, I'd wanted to say with the full force of my adolescent indignation. What about Beethoven's Ninth? Michelangelo's David? I searched my fourteen-year-old store of knowledge. What about Jane Addams? Thomas Jefferson. Joan of Arc. But I'd kept my mouth shut. Afraid of my uncle's taunts. *Stupid kid. You got any hair down there?*

Only once do I recall my mother uttering a critical word about Jack. "Crude," she said. "He's a crude man." Years later, Lil would tell me that she had come home one day unexpectedly early to find Jack pawing our mother on the sofa. The top two buttons of her dress were open and he was panting, my sister reported. At the time, I assumed Lil had saved my mother from Jack's predations, though now, thinking how my mother would have been widowed several years by then, I can permit other scenarios.

The top two buttons. Had Lil been that specific? I think about last night's dream—Maria with her buttons popping open. "Maria,

Schmaria," Merckin had said. "None of this has to do with Maria. You condemned and feared your Uncle Jack because he reminded you of yourself. You, your mother's baby, her only son."

When you told me you wanted to go to medical school and asked why I'd given up practicing medicine, I said simply that I'd learned I wasn't cut out to be a psychiatrist and there had been no other branch of medicine that interested me. Later, when you decided to pursue psychiatry, you asked what I meant by *wasn't cut out,* and I said something about being unable to endure the sense of responsibility I felt for other people, afraid of the impact I might have on them.

"What do you mean?" you asked. You were twenty-four. Still boyish with thin shoulders and a concave chest.

"It's not like fixing bones," I said. "Not to minimize fixing bones, but with fixing bones it's more focused what one worries about: the technique, did you set the bone correctly, place the pins in the right spot. With psychiatry, the patient reacts to things you never do, things that have nothing to do with you. Then there are the things you feel—the patient responds to that, too. All before you've said a word. That's the intrigue of it: the many layers of causation. But it's also what troubled me, the sense that even with the best intentions I couldn't be sure that my impact would be benign."

I don't think I said more than this. Certainly, I never mentioned any particular patient. But I wonder what you sensed, my feelings seeping out, past my own skin, past Maria, into you.

THE BUS LEAVES Todos Santos at four in the morning. I pack my things and lie on the cot fully dressed with the three blankets over me. There are no baby cries tonight, and I wonder if this is a good sign or bad. At three, I give up on sleep and make my way down the stairs. I urinate in the field behind the *pensión,* splash cold water from the courtyard pump onto my face.

The bus arrives twenty minutes early. Again, the driver shoos the people seated behind him to the back so I can sit in what I now understand must be the seat for anyone well-off enough to own shoes. Leaving the town, everything except the swatch of rutted earth lit by the headlights disappears so that the only way I can sense the road is by the groaning of the axle and brakes. I keep my eyes bolted to the windshield, terrified of the sheer drop to my right. Around me, a cacophony of snores as chins drop forward and back. Twice, the bus stops for someone standing by the side of the road. Twice, the driver descends to hoist baskets onto the rack on the roof.

In the dark, I return to the question of two afternoons ago: how could Carmelita have been murdered without anyone in the jail hearing her screams? On the one occasion Maria had talked with me about the encyclopedia salesman, she'd told me he'd held a pillow over her face. "I couldn't breathe," she said. "I was sure he was going to kill me."

Nausea rises from my stomach to my throat. Of course. How could I have not seen it before? Carmelita was suffocated to death.

The sky begins to lighten. Ink to slate to pearl until I can see the shapes of things. A golden glow forms at the horizon and then a band of orange. Looking down, I see a shimmering opalescence. We are driving right through the clouds. I open my window and inhale. I am breathing clouds.

It's fully light by the time we reach the lowlands and the highway that leads to the capital. I am exhausted. An exhaustion beyond lack of sleep. My eyes close and I do arithmetic in my head. Fifty-nine. Maria would be fifty-nine.

14 Rena

Tony Prankle with a "k," Rena realizes, is going nowhere. "I come here to get the Central American news bulletins. The guy who owns the newsstand carries them under the counter. The deal is, I buy a copy of every local and English-language paper he has on hand and he sticks what's under the counter in the stack."

"They're illegal?"

"Not technically. But they're not the sort of thing anyone wants to be known to carry. Nothing I don't know, but I like to keep up on what they're publishing in *El Norte*." He grins, revealing a brown incisor. He's good-looking in an ugly sort of way: a face with each feature flawed but somehow pleasing when pieced together on his large head. "The competition."

Prankle takes Rena's elbow and guides her to the street. He points toward an old convertible Morris Minor double-parked in front. Two street urchins are leaning on the hood. "My parking attendants." He hands them each a coin. "Where are you headed?"

Not wanting to reveal her aimlessness, she says the first thing that pops into mind. "The Museo Ixchel."

"That's near where I live. I'll give you a lift."

Prankle opens the door and Rena climbs inside. She can feel the heat of the seat through her dress, can smell the old leather cured, it seems, with tobacco.

"Are you into textiles?" Prankle asks.

"Not particularly."

"Well, that's about all you'll see there. But they're pretty amazing. Geometrics that give Escher a run for his money."

She recognizes La Avenida de la Reforma, sees the American embassy on the left.

"It's a God-awful city. But there are a few hidden treasures. Over there, at the Miga Deli, you can get a decent bagel. The only one in the country. And the Botanical Gardens," Prankle points to the right, "are worth a look. Skip the museum. A lot of dusty taxidermy. But don't miss the Popol Vuh. It's one room with nothing marked, so you have to guess what you're seeing, but my archaeologist buddy says it has some of the best Mayan artifacts anywhere."

He pulls in front of the Ixchel, looks at the clock on the dash. "It'll take me maybe three hours to get my story written and filed, but I could give you my infamous fifty-nine-minute tour after that. Say, four-thirty?"

Prankle writes down the address of La Posada de las Madres. Inside the museum, Rena sits on a bench and watches the few visitors diligently examine the weavings. With Leonard here, she'd been desperate to be alone. Or maybe it wasn't alone but unobserved. With Prankle, it's like being alone but with company. She could be anybody, any woman with a reasonably attractive face.

SHE WALKS BACK to the hotel. Sweating through his shirt, Hank paces in the courtyard, jiggling a whimpering Carlos.

"Where's Sonia?"

"Trying to get some sleep."

"It looks like he has some heat rash."

Hank peers down at the pink bumps on the baby's face.

"I'll get you a cool cloth." Rena unlocks her door and puts her bag on what had been Leonard's bed. Emptied of Leonard, the room feels different: calmer and cooler. She listens to the sounds embedded in the quiet—the hum from the wiring in the walls, a drip from the shower—and, for a moment, she regrets her offer to take Carlos for the night. Being with an infant, though, she reminds herself, is not the same. A baby's consciousness does not assert itself. Simply its demands: feed me, change me, hold me.

Rena wets a washcloth. She squeezes out the excess water, folds it in quarters lengthwise, brings the cool, wet cloth outside. Taking the baby from Hank, she dabs his blotchy forehead and cheeks. The whimpers stop and Carlos curls into her breast.

"You go rest," Rena says. "He can sleep on Leonard's bed. I'll bring him over after he wakes up."

Inside, she lays a clean white T-shirt atop the bed so the spread won't irritate Carlos' skin. Even though the baby's too young to roll over, she surrounds him with pillows before lying down herself to sleep.

When she wakes, Carlos is staring up at the ceiling. He's wiggling his fingers and toes, looking, it seems, at a wavering band of dark, a shadow from the blinds. Scooping him up, she heads over to Sonia and Hank's room.

Sonia opens the door, the freckled top of one breast visible at the neckline of her canary yellow robe. "You're an angel."

"All I did was lay him on the bed and take a nap. When I woke up, he was watching the shadows on the ceiling."

"You're kidding! He didn't scream?"

"Not a peep. I'm going out for a couple of hours, but I'll take him as soon as I get back."

PRANKLE'S TOUR IS heavily weighted toward churches. He begins with the Catedral Metropolitana, one of the oldest buildings in Guatemala City, spared from earthquakes—according to local lore—by a deal the Holy Virgin Mary, patron saint of the city, made with Santa Teresa. Next they visit La Merced, where Prankle points out the unusual organ and the colonial altar moved from a church in Antigua. Back in the car, they head up a small hill to La Ermita del Carmen. He has a smoke in the garden while Rena goes inside.

From a back pew, she studies the gold-and-mahogany altar. Shortly after they got married, Saul had gone through a cathedral phase, wanting her to accompany him as he visited every cathedral within a few hours drive of the city. He toyed with writing an article on the cathedral as an expression of man's narcissism, not the contemporary narcissism of self-absorption but the narcissism of grandiosity—a noble narcissism, Saul claimed. At the time, she had attributed this obsession to Saul's disappointment with his work, the way he felt himself to be a cog in what he called the psychosis gin: the circuit whereby families turn over their psychotics to the state, which then pays the pharmaceutical companies to wipe out their hallucinations like so many roaches nested in a wall. Now, though, she wonders if there'd been something more at stake, a questioning on Saul's part about the limitations of his and Leonard's (and, she supposes, despite her mother's vestigial Catholicism, her, too) ingrained secularism.

The last church on Prankle's tour is the Capilla de Yurrita, a Russian Orthodox structure built at the turn of the century by a rich religious fanatic. Prankle leaves the car running while Rena walks around the exterior of twisted pillars and onion domes, all proportioned so they look more like caricatures of themselves than themselves. Heading south, they pass the Terminal Market, where contraband monkeys and parrots are sold. Prankle ends the tour with a spin through the Aurora park, a misnomer, he tells her, since it houses an airport, a military base and a sad zoo.

"The only thing we missed is Kaminal Juyu, the Mayan burial ruins west of here, but there's nothing to see from the outside and you're not going to catch me dead, pardon the pun, crawling around in those tunnels." He looks at his watch. "How's a beer and a steak in an air-conditioned room sound? I know a place where the meat's more or less maggot-free."

THE STEAK HOUSE, it turns out, is in the posh section of Zona Diez, not far from the American embassy. It's softly lit and very cool. The bartender waves at Prankle. Two bottles of beer appear.

A waiter in a pressed white shirt approaches with menus. Prankle holds up a hand. He speaks in rapid Spanish. The waiter nods and does an about-face.

"I nixed the salads. The lettuce is an invitation for the runs."

Rolled *rellenos* arrive and Prankle opens them to spread hot sauce inside. Hot chilies burst inside Rena's mouth and her eyes tear. She rinses her mouth with beer.

"Sorry. I forget that other people's taste buds haven't been destroyed like mine." When the steaks are brought sizzling on metal platters, he reaches over to cut hers down the middle. "*Bueno,*" he says to the waiter. "You don't want them rare here. Save that for Peter Luger's."

Prankle polishes off half his steak in two minutes' time and orders more beers. He lights a cigarette and angles his body so the smoke blows away from her. "So, we journalists are all part detective. I thought maybe if I got two beers in you, you'd tell me why you're here."

Her stomach clutches as she sees that she's underestimated Prankle, assuming that he would, like Sonia, be content to have her serve as his audience. "What do you mean?"

"No one comes to Guatemala to stay in the capital. The old guy."

She scurries to construct an answer, then stops herself. This is irrational, she tells herself; her claim to Bernardo's remains has been sanctioned by two governments.

To her surprise, Prankle knows all about Bernardo. "The story broke the first time I lived here, 1976 to 1977. I wrote maybe half a dozen pieces about it for the *San Francisco Chronicle*. The wire services picked up a couple of them. It was right before the Carter administration halted support for the Guatemalan government. It was all a sham because once official support was withdrawn, the CIA simply had freer reign to do their dirty business."

"Did you meet the father?"

"A couple of times. They were here for a few months. Staying in an apartment in Zona Cuatro. I remember him telling me that Castro had been his student—and a lousy one at that. The mother was a red-diaper baby. A pianist, I think."

"Opera singer."

Prankle laughs. "Not too subtle, I'd say. Finding the body right after the father kicks the bucket. They must have assumed there was no one else who still gave a damn. Probably no one except the father had said boo about the corpse in ten years. So they figure once he's gone, they can close out the case, clear the shelf space."

"Who's they?"

"Bingo, babe. That's the million-dollar question around here. You answer that one and you'll get the Pulitzer. Don't worry. I'm not going to scoop you. Not because I'm chivalrous, but I couldn't sell it. A body in formaldehyde doesn't make good copy. You need fresh blood."

WITH CARLOS AS A reason for making it an early night, Rena declines Prankle's suggestion that they move on for drinks at one of the expat bars.

"Well, baby-sitting's a nobler cause than baiting the spooks, which is what I'll end up doing with my pals at El Establo. The bartender there makes sport out of tripping them up on their covers. But if you want to understand the adoption thing and see what this city is really about, you should come with me tomorrow to El Hoyo." El Hoyo, Prankle explains, means *the hole*: the place where the street children—beggars, prostitutes, addicts—live. "The reporting's done, and I've got a photographer lined up to do the shoot late in the day when the light's best."

Prankle pulls in front of La Posada de las Madres. Rena hops out before he can reach for her. "Five. Here in front."

She nods, unsure whether she's assenting out of hope that there's more she can learn about what happened to Bernardo or out of fear of insulting Prankle. She knocks on Sonia and Hank's door. Hank lets her in. Sonia is sitting on the bed, giving Carlos a bottle. Her hair looks wild. Carlos grips the sides of the bottle, eyes closed, as he gulps the milk.

Sonia hands the baby to Hank so she can show Rena the bottles she has left prepared in the kitchen. She yanks on the door of the rusted refrigerator, points to a plastic bin labeled with her room number. "I mixed three bottles. He'll probably need one around two and then at six and ten. There's a pot on the stove. I just boil the water and set the bottle in the pot for a minute or two to take off the chill. If you have any problems, knock. We'll be there."

"Don't worry. It's like riding a bike. It's all coming back."

"Are you sure you don't mind?" Sonia has begun to cry. She wipes her nose on the sleeve of her robe. "I'm just so tired," she whispers. "I'm scared I'll go out of my mind and do something awful."

Back in her room, Rena bathes the baby. Holding Carlos over the sink, she sponges him with warm water, first his face, then inside the folds in his neck, then his chest, back, bottom, legs and feet. Spreading a towel on Leonard's bed, she dries and diapers him, letting him lie and kick while she changes into her own nightclothes.

When she sees Carlos yawn, she cradles him in her arms and walks in small circles, singing softly to him until his breathing grows slow and deep. She sets him on the inside of her bed against the wall and curls around him.

Sleep, she instructs herself. *You'll have to be up in a couple of hours.* But she cannot stop thinking about Bernardo. About Prankle's implication that his body has been stashed in a basement these past fourteen years. That there was an American official somewhere who'd given that the nod. It makes her objections to the work at Muskowitz & Kerrigan seem trivial. Like complaining that radioactive apples are hard to digest.

AT FIVE, PRANKLE IS WAITING. He introduces the photographer, Jean, who is rifling through a camera bag next to him on the backseat of the Morris Minor. Jean glances up just long enough to avoid seeming rude.

They park behind the bus terminal and walk a few blocks south to what looks like an abandoned construction lot. Everywhere there are children, running, banging, stretched out asleep.

"Rubble never cleared after the earthquake," Prankle says. The stench is terrible, and Rena has to refrain from covering her nose. Prankle drizzles Tootsie Rolls into the hands of the children, who flock around them. Jean moves quickly, giving out more candy in exchange for the children letting him photograph them. The older children follow him, watching as he switches back and forth between the three cameras dangling from his neck. The younger children stay crouched in the dirt, digging with their hands through the rubble. A boy who looks like he can't be more than four years old is bare-bottomed. His stomach sticks out from under his T-shirt, hard like a filled balloon.

"Parasites," Prankle says. "They run around butt-naked over garbage and the worms climb right in."

Rena stays at the edge of the rubble while Prankle makes his way over boards and cinder blocks to catch up with Jean. Together they head toward the shanties in back. Corrugated boxes, sheets of tin, a discarded curtain. A pickup truck stops, and an Indian man dressed in western clothes goes inside one of the shanties. A few minutes later, he returns with two children. A boy and a girl. The man touches their backs with the flat of his hand as they climb into the truck.

After the pickup pulls away, Rena unclasps her bag and takes out a clump of bills. She walks over to a group of children and hands them each a bill: five, ten and twenty quetzals. The older ones glance back at the shanties before burying the bills in their clothing. The younger ones stare at them longingly, as though they might be food itself.

Nowhere an adult to be seen. Like a children's playground in hell.

Prankle approaches. Glass breaks under his boots. Backlit by shards of light darting off the tin roofs of the shanties, he appears preternaturally large. The children touch the tape deck he holds in his hand. He talks to them in Spanish and then plays back the conversation. They listen in silence, not one of them giggling at the sound of their own voice.

"Let's go. I've shown Jean what to shoot. He'll be here another hour or so."

In the car, Prankle cups her knee. "It's stupid to give them money. The big ones shake down the little ones. They take whatever money they find and use it for glue."

"They sniff glue?"

"Cheapest way to get high. It's a dog-eat-dog world. The bigger kids, nine, ten, eleven, work for pimps, mostly around the bus station and the Central Market. A night's work gets them two containers of glue and a couple of sandwiches. They control the younger ones, who beg outside the hotels. There's no fooling around. If the older kids don't turn over every quetzal, they can end up stuffed in a garbage can. The younger ones get thrown out of El Hoyo, which, hideous as it seems, is still their home."

Prankle starts the car and slowly backs away from the bus terminal.

"Where do they come from?"

"All over. The Guatemalans treasure children. Most adults spend their whole lives trying to provide for their children. But there's a war going on. Here, in the city, you can easily forget that. Out in the countryside, everyone feels it. A little girl I talked to last week told me that she hid under a crate while uniformed men set her house on fire with her parents and two older brothers bound inside. Afterwards, she just started walking and eventually ended up here. Another girl said she'd run away from the *finca* on the coast where her family had gone to work because she was being beaten with a horse crop by the foreman for not picking bananas fast enough."

Prankle glances at Rena. "You could use a drink. The Sheraton's around the corner. An Ugly American scene, but the bartender keeps a stash of good tequila."

RENA SURVEYS THE familiar atrium: the tight-seated chairs, the potted philodendron, the electronic pings of doors opening, elevators arriving, registers ringing. A woman standing in the doorway of one of the boutiques waves a bottle of Worth perfume. Her bracelets flash. "*Cuanto cuesta esto*?" she asks. The salesclerk behind the counter looks up from her magazine. "Eighty," she says in English.

Inside the bar, disco music plays over the sound system and the walls are decorated with American movie posters. Prankle leads her to a banquette beneath a *Casablanca* poster: Ingrid Bergman and Humphrey

Bogart on an airplane runway. A cocktail waitress brings a bowl of tomato-flecked guacamole surrounded by tortilla chips. Prankle presses a five into her hand. "*Para Renaldo. Dos margaritas. Dile que es para Prankle.*"

When the drinks arrive, Prankle clinks Rena's glass with his own. "To Bernardo Santiago. Whatever happened to him, may he rest in peace."

The salt stings Rena's lips, and she feels the tequila going straight to her head. Prankle puts an arm around her and then starts kissing her hair. She thinks about the brown incisor, about not being able to look Leonard in the eye, and unwraps his arm.

"I'll make you dinner. My famous mole sauce. You can stretch out on the couch and watch a video. My brother sends me *Saturday Night Live* without the commercials."

He'd planned it out. The visit to El Hoyo, then to bed. What a degraded idea of foreplay, she thinks, showing me children living in rubble. But she holds back a caustic comment because she suddenly feels nervous. Nervous because he seems to know everyone.

"I'll have to take a rain check. I signed on again to baby-sit."

Prankle runs a finger down her arm. She removes his hand and edges a few inches away on the banquette.

"I hope your friend's little bundle of joy is legit."

"What do you mean?"

"Baby parts brokers. It's big business here—stealing or buying babies and then selling their body parts. It's all mixed up with the adoption racket. The mothers think the babies are going to rich families from Philadelphia. Or the brokers get a baby and it's not healthy, so they turn it over to a lawyer for adoption." Prankle licks the edge of his glass, his tongue red from the salt. "There's big bucks in it, especially in India and Kuwait. For a male heir, some of those princes will pay a couple hundred K for a baby's liver."

"They kill the children for organs?"

"Depends on the part. Sometimes they sew them up and send them back."

She pushes her drink away, queasy and clammy all at once.

"The brokers, they're like ambulance chasers. They comb the Highland villages for pregnant girls. Seventeen-year-olds with two babies and another on the way and not enough food for even themselves. For two hundred quetzals, some of these girls will agree to give up a child at birth. Of course, they think it's for adoption. I've seen girls who were shown, no joke, pictures cut out of a magazine. One of those ads with the family who bought the Dodge minivan or the Mass Mutual Life Insurance. Fucking newsprint right on the back. Here, in the city, half the time the mother never even sees the money. The baby is stolen by a brother or uncle who handles the deal."

She excuses herself. In the back of her throat, she can taste the morning's bitter coffee. Doubled over the toilet, she heaves, an awful sound like the earth quaking.

Afterwards, she splashes water on her cheeks and rinses out her mouth. A woman in a starched apron hands her a paper towel. The woman holds up a finger. "*Un momentito.*" She lifts a folding chair out of the supply closet, motioning for Rena to sit. Rena lowers herself into the chair and closes her eyes. She feels the woman placing a cool towel on her forehead.

"*Bebé?*"

"What?"

"*Bebé?*" The woman arches her back so her middle sticks out. She pats her stomach.

"No. No."

The woman smiles as though in disbelief. Rena wills herself not to cry.

"No, no baby."

Returning to the table, she leans over Prankle. She touches his shoulder. Next to him is an empty shot glass. She whispers into his ear: "*La turista*, you'll have to excuse me."

He starts to rise.

"You stay. Please."

"I'll drive you."

"No. Really. It will make me feel worse to ruin your night as well."

The cocktail waitress arrives with another shot. Prankle looks over at the bartender, giving him a mock salute. "I'll get you a cab."

Rena places a hand over her stomach. "I'm just going to run. The concierge—it's already arranged." She takes her sweater from the banquette. Kiss him on the cheek, she thinks. One kiss and you're free. She brushes her lips on his scratchy skin and turns.

AT FOUR, SHE AWAKENS to a baby's cries. The high-pitched relentless cries she remembers from Gene, who'd had colic his first three months. A night when Joe was on the road and her mother shook her awake: "I can't take the sound. I'm afraid I'm going to put his head in the toilet." From her mother's room, Gene's two-week-old shrieks. The kitchen door banging as her mother ran out into the street. Bending over the crib, she found Gene red and blotchy from screaming. His skin hot. She held him firmly against her breastbone the way the neighbor had shown her. For an hour, she walked him through the house, bouncing him up and down, singing over his cries. Slowly his breathing calmed and the cries turned to whimpers. She laid him back in his crib and slept on the floor beside him.

After that, she'd not gone back to school. Her boyfriend Rusty would visit, and if the baby was sleeping and Eleanor was sufficiently alert, they'd drive to Stinson Beach, where she'd watch while he joined the other low-tide surfers. With Gene's birth, she'd lost all interest in learning more about what she privately called *this sex thing*. She was just tired, she told Rusty. Things would change when Gene started sleeping through the night. Or perhaps, she'd thought but not said, it was sadness at losing the little piece of her mother she'd still had before Gene's birth—afternoons when Eleanor would set a stack of forty-fives on the record changer and they'd dance together to the Beach Boys and Herman's Hermits, nights when Joe would be gone on an overnight haul and they would bring snacks into bed and watch *Green Acres* and *I Dream of Jeannie*.

Her second week home, she left a message with the school secretary that she had pneumonia and would be out for a while. When a concerned teacher called, she coughed into the receiver and said she was still pretty sick. As time passed, it became clear that her mother had erased the thought of Rena ever returning to school. In Eleanor's mind, she and Rena were the caretakers of the baby. It was only natural that Rena would be home with her, changing diapers and sterilizing bottles.

In a way, Rena didn't mind. The classes were boring, mostly busywork; she could easily keep up by reading the textbooks and doing the homework. As for the rest, the intrigues of the cliques and romances played out in the parking lot, bathrooms and cafeteria, her goal had always been simply to avoid notice or humiliation—to get by in whatever clothes she could pull together without drawing attention to her too-big breasts or lack of money. She'd been grateful to have a best friend, Cheryl, amazed when Rusty had picked her out of study hall.

In the end, it was an accident that intervened: Joe forgetting his wallet one morning and returning to find Eleanor in bed and Rena at the kitchen sink giving Gene a bath. "What the hell is going on here?" he yelled as he yanked Eleanor to her feet and grabbed Gene from the sink, all of which led to his taking Eleanor to the mental health clinic, where they began an antidepressant and arranged for a home aide to come weekdays.

Back at school, no one would catch her eye. Finally, a tearful Cheryl broke it to her that Rusty had been seen *more than once* driving MaryAnn home. To Rena, it made perfect sense. She'd wanted to say to him, it's fine, you can have sex with her, just keep taking me with you to the ocean. Keep letting me watch you cut the curves as you wend down to Stinson Beach. Keep grinning at me as you turn to hoist your board onto your shoulder and walk into the sea. Instead, she wrote him a note on lined paper torn from her history notebook: "It seems that things have changed. I'd appreciate your not calling me anymore."

By Easter, Eleanor had adjusted sufficiently to the antidepressant to completely take over caring for Gene. She'd gained some weight, but it seemed a small price to pay for the great improvement in her mood. By fall, she'd ballooned to one hundred seventy pounds and her skin had erupted in blemishes. Joe took to making nasty comments about Eleanor's appearance and once, drunk on beer, overturned a bag of cheese twists on her head.

SHE WAKES TO THE manager knocking on her door. When Leonard was here, the manager had seemed not to understand English, but he now speaks in a surprisingly clear British accent: "There is a Señor Prankle on the telephone."

"Please ask him to leave a phone number where I can call him back."

In the shower, Rena fantasizes about having Prankle talk with Sonia and Hank. They will listen to him. They will nod their heads sympathetically. Yes, they've heard about these things, but in their case they have used a lawyer of impeccable reputation who insisted they meet personally with the birth mother. Sonia will pull out pictures of the birth mother holding the baby, pictures they will save to show Carlos when he is old enough to understand.

Rena sits in the courtyard with a packet of postcards. She does not say to herself I am waiting for Sonia, though when Sonia's door swings open and Sonia wrapped in her yellow robe rushes barefoot out to the courtyard with Carlos on her shoulder, she realizes that this is what she has been doing.

"Can you hold him while I get a bottle?"

Rena reaches for the crying baby. She rocks him to distract him from his hunger pangs. Outside, she can hear the morning traffic, the screech of brakes, horns honking, as the day's commerce begins.

Sonia gives Rena the warmed bottle and goes to get a second chair. Rena rests the baby's head in the crook of her arm and brings the nipple to his mouth. He closes his eyes as he sucks, little gasping sounds.

"I can take him," Sonia says once she's settled in the chair.

"That's okay. I don't mind."

Sonia stretches out her freckled legs and folds her arms over her chest. "Each time, it's as if he's never been fed before." Her chin tips up as she looks at the sky. "Have you ever seen such a hideous sky? Like a stained tablecloth."

They sit quietly, Sonia staring up at the sky, Rena's heart beating too

fast. When Carlos stops sucking, Rena slides the nipple
and lifts him onto her shoulder. Immediately, he burps.

Sonia laughs. "Yes, coo-coo. My little barbarian." Sh
tom of Carlos' foot.

Rena moves Carlos back into her arms. Sated, he suck
enjoying the warm liquid on his tongue.

"Did you get to meet the birth mother?" she asks
sounds abrupt even to her own ears.

Sonia peers at her. "No. She was from a tiny village so
Highlands. She'd never been to the city. The lawyer
brought the baby to us."

Rena thinks about Prankle's stories of babies sold by
for the few hundred quetzals an adoption lawyer will pa
girls escorted to hospitals to have their babies and then
to sign that they learn only later are adoption consents.

"But you have her name? If you ever wanted to conta

A startled expression passes over Sonia's face. "W
Where are you coming from?"

Sonia stands. She reaches for Carlos.

Rena clutches the baby. The bottle falls and Carlos scr
hands are on Carlos' arms. She's pulling him.

Rena relinquishes the baby. She leans down to get the
it to Sonia.

Holding Carlos, Sonia steps back. She cleans the nipp
it in her mouth, puckered now like something charred. "H
baby."

TWO DAYS AFTER SHE graduated from high s
moved out. It was a Saturday afternoon, and Eleanor and J
Gene to the beach. She packed her clothes in two shoppin
the five twenties her mother had given her as a graduatio
note that she'd call once she was settled and walked to the

She remembers hitching a ride with a salesman headed to
who drank from a silver flask he kept in the glove compa

ared her by calling her chicky. She remembers taking the bus from San afael to San Francisco and getting off at Market Street. She remembers ıying a bottle of black hair dye (for reasons unclear other than that ıe no longer wanted to look like herself) from a Woolworth's clerk ith a cherry birthmark on her cheek. She remembers walking down xth Street and seeing the Alta Hotel: ROOMS—HOUR, DAY, WEEK, ONTH. YOU CHOOSE.

She fumbled to find a name to register, putting together Jane Eyre ıd Marjorie Morningstar to get Jane Morningstar. A man with a button missing from his shirt showed her a room with a bed and a dresser ıd a hard-back chair and a padlock on the door. He pointed down the ıll to two bathrooms, one with a toilet and sink, the other with only a ıb. Carrying the bottle of hair dye and a small white towel, she walked ward the one with the tub, past rooms with their doors flung open: an d guy passed out with his fly unzipped, two enormous women seated de by side on the bed playing cards, a boy with a boom box watching a television propped on the windowsill.

She remembers the banging on the door to her room an hour later hile she waited for the dye to set and opening the door to see Sammy ith her platinum hair, a red silk robe stretched over her ample hips.

"Gotta plug, sweetie?"

"Excuse me?"

"A tampon." Cigarette dangling, she fingered Rena's wet hair. Black ıme off on her fingers. "Jesus, what did you do? Run away from ɔme?"

Rena looked at the floor.

The woman laughed. She was young herself. "Don't worry. I'm not ɔing to rat you out. Last thing I need is the cops asking me questions. ıt you have to do something about that hair."

"I never did it before," Rena said apologetically.

"Go buy another bottle, brown, not black, and I'll redo it for you. n Sammy. Room 26."

In the end, because the Woolworth's was closed, Rena went platinum

like Sammy. "But you'll have to go short, because I don't have enough peroxide left for that mop." Sammy spread newspapers out on the floor of her room and sat Rena in a chair. In the corner was a card table with cosmetic bottles, a hot plate and a picture of a little girl with pigtails in a swing. Rena closed her eyes while Sammy snipped. Her head grew light as her hair fell to the floor.

When Sammy finally let her look in the mirror, Rena didn't know whether to laugh or cry. Platinum corkscrew curls sprang from her head. The next day, Sammy took Rena to Alil's.

"This is my cousin Jane from Barena. She needs a job."

"She has papers?"

"You have papers?"

Alil looked at Rena. Hanging on the wall behind him were black-and-white photos of girls dancing topless in glass enclosures like circus cages. "She is so ignorant, she does not even understand that I am from the royal Iranian family. My father is third cousin to the Shah and my mother is aunt to the sister-in-law of his wife. Before Khomeini, we lived in a palace with three swimming pools and our own heliport."

Rena nodded. Sammy rolled her eyes. Alil wore a starched white shirt with the sleeves folded up to his elbows. Fine black hair lay over his slender forearms. Narrowing his eyes, he studied Rena's chest.

"She's a kid," Sammy said. "Front room only."

"Turn her around."

Rena could feel Sammy touching her shoulder, pushing her gently. Dark flecks danced before her. Like a windup doll perched on a wedding cake, she pivoted around.

In the front room, the girls wore white satin hot pants, a black leotard and platform shoes. They served drinks, sandwiches and bowls of salty chips that made people drink more. The albino bartender poured the drinks strong, and after two or three most of the men dug into their wallets for the twenty-five-dollar admission to the back room. In the back, there were five glass cages where Sammy and the other girls danced in G-strings and spangled pasties. Passing through to pick up her kitchen orders, Rena would imagine the dancers were fish in an aquarium; the men who pressed their crotches against the glass, schoolchildren come to view the tropical specimens.

After Rena got her first paycheck, she moved out of the Alta Hotel into a share apartment she'd found from a card posted in a health food store: "Seeking nonsmoking roommate for meatless household committed to mind alteration without the use of substances. Large room three blocks from beach." Reed, returned to his moving company job after three months at the Mountain House detox center, was one of her two roommates. She bought a pot of geraniums for her windowsill and a Mexican blanket to cover the bed. When her day off fell at a time when Joe was on the road, she'd take the bus to visit her mother, whom she'd told she was working in a restaurant, and Gene, who cried the first time he saw her unfamiliar hair.

Afraid of her mind deteriorating, she ordered a subscription for the *New York Times*. She got a library card at the Tenderloin Branch near Alil's, where the reading room stank with the smell of the unwashed men who slept in the chairs but left the books untouched. She began with the A's and worked her way through the alphabet, picking authors either Reed recommended or she remembered from one of her English classes: Anderson, Brontë, Chekhov, Dostoyevsky, Ellison, Fitzgerald, Gissing, Hardy, Isherwood, James, Kipling, Lessing, Melville, Nabokov.

SHE SPENDS THE DAY visiting Lake Amitalán on the outskirts of the city. The lake is disappointingly ugly, with a power plant on the eastern edge and a string of decrepit vacation homes along the shore. Posted on the beaches are signs indicating that the water is *peligro por contaminación*.

All day, Sonia's words—*my baby*—ring in her ears. Once, while Eleanor was living in Eureka with the roll-towel salesman, drinking with him every night, and Gene was with Rena in New Haven, Eleanor said, "You think you're the mother, don't you? That you're better than me." Rena knew it was the scotch talking over the phone, but still she couldn't shake the feeling that she had stolen her mother's child. After

Gene returned to Novato, she felt self-conscious about their closeness, about the way three years of living together, just the two of them, left them able to finish one another's sentences. Although she's explained to herself the distance she's kept ever since as due to Gene's need for more privacy now that he's older, she sees now how, in fact, she'd removed herself for Eleanor's sake.

She skips dinner, bringing a banana and some crackers back to her room. It's the last night before Leonard's return and she eats in bed, reading from a copy of *The Age of Innocence* she'd packed in her suitcase. She hates the Countess Olenska for in the end honoring convention, wonders if this is how Sonia sees her: priggish and moralizing.

The Christmas before Mitch jumped in front of the train, Saul had broached the subject of their trying to get pregnant in the new year. They'd been married for two years. She was almost thirty-three. She'd put him off: she wasn't ready, she was traveling too much for her job. Could it be, he gently inquired, that with only Eleanor as an example she feared what kind of mother she'd be? "I took Gene," she retorted. "I took care of him." Perhaps, it occurs to her now, this is precisely the problem. Having taken Gene, she'd felt the edict was no more.

In her sleep, she listens for Carlos' cries. By morning, she knows they are gone. "They checked out yesterday," the manager tells her in his clipped accent. Rena rents their room. She moves her things across the courtyard, leaving Leonard the room they'd shared.

LEONARD RETURNS IN HIGH SPIRITS. He shows her postcards of Panajachel, the square in Chichicastenango, a panorama of the mountains with a waterfall trickling down the left quadrant. When he inquires about Sonia and Hank, she says only that they seem to have changed hotels.

On Monday, they return to the police station. Señor Padillo smiles broadly at them. "*Un minuto.*" They wait in the anteroom to Señor Perez's office. Rena watches a woman bring in a tray of coffee. A boy delivers a stack of newspapers. The phone rings and a toilet flushes. Leonard leaves to use a rest room. While he is gone, she hears a rattling sound which she imagines to be a dolly moving a casket. When she'd first received the letter from the State Department, she'd assumed that what had been found were bones identified as Bernardo's. Since meeting Prankle, though, she's envisioned a corpse soaking in formaldehyde in a basement room far below.

After an hour, the woman who brought the coffee motions for them to follow her into the office. Señor Perez stands behind his desk in a khaki uniform with green satin stripes. He extends a thin hand, a ring with a blue sapphire on his index finger. A scar runs down the middle of his left eyebrow, creating a ravine through the black hairs. The remains, he promises, will be turned over to them on Wednesday. Señor Padillo, he tells them, will handle the final paperwork. He bows slightly, the meeting they have waited six days for terminated in three minutes' time.

They spend the afternoon at the National Museum. Rena walks through the musty corridors hardly looking. On Tuesday morning, they go to the Central Market to buy presents: a blanket for Klara, a tablecloth for Ruth and Maggie, a carved wooden box for Marc and Susan. Not until they are back at the *posada* does it occur to her that they have bought nothing for Saul.

She cannot sleep. At five, she rises and dresses. Sitting in the courtyard in the hazy morning light, she wishes she had thought to bring something of Santiago's to have cremated with Bernardo. What would Santiago have wanted to go with his son? A copy of *Das Kapital*? A cross? A photograph of Bernardo with his parents? In the end, she takes a postcard of a quetzal bird and carefully prints: "Your parents loved you. May you rest with them now in peace."

ON THE BUS TO the police station, Rena tells Leonard what Prankle told her about Bernardo. Leonard looks down at his feet. "I'm not surprised."

The truck for the cremation company is parked in front of the police station. Two men lean against the back grille, smoking and drinking cans of soda. A guard escorts them to a small windowless room at the rear of the building. A few minutes later, Padillo appears. There are more papers to sign. More papers to be stamped. Afterwards, he speaks in Spanish to Leonard, who translates for Rena: "He wants to know if we want to walk with the casket from the building to the truck."

Rena looks at Leonard, but other than his slow recognition of what must be the alarm on her face, he does not seem taken aback that they will not see the body. Is it possible that this was not understood? She stands, her chair toppling as she rises. Her heart is beating so fast, she feels like she's being shaken. She imagines a casket filled with a sack of potatoes. "I have to see the body."

Leonard rights her chair. She is grateful that he does not question her. He speaks slowly and calmly to Padillo. Padillo reddens. "Señora," he says to Rena. "Please." He taps a nostril. "The nose, *cómo se dice, el olor?*" He continues in Spanish to Leonard, glancing every few seconds at Rena. Leonard does not translate their exchange. She hears *el embajador*. She sees Leonard point to a paragraph in one of the documents they have signed. Padillo shakes his head and then leaves the room.

"He says he will have to speak to Señor Perez. Apparently, the casket has already been closed." Nearly an hour passes before Padillo returns. Arrangements will have to be made. Workmen must be found. The earliest they can view the remains is after the siesta. *A la tres y media*.

Rena refuses to leave. If she leaves, she fears, the body will be whisked away. Padillo points Leonard in the direction of the street where he can purchase sandwiches. Leonard returns with cans of juice, cheese sandwiches on hard rolls and newspapers. Rena drinks the juice. She breaks the sandwich in half but cannot bite into it.

She sits in that room for seven hours. Once, she goes out to use the restroom. Twice, Leonard leaves to get fresh air. It is after four by the time Padillo returns. He beckons for them to follow. They walk down a long corridor at the end of which is a staircase blocked by a gate bearing a sign: NO PERMITIDO. Keys jangle as Padillo searches through the ring on his belt for the one that will open the gate. They follow him down a steep flight of stairs into the basement. Señor Perez and three uniformed men stand by a door marked with a skull and crossbones. In the dim light, the scar on Perez's eyebrow shines like something that has ossified. One of the uniformed men wears a hunter green beret. The other two have white surgical masks over their mouths and noses. The two with the masks peel off to flank Leonard. Perez and the man with the beret move toward Rena.

Padillo unlocks the door. Rena reels from the smell. Perez and the man with the beret have taken her elbows and are pushing her forward. It's pitch black and she fears she will scream. She can hear the heels of Padillo's shoes on the concrete floor and then a click as he flips on a surgical lamp. In the middle of the room is a metal table with a casket on top. The lid is swung so that she cannot see inside.

Perez guides her to the foot of the table. It is not clear if she is standing or being held upright. Sweat pours from her armpits, and her mouth and lungs fill with the taste of formaldehyde. Her eyes have clenched tight. *Look,* she says. She does not know if she has said this out loud or in her head. *Look.*

Inside the casket, gray strands like tangled seaweed jut from the head. There is no face. Only eye sockets and a bit of flesh on top of the cheekbones. A shroud is draped over the torso. What flesh remains on the limbs has turned yellow, like chicken meat gone bad. The hands folded over the shroud are only bones. One foot has a toenail grown wild. "Bernardo," she whispers, and then she hears a shuffling as Leonard's knees buckle and he is steadied by the two men at his sides.

A wedge of light cuts the floor as Leonard is taken outside. Rena does not move. She tries to plaster the photos she has seen of Bernardo onto the corpse.

Perez loosens his grip on her elbow, and the man with the beret moves to the side of the casket. *"La señorita ha terminado?"* Perez asks with no more expression than a waiter inquiring if she has finished her soup.

Rena nods. The man with the beret lowers the casket lid. He fastens the six latches. Rena crosses herself the way she recalls her mother doing when they'd see a hearse on the street.

In the hallway outside, someone has brought a chair for Leonard, who is sitting with his head against the wall. The men from the cremation company swing their black moving straps. Padillo leads them into the room. A few minutes later, they emerge hunched over with the casket strapped to their backs. The two men who'd worn the surgical masks help lift the casket up the steep stairs.

AT NIGHT, SHE screams so loudly that Leonard hears her across the courtyard. He bangs on her door to waken her and then holds her while she heaves and weeps.

"I forgot to put the note in the casket," she gurgles into his chest.

Leonard strokes her hair. "We'll tape it to the urn."

He guides her back to the bed. She does not know if she would have been able to ask. She only knows how grateful she feels when he pulls up the armchair where Sonia had sat rocking Carlos and is still there, asleep, when she sees the first morning light.

Part Four

A BODY RISING

15 Leonard

I pull into our driveway before six. I am thinking about Mrs. Smiley, trying to recall what I used to pay her. Opening the kitchen door, I hear footsteps in the basement. I call out a hello to Mrs. Smiley, only to hear your mother's voice in response. Racing downstairs, I imagine the disasters that have befallen Mrs. Smiley leading to your mother's departure from bed, but instead of calamity there is your mother, cheerfully folding towels.

"What happened to Mrs. Smiley?"

"Oh, I let her go. It was so annoying to have her here, puttering around." She rolls her eyes. "Good Lord, to think of all those years when she washed our underwear and poked around in our closets."

Your mother, it turns out, has risen from her bed with the furious energy of a cripple who's left her crutches at Lourdes. Upstairs, I discover the vacuum cleaner parked in the middle of the living room floor and curtains pulled down from the rods so they can be cleaned. The refrigerator, not defrosted since Mrs. Smiley's departure from our permanent employ, stands open with perishables tucked into an ice chest dug out from the garage. Despite my objection that she hasn't driven a car in nearly three decades, your mother takes the keys to her father's old Mercedes-Benz and heads off in search of vacuum cleaner bags and a new scrub brush.

Try as I might, I cannot discover the miracle font. When I left for Guatemala, your mother was twenty-seven years into her neurasthenia. When I returned, she was cured. It's not the transformation itself that troubles me. That strikes me simply as the proof in the pudding that the disorder had never been in her cells. (Did I ever tell you about the man on my ward who after three years of a hysterical paralysis of his lower limbs walked over to the nurses' station to request a tennis racket?) Ditto, your mother's *belle indifférence* to her recovery—the fact that she does not betray any amazement—which seems to me just another version of the comfort she'd had all along with the whole invalidism thing.

What troubles me is the cause, the pesky why questions. It seems too late, a year and a half since your arrest, to link this to you. I consider her upcoming sixtieth birthday and the way, or so I've read, that women suffer these transitions between the decades more than men. It takes me a week before I can entertain the idea that it's me. I'm in the shower, mulling it over, when I hear Merckin's measured voice: *We need to understand why you prefer to think of your wife as having atrophy of the cerebral cortex. You follow your daughter-in-law all the way to Guatemala. And you don't think your wife senses something's afoot?*

That she better get the hell out of bed?

Now you're thinking, Dr. Dubinsky.

Oddly, I sink into blackness. I can feel it coming like a flu settling over my muscles, leaving me lethargic and leaden with a clump of something hard and heavy, not in my throat but deep at the base of my lungs where the old breathing bags touch the diaphragm. Tired all the time, I cannot sleep except in snatches. Drained of appetite, I stuff myself from distraction.

At first, I think it is exhaustion from the trip. Latent exhaustion released by the travel like a hidden virus set off by a cold. Then, rising above my somatizing analogies, I consider the jolt to my system of so much intimacy: the sounds of Rena turning in sleep, brushing her teeth, her screams the night after we saw the corpse. Finally, I consider the most damning of possibilities—that I am sickened by the remarkable change in your mother.

Imagine, my self-approbation at not being thrilled by this turn of events. To feel only irritation at the disruption in my routine, the loss of the control I've had over the household. To wish that the old horse would climb back into bed.

The blackness filters inward, a tarry smoke that makes it hard to breathe. My environs, which even in the best of times strike me as lacking in charm, lose even their bland pleasantness. At moments, the sensation of everything being covered with grime is so powerful that I am surprised when the objects in my life still function: the keys on my keyboard depress, the gears in my watch turn.

We meet in early August. A Thursday evening in a heat wave, when most anyone with a decent bank account has fled the city for a square yard of beach or a wood cabin somewhere. Rena suggests a place on the uppermost level of the South Street Seaport. A tourist trap with mediocre food, she warns, but cool and breezy. I arrive early and am ushered to a table with knock-your-socks-off views of the mouth of the harbor. Party boats festooned with lights pass below, the reggae music blasting so loud I can make out the words, the lights of Brooklyn flickering—I can say it to you—like an ode to Walt Whitman.

She arrives exactly on time, and seeing her I think immediately of two things. That she is never late. That she always finds her way to the edge of water. She's wearing an ethnic kind of top and ankle-length skirt, her hair longer than I've seen it before, so that she looks less like a career girl and more relaxed and at ease. She kisses me warmly, once on each cheek.

We order chilled things to share: oysters and shrimp cocktails and lobster tails. She tells me that she went to see you ten days ago. We agree that you seem to have passed through the worst of it. Eighteen months. Nearly halfway.

She tells me that she's returned to her word-processing job. "The money's good and the hours suit me. In September, I'm going to France for two weeks. After that, they'll switch me from a temp to a permanent position."

She sees that I am perplexed about the trip, that she'd be off again less than three months after our return. "I guess I've been bit with the travel bug," she says. She doesn't smile and I feel a tightness in my chest, the way I did with you when you came to borrow my credit card and I knew there'd been a rupture between us, things you didn't want me to know.

(*You mean you knew I was lying.*

Yes.)

"I've never been, you know. Ruth and Maggie convinced me that September's perfect. The college kids will have left, but it's still warm."

She pushes her hair back from her face, and I can see in that moment the way she will age: the tight muscles weakening and the skin growing loose and delicate but, like Katharine Hepburn, the great bone structure holding its own to the end. A despondency at the sense of a secret settles over me, and I don't even ask for the details of her trip. The conversation turns to books, and I have the distinct impression that this is purposeful on her part. When she inquires about my book, I fall for it the way a vain woman will for a compliment.

I order a brandy with coffee and indulge myself in your wife's attention, in the sound of my own voice—knowing all the while that tomorrow I will feel sick with humiliation at my own pomposity. "There is always a personal story behind the public one," I intone. "Only we're usually too simplistic in the way we look for the parallels. The logic is more like that which operates between a dream and psychic reality: opposites and similarities are the same, contiguity is the signal of cause and effect, positives and negatives dissolve in a common pool."

In the dim light, she looks like an apparition. Across her face, I can see the traces of your eager visage when you still believed in ideas. Hour after hour around that duck pond and then later, as a medical student, stuffed with facts but starved for thought, your vacations spent reading Adorno and Habermas and those dense literary critics with their hodgepodge of deconstruction and Marx and Lacan. My own secrets swim up from their hiding places and for a moment I feel tempted to use them as a rope to reach out to Rena, but I stop myself, sheer will, as I see the betrayal in telling your wife about Maria before I tell you.

THE FOLLOWING SUNDAY, I go to see you. To my relief, your mother, still in her cleaning frenzy, every closet and shelf emptied and scrubbed, does not ask to come along. I leave at dawn, a day when light does not so much appear as darkness fades. I rifle through the night's dream: quarreling with your mother, you two still children, about the reprehensibility of her buying every toy you so much as graze with a glance. *You'll ruin him,* I say about you, *turn him into God knows what.*

At eight, I stop for breakfast at a diner outside Fairfield, empty save for a group of golfers in pinks and greens and two tables of truckers chewing with their caps still on. The waitress passes her eyes over me with no more interest than I've been able to give to the landscape around me—a paunchy old geezer.

I order a geriatric breakfast of grapefruit juice and Special K.

"No Special K." Her scalp shines under sprayed red hair. "Flakes, krispies or bran."

For a moment I miss your mother, who would have ordered more respectably. The Number Two with Canadian bacon. The Number Five with flapjacks. Or perhaps I feel badly about the dream, the transparency of the wish to point the finger about you at her. The wish for an excuse not to tell you about the ghost in the attic, the spectral Maria, safely hidden, I'd pretended—as though there were ever a child who'd not found the key.

YOU REST AN ELBOW on the metal table, assume your chin-in-the-sling-of-the-hand pose.

"Did it occur to you that she might have worked it through with you if you'd stayed? That what happened between the two of you might have been understood in a way that would have helped her?"

Either you've been dabbling in the same theoretical waters I still dip into from time to time (the new models about illness being a two-person construction, about the treatment having as strong an impact on the treater as the treated) or your intuition lands you where I've been since seeing your mother's return to the living: at the way we sacrifice parts of the self to protect, or so we believe, the rest.

"I couldn't," I say. "It was a vicious circle. She needed me to provide the words for her feelings. But I couldn't step outside the force of my own responses. Had I admitted more than the skin of my feelings"—a shiver passes over me just thinking about it—"I would have been thrown out on my tail. Or at least thrown off the case."

"Did you consider that? Stopping working with her rather than stopping working completely?"

"If I'd been able to consider, it wouldn't have happened. Not that I stopped thinking. I couldn't stop thinking. But my thoughts had lost their influence, like soldiers stripped of their weapons. All I had were my feelings and, thank God, enough conscience not to act more grossly than I did."

"Did you act?"

"Not in a sense that a behaviorist would call action. More in a Catholic sense. I violated her in my thoughts. And my feelings—I'm absolutely certain—seeped through. Had she been better put together, she would have screened them out. But she was like a high-power radio receiver when it came to carnality. She could detect a fraction of a megahertz."

You grow silent. You look remarkably well for someone who's just spent a year and a half in prison with two plus years to go. As though receiving the punishment for your misdeeds, real and imagined, has been a liberation.

"So," you say, "you had Maria and I had Mitch."

We stare at each other.

"What do you mean?"

You laugh. The guard peers through the window. He holds up the familiar two fingers. You hold up three in return. I notice that you're no longer wearing your wedding band.

"Tell Mom thanks for the clippings."

I raise an eyebrow.

"She's been sending me articles from the *Times* on topics related to health care. Controversies over vitamin B_{12}. New theories about serotonin reuptake. Utilization of physician assistants in rural areas. It's actually been very helpful. Motivated me to get Morton to start looking into what options I'll have to practice after this."

You point to the green walls around us. The door opens and the guard cocks his head. I follow you out, the guard as always at the rear. At the turnoff for the lockup, a second guard is waiting. He shadowboxes with you, and I watch in amazement as you return the punches.

I MAKE MY WAY to the car and drive off the prison grounds. Exhausted, I could be asleep by the count of ten. I find the throughway entrance and head south. At the first rest area, I pull in and park in a distant corner. I lean the seat back, check that the doors are locked and close my eyes.

A tapping sound wakes me. A state trooper is knocking on the glass next to my ear. Groggily, I raise a hand to roll down the window. I smell the exhaust from the trooper's car pulled perpendicular to mine, hear the hiss from his two-way radio. It's neither light nor dark. I'm confused as to whether it's night or day.

"You were sleeping so long, we got worried something was wrong. Folks don't usually do more than an hour shut-eye in these places."

I inhale deeply, close and then reopen my eyes to regain my focus. "No, no. I'm fine." I look at the clock on the dashboard. It's nearly seven. Seven at night.

"Maybe you best go inside and get yourself a coffee and sandwich."

Inside, I call your mother and tell her when I'll be home. In the background, I can hear a Frank Sinatra record. Records she dragged up from the basement and has been playing on an old turntable of yours.

Obediently, I order a coffee and tuna sandwich. I set the sandwich on the passenger seat and prop the coffee between my legs. Other than the sixteen-wheelers speeding past on my left, there's little traffic. I sink into the drone of the engine, let my eyes adjust to the dark.

You had Maria and I had Mitch, you said, the idea so effortless it was as though I'd told you something you already knew.

I want to argue it out with you. A useless exercise, I realize. As if the unconscious could be evaluated like a legal brief. Still, I cannot resist imagining the exchange:

A faulty analogy, I insist. I knew Maria. I was by any reasonable construction of events the motive force behind her slitting her wrists. You never met Mitch until after his jump. It's not a parallel.

Oh, really, you counter. *But Mitch knew of me. He knew I'd chosen not to see him my first day on the job. He knew I was no more going to be his Prince Charming than you would be Maria's.*

That's not what happened. She tried to kill herself because she'd trusted me and then I turned out to be no different from the encyclopedia salesman.

That's how you saw it. That you'd caused everything she experienced. Her desire for you. Her disappointment in you. Her fear of you. Her fear of her desire.

I am nodding. Goddamn idiot that I am, I am nodding as I approach the Henry Hudson Parkway, the George Washington Bridge and New Jersey now in sight.

I felt exactly the same. That I was the cause of Mitch losing his legs. And now you feel the same way about me. That you are the cause of everything I did. That it was all because of you.

The megalomania of this washes over me. The madman's trick of turning the wish to disavow all responsibility into assuming it all. The pleasure of self-flagellation. The comfort of mea culpa, of a world completely under one's own control.

Not until I'm in bed does what you've told me, that you are going to attempt to return to working as a doctor, sink in. That you, braver soul than I, are going to try again.

16 Rena

For a week after her return from Guatemala City, she'd not gone back to work. Bernardo's ashes sat in their urn on her dresser. She considered sprinkling them in the orchard adjacent to Ruth and Maggie's country house. She considered donating them to a library or some kind of archive. Then, one morning, she woke with an idea fully in mind. She opened the urn and removed the plastic bag. A body reduced to a few pounds of silt. With the bag in her backpack, she took the Broadway line to the last stop and boarded the Staten Island ferry.

It was early morning, just a little past seven, and the ferry was empty save for a handful of night workers returning to their homes. She buttoned her sweater and pulled open the glass door that led out to the deck. The sun, still low in the sky, cast an amber sheen over the water. Gulls dipping for fish screeched in anticipation of their kill and a foghorn blasted from the east. The ferry traveled quickly into the channel, and within a matter of minutes they were in open waters.

Moving toward the back of the boat so she would not be in view of the captain, she took the bag of ashes from her backpack and held them close to her body. As a child, when she was scared, her mother would whisper, *Just close your eyes*. Rena had done this with Nick. She'd done this with Joe. She'd done this with Saul for most of the year after Mitch. Not until Bernardo had she forced herself to look.

They were passing between Ellis Island and Fort Jay. To her right, she could see the crowned head of the Statue of Liberty, the green hand hoisting the light. Her mother's mother, Filomena, had made the passage from Italy to New York in 1912 at the age of four. Her mother's father, the drooling old man she'd met at Betty's house, had done the same eight years later. And her father's parents? If Eleanor had even known, she'd not said.

Rena opened the plastic sack. Inside was a gritty white substance with small pieces of bone. She leaned over the rail of the boat and let the ashes fall. They blew back, some catching on the wet side of the boat, some drifting down to the water. She thought of Santiago weeping as he told her that his wife had died of grief.

To the east, the sky was fully lit. To the west, dark clouds, the remains of the night, moved toward the sea. A fleck of sandy ash stuck to her palm and for a moment she saw eye sockets, thought, *are you there,* but then the wind lifted the ash and as it disappeared in white air she whispered, "Bernardo, rest in peace."

At home, she drew the blinds and closed her bedroom door. She pulled open the top drawer of her file cabinet and lifted out the folder marked G. She counted the remaining giraffe money: six thousand two hundred dollars.

In the afternoon, she called Sari. "Thank the goodness you're back," Sari sighed in her Urdu-inflected English. "The girl who filled in for you is too stupid to even use the spellcheck properly. Last week she made a typo on the word *formulate* and then selected *fornicate* as the replace option. The partner whose brief it was yelled so loudly that people ran in, thinking there was an emergency. And you won't have Mr. Beersden breathing down your neck any longer. He's been transferred to the Chicago office."

Rena returned to work the following night. She slipped into the old routine with the ease of a swimmer rediscovering her stroke: the evening walk, the stop at Grand Central, the wee hours chamber music, the walk home at six. On the weekend, she went to see Saul. When he asked about Guatemala, she could think of nothing simple to say. "They showed us a body. I hope it was his."

There was something new and hard in Saul's face. Not hard in a wizened, scarred way, but hard like a diamond blade.

"I threw his ashes over the water. Next to the Statue of Liberty."

Saul took her hand. Out in the open. His hand felt like a stranger's, the delicate fingers now thickened and rough. She peered at the skin showing over the vee of his uniform shirt, wondered if the bird's-nest hollow had disappeared under a shield of muscle, flushed at the thought that he would feel different now.

THE SECOND GIRAFFE had arrived in late July. A box again from Barcelona. Again, she drew the blinds. Using sewing scissors to cut the puckered stitches at the base of the giraffe's neck, she pulled out a piece of folded paper. Two words—LA TRINITÉ—with a cross drawn underneath.

She crumpled the paper into a ball. This is lunacy, she tried to reassure herself. He cannot expect me to find him from two words on a scrap of paper.

She took the wrinkled paper to the travel bookstore in Rockefeller Center, where she unsuccessfully searched the Spanish guidebooks. Reluctantly, she approached the information counter.

"I'm looking for a place called La Trinité," she told the woman behind the counter. "I think it's near Barcelona."

"Are you certain it's Spain? La Trinité, that sounds like France."

She thought about the *Atlas Routier* she'd taken from Bria's apartment. The dashed lines for the pedestrian routes through the mountains. "It could be."

"La Trinité," the woman murmured. "I wonder if that's the name of a church." She stood. Her silver pageboy swung beneath her headband. She led Rena to the back of the store. Climbing up on a stepladder, she reached for a book on the top shelf: *Guide des Églises et Chapelles de France*.

She flipped to the page. A paragraph entry and a dark photo of an engraved iron door. "The Pyrenees Orientales. That's about as close to Barcelona as you're going to get in France."

Rena bought the book. At home, she read the brief entry about La

Trinité. A Roman church from the twelfth century that had been a stop on the hermitage journey for the Catalans. Renowned for its elaborate iron door and the wooden altarpiece carved by a Monsieur Autel. Perched in the foothills of the Aspres, near Mont Canigou. Near the village of Prunet et Belpuig.

She found Prunet et Belpuig in the *Atlas Routier,* studied the map the way Reed had taught her to do. The towns thinned out as the white along the Mediterranean coast shifted to green. There were mountain peaks near La Trinité, the Spanish border close below.

For a week, she alternated between astonishment at Reed's assurance that she would find him and the awareness that she did not want to go—not so much out of fear (it seemed unlikely that now, nearly a year and a half since Saul's arrest, anyone was watching her) but rather because it was too soon after Guatemala, those sights and sounds not yet digested. On her walks home from work, though, she was flooded with memories of Reed: how after three nights sleeping on the floor of her room in the apartment they'd shared by the beach, she'd come back from Alil's to discover a mattress and dresser he'd hauled home for her, discards, he'd claimed, from the moving company, but now, it occurred to her, things he'd probably bought. His taking her to Yosemite, the first time she'd ever seen a mountain, where they hiked through Alpine meadows blanketed with wildflowers and he hung their food from a tree to keep it from the bears.

She'd planned her trip for September, after the crowds but before the snow. She mentioned going to the mountains to no one. Instead, she booked a flight to Bordeaux and said she would travel on to Nice. A reasonable journey, traversing the country west to east. Not a trip anyone would expect to involve a detour into the Pyrenees.

Everyone had their hidden South of France they wanted to share: Maggie's list of the best *auberges* in the Dordogne for eating the real Quercy fare, her mother's boss's itinerary through the *villages perchés* of the Luberon, the Roman ruins at Arles, the Gorge du Verdon. Saul threw in his two cents—Bregançon, the campers' beach beneath a château that served as the southern residence for the president of France

—and then, to Rena's amusement, a note from Klara with a clipping from *Vogue* on shopping in Saint-Tropez. Only Leonard, whose narrowed eyes had betrayed his disbelief at her bitten-by-the-travel-bug claim, offered no advice.

SHE LANDS IN Bordeaux at noon. Driving east, she crosses the Garonne in full view of the Pont de Pierre. A haze of heat hovers over the water, the bridge, older than anything outside a museum she's ever seen before, a hallucinatory quality to entering a world where the centuries are layered on top of one another and schoolchildren race through thousand-year-old arches and plazas laid out in the time of kings. In San Francisco, the Victorian houses had been their ruins. In Novato, antiquity had been the shopping center on Route 101.

It's an hour's drive to the inn at Tremolat where she's reserved her first three nights' stay. She follows the innkeeper upstairs to her room overlooking the gardens behind the church. Closing the shutters, she bathes and climbs still damp under the cool white sheets of the bed. She sleeps until dusk and then, in the evening, walks to the café on the square where the college French she'd boned up on this past month works for an order of grilled trout that arrives with string beans fine as matchsticks.

For two days, she lackadaisically follows Maggie's itinerary for the region. She visits the medieval towns of Domme and Sarlat and the monastery in Souillac, picnics on white peaches and soft cheese from the *épicerie* on the square. Dimly recalling a canoe trip she'd made with Reed when he'd joked that he was going to have to teach her the things kids learn when they go to camp and, lucky her, she'd be spared the bug juice, she rents a canoe in Limeuil, where the Dordogne and Vézère converge and families of ducks make their home. Mostly, though, she is watching: watching to make sure there is no one watching her.

At night, she reads guidebooks and studies maps. Not about where she is, this gentle cultivated landscape, but where she is going: into the rugged mountains, where heretics and revolutionaries and resistance fighters have hidden and, she presumes, where Reed now lives.

She leaves at dawn, fighting to keep the little pit, half fear, half excitement, deep in her stomach. The fields are filled with people picking grapes for the annual *vendange*. Driving south, the farms grow scrappier, the picturesque yielding to light industry. At Montauban, she picks up the autoroute. She stops for gas and a sandwich in a futuristic rest area that abuts the Canal du Midi. Pleasure boats dock adjacent to the pumps, and families eat on outdoor tables surrounded by fierce flies and the roar of the highway. She abandons her sandwich after two bites.

Fifteen kilometers north of the Spanish border, she exits the autoroute and cuts back to the west through the red clay town of Ceret, where she'd read that Picasso had fled one beautiful lover accompanied by another, toward the foothills. The fruit orchards disappear as she climbs and the towns thin to an occasional hamlet. The bends in the road sharpen and she downshifts, using the gears to control the curves.

It's nearly five by the time she reaches La Trinité. She leaves the car in a turn-out across the road from the church, hugging her arms in the cooling air. Across the valley, she can see the jagged peaks of the Pyrenees, the tallest already snowcapped. She'd expected a village, but there is only the church, a phone booth and a bulletin board with postings about the surrounding parkland. The little pit, now almost all fear, rises up as she thinks about how many leaps there'd been between the scrap of paper and this church.

The iron door is open. Inside, it's dim, the only light coming from a stand of prayer candles. A coin box requesting money to help pay for the electricity hangs next to a switch. She puts in a five-franc piece and flips it on. A faint spot shines on the altar where Jesus with outstretched hands is flanked by a man and a woman. Serpentine columns laden with marble grapes surround the threesome.

A woman with a lace kerchief tied under her chin plods flat-footed through the doorway. She turns off the spot. "*C'est fermé, mademoiselle.*" Rena follows her out to the courtyard. She asks if there are lodgings in Prunet. The woman shakes her head. She points up the road. "*Il faut aller à Saint-Marcel.*"

It takes twenty minutes to reach Saint Marcel. Two men drink and smoke under a Cin Cin umbrella in front of a grim auberge. Inside, the proprietor leads her to a room on the top floor dominated by a massive armoire with a crack in the mirror. She leaves her bags and then, in the waning light, takes a walk through the village. Women sit in their aprons on the steps of the ancient stone houses. Teenagers with a tape player have congregated near the phone booth outside the post office, the girls smoking and dancing, the boys just smoking.

She eats at the *auberge,* one of three diners. She watches the bar, which by the end of her meal is populated by a weathered-looking couple, a man in a leather vest and a young couple with their baby in a stroller. She knows that Reed will not simply walk through the door. Yet she half expects him to.

She waits until after the proprietor's wife has cleared the table to inquire: the cousin of a friend, she's forgotten his name, who lives nearby. Tall with blond hair.

"*Non. Il n'y a pas d'américains içi.*" The proprietor's wife tilts her head in the direction of the weathered couple. "*Ces gens sont des hollandais. Le seul autre étranger de la région, c'est un canadien qui loue le Mas Gontine. Il est très grand mais il a les cheveux noirs.*"

A Canadian. Very tall with black hair. Inside, Rena laughs. Sammy's laugh when she'd seen Rena's shoe-polished curls.

IN THE MORNING, Rena carries Reed's *Atlas Routier* across the street to the *épicerie*. She buys fresh figs and a bottle of water from a man in a butcher's apron stiff from starch. After she pays, she asks for directions to the Mas Gontine. The man directs her back toward Prunet. Left at the sign for Col Fortou and then the first right onto an unpaved road. *Au bout de la route.*

She packs up her things and pays for the room. Driving toward Prunet in the morning light, she can see the wild blackberries in the bushes along the road. Every hundred feet, the trees open to reveal the valley dotted with squares of farmland. It's a landscape with extraordinary depth, one thing rolling into the next: grazing pastures for sheep, bales of hay ready to be moved into the barns for winter, always, at the horizon, the mountains stacked like dishes.

Turning onto the dirt road, she's uncertain if she feels more nervous about finding Reed or a large Canadian with black hair. The lane leads into a ravine edged with the gnarled roots of the trees above. The car bumps over the stones. At the end is a wooden gate with a sign: MAS GONTINE.

She parks outside the gate, from where she can see the back of the old *mas,* so laden with vines that it appears to have grown right into the earth. She unlatches the gate and walks down the path, past an abandoned henhouse and a clothesline with dish towels hanging to dry. She can hear music. John Coltrane. Her heart pounds. Rounding the bend, she sees the stone steps leading to the open door. She climbs the stairs and peers into the dark.

"Yoo-hoo," she intends to holler. Her voice is barely above a whisper. She knocks on the doorjamb.

A figure wrapped in a towel approaches. A shadow shades his face. He squints into the sunlight where she's shivering. Rolls of fat drape his belly; his hair, an inky black, is thin and coarse. Only in the fine nose and the sweep of his athlete's shoulders can she detect the traces of Reed's past leonine beauty.

He puts his arms around her, lifting her slightly. His skin smells of things fermented, his breath of nicotine. Releasing her, he grins. "Well done, Giraffe."

WHILE REED SHOWERS and dresses, she surveys the kitchen: an ancient fireplace flanked by pots large enough to boil laundry, a modern stove, a small window adorned with a spider's web, a bachelor's refrigerator stocked with wine and cookies and a bag of espresso beans. On the shelf, she finds a carton of sterilized milk. No tea. While the coffee brews, she walks to her car and brings in her things. She washes the figs and makes a tray of coffee, sliced figs and cookies.

They breakfast on a table in a grassy clearing in front of the house. From here, she can see how the *mas*—in parts, Reed tells her, over nine hundred years old—is built into the hillside. Wooden doors with metal closures lead to the place where the animals were once lodged, home now to an old washing machine and a pair of fruit bats. Among the peaks in the distance, Reed points out Canigou, a sacred site for the Catalans. To the left, a peach orchard. To the right, a pasture for a neighbor's sheep.

In the sunlight, she can see the crow's-feet that spread out from Reed's eyes, the skin underneath soft and bumpy like the rind of an overripe fruit.

He sees her looking. "I know. I've gone to shit. Penance for my sins." He touches his brow. "Saul the innocent probably has a brow like a baby's ass."

"He does look pretty good for someone locked up for four years."

"Four years?"

"Yes."

Reed closes his eyes, presses the lids with his fingers. A minute or more passes before he speaks. "I reached Bria in Tenerife right before I came here. She told me she'd informed the police about Saul. His role was so small—I assumed he'd gotten off on parole." He lowers his hands. "Four years. Long time behind bars."

"You didn't expect she'd tell them about Saul?"

"No. First of all, I never thought she'd get nabbed. She grew up on smuggling; her old man used to smuggle diamonds out of Cape Town. Christ, she remembers diamonds taped inside her diaper. And I'd scripted this whole worst-case scenario for her—what to do if she got caught. How to call me, pretending I was her lawyer. I figured it would take them a day or two after no one showed up to realize it was a ploy, but by then I'd have gotten the loot in Tenerife and hightailed it out of there. She could tell them about me and try to use that to bargain her way out."

He pushes his chair back from the table. His shoulders are slumped, his eyes cast down toward the lax gut. "I still can't figure out what happened. I couldn't believe it when she told me she'd given them Saul. I was sure he was home free on this one. His role was such small change.

He supplied the list of drugs and the pharmacist's schedule, in exchange for which he got his tab with Fabio—that was the dealer he owed money to—wiped out and just enough stash to detox himself with."

Reed takes a pack of Gauloises from his pants pocket. "My best guess is they played hardball with her and she got scared. Or maybe Fabio got to her and threatened that if they found out about him, he'd get back at her so she gave them Saul as a diversion."

"How'd you end up here?"

"From Tenerife, I caught a boat to Agadir in Morocco. I hid out for a couple of months in Marrakech, used some of the pills to wean myself from the cocaine, then sold the rest in Tangiers, where someone got me a Canadian passport. I came here on that. Robert Allen. A bookkeeper from Ontario with a small inheritance from an aunt." He puts the cigarette to his mouth but doesn't light it. "Why four years?"

"It was the manslaughter charge."

"No one was hurt."

"The pharmacist, Kim Sun, miscarried. She was nine weeks pregnant. She lost the baby a few days after the burglary."

They sit in silence, Reed staring off at the horizon, the unlit cigarette still dangling from his lips, the platter of figs browning in the sun.

IN THE AFTERNOON, he takes her on a drive along the treacherously windy D618. They're in his car, a used Fiat he bought for cash in Marseilles. They round hairpin turns without guardrails, the rocky riverbed a sheer drop below.

Reed rolls down the window, lights a cigarette. "That asshole Fabio. He sent an idiot to do the job. We had a list typed up of the pharmaceuticals that were supposed to be handed over. A robot could have done it. Then, at the last minute, this moron asks her to throw in something for his girlfriend's period cramps. So he can save the four ninety-nine."

"So he pulled a gun?"

"Something she said made him think she was messing with him."

He's driving with one hand, smoking with the other. He takes the single-lane blind curves without slowing first.

When she gets back, Reed is cleanly shaven, his wet hair combed back from his face. He's dressed in khaki shorts and hiking boots. He points to a backpack on the kitchen table. "I'm going to take you to Canigou. You can't come to this region without paying respects to the great lady. If I don't have a heart attack climbing up, we'll picnic at the monastery."

They drive to the orchard town of Casteil, a hiker's outpost to Canigou, from which, Rena reads, visitors can either hire a jeep or begin the three-quarter-hour climb to reach the monastery of Saint-Martin.

"We can take the jeep," Rena says.

"No. Goddamnit. I played football at Stanford. If I croak on the way up, I deserve it."

It's a steep walk through patches of sweet-smelling garigue and thick green pines. Reed, panting, falls behind. Halfway up, Rena stops at an overlook to wait for him. When he reaches her, his face is red and dry. She pulls a bottle of water out of his backpack, and he drinks without speaking.

At the top, Reed rests on a bench while Rena takes the tour of the monastery, where the inhabitants live under a vow of silence. To start, a priest ushers the visitors into a small room where they are shown a film about the history of the eleventh-century structure built atop a huge rock outcropping by the Comte de Cerdagne, for whom the mountain range is named. Then, in silence, he leads the group up a path toward the monastery itself. Looking down, Rena can see wooded ravines and a stream. The cragged peaks of the Pyrenees hover above. An amazement, she marvels, that anything was constructed on this wild remote spot, that materials were hauled up the mountainside, that people have lived here for more than a millennium.

They picnic on a bed of brown pine needles: the Camembert and apples Reed packed, a *pain de campagne* bought along the way.

"I could do it," Rena says. She sweeps an arm outward. "With all this to look at every day, I could do it—live here without talking." What she does not say is that not only could she do it, she'd had to control herself from taking the priest's arm and pleading to be taken in.

"What are you going to do?"

She can see the light roots at his scalp and the blond hairs on his arms. He taps his cigarette pack and pulls out a cigarette, which he holds but does not light. "I don't know. All my life I've been scrambling to pick up the pieces. Never deliberately choosing."

"I used to look at you, when you were working at that topless joint and it was just a job for you, a way to make money, and think how it would be a lot simpler to just have to make money. That was my downfall: this idea that I needed to find a calling. All these lies to myself about what I'd be able to do with a law degree. Then, like everyone else, getting greedy and going for the big money the first year out of my clerkship. That's what I admired in Saul. He never sold out."

"In a lot of ways, he felt just like you—somewhere along the way what he'd wanted to do got swallowed up by a career. That's why he wrote me after I did that op-ed piece. He was trying to get back in touch with the ideas he'd put aside to get through his residency."

It's late, nearly six, and the light is beginning to pearlize in the cooling air. Reed stuffs the cigarette back in its pack. He washes an apple under a stream of Badois. "You could write a book about Saul's and my botched attempt at crime. Hell, you can't have a crime in America without someone writing a book about it. I'd do it myself if it wouldn't lead the DEA to my door. Write a book, retire and have yourself a baby."

"A baby? Where'd that come from?"

"Turning forty, this past year. The black stuff hides the gray." Reed pats his hair. "You're not that far behind."

"Four and a half years."

Reed hands her the apple and she bites into it.

"It wouldn't take too much arm-twisting to get me to make the necessary contributions."

Startled, Rena looks up to see him laughing. She chews and then wipes her mouth. "Thank you, sir. I'll keep that under consideration."

• • •

SHE SLIPS BACK into her life in New York without a sign of anyone having traced her steps. Returning to work, she's restless, no longer comforted by the night hours, by the solitude.

She spends her first Sunday back walking. She traverses the city ablaze in its autumnal glory: across the park at Ninety-Seventh Street, the trees all yellows and oranges; south on Fifth Avenue, the museums decked with the banners for their new exhibits; west on Central Park South, where the horse-drawn carriages begin their thirty-five-dollar jaunts. Not until the last lap north along the river promenade, past the boat basin, past the flower beds, past the hippo park, does she acknowledge what she is doing: fighting with her feet. Seven miles. One foot after the other. Fighting the hole she'd watched swallow up her mother. A state she's always privately viewed as in some essential way morally offensive. A debate she and Saul had when they first met—her belief that depression is philosophically incorrect. As though we are justified in the assumption that we will not suffer. As though our fate is to be content, and indignation is therefore due when disappointments heap at our feet. "You're an existentialist psychologist," Saul had quipped. "Rollo May with a little Albert Ellis thrown in." But once, when he looked at her with an eyebrow slightly raised and a strained smile on his lips, she'd had the thought that he saw right through her: her disapproval, the way she'd managed those months when her mother had sunk into the couch like a corpse settling into its coffin.

Her second week home, a headhunter for a Washington political consulting firm approaches her about a job. A small but dynamic group: two researchers from Rand, a Madison Avenue whiz kid, a statistician out of MIT. Rena would be the hands-on person for the candidate. Working with the staffers to translate the group's recommendations into action. A salary starting in the six figures. Excellent benefits. Partnership opportunity.

On the weekend, she can't sleep. Fully dressed, she lies on her bed with a blanket over her. She can feel Braner's sticky hair between her fingers. She flings back the blanket, thinks, I'd sooner go back to Alil's.

There is no sunrise, just a gradual shading of the black sky to gray and then an iced white. Joggers appear in the park below and an oil barge floats on the choppy river. Dots of rain mark her window. For a few days after her return from France, she'd imagined that Reed's plan for her had already been executed. When her period finally came, she was relieved—relieved not so much to discover that she was not, in fact, pregnant, but to not be pregnant by Reed, golden boy, no longer golden, now only tarnished. She thinks about herself. No longer the waitress's kid banished to the kitchen during Nick's *little visits,* the school truant, the barmaid at a topless joint. Not even Saul's arrest could reverse that.

There's a truck backing up on the street. A dog barks. The pipes creak.

Once, when she and Leonard were eating dinner in Guatemala City, working hard to find something to talk about aside from the embassy bureaucrats and how long before they could retrieve Bernardo's body, they'd taken to talking loosely about biology and reproduction. A baby girl, Leonard had told her, is born with all her eggs. From the perspective of the gene, life is no more than the spring on a windup clock, an egg released with each rotation of the hand on the dial.

Four more years until forty, Reed had admonished. On her palm, there are little paper cuts, a web of lines. How much easier if she could believe in destiny. If she did not believe that her life is her own creation. No, more than her life. She. Her very self.

SHE TURNS DOWN the job. "I'm thinking about having a baby," she tells the headhunter, taken aback by her own words.

When she goes down to the lobby for her mail, Pedro hands her another box from Barcelona. "Your Spanish friend?"

Rena nods.

Pedro points to the return label. "She likes toys, yes?"

"Yes."

Upstairs, Rena opens the box. It's a large doll made out of cloth. The puckered seam is underneath the pink pinafore. Inside is a wad of hundred-dollar bills and a typed note. *Para el bebé.*

She waits until five, when the cell blocks return from their work assignments, to call Saul.

"My father said you were back. I was wondering when I'd hear from you."

In the background, men are yelling. "I'd like to come tomorrow."

"I'll have to check my social calendar. Let's see . . ."

"I'll come in the morning."

"Whenever you'd like, Rena dear."

She goes straight from work to the bus. She sits in the rear, behind the bathroom and away from the other passengers. She stares out at the highway, imagining a family tree of Eleanor, her father, Klara and Leonard spread out across the lanes: the Italian-Catholic daughter of a fishmonger, the second-generation son of prosperous German Jews, the daughter of an Episcopal surgeon from Baltimore and the only son of Ukrainian Jews come through Ellis Island. Lines dropping to Saul and her and then, from Saul and her, to a dot with a name in letters too small to see.

FROM A DISTANCE, she would not have recognized him, his lanky physique now entirely hidden under an armor of muscle.

"It's an amazing sport, lifting weights. I always thought it was about vanity and a stupid kind of fanaticism. But there's a true zen to it. To lift correctly, without injury, you have to visualize your anatomy and the entire sequence of your movements. It's like a meditation. I've been learning from a guy here who used to be the number one bodybuilder in northern Jersey. I'm teaching him algebra and he's teaching me how to lift."

Rena feels a wave of nervousness pass over her. The same nervousness she'd felt when she first took Saul to visit her mother and Eleanor greeted them in loose cotton pants, a look of serenity on her previously frenetic face. An anxiety about change, a suspiciousness that seems almost innate, an inborn xenophobia.

When Saul asks about her trip, she tells him about Tremolat and canoeing on the Vézère. She talks about visiting Domme and Sarlat and the castles in the Lot. Afraid that the room is wired, she says nothing about driving south into the Pyrenees, about climbing Canigou.

Saul watches her carefully: her fidgeting, the ways she sucks her pinkie nail. Her sentences grow awkward, jagged clause after clause, as she sees that he knows she's holding something back.

"I saw him."

Saul folds his arms.

"He didn't know about you. He didn't learn until five months later." She stops, worried about saying anything more.

"I take it you believe him."

"He never expected what happened. He thought you were safe." She watches Saul's face, the clenched jaw, the eyes held too still. "He wants you to write to him. He said it would be music to his rotted soul."

"His rotted soul."

"Actually, what he said was his rotted little soul."

"Oh, I see. So that implies that it was never much of an organ to start with."

Saul leans back in his chair. "The truth is, what happened afterwards is irrelevant. I've had too much time to think about it. Blaming him is just a way of not blaming myself. I'm the one who wrote that list, who told them Kim Sun's schedule. What he did, he can grapple with."

"You'll be free in two and a half years. He's away forever." She averts her eyes, but not before Saul has seen her pained expression.

"Survivor guilt. We'll go on. He won't."

They sit in silence. Then Rena says, "Still, you must be mad at me. Since I introduced you."

"Well, I never thought about that. That might be entertaining. To be mad at you. Only the argument doesn't hold water, since you didn't set about introducing us. Remember? We bumped into him at the Whitney."

"The show with bottles of urine set up on a table. You went into a dissertation on the brilliance of the exhibit."

"One thing's for damn sure. If I make it through four years here, I won't waste another two minutes on intellectual masturbation like that."

"What will you do?"

"Try and get my license back. If I can, I'm going to leave the head business. Do a second residency in primary care or something like that. My father told me a story about this patient he treated when he was an attending, right before he met my mother. It made me think this shrink thing is a family business gone bad."

The guard raps on the window. The familiar two fingers.

"You're the one," Saul says, "who's got to figure out what's next."

"That's exactly what he said. He thinks I should have a baby before I'm too old."

"He's right, you've put it off all these years."

"Actually, that's why I came here today." She pushes her hair off her face. "I've been thinking," she says slowly, "that you'd be pretty good genetic fodder."

Saul stares at her.

"I'm not talking about getting back together. Just having a baby together."

He places one hand on top of the other, his ringless fingers now half again their former size. "And how do you imagine this happening?"

"Nothing fancy. The old-fashioned way."

Outside, keys are jangling. Rena stands.

"I asked Monk. You can request conjugal visits. As far as they're concerned," she points at the guard now unlocking the door, "we're still husband and wife."

17 Leonard

On the eve of your mother's sixtieth birthday, she announces that I am to take her to see you the next day. Russian caviar. A new handbag. Dinner at Dantelli's. These I would have expected. All evening, I watch her prepare. She bakes Toll House cookies and packs them in a Christmas tin even though it is only early November. She presses her Irish linen handkerchief blouse with a steam iron. She polishes her navy pumps and lays out her stockings and underwear.

In the car, she sits silently with her hands in her lap. Since she's abandoned her invalidism, her face has lost its puffiness and remnants of her former handsomeness have returned. I try to prepare her by describing the visitors' setup: the room with the reinforced window, the table where arms and possessions are to remain in full view. She listens politely, the way one might to the safety directions on an airplane.

Arriving at the prison, I sign in only her as the visitor. When they call her name, I rise but she motions for me to stay. Head erect, her girls' school posture, she walks toward the guard. I watch her from behind—a tall woman in a powder blue suit, broad in the back and the beam. She wobbles slightly on her pumps and then stands very still while the guard rummages through her pocketbook and the little shopping bag in which she has placed the cookie tin.

Fifty minutes later, your mother returns, escorted by a guard carrying a box of books you have asked us to take back. I see the blue covers of my Standard Edition, paperbacks by R.D. Laing, Searles, Lacan, Erikson. Your college philosophy texts. Dostoyevsky's *Crime and Punishment.* Driving home, your mother tells me how well you look. Fit and handsome with your new muscles and inch-long hair. How you told her that you have been in correspondence with the medical board and may be permitted to work as a physician's assistant in a rural area in upstate New York. About your hopes of doing a second residency in primary care.

For a moment, I dread her saying something horrid like *who knows, maybe he'll become a surgeon,* but instead she smiles at me. Cars around us have begun to turn on their headlights, and in the refracted light her brow appears smooth and her eyes shine and I recall her snow-white skin one moonlit night, the sheer length of her, shoulders to toes, against creamy bedsheets, the chestnut triangle, those early years when our sexual life together was the one consolation we, mismatched souls, could offer each other. I swallow remembering her great appetite. Her violent orgasms.

Your mother rests her head on the window glass. She places a hand on the armrest between us, but I keep my fingers, all ten of them, on the wheel.

I think again about my dream in Todos Santos. Your mother with hair sleek as a ferret's. Always I've thought that we ceased relations after her father died, but now I wonder if it was before. For her thirtieth birthday, her parents had come to stay with the two of you while we had a weekend in the city. There were opera tickets, *La Traviata,* gifted by them, and a suite at the Waldorf. A negligee she'd bought for the occasion. Her preparations in the pink marble bathroom that night. Her muffled sobs when, climbing into bed, she discovered me in feigned sleep.

Why, I wonder now, this refusal? Retaliation for her having allowed her father to make her decisions? Anger that she would never grant me the adoration she'd given him?

Lulled by the movement of the car, your mother has fallen asleep. I touch her leg. It was a lavender gown, that night at the Waldorf. Lavender silk with a lace décolleté. Getting up in the middle of the night, I saw the candle she'd placed on the bedside table. She'd known. That with our bodies we could have made pockets of love in our lives. This was her choice. A brave choice for a woman with stretch marks on her belly from carrying two sons and a husband whom she'd been raised to view with contempt. I stood watching her, my fingers quivering inches from the lace, inches from awakening her, but instead, revenge the last word, I crept alone into that pink marble sarcophagus to relieve myself.

I WAKE AS I DID the night after your arrest, thinking about the dream of the burning child in *The Interpretation of Dreams*. I go downstairs to the kitchen, where the box of books sits by the door. At the kitchen table, I search the index for the dream. My eye settles on the entry for the dream of smoked salmon. Flipping to the page, I laugh aloud, a weird laugh at three in the morning against the refrigerator hum, remembering my Uncle Jack with his creamed herring dreams. "All my dreams are of eating vats of creamed herrings and *shtupping* red-haired girls from behind," he said when I first told him I was going to study psychiatry. "What would your Dr. Freud say about that?"

In the story about the dream of smoked salmon, a butcher's wife challenges Dr. Freud's theory that every dream is the fulfillment of a wish. Not the case, she argues, with her dream of being unable to have a dinner party due to having nothing in the cupboard save a single slice of smoked salmon. Tracing her associations, Freud easily trumps her: her wish had indeed been fulfilled in that her unconscious desire was to *not* have the dinner party since it would provide an opportunity to fatten up her skinny friend whom her husband, with his taste for stout women, would then only find more attractive than he already did.

In the margin, you have penciled *Lacan's Écrits* and a page number. I dig through the box and find the book and then the page with a circled asterisk next to Lacan's discussion of the same butcher's wife's dream. I struggle through the odd terminology, shocked by the easy, vulgar tone. The butcher's wife whom Lacan calls "our witty hysteric."

The butcher, a man, Lacan writes, whose wife, after he fucks her, does not have to masturbate.

You have drawn little arrows into the margins. From the butcher's wife, an arrow to the initial K. From the skinny friend of the butcher's wife whom her husband admires too well, to R. From the butcher, an arrow to a smudge mark where something has been erased.

I wait until the sky lightens. Then I climb the stairs. I listen to your mother's *clu-hah*. Slowly, I pull back the covers. I place my hands on your mother's still lovely shoulders. I think of lavender silk. Of a lace décolleté. Of her girlhood hair. Because she is, after all, your mother, I say no more.

IN THE MORNING, she beams like a newlywed. She dresses in black slacks and a loose blouse that flatters her tall figure. She puts Vivaldi on the stereo. She makes pancakes with frozen blueberries. She sets the breakfast table in the dining room with her Wedgwood china.

Your mother pours me coffee in a long fragrant stream. A bowl of red apples gleams on the sideboard. "I would like to go to Italy, Leonard," she says. "We have never traveled. The jewelry I inherited. The boys will never want that old stuff. We could sell my grandmother's pearls and go on a trip. I haven't been to Europe since I was nineteen and went with my mother and brother. I would like to go to Florence with you. To Venice. Siena. Rome."

Your mother's eyes are shining. Had you asked me if she knew the names of four cities in Italy, I would have said no.

"I would like to learn Italian. We could rent a villa in Tuscany."

My face is collapsing. Your mother rises. I bury my head in her stomach. I am weeping. She lowers herself to her knees and holds my face in her hands. Her horsewoman's hands.

"Forgive me, Klara," I whisper.

Tears cascade over her cheekbones.

"Forgive me, Klara," I repeat.

"Forgive me, Leonard," she whispers back.

• • •

After lunch, we walk together. Your mother remarks on the names of trees and the architectural styles of the neighborhood houses. It is so strange to be walking together, we might as well already be in a foreign country. Three girls, maybe thirteen, fourteen, pass arm in arm. They're dressed in the plaid skirts and saddle shoes of a parochial school, coats and book bags swinging loosely from their bodies, hair arranged in the way that uniformed girls learn to signal their sexual knowingness.

"That was me. We had to stand in line, shortest to tallest, and the headmistress would measure from the bottom of our kneecaps down three inches to the required skirt length. Of course, I was always the tallest and therefore the last. I'd write limericks in my head, anything to kill time while the headmistress went from girl to girl. Once, I developed a terrible crush on a man I glimpsed through a doorway while I was waiting. I was composing a limerick about this girl in my class, Carol Jerginn, who kept straight pins and lipstick in her coat pocket so after school she could shorten her skirt and redden her lips. All I could see from my place in the line was his profile and his thick black hair. For weeks, everywhere I went, I looked for him. I described him to all my friends, and they would point at men and ask if that was him."

"What was the limerick?"

Your mother laughs. A big-throated laugh. How could I have forgotten what a hearty girl she was? Blue ribbons for dressage. Gold ribbons for girls' basketball. How unexpected her taking to bed really was. "Let's see. 'Carol Jerginn shows her knees. Always looking for the he's. Carries lipstick in her pocket. Got a boyfriend, cannot knock it.' "

"I'm impressed."

"Oh, I had a whole notebook of them. 'Miss Flanner measures floor to hem. Worries, worries about the them. Thinks a girl who shows too much calf. Won't be able to learn her math.' Not the best. Calf and math."

I always knew your mother had been bold and popular, but never have I thought of her as a wit. *Our witty hysteric.* "What happened?"

"With what?"

"With the man in the hallway?"

"Oh, nothing. Some other distraction came along. My friend Margaret Nunce started going out with a boy who worked in a gas station. That was very risqué. He might as well have been an ex-con."

Your mother's hand flies to her mouth.

I smile and take her arm.

"Margaret came into school one day all in a tizzy because this boy had told her he was going to get her name tattooed on his arm. Everyone said he wouldn't really do it. Then I had a dream that my father got a tattoo. I joked about it to everyone. In the afternoon, Margaret begged me to walk with her to the gas station. We must have walked two miles out of our way to see this boyfriend of hers. We get there and first thing we see is Margaret's name tattooed on his arm. I don't know which of us was more shocked."

I steal a glance to see if your mother understands what she is revealing about her feelings toward her father, but if she does, she keeps a poker face. I hear my Uncle Jack when my Aunt Mindyl would go on and on about a slight from forty years before: "Goddamnit, my lawyer, he tells me there is in this country something they call a statute of limitations. After that, what do they say, let sleeping dogs lie. Let sleeping dogs lie in the sun and dream their farty dreams or whatever it is they dream."

It's nearly dark by the time we get back to the house. Seeing the box of books by the kitchen door, I recall what had sent me downstairs last night: the burning child in *The Interpretation of Dreams*. I take the box up to my study and settle into my desk chair. Downstairs, your mother is listening to an old Beatles album of yours while she layers a lasagna. I find the dream and slowly read:

> A father had been watching beside his child's sick-bed for days and nights on end. After the child had died, he went into the next room to lie down, but left the door open so that he could see from his bedroom into the room in which his child's body was laid out, with tall candles standing round it. An old man

> had been engaged to keep watch over it, and sat beside the body murmuring prayers. After a few hours' sleep, the father had a dream that *his child was standing beside his bed, caught him by the arm and whispered to him reproachfully: 'Father, don't you see I'm burning?'* He woke up, noticed a bright glare of light from the next room, hurried into it and found that the old watchman had dropped off to sleep and that the wrappings and one of the arms of his beloved child's dead body had been burned by a lighted candle that had fallen on them.

Never have you reproached me. You never would.

I WRITE YOU the whole damn thing. The dream of the burning child copied verbatim. A diagram with my name on one side and yours on the other. Maria at the bottom of the page in my column. Mitch at the bottom of the page in your column. Me, asleep, while you went up in flames. The words *murderer* and *murdered* floating everywhere with colored lines in between. An echo chamber of accusations: Leonard murders Maria. Saul murders Mitch. Leonard murders Saul. Saul murders Saul.

The wish indulged is the dream. The dream enacted is the crime. All the times we don't see because what we see is not what we want.

I stare at the paper. What was it Merckin had said in those last sessions before I jumped ship? His voice from behind the couch, slow and deliberate, as though he were talking to someone in a state of shock: "You did not try to kill Maria. Maria tried to kill herself. It was your lust for her that made you think you were the one slicing her wrists."

I didn't laugh, did I? I didn't taunt, No job-y, no couch-y, right, Doc?

"Guilt that fed on guilt you'd felt about earlier fantasized crimes. The revenge you wished you could take on your Uncle Jack for fucking your mother."

He did not fuck my mother.

"Dubinsky. You are playing the idiot. You know we are not talking facts in this room."

Only Merckin never called me Dubinsky. And Merckin would never have said fuck.

I wait a week to mail this to you. By then, I've expanded the diagram to include my own oedipal and infanticidal crimes. I scratch out these sections and add a long postscript begging your forgiveness for my indulgence in this all.

YOUR MOTHER COMBS through guidebooks. She charts our itinerary. Three days in Milan. The train to Venice. Six days in Venice. A car to drive to the Amalfi coast. A weekend in Portofino. Five days in the Tuscan hills. A week in Florence. Battling a cold, I lie on the couch with a blanket pulled over my chest while she reads aloud passages about twelfth-century walled villages and palazzi converted to hotels. I am happy to let her make the decisions, grateful that my cold provides a shield for this feeling of things rapidly decompressing, this sense of the pressure suddenly released.

I alternate between excitement about what lies ahead and a desperation to do anything—sleep, eat, drink—so as not to think. Waiting for your response, I am unable to touch my book. The putrefied, morbid agenda of the historian hidden behind the dictum to examine the past lest we otherwise repeat it: set the bones in death that were left broken in life.

As a youth, when I was anxious, before certain important exams, before certain difficult encounters, I would close my eyes and wait until I saw a third eye, a pale shimmering blue light. Seeing the blue, I would have the sensation of having found my deepest self, of being bathed in a cool protective calm. Now, my skin burns and everything is colored hot hues. Oranges, yellows, reds.

When you write back, it is only a few hurried lines. I have to remind myself that you are not a man of leisure. That by day you make shelving brackets, that by night you wear foam earplugs.

> A brilliant case analysis, dear Father. But aren't you committing a kind of genetic fallacy? The fact that there are parallels between Mitch and Maria does not mean you caused me to aid some two-bit hoodlums.

> P.S. I should be more ceremonious about telling you this, but we seem to be cutting to the chase on all matters here. Rena has asked me to father her child. I have decided to do it. Perhaps, after all, you will be a grandfather.

To my surprise, I am not really surprised. Rather, I am anxious, afraid that any intrusion on my part will cause one or the other of you to change your mind. It takes every ounce of self-control to wait until Thanksgiving day to call Rena. We make small talk for a few minutes. Then, without segue, she announces that you have begun your conjugal visits. Conjugal. Conjugate. A word you can push back and forth like the disk on a Catskills shuffleboard court.

"And the divorce?" I say it so hesitantly, so softly, that for a moment I think she hasn't heard me.

"Morton's doing the paperwork. We'll file after I get pregnant. If I get pregnant."

I touch wood. Three times.

We don't talk again until New Year's, when I call again. She says nothing about your visits. Instead, we speak of the trip to Italy your mother and I will make in March. At the end of our call, she says, "Don't even think about Saul while you're gone."

Afterwards, I don't know if she was telling me that I'm not to call her until I get back or that she'll watch over you or you don't need watching over or I should think only of Klara or I should leave the two of you alone.

I TELL YOUR MOTHER about Rena's plan the night before we leave. She crosses herself—something I've not seen my High Anglican wife do before. She smiles seeing me watch her, then takes my hand.

For me, Italy is an endless mother and child, a chamber of funhouse mirrors for Mary and the baby Jesus. Mary lush as fruit, the baby plump as a sausage. Mary with tilted head and tragic eyes, the baby with a golden halo overhead. Your mother amazes me with her energy. Every morning over breakfast, she lays out the day's itinerary. In Venice, walks through the maze of medieval streets and hidden courtyards. The vaporetto to Murano, Burano and a meal on Torcello. A footbridge across the Canareggio to find, my one request, the Ghetto Vecchio, where for half a millennium Jewish life has survived.

In Florence, I get the flu and lie feverish on a feather bed, the windows to our room flung open onto the garden so I can smell the early flowering vines, while your intrepid mother sets off on her own. She comes back with postcards from the Uffizi and a book about Michelangelo for you. She shows me her flea market purchases: a cashmere sweater for Marc, a leather satchel for Susan, a silk scarf for Rena, a packet of notepaper for Mrs. Smiley. A lace tablecloth, beeswax candles, a leaded glass picture frame for us. Buried at the bottom of her bag, a yellow baby's bonnet.

WHEN WE GET HOME, there's a letter from you. The baby is due in September.

Your mother counts the months on her fingers. "Four," she announces. "She's four months pregnant." At night, we talk about our fear of telling Marc and Susan with their too ardent advocacy of their *lifestyle*.

I spend a day in the stacks at the Columbia library and then meet Rena for an early dinner before she begins work. Except for a new high color to her cheeks and the slightest thickening of her middle, the pregnancy is still imperceptible. She drinks a glass of milk and eats a spinach salad. She tells me that her mother will come for the first two weeks after the baby is born. How she will have to return after twelve weeks to her night word-processing job if she is to keep her excellent health insurance.

"Who'll watch the baby?" I ask.

"I'll have to find a sitter." An anxious look passes over her face and, I imagine, over mine, too, as I wonder who she'll be able to find for the hours she works and how she'll afford it all.

On the train home, it occurs to me that I could do it—watch the baby. By the time the train pulls into my station, the idea has become a plan: I'll stay with Rena Monday nights through Saturday mornings so that I can take care of the baby while she's at work.

I cannot sleep. Tossing and turning, I interrogate myself about my motivations. By four, I'm longing for Merckin who compared to my own accusations would have been a lamb: I'm trying to castrate you, I'm trying to destroy what's happening with your mother.

I skip my morning work session and join your mother at the kitchen table. She lowers the paper. Too far gone to be politic, I blurt out my proposal.

Your mother swallows. She touches her neck, then folds her hands. "Now that we have this . . ."

"I'll be home Saturday morning to Monday night. Nearly half the week."

She inhales deeply, releasing the air through her nose.

"It's just for a year, until Saul gets out." I take her hands in mine. "It's not about you, Klara," I say, realizing only now that this is the truth. "It's about doing for Saul what he cannot do for himself."

Slowly, your mother nods. I don't even know if she knows she is nodding.

"Perhaps I could come in for a day each week to give you and Rena a break." Her voice buckles on the last word.

Now my eyes fill. "Of course, dear. Of course."

SUSAN, RISING TO HER best self, insists on throwing a baby shower, which your mother insists we have at our house. Your mother is terribly excited about it. For a week, she dusts baseboards, irons napkins, arranges chairs. Long conversations ensue between Susan and her regarding the menu and your mother's decision, at the eleventh hour, to bake the cake herself.

Rena wears a pale green dress with a white collar. Her hair falls in curls around her newly rounded face. For the first time, I feel the baby's presence: asleep in the mound under her dress. Susan places her hands on Rena's hips and moves her to an armchair surrounded by pastel packages with rattles and tiny stuffed animals attached to the bows. Rena coos over the baby blankets from her Aunt Betty, the hooded towels from my sister Rose, the Mother Goose clock sent by Lil. Ceremoniously, the larger items are paraded before her. A car seat from Ruth and Maggie. A high chair from her former bosses, Muskowitz and Kerrigan. A carriage from Marc and Susan. From your mother and me, a check to buy the nursery furniture.

Wiping her eyes, Rena looks up at us all. Ruth and Maggie move to her side. Your mother shuffles out to get a tissue. Rena talks about the way so many people have helped her over the years. Rebecca. Ruth and Maggie. "And now Leonard," she pauses, then catches herself, remembering, I presume, your mother's promise of weekly visits, "and Klara, who will come to watch the baby after I go back to work."

Your mother beams. Backlit from the open window, her silver hair shines. She touches Rena's arm. "Come, let's have the cake."

WHEN RENA GOES into labor, she calls us and we call you. Ruth and Maggie take her to the hospital, stay with her through the labor and delivery. It's a boy. Seven pounds, nine ounces: Bernardo Dubinsky Peretti.

Your mother and I go to see Bernie the next day. I cradle him in my arms, examine the ten little fingers, the tiny nails, the surprisingly long toes. He has red hair and fair skin. My sister Eunice's complexion. He opens his watery blue eyes and they focus on something on my face—perhaps the circles of my nostrils, perhaps the line between my lips.

"Grandpa," Rena whispers to the baby. "This is your grandpa."

She smiles at me with her huge thyroidic eyes and I think of her weeping in La Posada de las Madres the night after we were shown the body and our sitting together across from Charlie Green when he announced that I would have to put up the house to get the bail money and the first time we met in the Chinese restaurant near your old apartment.

"Remember," she says, "how you told me that our personal histories begin with our grandparents' memories?" Oddly, I am not surprised that her thoughts, too, have drifted to our first meeting. We used to call it the intermingling of the unconscious—something that always struck me as a scientized label for magic. "For Bernie, that's you."

My grandson slips back into sleep. I lean down and kiss his forehead, the sweet infant smell. My mother and her immigrant spunk. My father and his noble politics. My sisters and their adoration of me as their little brother. My Uncle Jack, who would have been happier somewhere lower on the animal chain than owning a *shmatte* factory. Merckin. Klara's father. Maria. All of this, Bernie, I will tell to you.

BY THE MIDDLE of Rena's second week back at work, we've fallen into a pattern. Because of her night hours, I mark the beginning of each day with dinner. We eat together while Bernie has his early evening nap. Afterwards, I do the dishes and Rena breast-feeds the baby before leaving for work. He stays alert for an hour or so and then we begin to prepare for bed in the living room, which is now Bernie's room. At ten I give him a bottle and we sleep until three, when he awakens like clockwork for another bottle. He then usually sleeps through until Rena returns at seven, when he nurses again. She bathes and dresses him while I shower and make preparations for the day. By nine-thirty he's ready for his morning nap and she goes into her room to sleep. When he wakes, I take him in to nurse and then bring him with me so she can sleep for a few more hours. She gets up by four, after which I head out alone for a walk and the day's errands.

Since tomorrow is Rena's birthday and the day your mother visits, I stop first at a bakery to order a cake. Ruth and Maggie have called to say they'll bring prawns and a salad. Your mother has promised to bring candles and the presents: two pairs of nursing pajamas and a gold locket that belonged to her grandmother for which she's had a miniature photograph of Bernie made.

Leaving the bakery, I walk north to Riverside Church. Inside, I take the elevator up to the bell tower and climb the three hundred steps past the enormous iron bells of the carillon to the observation platform, where I can see all the way to Connecticut. All the way, I like to think, to you.

A crystalline day, the river is the rippled blue of an eye. The sun hovers above the horizon, preparing for a glorious descent. Last night, giving Bernie his bottle, it occurred to me that you are the one who knows everything. About myself, I have told you everything of import. Were I to die tomorrow, I would feel that you know what you need to understand me and therefore yourself. Rena, I would wager anything, would say the same. That is why she was so devastated by your arrest: not simply because of the violence it did to her life, not even because of the way you brushed lips with danger, but rather the way you damaged yourself as her touchstone—one of the few people she had chosen to know her. In a way, I feel sadder for you than for her; she will either learn to rely more deeply on herself or find someone else. It is you who will have to live with having disappointed her. It is a hard cross to bear: that I tell you from experience.

Still, my son, you are the one who knows—the true historian—and because I believe that when you are freed next year, you will go on to be a fine doctor (I feel certain that you will make this happen) and a fine father (Rena told me how Bernie let you hold him right off, how you rocked him back and forth so that he fell asleep in your arms), my grief at your plight has begun to dissolve into my faith in you.

When I come in, Rena points to the floor, where she's spread out a quilt. Your son is on his belly and he's lifted his head up in the air. "Look," she says, "a body rising."

Over dinner, Rena reads to me from one of her books about the settled baby, the baby who has acquired a rhythm for sleeping and eating, whose distress has shed its mystery. The baby for whom the world is no longer a trauma but contains within it the possibility of the womb, who now finds pleasure in an array of activities, whose caretakers can interpret his cries and without thought do what it takes to comfort him.

Rena laughs. "That sounds like Bernie. Only it's hard to know who it is that has settled. The baby or us."

"All of us," I say. Were you here, across the table, you would provide the catalog: Rena, your mother, yourself. Me. I suppose you would include me. Rena allows the *us* to hold who it may.

The baby wakes, and Rena lets him nurse while she finishes eating. The phone rings, your nightly call guaranteed by Marsden Stem, Grand

Marshal of the Blackjacks, who insists that now that you're a father the others give you first chance at the phone. Rena holds the receiver next to Bernie's mouth so you can hear the gurgling sounds, and it is as if you were a father away on a business trip. Not in prison, not on the way to being divorced.

"It's been three years tomorrow," you say when I take the receiver. For some thick-skulled reason, it is the first time I put it together, that you were arrested on Rena's birthday. Despite everything, your mother was always the one who remembered birthdays, who wrote the cards. And even though it would be me she'd send to the mailbox, I never looked at the envelopes, never let the names and dates sink in.

IT WILL SURPRISE YOU, given all that I've said, to learn that every night I say a prayer for my grandson. *God bless our baby. God grant him a long happy happy healthy healthy wonderful life. God grant us all the wisdom and self-control and goodness*—yes, I do believe in such a thing—*to provide for him a joyous home in which he will flourish and thrive.* I repeat these words, shamanistically, ritualistically, superstitiously three times. I am embarrassed to reveal this piece of irrationality to you, and I hope you will only smile and be amused and perhaps touched but not disdainful of me.

I repeat these words three times lest, should I not, they not happen. I repeat them because I did not do these things for you. I repeat them because I love you, my second-born son.

Epilogue

It's two in the morning, her nightly break. No clock is needed. She knows. The tingling as her breasts fill, the dampness inside her nursing bra. She locks the door to the secretaries' lounge and unpacks her electric pump and the plastic bottles she carts back and forth from home. She pumps—the relief of her glands emptying, the satisfaction of watching the containers fill with the milk that will feed Bernie tonight while she's gone.

Afterwards, she places the bottles in her cooler pack, washes the pumping tubes, and gathers up her coat and gloves to get the taste of night air her lactating body has demanded since her return to work. She presses the down button, watches the panel as the elevator rises to the twenty-sixth floor.

Inside, she leans against the rear wall. There's a flutter in her heart as she detects the fall, her breath and muscles locking, her body knowing it first that the descent is too fast. Frantically, she pushes the red STOP button but the car continues to drop. She pulls the alarm, hears the bell sounding through the popping in her ears, crouches to the floor, arms covering her head. She screams. The elevator hits the bottom and like a yo-yo starts up again, all the lights flashing at once and then suddenly nothing as it comes to a halt.

She stays crouched, afraid to move. Five minutes, maybe more, then a man's voice: "Okay, we'll try and bring it up a little closer to nineteen."

The doors open and she sees above her the scuffed tips of two work boots. Slowly, the car inches upward. A man's dark hands reach down to steady her as she climbs, first one knee, then the other onto the landing.

He cups her elbows as he brings her to her feet. "Got her," he says into a walkie-talkie. He looks her over, head to toe. "Anything hurt?"

She shakes her head. Her teeth are chattering.

"Here." He keeps an arm out for her to hold on to as he takes off his shirt and drapes it over her shoulders. The cloth smells of tobacco and sweat. On his other arm, there's a mermaid with a snake coiled around the tail.

Dizzy, she leans into him and then begins to heave, her face pressed against his white undershirt, her fingers squeezing the mermaid, as she thinks about the cable snapping and how she was certain she'd plummet, a free fall, to the bottom. The fear not so much of having all of her bones smashed, that would last but an instant, but of Bernie losing his mother, his future stamped with grief.

When she gets home, both Leonard and Bernie are sleeping. Still shivering, she puts on pajamas and wool socks. With Bernie's cry, she tiptoes into the living room and lifts him out of the crib. Settled in the rocker in her room, her breasts fill immediately. Bernie sucks avidly, happily, greedily. Outside her door, she can hear Leonard moving around. "Hungry little monkey," she whispers. "Say happy birthday to your mummy."

Leonard knocks while she's burping Bernie.

"Come in." He's smiling, carrying a tray with a glass of orange juice, a mug of tea and a bud vase with two yellow roses. Tucked under his arm is a tube wrapped in Venetian paper.

"Happy birthday. The present is from Bernie and me." Leonard puts down the tray and tube and reaches out his arms for the baby. With Bernie on his shoulder, he continues Rena's pats.

Rena takes the gift. Carefully, she undoes the wrapping. A sea swirl: lapis, moss, coral, sand. She pulls the rolled paper from the tube and spreads it out on her desk, weighting the corners with books.

It's an antique map, prepared for the *Valentine's Manual* of 1865 by a Mister M. Dripps. "Oh! It's wonderful."

"Look at your neighborhood. The grid of streets was laid, but there was no Riverside Park, no Riverside Drive."

She leans over the map. "The only marked buildings are a lunatic asylum and an orphanage."

"The New York Lunatic Asylum. And the Leeke and Watts Orphan Asylum."

Bernie burps. He twists to look at her and then breaks into one of his radiant toothless grins. "I'll give him his bath," Leonard says. "You get some extra sleep."

Rena kisses Bernie on the nose, Leonard on the cheek. "Thank you, my dears."

Warm now, she cracks the window. There's a fresh dusting of snow on the sill. Icicles descend from the upper tree branches. Shimmying on the river are the reflections of the New Jersey shoreline, the towers doubled on the water.

She studies the map. The dozen ferry crossings from before the bridges. Downtown, Thompson Street where her mother grew up, Fulton Street where her grandfather's fish market had been. Leonard's West End Avenue not yet paved. The Bronx, where her father was raised, still farmland. The street where he resided as a law student, where, presumably, she was conceived, sandwiched between the lunatic asylum and the orphanage.

She finds the block where she and Saul had lived together. Crossing the parchment, west to the Hudson, north along what was then called Strikers Bay, she finds herself, where she is now.

Acknowledgments

My sincerest thanks to my agent, Elyse Cheney, who found my novel its perfect home, and to Antonia Fusco, dream editor; our collaboration has extended through every aspect of this book. For their generosity of spirit and time, I thank the many people who read the manuscript in various drafts or helped in other ways to shepherd it into being: Ann Braude, E. L. Doctorow, Mark Epstein, Candida Fraze, Alejandro Gomez, Marian Gornick, Vivian Gornick, Ken Hollenbeck, Lila Kalinich, Amy Kaplan, Carole Naggar, Michele Nayman, Arlene Shechet and Barbara Weisberg. Finally, my deepest gratitude to Shira Nayman and Jill Smolowe without whom this work would not have seen the light of day.